SO-DZL-541
3 4028 09170 7662
HARRIS COUNTY PUBLIC LIBRARY

Ramakr
Ramakrishna, Kamesh
The making of Bhishma :
   Book 1 of the great war
   re-imagined
                        $24.95
              ocn976177755

DISCARD

...[if there are three hundred Ramayanas] there might be three thousand or thirty thousand Mahabharatas.

A.K. Ramanujan

DISCARD

THE MAKING OF BHISHMA

BOOK 1 OF
THE GREAT WAR, RE-IMAGINED

KAMESH RAMAKRISHNA

KASHI PUBLISHING CAMBRIDGE MA

USA ISBN: 978-1-939338-05-1
USA Retail Price: US$24.95
Copyright © 2015–2016 Kamesh Ramakrishna
URL: www.thelastkaurava.com
Discussion: www.facebook.com/kameshramakrishna
Email: Kamesh@kashipub.com

US Edition, Published: December 15, 2016 by

Kashi Publishing
Cambridge, MA 02139, USA
Telephone: +1-617-335-1520
Email: publisher@kashipub.com

All rights reserved. No part of this publication may be reproduced, stored in, or introduced into a retrieval system, or transmitted, in any form or by any means (electronic, mechanical, photocopying, recording, or otherwise) without the prior written permission of the publisher. Any person who does any unauthorized act in relation to this publication may be liable to criminal prosecution and civil claims for damages.

Disclaimer: This is a work of fiction based on an ancient Hindu epic. Names, characters, places, and incidents are based on the original stories from the Mahabharata. All changes are products of the author's imagination. Any resemblance to actual persons, living or dead, is entirely coincidental. The views expressed in this book are those of the author alone.
Illustrations: Junuka Deshpande
Map: Harshad Marathe

Typeset in Palatino Linotype.

For my parents

ACKNOWLEDGEMENTS

My grandmother introduced me to stories from the Mahabharata. In a traditional dinner-time routine, she would seat my siblings and me around her on the floor and efficiently get us to eat, doling out a tablespoon of *thayir-sadam* with a spoonful of *sambar* into our hands. With each spoonful came a bit more of an episode from the great epics.

My father introduced me to reading. He did not control the quality or quantity of the books I read, both bought and borrowed. As a boy, I often spent hours in the India Book House in downtown Mumbai and the British Council and the USIS libraries in Delhi, while he completed errands.

My mother scolded me when I told her that I was "writing the Mahabharata" as this epic tale of intra-family war is believed to bring bad luck to the extended family of the writer. So I was surprised when she asked for a copy of my work-in-progress and read the whole manuscript in one long sitting. She then told me that we need not worry – what I had written was not the Mahabharata after all – the curse would not apply. She was the first reader of this curse-free version. She even said she enjoyed the story, an accolade never bestowed easily. After that ringing affirmation, I had no choice but to get on with it and publish the book.

My wife and daughters have been tolerating my obsession with the Mahabharata for a long time and are overjoyed that I am finally done with this book. I appreciate their patience; through their love and support, they created a world in which I could write.

Many writers and texts have influenced me. The great scholar and poet A. K. Ramanujan's collection of folktales acted as an inspiration; likewise, Iravathi Karve's analysis of the main characters of the epic in *Yuganta*. J. A. B. van Buitenen's translation of the critical edition produced by the Bhandarkar Oriental Research Institute was a key reference. Information about ancient India came from the *Brihatkatha*, the *Jataka* tales, and the *Panchatantra*. the controversial anthropologist Marvin Harris (*Cultural Materialism*) provided a theoretical foundation. Insights into ancient cultures came from Robert Graves (*The Greek Myths* and other works). The amazing novelist Gore Vidal (*Creation* and *Julian*) provided a model for the writing.

Harshad Marathe illustrated the map of South Asia that is the frontispiece – he admirably translated my comments into a visual. Junuka Deshpande provided the small, evocative and creative illustrations used to introduce major sections in this book. Finally, my thanks go to my editors Jayashree Anand and Padmini Smetacek for their careful reading and their encouraging comments. Their critiques have been crucial for finishing this work.

I take full responsibility for this work of fiction. Its contents and the opinions in it are a product of my imagination. All my life I have read widely in the fields of history, archaeology, mythology, philosophy, science, and technology, and I drew on these to create this story. I do not claim historical authenticity or scriptural validity. The novel does not represent my beliefs about what may have "really" happened.

This novel does not represent the views of the Publisher or of anybody else. It is not endorsed as authentic or historical by the Publisher or by anybody else.

INTRODUCTION

As a child, the Mahabharata fascinated me – not only did it have heroes, heroines, villains, and fast-paced action, but it also raised profound human questions about fairness, the thirst for revenge, the horror of war. When I became interested in history and pre-history, I struggled to fit the stories into what the archaeological record showed. The histories of other vanished cultures of the ancient world—Greece, Egypt, and Sumer—seemed to be grounded in verifiable fact while the Mahabharata, a self-proclaimed *historical* epic of a still-alive-and-breathing culture in South Asia and Southeast Asia, seemed to lack any foundation in the reality we could unearth.

This book is a revised version of *The Last Kaurava* a novel published in November 2015 by Leadstart Private Ltd. in India. The original was published in India for Indian readers who have easy access to the story of Mahabharata through books as well as in school, or as stories told by parents, grandparents, or the many uncles and aunties who populate the family environment. To many of these readers, the world of the Mahabharata is exotic but not excessively so— metaphors and allegory from the epic often appear in ordinary conversation. My hope is that this revision can still make sense to readers outside India who know the basic story of the Mahabharata but who only experience it as exotica. Mostly these readers will be from the South Asian diaspora, but others, not of South Asian origin, may find my book interesting as well. An extended summary of the original Mahabharata is included in the boxes below. It is an introduction to the reader completely unfamiliar with the original as well as a reminder for readers who know some of it.

The Mahabharata: Summary of the Original Epic

Shantanu, the king of Hastinapura falls in love with Satyavati but is unable to marry her because her father asks that Shantanu should disinherit his son Devavrata and pass on the crown to her sons. When Devavrata finds out, he voluntarily relinquishes his inheritance, but that does not satisfy Satyavati's father who is concerned that Devavrata's own children would not accept this. In response, the young Devavrata vows celibacy, which earns him the title *Bhishma* (usually translated as "The Terrible").

Satyavati's sons Chitrangada and Vichitravirya die childless but Satyavati arranges for Vichitravirya's two wives to bear two sons fathered by her pre-marital son Vyaasa (also the author of the epic). These two sons are the blind Dhritarashtra, the elder, and the pale Pandu. Dhritarashtra, being blind, cannot be king, so Pandu inherits the throne. Pandu exiles himself as punishment for a murder that he commits. Bhishma is Regent during the various periods when there is no functioning king on the throne of Hastinapura.

Dhritarashtra has a hundred sons, called the Kauravas, headed by Duryodhana and Dushasana; Pandu in exile has five sons, called the Pandavas, named Yudhishthira, Bhima, Arjuna, Nakula, and Sahadeva. After Pandu dies, the Pandavas return to Hastinapura with their mother Kunti and are raised with the Kauravas. Duryodhana who had expected to inherit the kingdom by default resents the return of the Pandavas as Yudhishthira becomes the crown prince. The result is enmity between the Kauravas and the Pandavas.

Duryodhana plots against the Pandavas, who escape a burning palace and disappear. They come out of hiding at the wedding of the princess Panchali Draupadi, the daughter of Drupada, king of Panchala. Panchali chooses Arjuna as husband, but in order to fulfil their mother's mistaken injunction to share his "winnings", all five Pandavas marry Draupadi. The reappearance of the Pandavas with a powerful new ally leads to a compromise. Hastinapura is divided and the Pandavas are given the barren south-eastern half where they establish the city of Indraprastha.

Duryodhana's plots continue. Yudhishthira is invited to play a game of dice and finds himself facing an expert opponent, Shakuni. Yudhishthira loses everything, including his brothers, himself, and then Draupadi. In a confrontation, Draupadi is assaulted and Bhishma refuses to intervene. In order to settle the conflict and prevent war, the Pandavas agree to go into exile for at least thirteen years, with an additional twelve years of exile if discovered during the thirteenth year.

After thirteen years, Duryodhana refuses to return Indraprastha to the Pandavas. War is unavoidable. This becomes a Great War in which many, many kings from all over the world (i.e. India) participate – almost two million warriors converge on the field of Kurukshetra. The war lasts eighteen days, with almost all the warriors dead.

Bhishma fights for the Kauravas and is fatally injured on the ninth day, but stays alive on a bed of arrows for another fifty-six days, well past the end of the war. Yudhishthira comes to him for advice and receives it – almost fifteen thousand verses out of the canonical total of one hundred thousand verses of the epic are Bhishma's advice to the newly crowned King of Hastinapura.

Many scholars have viewed the vow of celibacy to be the root cause of the chaos described in the epic. In that case, one would expect Bhishma to be a central character of the narrative. But he is not. After the vow, there are only three occasions on which Bhishma appears and makes a fateful decision. These three episodes span three generations! For a central character, he receives little time on the stage leading to the war. But after the war is over, Bhishma's instructions are a sixth of the verses in the epic!

The reader of the Mahabharata may be confounded by the setting of the story. Technologies from a variety of stages of development (Iron Age or Bronze Age or even Stone Age) are indiscriminately mixed together. Social organizations from different social systems are placed in the same time period. Tribes or peoples from different eras take part in the Great War. The war takes place within a few weeks of the end of the period of exile, but armies and warriors come from thousands of miles away to take part in it.

So what is the truth? Archaeology provides some hints.

We know from satellite images and excavations that around 2000 B.C.E. in South Asia, a great river with over a thousand urban settlements on its banks dried up and disappeared. This river, the Sarasvati, is mentioned in the *Puranas* and the *Vedas*. The vanished settlements were the Sarasvati-Sindhu Culture (SSC), which had been called the Indus Valley Civilization after the settlements first discovered on the banks of the Indus. These settlements were spread out over modern-day Pakistan and western India. When the river dried up, the SSC towns collapsed, sending refugees in all directions. Refugees moving east into the Gangetic plain would have encountered a native, forest-dwelling, non-urban population, leading to conflict over land and its uses. These were unresolvable conflicts with no compromise – one side had to lose and the other side had to win. War would be the solution, both awful and unavoidable; with peace would come a new way of life.

The Great War, Reimagined is planned as a series of novels that tell the story of this crisis. *The Making of Bhishma* is Book 1 of the series. Changing the context has resulted in many differences between this book and the story in the original Mahabharata. This novel is set in 2000 B.C.E. against the backdrop of the crisis caused by the drying up of the Sarasvati. Hastinapura on the Ganga is a frontier town that is overwhelmed by immigrants. Social policies set to manage the crisis fail and set the stage for the Great War that ended one civilization and established the first empire in the region.

The story is told in this book was memorised by the *Kavi Sangha,* an organization of bards and poets, whose annals comprise the historical archives of the cities in the Panchnad culture. The archives of Hastinapura contained the memoirs of Devavrata, also called *Bhishma* ("the Terrible"), who was a central figure of the time leading up to the Great War. The head of the Kavi Sangha, called the Vyaasa, was a respected figure who also played a part in this story.

I followed some ground rules for establishing the context. Fantasy has been eliminated – there are no gods, goddesses, or demons; there is no magic or magical weapons; there are no miraculous conceptions or divine reincarnations; the *Law of Karma* (that depends on the concept of rebirth) is not used to explain behavior. Situating the Great War in 2000 B.C.E. has limited the technologies available. For instance, no nuclear weapons, but more to the point, no horses or iron or million-man armies. Iron was scarce or unknown; armies were small; horse-drawn war chariots would not exist for another two hundred years; transportation was by carts drawn by oxen or onagers (the "Asian wild ass"). The people were not all that different from us – they loved, they hated, they were kind, they got angry, they acted without thinking, they plotted, they lied, they demanded the truth, and so on. In short, they were not better than us, or worse than us, but just like us. The one big difference was that the culture did not use writing but was an oral one – history was memorized and recited, not written and read.

This book, *The Making of Bhishma,* is a significant part of The *Last Kaurava a novel,* published in India by Leadstart in 2015.

What is the difference between *The Making of Bhishma* and *The Last Kaurava a novel? The Making of Bhishma* tells the story of Bhishma's life as narrated by Bhishma lying mortally wounded and a prisoner of his grand-nephew. *The Last Kaurava a novel* embeds this same narration within the context of a second crisis over twelve hundred years later. That second crisis results in a project to write down the history of Hastinapura. The advanced and sophisticated culture of South Asia in 850 B.C.E. was non-literate (to the best of our knowledge) and a script had to be invented – the frame story is the story of the invention of a syllabic script (called *abugida* by linguists) that is the presumed root of all later South Asian and Southeast Asian abugidas.

Readers of *The Last Kaurava* felt that the frame story interrupted and slowed down the main story and was a significant barrier to continuous reading. I felt that the frame story also distracted readers who might be struggling to map the reimagined life of Bhishma to his life described in the original Mahabharata. I concluded that the frame story, though intriguing to many readers, would detract from the experience of reading for most readers. I decided that readers in the South Asian diaspora as well as people unfamiliar with Hindu mythology would be better served by a condensed version of *The Last Kaurava a novel.*

There is one other major modification with respect to the original epic – I have changed many of the conventional names used for characters in the original. The Mahabharata often uses descriptive names or titles for the characters rather than their given names. Some characters are never called by their given names! Some of these names are simply descriptive or honorific. Devavrata is called *Bhishma* ("the terrible"), *Pandu* means "the Pale", the wife of the Pandavas is *Draupadi* ("daughter of Drupada") or *Panchali* ("Princess of Panchala"), and so on. But some names are clearly invented to label the villains. Thus the eldest Kaurava is *Duryodhana* ("bad warrior") and his brother is *Dushasana* ("badly seated"). Some names may have been put-downs that have lost their sting. For instance, the martial arts teacher who fights for the Kauravas is called *Drona* (a wooden jar that holds the intoxicating drink *soma* during rituals). Conversely, some names for the heroes are intended as praise. *Yudhishthira* means "firm in war. Some names may have been humorous. Bhima is called *Vrikodara*, or "eats like a wolf."

I have tried to identify the given names of the major characters in the original Mahabharata. For example, Duryodhana is also called *Suyodhana*, meaning "good warrior", and his brother is *Sushasana* ("well-seated"). The teacher Drona is sometimes called *Kutaja*, which means "mountain peak" but also means "jar." It is possible that the teacher's name Kutaja was transformed to Drona by his detractors. I have provided below a list of the names that I felt needed this treatment, and in the body of the book, I will use both names when possible. Note that the new names appear somewhere in the original Mahabharata, except when noted.

Original Name(s)	Modified Name(s)	Reference(s)
Pandu: The Pale	*Mahendra*: Indra, the Great	Father of the Pandavas
Vidura: The Wise	*Dharmateja*: Illuminated with Law	Half-brother to Pandu and Dhritarashtra
Duryodhana: Bad Warrior	*Suyodhana*: Good Warrior	Eldest son of Dhritarashtra; leader of the Kauravas
Dushasana: badly seated	*Sushasana*: well seated	Second son of Dhritarashtra
Dharmaputra: Son of Dharma	*Yudhishthira*: Firm in War	Eldest Pandava
Panchali: Princess of Panchala *Krishnaa*: Dark Woman *Draupadi*: Daughter of Drupada	*Agnijyotsna*: From the Heart of Fire (In this book, she is NOT the daughter of Drupada)	Future matriarch of Panchala, who marries all five Pandavas; one of her titles is "The Dark Lady"
Drona: Wooden Soma Jar	*Kutaja*: Jar, or Mountain Peak	Martial arts teacher

THE PRISONER

AMBA'S VISIT

"I am Amba."

The voice rang in Devavrata's ear like a forgotten melody. It first evoked in him a sense of lightness, enveloped him in a warm glow like dawn breaking out, cradling the river Ganga. Images stuck in lost time veered in and out of focus. Questions came flooding in. *How could it be Amba? What was she doing, here and now?* The questions stuck in his throat, refusing expression. Then the voice in his ear shattered and a grey miasma crawled out of it, a grey that he associated with pain and anger. The glow faded, and the grey fog grew until it shadowed every color. *Amba. She is here. I must see her.* He tried to turn. The stub of an arrow, under the pit of his left arm, made him pause at every movement, however slight.

"You killed Shikhandin. You killed my son."

The greyness increased. *Yes, he had killed Shikhandin.* His mind raced. Shikhandin had lured him into an ambush. He had dealt Shikhandin a fatal blow. Then the ambushers attacked and a well-aimed arrow had penetrated under his arm to his lungs. His arms rendered useless, he had fought and fallen by Shikhandin's side. He was now a prisoner. Shikhandin and he had been transported to the Pandava camp in the same cart and he had listened to

Shikhandin moan as he died. *Shikhandin was Amba's son?* He should have known. It explained so much. He understood now why trusting Shikhandin had been so easy. An image of Amba's profile as she looked out at the sunrise over the garden town of Varanavata, his model town for resettling the Panchnad refugees, melded into a profile of Shikhandin looking out over the Ganga at the remains of a settlement burnt in the war. That was why he had dropped his guard as he followed Shikhandin into the ambush. He recalled the surge of anger when he discovered Shikhandin's betrayal; that was why he had slashed Shikhandin. *Shikhandin, the arrowhead, well-named and well-aimed, truly an arrow aimed at him,* was the only person he had killed in this war, for at his age, he was useless in battle but an asset in conducting the war. *But... there were so many buts.*

"You killed your son. Die."

The greyness turned darker. Devavrata wanted to face Amba and deny the astounding charge. But then he felt her hand push on his left shoulder, the one with the arrowhead. The bed pushed back against the broken shaft of the arrow.

The pain... the pain exploded all over his body, a burn that would not stop. He was a warrior. He said to himself, *I will not scream,* and he threw himself into this struggle against the scream with the roar he had used in battle. He was *Devavrata Bhishma,* Devavrata the Terrible, four times Regent of Hastinapura, the bulwark of an empire built to last an eternity, an empire that must save the refugees fleeing from their ancient home of Panchnad in the west into the embrace of the Ganga and the Yamuna. He was the savior of that civilization, and he would not scream.

His challenge did not stop the arrowhead – *Shikhandin!* – from pushing deeper past his lungs to his heart already torn by Amba's presence. His last memory was of a glimmering haze in which guards rushed in and pulled Amba away, and regret that he had not been able to look at her face.

A FATHER'S BOON

"I give you this boon, my son – you can choose the time of your death."

On his deathbed, Shantanu had labored to whisper these words to Devavrata, his son.

If it sounded like nonsense to Devavrata then, it was definitely nonsense now. He must be dead, for he was floating. All about him was a white nothingness, unrelieved by shadow or color. This must be death. That was not possible; he had not chosen to die. Then he heard something, off to his left and behind him.

"Will he die?"

Devavrata couldn't see anything, but his hearing was good enough that he recognized the speaker; it was his grandnephew Yudhishthira. His thoughts formed questions. *Was this a dream? Why am I floating? Who was Yudhishthira talking about?*

An unfamiliar voice came from his left.

"Not right away, sir. When he wakes up, he may be in pain. I will do my best to help."

The whiteness started to fade into grey. Where am I? How can I hear a discussion between my grandnephew and a stranger? The greyness turned darker. Somebody was going to wake up soon. Who? Who were they talking about?

Devavrata felt a touch on his chest. He looked down. There was nothing to see. He could feel four touches close together on his invisible chest. The greyness was definitely darker. *If it gets any darker I won't be able to see anything.* It wasn't a greyness anymore; it was a blackness. Meanwhile, the touch continued and moved. *Are they really touching my chest?* If so, there was a spot just below his left nipple that was sensitive. If they touched it, he should feel ticklish. A short time later, he felt a touch on the sensitive spot. To his relief, he twitched. The voice continued.

"His heart is in good shape. I don't hear any worrying sounds. The tip of the arrow is almost touching his heart. Do not move the arrow. At the first large movement of the arrow, his heart may be punctured, blood will pour out into his lungs, and he will die."

Now Devavrata could place that voice. It was the doctor who had worked on Shikhandin when they were first brought in. The conversation he was listening to was in the medical tent. He was floating again, in another blackness somewhere near the medical tent. He still couldn't see, but he could hear. Yudhishthira and the doctor were discussing some injured person. *Who could it be?* Whoever it was, he had a lung injury from an arrow. *Just like me.*

"Will it heal at all?" Yudhishthira said.

That was like Yudhishthira. His voice reminds me of his father. Caring for everyone, even a wounded prisoner.

"No," said the doctor. "The Regent will die of it sooner or later."

The Regent was going to die. The Regent? I am the Regent. They are talking about me. He must be in the medical tent and not floating around. He was not dead. He was dying. *What happened to my father's boon?* It had been a strange utterance, possibly the strangest from his father, delirious on his deathbed. Even in delirium, his father had been completely serious and convincing. Occasionally, in idle moments, Devavrata wondered what his father had meant. Apparently nothing, for here he was, fatally wounded and soon to die.

Why can't I see? He was prepared to die, but he had always imagined himself entering death with eyes wide open, seeing everything. Moments passed; it felt like an eternity and fed a growing sense of panic. He found himself back in his body, and now he could feel the pain in his shoulder pulsing and alternating with his heartbeat. It refused to be ignored. He opened his eyes. The doctor was sitting by his side, along with Yudhishthira. The doctor had bent low and leaned in to place his right ear on Devavrata's chest. Devavrata closed his eyes.

After the doctor raised his head, Devavrata heard Yudhishthira say, "How long?" The doctor said, "Two days, a week, perhaps. Not more than that. I'll be back tomorrow to check." Then there was quiet.

The first thing that struck Devavrata when he opened his eyes again was the sunlight streaming in through the open door-flap. His bed had been turned around. Now he faced the entrance of the tent and could no longer see the mat on which Shikhandin's body had been laid out. His left leg was tied, as before, to one of the tent-poles. He could turn a little more freely to the right, but a roll of felted cotton placed behind him prevented him from rolling onto his left side. The cotton was matted and felt rough on the skin of his back. His shoulder was sore and he found he could not move his arm.

"He has opened his eyes," Yudhishthira said.

Devavrata knew now that they had been talking about him all along. *I am going to die, and fairly soon at that.*

Amba was nowhere to be seen. Yudhishthira, his grandnephew, smiled at him, but his grave eyes gave the lie to the smile. Calmness radiated from Yudhishthira and seemed to calm the people around him. That alone made him different from his cousin Suyodhana. A sensuous pout of the upper lip characterized the descendants of the old Queen Mother. *My stepmother*, he thought. She had it, and so did her father and her brother Shukla, the current Vyaasa. It marked her descendants, made them attractive, and encouraged people to defer to their wishes. Her grandson Dhritarashtra had the pout, and despite his almost-complete blindness, women came to him, and he did not turn them away. Dhritarashtra's son Suyodhana had the pout. It made him look dissatisfied, which he was much of the time. Yudhishthira, also her great-grandson, had not inherited the pouted lips. That had settled the matter for the Queen Mother – she demanded proof that Yudhishthira was truly Pandu's son and, therefore, the legitimate heir, *her* heir. There was no proof and no known way of establishing the truth. "Yudhishthira is not my descendant," she said. "You must support Suyodhana's claim, he is my only true heir." His stepmother was another reason the cousins could not compromise.

That curve of the lip, with its hint of subtle pleasures, also drew people to Suyodhana and his brothers. Devavrata knew the look, for despite all that had happened, it had the power to make him want to please his stepmother. After his father's death, he and his stepmother had clashed frequently, but he compromised even when a compromise was not warranted. Even when his anger at his stepmother was so great that a compromise seemed impossible, her brother Shukla, with the same facial feature, could bring him around. Because of that look.

The unanswered questions about Yudhishthira's legitimacy was one of the reasons Devavrata supported Suyodhana. *That's not the only reason for this war,* Devavrata thought. *The Pandavas will destroy what I have built.* His life's work, accomplished during four long terms as Regent for one descendant or the other of his father Shantanu, was the empire he had constructed around Hastinapura. The refugees fleeing the famine in the west caused by the loss of their great river, the Sarasvati, could have been sent back to certain starvation and probable death; they could have been forced to go further east into land inhabited by the forest-dwelling Nagas[1] and Rakshasas[2] and left to fend for themselves, to die or to survive on whatever terms they could get. His father had tried and failed at that, for the forests were not easy to clear, the land was hard to till, and, bar some, the refugees were urbanites, not farmers. They all wanted to immigrate to Hastinapura. Despite their poverty, they did not consider themselves refugees – they were immigrants. Before the crisis, immigrants were welcome in Hastinapura. The Kauravas[3] were immigrants. All the non-Naga residents of Hastinapura were immigrants. In normal circumstances, immigrants would have been welcomed in Hastinapura.

However, the circumstances were far from normal. The river Sarasvati[4], which hosted most of the Panchnad cities, used to receive snow-melt from the Yamuna, which flowed about ten

---

[1] The Hastinapuris gave the name *Naga* to the forest-dwelling, matriarchal bands living along the Ganga. The Nagas had many names for themselves, derived in different ways such as from a totem animal (Matsya, Naga, Meena, etc.) or from the name of the founding matriarch and sometimes her spouse.

[2] The Nagas gave the name *Defender* (in their own language) to the hunter-gatherer tribes that dwelt in the forest to the east of modern-day Patna. The Hastinapuris translated that name into the Panchnadi language as *Rakshasa*.

[3] *Kaurava* means "descendent of Kuru," but the term is usually applied specifically to Suyodhana and his brothers.

[4] *Sarasvati* is the hidden river of Hindu legend, flowing invisibly to merge with the Ganga and the Yamuna near Allahabad.

yojanas[5] to the west of Hastinapura, and from the Sutudri[6], which flowed even farther west. The earthquakes in the Himalayas had changed this. The Yamuna had shifted east, and the Sutudri had turned west, depriving the Sarasvati of water. That had forced the migration.

The Yamuna's eastward shift was not an immediate gain for the eastern lands – the waters had no channel to flow in and flooded the land. The Khandava forest to the west of Hastinapura and areas further south were flooded and could not house the immigrants.  Instead, any settlements they built would have to be in the lands to the east and south of Hastinapura – lands already occupied by the Nagas, hitherto friendly.

These immigrants did not want to be pioneers creating new settlements that would take a generation or more to become as livable as the towns they had left. They wanted to live urban lives rather than frontier lives. Devavrata's accomplishment had been to marshal the unhappy refugees into work crews that built dams, created lakes, constructed waterworks – thus creating the infrastructure to support new settlements.

All this had come at a cost – the Nagas, who had been friendly to Hastinapura, were being squeezed out of their traditional land. Permanent immigrant settlements took over the lands that the Nagas left fallow to recover from the stress of slash-and-burn agriculture. As each new settlement grew, all the arable land near water bodies would be taken, and the Nagas would not be able to live the way they used to. Either they would give up their way of life or they would leave. If necessary, they would be pressured to leave.

---

[5] *Yojana* is a measure of distance, estimated variously to be between seven and ten miles.

[6] *Sutudri* is the river Sutlej.

The Pandavas might, no, they *would*, undo all that he had accomplished. They would justify their rebellion, just like their father had justified his, in the name of fairness and justice for the Nagas. Suyodhana would not do that. Suyodhana, like his father Dhritarashtra, did not care about the Nagas. Like his father, he had many ties to the immigrants. Some friends, many lovers, many allies. *He will soon outdo his father in the number of wives and concubines from among the immigrants.* Hastin's descendants had come a long way, transitioning from the trading family that founded Hastinapura to the warriors they now were as rulers. Suyodhana would not interfere with the administration of the empire that Devavrata had established.

The doctor spoke to him. "Do you feel any pain?"

Devavrata's heart was no longer racing as it had done when Amba had pressed on his shoulder. *Where was she?* His breathing was still ragged. He could feel the stubby edge of the broken arrow against his upper arm. *It had not gone away; it was still there.* He shrugged and essayed a smile.

"A little," he said.

The doctor's face did not change.

Yudhishthira said, "I have bad news for you."

"Uh-huh."

"Your injuries continue to worsen. Not because of what Amba did," Yudhishthira said. "She was upset over her son's death. I approved her request to collect her son's body. I did not anticipate her actions."

Did they know what Amba had told him? Did anyone? Had Amba told the truth? *I must talk to her. I must reassure Yudhishthira that I am not afraid of her.* Devavrata tried to smile, but the pain turned it into a grimace. He said, "She should be angry. He was her son. I still want to talk to her when her anger cools – perhaps in a month."

Yudhishthira's eyes dropped away from Devavrata. His shoulders slumped a little. Then he slowly raised his head and looked straight at Devavrata, "That is not likely."

What did he mean?

Yudhishthira said, "You will die soon, Grandsire." For a brief moment, Devavrata saw a ripple of worry move across Yudhishthira's face and his calm eyes.

Devavrata frowned and his eyes narrowed. Yudhishthira continued, "The doctor here refuses to remove the arrow. Amba pushed the arrowhead past your lung, and it is now near your heart. It missed all the vital spots along the way. If it hadn't, you should have bled to death. You are alive because the arrowhead is plugging its own hole. The doctor does not expect you to last a week."

Was that all? He had listened with his eyes closed.

"You would probably die immediately if the arrow were removed. At best, you will last a few ghatis[7]."

Was this how my father's boon manifested itself?

"You mean to say, I can choose when I will die."

"Yes. That is one way to put it."

YUDHISHTHIRA'S REQUEST

Devavrata had not expected it to hurt so much. He was a warrior, and an old one at that. He had survived much. He had been cut by a sword and had lived through that. He had felt the sting of a sharp arrow before. He had felt the bone-numbing pain of slipping down a hillside after missing a step and yet recovered his balance to keep fighting. That was physical pain and only physical pain – he knew he could overcome physical pain.

This time, it was different. The thoughts that echoed in his mind could not be subdued unlike bodily pain. They grew with each reverberation and tore open an old wound that he believed had been cauterized by the passage of time – over five hundred

---

[7] A *ghati* is defined as one-sixtieth of a day (from sunrise to sunrise) and is twenty-four minutes. A *vighati* is one-sixtieth of a ghati and is twenty-four seconds.

moons[8] – yet Amba's visit had re-opened that one. She was angry because he had killed her son. He could understand that. *Why did she leave in the first place? That was a puzzle.* If he had known that she was pregnant, he might have... he was surprised that he did not recall anymore why he had been absent when she disappeared, but if he had known of her pregnancy, he would not have been absent. *Shikhandin was my son!* He thought he had become inured to surprises. The onset of war at Suyodhana's instigation, the Pandavas' escape, their alliance with Panchala, the alliance of the Yadavas, led by Krishna Gopala, *the cowherd,* with Panchala: the list of surprises was long, but this one beat them all. The dead Shikhandin was his son. *I killed my own son.* Shikhandin was the son he had vowed would not exist and now he had made good on that promise. He had no son. *Truly, I deserve to be called Devavrata Bhishma!*

It appeared as though Shikhandin's paternity was a secret from everybody else too. His great-nephew Yudhishthira had apologized for the attack – he had approved Amba's visit to take her son's body and had not imagined that she might find an opportunity to kill his killer. The apology revealed nothing more – nothing in what Yudhishthira said indicated that he knew that Shikhandin was his granduncle's son, an uncle of a king in his own right, or even that he knew of a past relationship between Amba and Devavrata.

Yudhishthira had taken care to see that Devavrata was safe and comfortable. The other Pandavas — Bhima, Arjuna, and the twins — had come by, their voices subdued and their shoulders slumped in his presence. The nurse assigned to him was brusque and abrupt in his actions – there was no love lost for the enemy commander. *Only my grand-nephews, the leaders of this camp, care if I live or die. To the rest, I am the enemy, better off dead.* The feeling was different in Suyodhana's camp – Suyodhana, his brothers, and their hangers-on did not seem to care if he lived or died, but

---

[8] A solar year is about thirteen moons, or lunar months. So five hundred moons (or months) is about forty years. Bronze Age cultures appear to have used a calendar that used the month to measure the passage of time and the years for agricultural purposes. In the interest of readability, I will use "moons" when characters are conversing but "years" during description.

the rest of their army had deferred to him. Who, indeed, was his ally?

The entrance to the tent slit its eastern side. A flap of leather stopped the rays of the morning sun. Devavrata's bed was laid along the southern side with his head towards the entrance. Alongside the western side, there had been another bed with Shikhandin's body, laid out on its back. Devavrata had puzzled over the profile, how it seemed to tug at a corner of his mind. With Amba's revelation, that mystery was explained. Amba must have taken the body away the previous night and come back when she realized that Devavrata was in the same tent. She had returned to kill him. Once upon a time, those wide eyes and high cheekbones had touched his heart to give it life; now they had returned to reclaim that life. *No matter, I am a fortunate man.* Before death claimed him, memories, from so far back that he almost doubted their reality, had materialized to lighten his heart. Those memories would assuage the sorrow that now welled up within him as he recalled watching his son die. The son he had not known he had. *Just once, before Yama takes me,* he thought, *I was permitted a glimpse of a small pleasure from lost time. I do not blame Amba; she has been the only light in my life. That is enough.*

His grandnephew posed a different problem. Yudhishthira looked subdued, as though depressed by the thought of Devavrata's imminent demise. If there were one thing Devavrata could change, it would be this – to relieve Yudhishthira of this misery. He had liked Yudhishthira as a boy and he liked him now as an adult – the slight youth with faraway eyes had changed into a dignified man who held himself like a warrior and behaved like a commander of men. However, the legitimacy of his claim was in doubt. The compromise Devavrata had forged once, many years ago, that made Yudhishthira the Chief Magistrate of Indraprastha, the breakaway republic, the "city of Indra", had collapsed under the weight of Suyodhana's ambitions. Devavrata had not expected the compromise to survive forever, but it did not even survive the first generation. His plans for the continued growth of the empire envisaged that Hastinapura would eventually rule all the surrounding lands, including Indraprastha – but the compromise had barely lasted a few years.

Yudhishthira's manner expressed genuine concern for his granduncle. He said, "Grandsire! I wish the doctor had said something different."

"Yudhishthira, my boy! I am an old man and have seen much. That my wound is fatal, I know myself. Your doctor is right. I do not have much time left. I accept it."

"I am sorry we had to capture and disable you, but that was necessary," Yudhishthira said. "This war was... is, unnecessary. No matter, now we must win it."

"You did what you had to, my son. I am sworn to protect the dynasty and ensure legitimate inheritance. As long as I live I would have to oppose you."

Yudhishthira did not respond. Devavrata's public oaths were known to all – his acceptance of his own disinheritance – but they made for whispers hinting at treason. There were secret oaths as well – celibacy and unquestioned support for the Queen Mother's children – made to his father and stepmother, which were only known to a few. Sanjaya, the family bard would sing publicly of Devavrata's vows were he not terrified of Devavrata *Bhishma*. The Vyaasa Shukla, the golden-voiced head of the Kavi Sangha, knew all that Devavrata knew and probably more. Lastly, the secret oaths were known to his nephew Dharmateja *Vidura*[9], who was known for his wisdom, intelligent, of closed mouth and open mind, born alongside his royal brothers Mahendra *Pandu*[10] and Dhritarashtra, the child of the royal wet-nurse, perfect in every way that the other two were not, but ineligible to be king because his mother was not royal, not a wife, merely a maid-servant of the queen, occasional bed-mate to their father, the dead King Vichitravirya, and wet-nurse to his sons. *Did Yudhishthira know of these vows? Was he about to question my decision to oppose him?*

Devavrata did not expect Yudhishthira to say anything. *Why should he touch on the subject?* The question of succession would be

---

[9] *Dharmateja* was called *Vidura*, meaning "the Wise." He was not a warrior, but due to his intelligence and wisdom, he was appointed Chief Minister to Devavrata Bhishma and later to Mahendra Pandu and Dhritarashtra.

[10] *Mahendra* was called *Pandu*, the Pale, possibly because of his albinism.

resolved through battle. Yudhishthira had refused to be drawn into the ancient debate over legitimacy. His father had acknowledged him as his son, eligible to be Master Trader of Hastinapura, and that was the final word.

"Our dynasty will live on," Yudhishthira said, "Its survival is not my worry. What am I worried about? The crisis that began in your time continues to confront us. My father rejected your path, and now I reject it as well. We may not undo all you have done – but we will stop the continual grab of Naga land and the eviction of the Nagas. The Yadavas have promised not to come further north. We have more than our share of refugees, immigrants or not. The next batch can go further west, beyond the mountains to Bahlika.[11] I want you to explain why you chose to create this empire. It will perhaps help us follow a wiser path, one that the Matsyas, the Yadavas, and Panchala can support. My cousins felt threatened by our proposals. You did too. War was inevitable. You may be too old to fight, but your mind is revealed in all their strategy. That is why we plotted to capture you. We only intended to capture you – we did not intend to injure you thus, let alone kill you. We thought that with you as our prisoner, Suyodhana would be left with Kutaja *Drona*[12], the master of weapons and the martial arts teacher, as the only competent advisor on the conduct of the war."

"What grieves me," Yudhishthira continued, "is that your injuries are fatal and you will die as my prisoner. I have no options in this matter. I cannot send you back. I must keep you a prisoner. My men are afraid of you and your cunning – even now I am being asked when we will execute you."

Cunning? Devavrata mused at that description. Of course, they were right. Only the cunning survive to an old age. He had survived. I must be cunning.

---

[11] *Bahlika* is believed to be either Bactria or Baluchistan. It is said to have been founded by Shantanu's brother Bahlika who abdicated and left Hastinapura.

[12] *Kutaja* means "mountain peak", but also "jar". Later, the martial arts teacher would be called *Drona*, which means "jar", specifically one used to hold the hallucinogenic drug *soma* used in Vedic ritual. Drona is possibly a pejorative name.

"What do you want from me? As you say, the crisis continues. Clearly, we have not been wise enough, for we have added war to the furnace."

"I want to know the history of the crisis. How it came about, what was tried, and what did not work. You are the only person whose knowledge goes that far back."

"Not the only person..."

"The only person I can talk to. The Queen Mother refuses to have anything to do with us. Uncle Dharmateja Vidura tells us that he supports our claims but then, being Vidura, chooses to stay in Hastinapura, at Suyodhana's side, and refuses to explain his actions. He has always helped us when we lived in Hastinapura. My mother Kunti says she will not move out of Hastinapura but that I should fight for my rights. The Vyaasa Shukla can move freely within the city – he comes and goes as he pleases – he takes care to speak in parables that nobody understands.

A sour taste rose in Devavrata's throat. He was being asked to remember on command. Remembering was what he had been doing ever since he had been captured, but those were not the memories anybody wanted.

"I need time to think. I am tired, and it is late. Can you ask me tomorrow?" *With luck I shall be dead.*

"Yes, I will," said Yudhishthira. "I will come ten ghatis after sunrise. I will bring along Indraprastha's Archivist."

An archivist! So they were getting some help from the Kavi Sangha. Devavrata mused as he carefully eased his shoulders back on the cotton roll.

THE ARCHIVIST OF INDRAPRASTHA

Lomaharshana[13], the Archivist, woke up that morning to find one of his younger colleagues sitting by his bed.

---

[13] *Lomaharshana* means "one who makes hair bristle or stand on end."

"We have a message from the Vyaasa," the junior said. "He will visit us soon, a quiet visit, without any ceremony. The Pandavas are rumored to have a senior prisoner in their camp. It is imperative that you archive his memoirs. Ask the eldest Pandava, Chief Yudhishthira, for permission and for any questions he might want answered. There cannot be any delay."

As Lomaharshana prepared himself for the day, a messenger came from Yudhishthira. "We have a prisoner whose memoirs you must archive soon for he is on his death-bed. I've told him what I want to know and he understands my requirements. You must start as soon as you can."

Lomaharshana hurriedly completed his morning rituals and meal and went to the hospital tent. He recognized the prisoner. *The Regent. Bhishma.* It was a shock to see the man, whose name had been used to scare him as a child, tied and confined to a hospital tent. Then it hit him that this capture could well mark the end of the war. The morning meal weighing down his belly suddenly felt lighter. *Capturing Devavrata the Terrible was a great achievement. If this will not make peace, what will?* The Regent was still asleep. A nurse was replacing a bloodied cotton roll placed behind the Regent with a fresh one.

"There is an arrow still stuck in his shoulder," the nurse said. "He will act as though it doesn't matter, but from time to time he will admit discomfort. The doctor says he will die if we extract the arrow, but then, he will die in a few days anyway. Why they don't let him die, I don't know. They aren't even questioning him – I would put him down on the ground and jiggle the arrow until he told us everything. Instead, we've been taking care of him, doing what we can to comfort him. I clean the wound with fresh turmeric water and keep it covered. While you are with him, just do whatever makes him comfortable. Not too much though," The nurse gave a crooked grin and left.

Lomaharshana sat down at the foot of the mat and waited for the Regent to wake up.

"Amba!" the sleeping Devavrata mumbled. Lomaharshana leaned forward to catch the word. *Who or what was Amba? Maybe he said Amma? Was he calling for his mother?* Despite the coolness of the autumn morning, Devavrata's face and throat showed beads of sweat. His cheeks glowed with a thin sheen of moisture. Lomaharshana cleared his throat loudly, but the Regent did not respond. The nurse came back and said, "He's up. Look," and before Lomaharshana could protest, he pushed the sleeping Regent's arm with a finger. Devavrata flinched and tried to turn his head. The pain brought him completely awake, his eyes wide in the effort to control his response. He saw the Archivist sitting near his feet. His eyes narrowed again and he said, "Who are you?"

The Archivist said, "Lomaharshana, sir. I am the Archivist. I have been asked to work with you. Please don't trouble yourself; there is no reason to hurry. The Commander will explain it all to you. I am waiting for him."

"Commander?"

"Chief Yudhishthira, Consort and Head of the Queen's Council. He will be here soon, sir. I would like to wait for him. I am ready, otherwise."

The Regent said, "Yes, you would be ready! You are the Archivist. Does Shukla know you are here?"

"Shukla, sir?"

"The Vyaasa, Shukla. Your leader."

"Yes, sir, he does."

"Where is he?"

"I don't know, sir. These days, his movements are secret."

Devavrata looked around the hospital tent – it was large and empty, as if erected just for him. The sun was bright outside. It was still early. Outside the shelter, the shadows cast by the early morning sun had grown shorter, and their fuzzy edges had become sharper. It had been a month since the monsoon had ended and the autumnal equinox had been celebrated. In a normal year, the harvest should be in progress. In a few days, the farmers would be busy again, preparing for the winter crop.

I am a warrior, not a farmer! That was what Suyodhana, encouraged by his friend Karna, had proclaimed when Devavrata had counselled patience. They are wrong. A warrior needs to know all that a farmer does about the cycle of the seasons. It would not be easy to satisfy Yudhishthira – what did he want to know? It was not as though Devavrata had had many policy choices. First Yudhishthira's father and now Yudhishthira acted as though there were choices. The supply of easy-to-till land was limited. The Nagas, with their slash-and-burn practices, had used the forested land inefficiently. They did not create permanent settlements, just ramshackle villages that were abandoned after ten to twenty years,[14] the spent field left fallow for at least two generations, until no one in the band recalled living in that spot. Any itinerant settler could exploit the situation; all he had to do was occupy the fallow land and scream if a Naga threatened. Yudhishthira's father had rejected patience. He, Devavrata, had tried his best, but there was no "fair" solution.

Now Yudhishthira seemed to be in a hurry. Devavrata looked around the tent. The archivist had closed his eyes and appeared to be meditating. He had assumed the *nishkamkarnarpana* [15] pose. *He has the right idea – use our training. There is no hurry. I, too, can be patient.*

Yudhishthira came on time, and alone. Again, Devavrata was struck by the difference between the cousins. A king had an entourage. Suyodhana was a king. He called himself King. He moved in Hastinapura with a coterie of courtiers who waited on him. Yudhishthira did not call himself King, or for that matter, Emperor, as some of his troops called him. He walked around the camp without an entourage. He had chosen to make his city a *janapada*, a state governed by a council chosen by the people. That had been the practice in the cities of Panchnad, the land between the Sarasvati and the Sindhu. A hereditary matriarch, advised by a council, headed the janapada. A matriarch had never ruled Hastinapura, with its unusual evolution from caravanserai to city.

---

[14] For agricultural purposes, the solar year is defined from one winter solstice to the next winter solstice.

[15] *Nishkamkarnarpana* pronounced niche-calm-cur-narp-un-u(h) means "paying attention without attachment" were a set of skills to memorize. This is one of the techniques the Kavi Sangha teaches its bards to enable them to memorize, recall, and forget what they heard.

Indraprastha, Mahendra Pandu's town, a new settlement born of Hastinapura, had chosen to return to Panchnad practice, but with some changes.

Yudhishthira sat down by Devavrata's head. His voice was soft. "Did you sleep well? Are you comfortable?"

Devavrata found himself smiling at the courtesy; he had become used to the forceful language that ruled in Suyodhana's court.

"Your people carried out your instructions perfectly, my son. You have competent hospital staff. They propped me up so that the arrow would not be dislodged. A boy attended to me every time I woke up. Why care so much for a dying man, an enemy at that?"

Yudhishthira smiled. "Should I torture you to get information about Suyodhana's war plans? I have been asked to do that. Fortunately, I do not need that from you. I have other questions, as I said yesterday. Do you remember our conversation?"

"Yes. I've thought about it all evening, and I was concerned that I would not be able to sleep. Then night fell and, fortunately, sleep took me. You want me to regurgitate ancient memories?"

"Yes," Yudhishthira said. "There is much I do not know. I was young, perhaps too young, when my father told me some of the history. He died just as I came of age. When we returned to Hastinapura, my mother was concerned that all the children were only being taught martial arts. She asked Uncle Dharmateja Vidura to take charge of our education, but he had to deal with all five of us. He taught me about the administration of your Hastinapura Empire. There was no time for anything else."

"True, we did not have any time for you. Or, for that matter, for your innumerable cousins."

"Grandsire, that isn't the past history I want to hear about. Tell me about your childhood. Tell me about your father, great-grandfather Shantanu, and what he did."

It's so easy to like this man, Devavrata thought. He is very direct, just like all of Satyavati's descendants. Maybe we are wrong to doubt his parentage, lip or no lip. There are differences

– he is polite, whereas Suyodhana and his brothers are arrogant. He wants history, not an artful story with the twists and turns that please storytellers. I cannot give him either version.

"My childhood? You cannot understand my childhood without knowing everything else that was going on at that time."

"I can listen. Begin as early as you have to. Begin with the founding of Hastinapura, if you will."

"I'll need some time to collect my thoughts."

"You can work with Lomaharshana here," Yudhishthira said.

"Yes, I have met him," Devavrata said and nodded to the Archivist who was standing silently at the foot of the bed.

WHERE IS DEVAVRATA?

Suyodhana could not stop pacing. Karna watched him range across the entire room.

"Damn it! Damn, damn, damn, Karna! I do not want to make peace with those Naga-loving Pandavas. Don't they get it? I want war!"

"Suyodhana, my friend. Cheer up!" Karna said. He had come as soon as he was called, for Suyodhana had stormed out of the council meeting.

"That meeting was a waste of time. Why did I call it?"

"It was a waste. We got what we needed, though. Permission!" said Karna.

The morning had begun with bad news. Devavrata Bhishma was missing. He had left on a secret mission with Shikhandin. It had been a week, and he had not returned. It was frustrating to work with the old man. He had ruled as Regent for so long that he could not stop ordering people around and doing things without permission. Now he had gone off on a mission that Suyodhana and Karna had tried to ignore, a fool's errand to make peace.

I do not want to make peace with those Naga-loving Pandavas. Only Karna understood how Suyodhana felt; only Karna had tasted the bitter fruit of rejection by his inferiors that Suyodhana swallowed every day. Suyodhana's spies relayed to him the word on the street – though watered down, for Suyodhana's anger would scorch the messenger. Yudhishthira was wise, Suyodhana was not; Yudhishthira was a mature adult, Suyodhana was a spoilt boy; Yudhishthira tried to be fair to all, Suyodhana favored his immigrant friends.

The siege of Indraprastha the previous year had been an extraordinary success, bar one inexcusable failure. The Pandavas had been trapped and their allies, the Panchalas and the Yadavas, had been unable to come to their aid. Blocking the upstream dam had cut off the water supply to the city. Then they had diverted the excessive snowmelts of the spring into channels that went a long way away from the city. The Pandavas' *City of Indra*, Indraprastha, had become a cemetery with thirsty and starving people and dying children. In another day or two, all the people, both the citizens of the republic, the *janapada* whose *janas* ruled, as well as the common people, the powerless and leaderless *ganas* whom the Pandavas had so publicly championed, would have handed the Pandavas' heads to him on a platter. *Five platters*, he corrected himself. *It could even have been seven if his guards had not been tricked by the wily Yadava chief Krishna, and the arrogant Panchala Matriarch, Krishnaa Agnijyotsna.*

The inexcusable failure had been to permit the Pandavas' successful escape from the city into the surrounding forests. *The fools had let them go!* After they left, Suyodhana's troops had looted the city and he had ordered its destruction. The citizens were ordered to settle elsewhere. Granduncle Devavrata, *Regent* Devavrata, had objected. *For somebody called Bhishma, he was soft.* The victory would have been a celebrated one as the Pandavas had left everything behind – wealth, clothing, slaves, and all that made life worth living. The victory should have made his, Suyodhana's, life a glorious one, but for the virus that had infected his own people – the virus of singing Yudhishthira's praises spread by exiles from the destroyed city – and had made victory taste like mud in his mouth.

Recalling the botched victory reminded him of the debacle earlier that morning that had left him angry and despairing. *I need*

Karna here and now. Karna was the only one who could pull Suyodhana out of the depression that gripped him whenever he thought of the Pandavas.

"Send for King Karna," he had said to the attendant at the door. The man had gone to find Karna. That was when the news of Devavrata's disappearance was brought to him.

As Suyodhana waited for the arrival of his friend, he heard a commotion outside. He went out and found a man lying sprawled on the ground near the door to the chamber. He was panting.

One of the gatekeepers said, "He asked for King Suyodhana!"

"Bring him here," said Suyodhana returning to his chamber. The guards picked up the man and brought him into the almost-empty chamber. Suyodhana recognized him as one of Devavrata's attendants.

"What exactly did he say?"

"The Regent Devavrata has disappeared. He says he was last seen with the stranger Shikhandin, who has also disappeared," said a guard.

Suyodhana shook his head in disgust. The old man could not do anything right!

"Karna!" he said as his friend appeared at the door. "What are we to do? The slippery Shikhandin has disappeared. Our field marshal, Devavrata Bhishma, too. I knew we should not have trusted that Naga. Bhishma! He may even be dead."

"Does it matter?" asked Karna.

"You are right; we don't need the old man. We captured Indraprastha without his help. If it had not been for the interference of my treacherous uncle Dharmateja – I should call him Vibhishana, not Vidura – we would have the Queen of Panchala serving us. We do not need him, but we cannot lose him. Granduncle knows all our defenses. If he is not dead but is a prisoner, they will torture him and extract that knowledge from him."

A meeting of the war council was in order to deal with the crisis. The council consisted of Devavrata, who was absent, Kutaja

Drona, Suyodhana, Suyodhana's brother Sushasana, and Karna. Sanjaya, the court poet, attended in place of his father, the blind King Dhritarashtra, *"King" by the grace and sufferance of Devavrata, the generous, abstemious, self-sacrificing, ever-critical Regent.* All his life, Suyodhana had endured the taunt "the son of a blind king". His uncle Dharmateja Vidura was on the council, but Suyodhana arranged for his uncle's absence by not informing him of the meeting. *What was the point of having an avowed critic of war on a war council?* He had been one of Devavrata's appointments to the council, and Devavrata was not there.

Suyodhana called the meeting and asked their martial arts teacher, Kutaja Drona, to chair it. He had all but begged him to focus on the immediate crisis caused by Devavrata's death or capture. Kutaja Drona was an obstinate, unyielding disaster as a chair; nothing that Suyodhana or Karna proposed was to his liking. *What did he think, that he was the king? His attitude was wrong. He made negativity the order of the day.* There was no point organizing an expedition to find Devavrata and rescue him if he was still alive, for they did not even know where the Pandava camp was. Nothing was possible if it was in Panchala territory. It might be in Yadava territory. They should collect intelligence from spies before trying to find the Pandavas. They could even be hiding out with the Matsyas (though Suyodhana could not imagine a drearier part of the country). Only Karna and he wanted to send out a full-scale war party.

The council wanted more information before they decided. Devavrata's guard who had returned was suspect. He said the second guard had run away, but how could he prove that? He had revealed very little useful information. Suyodhana thought it might be necessary to threaten him with torture. Kutaja Drona recommended that a small troop investigate the site of the kidnapping. The council had agreed. *They'll support anybody but me.* Suyodhana had left the session in a rage.

It had been a waste of time. It made him furious. *Investigate first, indeed.*

"What am I going to do, Karna?"

Karna said, "My friend, calm yourself. What you have is good. The council has not appointed an investigator or specified the size of the troop. Until the council meets again, you are in charge."

Suyodhana smiled. "Of course. I may not be King yet, but the Regent is absent. My father will do whatever I say. You can be the lead investigator."

"I will need a team of three hundred men."

"Good. You be the investigator. I will mobilize the rest of our army so that we are prepared to act on whatever you discover."

THE PAST THROUGH

SHANTANU

DEVAVRATA'S EDUCATION

"Tell me about your childhood. Tell me about your father."

At Yudhishthira's request, Devavrata narrated the story of his early days. Much came to mind, the memories of a child. Like the memories of some children, there was no trace of crisis or turmoil, either then or to come. He knew that his mother was sometimes pregnant, and as he grew older, he realized that his brothers or sisters disappeared soon after their birth, but these events hardly had an effect on him. He did not see his siblings when they were born, and then, suddenly, they were gone.

He skipped past his earliest memories with brief descriptions – the occasional regal visits from his father, King Shantanu, and his mother, Queen Ganga, interrupting an endless routine of playing with the attendants who took care of him, of crying when his parents or his attendants demanded obedience to some rule, of ordering the servants around the house, of running along the riverbank and building sandcastles. As he learned to talk, visits from his mother became more regular and patterned. She hugged him and called him *laḍla*, "sweet boy." He, in turn, called her *avva*, "mommy". He would wait for her hugs even as he moved from one caretaker to the next and from one teacher to the next.

In the beginning, the King did not seem to know what to do with a toddler. Devavrata was his one and only son, and Shantanu envied the boy's easily expressed affection for the Queen. As Devavrata learned to speak and became articulate, his father came by more often. He asked his son to call him *bābō*, "papa", rather than *Rājan* or *Mahān*,[16] or other names that Devavrata had used, imitating the people around him who were always deferential to the King. The switch was awkward at first. But Devavrata wanted to please his father and tried to be informal when at home with his father.

Shantanu took Devavrata to public events, and Devavrata took pleasure in his father's pride in him. The king took Devavrata to council sessions where the boy sat quietly to the right of and behind his father's high seat. It seemed reasonable to be proud of this indulgence and to observe how his father conducted himself as the leader of the council, a role Devavrata was being groomed for. He observed the decisions involved in being the Chief – judging, rewarding or punishing, and finally, facing up to the consequences of those decisions. His family seemed happy and secure.

Then his mother died.

Devavrata's voice trailed away. Yudhishthira watched him as he stopped speaking.

"If it pertains to this war, you must tell me," Yudhishthira said, his voice still soft and quiet, but with the authority of a Ruler.

Why am I telling this story? Devavrata thought. *Is what happened to my mother relevant today?* It might bother him like the incessant flapping of a hummingbird sipping from a jasmine flower, but that did not make it relevant to others. What had happened to his mother that day was not inconsequential; it had cast a shadow on the rest of his life. The events of that day made him the Regent he had become. They influenced his key decisions that led to certain actions and forced more decisions. It could be said that the events

---

[16] *Rājan* is usually translated as "King," with the connotation of "Glorious One" or "Resplendent One;" *Mahān* means "Great One".

leading to his mother's death also led to this war. Those events were relevant to Yudhishthira's questions about policy.

Devavrata said, "When my father and mother had a disagreement, the house would darken and the air would become hot and humid like the herald of a monsoon storm. I am sure this was only in my mind, for the mansion itself was never heavy and oppressive. All the staff walked on tiptoe when my parents fought, trying to avoid attention. Even though I was only eight years old, Mother and Father would be short with me. My Mother tried to make up for the irritability with an impulsive excess of unexpected hugs. I made occasional attempts to ask my mother what the matter was, but she did not answer. I later concluded that she was preoccupied and did not listen to my questions. I was not used to being taken seriously by my parents, so that was no surprise. This is a report of my observations. I understood the situation many years later, and my memory is undoubtedly colored by that later knowledge.

"I was eleven years old when my mother died. I understood everything that had led to her death. You may be surprised at that. It was a consequence of my education, which had deviated from the traditional. I had learned to memorize conversations that I heard, even if I did not understand them then, I could recall and understand them later."

"What was different about your education?" Yudhishthira said.

Devavrata continued, "As was customary for the first son and heir of a great trading family, I had started my schooling at the age of six. Yes, the Kauravas were becoming warriors, but they continued to be a trading family. My schooling would follow an established pattern appropriate for the future master of a caravan. That pattern has changed now, for the Kauravas have become warriors, as our ancestor Samvarana wanted. Suyodhana's cohort, warriors all, looks down on traders. My father's descendants today would not recognize the kind of education I received.

"I received a trader's education. It started as soon as I could speak meaningful sentences describing actions by others. Speech proved that I was not mentally disabled. The test showed that I could interpret simple actions and sequences of actions performed by others and describe them in simple sentences. Once schooling started, I did very well and advanced rapidly in comparison to the other traders' children of my own age. I had little to do and, being bored, I joined the bards in their training sessions. By the age of twelve, they were expected to accurately memorize complete conversations that lasted for at least a half-ghati, recall shorter conversations with intonation, and the core content of longer conversations of up to three ghatis. I enjoyed these classes.

"Trading families believed in training[17] their children in multiple skills. Trading was the only guild to do that systematically. Memorizing the manifest of a caravan was one skill; being prepared to fight off bandits to protect the caravan was another. Both were necessary. Thus, we also trained to fight, which consisted of exercise routines to develop the strength of various muscles in the body so that the hands and feet became fighting instruments, the centre of the body the source of power, the eyes as windows that not only let one view the world, but could also expose an enemy's innermost thoughts.

"After memorization and martial arts, the third aspect of my education was unique to me as the son of the Kaurava ruler of Hastinapura. We Kauravas had to do more than defend ourselves; we had to inspire the warriors we led into battle. The guild of mercenaries selected promising apprentices to undergo training in command, called officer training. Guru Vasishtha, the first Vyaasa, had persuaded the master of the guild of mercenaries of his time to train the officers in Samvarana's army. Guru Vasishtha had also persuaded the senior-most Matriarch of Panchnad that a form of the training that prospective matriarchs received should be provided to Samvarana, the Master Trader of Nagapura, as well as his chosen descendants, as long as they were the guardians of the Panchnad frontier. There is much superstition about this training. No, we do not have a command voice that compels obedience. We do not enter a mystic trance in which we consult with past matriarchs before we come to a

---

[17] More details on the training of an apprentice trader may be found in Appendix A.1.

decision. We do learn what it feels like to be at the reins of a runaway cart. We learn to steel our gut and take decisive action in the face of uncertainty.

"This brings us to the greatest change between our world and that of Panchnad: The Master of a caravan is a man who wields supreme power, while in a Panchnad city, the Matriarch wields power with the advice of her council. This is as it should be, since a caravan may have to go through hostile territory controlled by bandits or meet criminals who pretend to be friends and act as spies for enemies. The Master must have a free hand to make crucial and deadly decisions under pressure. Guru Vasishtha and King Samvarana made this the model of governance for Hastinapura. The ruler of Hastinapura, like a caravan Master, is ever ready for battle. Panchnad was a land in which cities settled conflicts without war; Hastinapura and its neighbors will settle conflicts by war and nothing else."

"Granduncle!" Yudhishthira said, "You've talked about this before. I recall quite distinctly your telling me many years ago that in Panchnad conflict was not settled by wars. I was unable to understand you, for all my life, the prospect of war has never been far away. How did Panchnad settle conflicts without war? All the foreign cultures that I have heard about from travelers and traders engage in war. How did Panchnad become a war-free culture?"

"As you may have found," Devavrata said, "Traders who have gone on caravans to the West attest to the unique features of Panchnad, the most unusual being the way society was organized. This organization was the key behind the absence of war. Most of the ordinary citizens, not being traders, did not know that these were unique features of their culture. The people of Panchnad did not understand how special they were.

"The practice of war, so common in the west, was considered strange in Panchnad. The scholars in Takshashila have an explanation. They call the period in which Panchnad developed the Third Age. It is tempting to call these present times that we live in the Fourth Age. What the Fourth Age will be like, nobody knows. But it is likely to be the baleful Age of Kali, the Age of Strife. I say this with conviction, because the world has been at war for most of my life. The coming of the Age of Kali was presaged by its shadow on the lands to the west. Parsaka[18], Sumer[19], Elam[20], and even powerful Lauhityapada[21] abandoned trade as the path to prosperity and succumbed to war, with external enemies as well as internal ones. The effluent of war clogged and then blocked the river of trade and then stopped it completely.

"My son, you want to know how this one-of-a-kind society came about. I will tell you, but remember this: it will be impossible to recreate. That was your father's confused goal."

Yudhishthira said, "I want to know more about Panchnad and the world in the Third Age. Tell me what you know of the Third Age: the world at large and Panchnad in particular."

PANDAVAS WILL LOSE THE WAR

Devavrata paused in his narration. He said, "Yudhishthira! Your own world is disintegrating around you. You are struggling to save yourself and your brothers. In my opinion, you are losing. Why do you want to know about the world and the Third Age?"

Yudhishthira said, "Grandsire! You are one of the few people who know the greater world. The immigrants and the Nagas struggle to maintain themselves. Suyodhana and his cohort have no interest beyond the immediate. The Kavi Sangha keeps its secrets. When peace returns, we will need to know more about the rest of the world. It is not idle curiosity."

Devavrata said, "Once again, I regret your father's decision to separate himself from Hastinapura. That is in the past. My

---

[18] *Parsaka* is the ancient name for Persia in South Asian literature.

[19] *Sumer* is the name for the group of city-states that began the urbanization of Mesopotamia (around 3000 B.C.E.).

[20] *Elam* was an ancient non-Semitic culture in southern Iran that frequently came into conflict with the Semitic Sumer and Mesopotamia. In 2000 B.C.E., Elam was the hegemon, and the once-powerful Sumer was reduced to poverty.

[21] *Lauhityapada* means the "Land of the Children of Red (soil)," or maybe "People of the Red Way." One of the names used by Egyptians for their country was The Red People's Land.

narration may fill this hole in your education. I regret that it may be wasted in your lost cause."

"I am grateful for your courtesy, grandsire."

Devavrata continued, "My education, as I've described, was very different from what is taught now. As a trader, I learned some bardic skills, some warrior skills, some linguistic skills, and some skills in observing cultures. Now the Kauravas are warriors and this war, your war, is like no other war in Panchnad's history. The Kuru family are not traders anymore; they are warriors and empire builders.

"To repeat, this change has its origins in the exile of Samvarana by the Panchalas, your ally. Hastinapura was a border town that was treated as a glorified caravanserai. The Nagas of Panchala drove out the Kuru leader Samvarana. He returned and re-took Hastinapura with the first Panchnad army that was trained to kill its opponents, not capture them. Samvarana's guru, Vasishtha, helped create and train this army. The army became a permanent institution to protect Hastinapura from the Panchalas. Hastinapura was no longer a Panchnad town, but a militarized state, perpetually ready for war. Meanwhile, Vasishtha's organization, the Kavi Sangha, became the foremost advisor of the Kuru family."

"I understand now what my father was talking about," Yudhishthira said, "when he denounced the patriarchal city. It came about through war and was sustained by an army. In turn that army presented a fierce face to the world and ensured the continuance of hostility."

"Yes," Devavrata said, "the Kauravas were traders and warriors, but we also created the first patriarchal state in our world. My policies were built on this framework. As you point out, your father disagreed: strongly enough that he exiled himself rather than work in a state that he could not change. He took you away and raised your brothers according to his values. In hindsight, that was a mistake; he should have stayed. You would have been educated and not been ignorant of necessary knowledge and skills.

"As it was, when you and your brothers turned up in Hastinapura, we could still train your bodies. Bhima and Arjuna have become formidable warriors. Your minds had developed according to what your father taught you. You could not have become traders even if you had wanted to. There is much more to being a warrior than brute strength, and we left you to learn those other skills on your own."

"For what little I have learned, I have to thank Uncle Dharmateja Vidura," Yudhishthira said, "I know, though, that you are right. My brothers were enamored of the warrior's path that you showed them and did not choose to learn from their wise uncle."

"Yes, your uncle tried, but I do not believe he could have succeeded," Devavrata said. "I was surprised when he took such an interest in your education. For most of his life up to then, he had been like a restrained version of Dhritarashtra. I knew that Mahendra Pandu's defiance of my policies and self-exile had impressed Dharmateja Vidura. He paid many visits to Indraprastha and brought back useful information. He is truly Vidura, the wise. If only Dhritarashtra and Suyodhana would listen to him."

"His visits were welcome ones," Yudhishthira said. "When I was young, I had no idea who he was. He played with us, brought news of events in Hastinapura to my father and my mothers, Kunti and Madri. He was a kind uncle. He taught me a great deal."

"Dharmateja Vidura was the child of a servant, not a Kshatriya, so even though he was the son of the King, he was not educated as a warrior," Devavrata said. "He was raised alongside Mahendra Pandu and Dhritarashtra, so he learned things he would never have learned otherwise. Even so, he could not have made you a greater warrior than Suyodhana. Do you understand why I think you will lose to Suyodhana? Forgive me for saying that, but I have no use for tact now. Suyodhana received the education you and your brothers did not, education as a warrior."

For the first time, Yudhishthira raised his voice and interrupted Devavrata's remarks.

"Grandsire! I do not take offence at your critical statements about my education or that of my brothers. Surely, it is irrelevant to the story you were telling, isn't it? How does this relate to the immigrants? How does it relate to this war? What, in your opinion, do I need to know and can you teach it to me now? Can you tell me why the Nagas opposed the establishment of Hastinapura and the consequences of that opposition?"

"The deficiencies in your education and that of your brothers are relevant," said Devavrata. "Suyodhana is a skilled warrior. He has skilled strategists working for him. His education, just like mine, trained him in war. Unlike me, he has trained to be nothing but a warrior. He is capable of recognizing a thousand distinct sounds in their context and reacting accordingly. His hands and fingers were trained to be flexible and strong – sensitive enough that, blindfolded, he can identify objects by touch, strong enough that his grip is unshakeable. That is the origin of his battle-name *Duryodhana*[22]. I know that the name has been used to mock him, and he is easily irritated by the insults. He had the best teachers on strategy we could get from Parsaka, where war is a persistent way of life for the cities. This, too, I don't expect you and your brothers to have learned and maybe you do not appreciate it. You may have tactical successes like my capture, but you will fail to win the war."

"That may be. If we fail, we fail. Our consolation will be that we will have tried to move the world down the kinder, gentler path that my father wished to take."

Devavrata sighed. Had Yudhishthira not understood him? Had his bluntness clouded the message? Yudhishthira had asked to be educated and in that he could help.

"I will answer your questions and then continue to tell the history leading to my father's policies," he said.

---

[22] *Duryodhana*, means "Bad Warrior". However, the connotations of the adjective "Bad" are controversial. It could be interpreted as "difficult" or "malevolent" rather than "unskilled," the last being pejorative while the first two might imply great skill.

Annals of the Kavi Sangha

One thousand and two hundred years after the start of what would be called the Kali Era, Hastinapura suffered a crisis – a flood destroyed the city, killing most of the kavis. The oral archives, memorized by the kavis, were in danger of being lost. The Vyaasa Vaishampaayana initiated a project to write down the oral archives.

In addition to stories with heroes and heroines and gods and goddesses, these archives contain information of interest to historians. The answers to many of Yudhishthira's questions fall in this category. These questions and answers are rarely recited in public, but they are an important piece of the archives. These are the Annals of the Kavi Sangha.

Appendix A.2: The Four Ages of the World

Yudhishthira said, "What did people believe about the state of the world, in particular, the concept that we were on the brink of a Fourth Age of extreme evil; that the transition from one Age to the next would be calamitous and traumatic; and, that all humanity would be destroyed at the end of the Fourth Age."

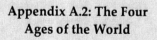

Appendix A.3: The Rarity of War in Panchnad

Yudhishthira said, "All my life the prospect of war has never been far away. How did Panchnad settle conflicts without war? All the foreign cultures that I have heard about, from travellers and traders, engage in war. How did Panchnad become a war-free culture?"

Appendix A.4: The End of the Third Age

Yudhishthira said to Devavrata, "I want to know more about Panchnad and the world in the Third Age. Tell me what you know of the Third Age: the world at large, and Panchnad in particular."

Appendix A.5: Naga Reaction: Panchala and Nagapura

Yudhishthira asked Devavrata how Hastinapura had been established despite the hostility of the Nagas. The Annals record Devavrata's opinion.

MOTHER

DEVAVRATA LISTENS

Devavrata said, "You have now heard all there is to know of the history of our family's city. Do you have any further questions, my son?"

Yudhishthira said, "Grandsire! Let me ponder on what you have said. I have many questions, but I will wait as I would rather know how your father's policies affected the people and the state. Please continue with your memories of childhood."

Devavrata said, "Out of boredom with my teachers in the guild of traders, I had joined the guild of bards in their classes. I began as a precocious student in listening. Less than thirty moons[23] into my education, I could report conversations lasting as long as a ghati. I could memorize lists of words exceeding one hundred. I could identify over a hundred sounds. I had arrived at the level of expertise expected of an eleven-year-old apprentice bard ready to enter a period of intense study under the tutelage of one or more teachers. I was still a child; I thought my parents knew of

---

[23] About two-and-a-half years.

this precocity. But, in retrospect, it seems that perhaps they did not. Many of my interactions were with servants and teachers who reported remarkable progress, but my parents must have immediately discounted it. When my parents quarreled, they seemed unaware of my presence nearby. A normal eight-year-old would not have understood their conversations. I certainly did not. But I memorized them and retrieved the memory later, at a time when I did understand.

"Why is this relevant, you ask? I was an eight-year-old with the memorization skills of a much older boy. I spied on my parents, and what I heard went into some dark corner of my mind. Over the years, I came to understand those words better through replaying the conversations in my mind. I finally understood the events of the year my mother died."

It struck Devavrata that something had changed in Yudhishthira. He had come in abruptly without the usual polite excuses. His eyes frequently darted to the entrance and when they came back to focus on him, they seemed to have lost their brightness. *Was he even listening? What was the hurry?* He would have to solve that puzzle. In the meantime, Devavrata did not want to change his narrative. Whatever hurry Yudhishthira was in, that hurry could wait.

"May I continue?"

Yudhishthira's forehead furrowed as he tried to grasp what Devavrata had said. He summarized in his mind: Devavrata's memorization skills were not public knowledge, and he did not display them. The rulers of Hastinapura no longer trained to be anything other than warriors. They trained to be warriors and nothing else.

"Yes, of course."

Devavrata went on:

"I listened to all the conversations that went on in my house and memorized them. I was young and had not developed the moral measuring stick by which to judge a person's actions, whether the person was my parent or my teacher or even the staff with whom I spent most of my time. That judgment came later. That is the power of memorization skills – the past is not a closed book, you can retrieve saved memories and learn from it again and again.

"One day, I was about to enter my mother's private chambers. That morning she had gone to the river-side cottage where her father lived. I knew she had returned when one of her maids ran out to moisten the *kusha* grass screen and to fetch the fan. I heard my father's voice and stepped back. There was an edge to his voice – of pleading – he sounded as I did when I wheedled a sweet from the cook. I stopped and listened. I automatically memorized what was said, but I only understood some of it then.

"My father said, 'Gangu, Gangu, Gangu! Why can't you understand?' I recognized the signs of a major breakdown – my father called my mother Gangu only when he was aroused or overwrought. "We face a crisis! For fifty years, from the time of my grandfather, we have been struggling with this problem. We chose to be generous to the refugees as they came here. Everybody agreed to make the sacrifice – that is what makes us great. What's the use if we cannot...? We have become poorer. Our enemies grow stronger. Every day I hear about some Panchala demagogue who wants to create a new army to liberate our Nagas. We need to be more practical, more pragmatic. You know that the Kavi Sangha felt that we were being too kind – they had proposed exiling all refugee families that had children, or killing their newborn children. That would encourage them to go further east. I disagreed – they would be going into a wilderness with no support from us. I said... we said, *No, we must all bear the burden*, and softened the law that the Kavi Sangha had formulated. We made the law that each family would be allowed one child to replace each adult in the family. We applied this to everybody! We stopped referring to them as refugees and called them immigrants. We voluntarily treated them as our equals, even though we were the overwhelmed hosts and they were the desperate and impoverished guests. We all took a risk – all we need to do now is survive this drought and the threat of famine. We will survive, and in a few years, when the crisis is past, we can repeal these laws. If not me, it will be my son Devavrata who will repeal the laws!'"

Yudhishthira said, "Grandsire, your voice changed and you did not sound like a wounded warrior. Are these truly the exact words you heard? How can you reproduce it with such fidelity?"

Devavrata said, "My memory is perfect. That is exactly what he said, but I have often wondered at those words – that I would repeal those laws? You may not realize it, but much is lost in this recitation. Was he proud that I would repeal his laws? Was he chagrined that he could not? What else was hidden in those words? I had learned to memorize speech after a single hearing, but teasing out the inner meaning had not figured in that feat. It took some time, but I had learned to memorize the intonation, but did I have all the elements that convey emotion? It was the first time I had put a learned skill to use, and there was something magical and wonderful about it. I stood there memorizing my father's words even as he spoke, even as in my mind I observed myself memorizing, full of wonder at my ability.

"You ask how this memory works. I don't know but I have an image that provides a metaphor. Perhaps it will help. The sounds come in and are transmuted in my mind into the parts of a giant tree, an awe-inspiring banyan tree that provided the framework for that memory. With loving care, the sounds were deposited, one on this leaf, another on that branch. Some made their way onto the hanging roots and clung to them like butterflies. Others fluttered about for an absurdly long time, tiny jeweled hummingbirds refusing a perch until the right one was found, and they too transmuted into butterflies. As the tree filled up with sound that created a background chorus, the butterflies would sparkle and light up, providing hooks for unravelling the chain of a melody. The shortcomings of memory that I complain about are afterthoughts; in hindsight, the most magical acts become mundane and tiresome. Meaning was in the melody, and it had to be played, or as in this case, replayed, to extract content.

"The beauty of what I imagined overwhelmed the child that I was – it was a long time – years before I went beyond memorizing the sounds to understand the words. That required rehearsing the words, and that is what I did. I rehearsed not just this but many other conversations that I chanced to overhear until I understood them. With understanding, they lost the sparkle of wonder.

"For a long time, I felt that I had committed a crime, a crime of omission. If only I had allowed myself to understand this dialogue that I had memorized with such pleasure, I might have been able to protect my mother. There were days when I searched desperately through the stock of remembered conversations, rehearsing each one looking for more evidence of my culpability. Most of them revealed little that was worth remembering forever. However, I found the mundane exciting for it revealed details of lives that as Regent I would never experience for myself. When I was done with a memory, it would return to its assigned spot in the banyan tree of my mind. Then I recalled a few that showed the repeated conflicts between my mother and my father. I had memorized much that could only be retrieved by invoking the feelings of the time. Even as I grasped the meaning of some significant narrative, I discovered that some of them seemed to become lost and were forgotten. The act of rehearsing could result in forgetting these highly charged memories; that is one of the methods for managing memory that the Kavi Sangha calls *nishkamsmaranadharanam*[24]. Luckily, not all of them vanished, and I stopped rehearsing. The memories were depressing to review in this manner. But despite that, there were days when I would return like an addict to rehearse just one more conversation and then one more and then another until I hit one between my father and mother. When that memory faded in the act of rehearsing, I would react with self-accusation and vow never to do it again."

Yudhishthira said, "Grandsire, are you saying that what I have asked you to do risks your memories being lost forever? In that case, I should…"

Devavrata said, "I am dying, and these memories will be useless and lost. Let me judge for myself what memories I wish to die with and what I wish to hand over. If you win this war, they may be of use to you."

"Your death will be a burden I must carry."

---

[24] *Nishkamsmaranadharanam*, pronounced niche-calm-smur(f)-run-u(h)-thar-run-um, means "holding on to memory without attachement". They were a set of skills to manage memory. This is one of the techniques the Kavi Sangha teaches its bards to enable them to memorize, recall, and forget what they heard.

"Such are the unique burdens that only a ruler can carry. If my memories are to be of any use, Yudhishthira, you as the King must carry this burden."

Yudhishthira took a deep breath. Yes, I do want to understand this part of the past. He nodded.

Devavrata continued, "In any case, I listened. I had three choices – I could leave, but I did not have the desire to do so. In the beginning I felt that this conversation made sense and revealed secrets to me that I did not know. I could go in and interrupt a quarrel that I did not fully understand. I could stay and listen to the conversation. Much of that conversation was new to me. We had been suffering a crisis since the days of my grandfather Pratipa; I had not known that! There were refugees. I wondered: who were they? How could I identify a refugee? What made them different from non-refugees? My father had said *We...call them immigrants now.* I knew about immigrants, they lived in the immigrant quarter of Hastinapura. I did not know that they did not belong there, that they were not just another guild that provided a ghetto for its members, but people who were guests at first, and whom now it was difficult to feed.

"The conversation continued with even more worrying statements: *We have become poorer. Our enemies grow stronger.* What was this crisis, and why did I know nothing about it? Then, that the Kavi Sangha had proposed a harsh law. I knew about the Kavi Sangha. They were the intellectual bulwarks of the Kuru family ever since Guru Vasishtha, the founder of the Kavi Sangha, had taught King Samvarana a new way, the way of the warrior. Every day, a Kavi Sangha member would be a guest at our dinner ceremony. A brief session with the King would be followed by the recital of poetry. Dinner would follow. Occasionally, the Vyaasa Parashara came and told stories while the children of the palace ate dinner. Once I had asked him what he did when he was not telling stories. He said that he wrote poetry. I had asked him what the Kavi Sangha did, and he answered they told stories and remembered everything. They were especially good at memorizing and repeating stories. Knowing my own ability for memorizing, I had asked him if I should join the Kavi Sangha. My mother had frowned, but the Vyaasa had smiled and said, 'Yes, of course. You will be a great leader who will do great things.'"

Yudhishthira said, "Grandsire! Our time is limited. Did you find out what the law was?"

"You are right, I digress. What had my father said? That they had proposed applying a much harsher law restricted to the immigrants just to encourage them to go east. I knew about 'going east'. That has been the Kaurava mission since the founding of Hastinapura. Every year at the Spring Festival, the directive of the Name-giver, Hastin, would be recited. It talked about the historic role of all the descendants of Puru to keep the Panchnad culture alive, of the Bhaaratas to spread it in all directions, and the particular mission of his own descendants to populate the East. The only descendants of Hastin who had whole-heartedly accepted this mission were Kuru's descendants, the Kauravas. The others had been killed by the Panchalas, or had abandoned Samvarana, or like my uncle Bahlika, accepted the offer of leadership elsewhere. There were many other directives, but this was the strangest one, for in those days settling in the East was an unthinkable fantasy. 'The Kauravas cannot go east from here.' The last assertion was by my mother's father, a man who said little, and what he said was difficult to understand. My father disagreed. Neither the Naga nor the long-term settler could be coerced, but the immigrants could be. The immigrants had to go east and relieve the burden on Hastinapura. My father just did not know how to make it happen."

"Grandsire!"

"Yudhishthira, I hesitate to describe the law."

"Grandsire! You are called Bhishma. What law could be so beyond the pale that it makes you hesitate?"

"Yudhishthira, please be patient. Let me tell you at my pace."

"Of course, Grandsire."

Devavrata continued, "The Nagas and the immigrants were a study in contrast. The Nagas moved often but did not want to migrate; the immigrants had migrated but did not want to move. Once a month, the King and I would make a trip to the Naga temple that was at the center of the city. To get there from the King's mansion, we had to ride a bullock cart through the newly formed immigrant quarter and then through the Naga quarter. Sometimes I would sit with the carriage driver, a family fixture named Bakakula. Bakakula gave a pithy description: The immigrant quarter looked like the residents had come to stay, while the Naga quarter looked like the residents were passing through. I don't know whether Bakakula was trying to impress me with his wisdom or repeating a common observation.

"At other times, I would sit with my father and as we exited the immigrant quarter, my father would make his observation. 'Compare the immigrant quarter to the Nagas,' he would say. 'We, the city dwellers, love the immigrants. They keep everything so neat and tidy, unlike the Nagas. Take note, however, that it is the Nagas who go into the forest to hunt, it is the Nagas who cultivate crops, no matter how inefficiently, and it is the Nagas who will forgo neatness and control to settle in the jungle.'

"It took me many years to realize that my father and the driver were not disagreeing with each other. The Nagas are the ones prepared to settle a new frontier land, while the immigrants hope to join a developed culture, and this can make all the difference.

"At that time, their statements left me confused. What did father approve of? He would get upset if the house was not maintained meticulously, occasionally calling the house manager in for a lecture on some shortcomings – cobwebs in the corner, dust not swept off the hearth. This upset everybody, beginning with my mother, as she was the one who gave the orders to the house manager. My father's intervention would then lead to a private discussion between them, my mother calling my father's actions unbecoming of a chief. At these sessions, I would be a lamppost, listening, saying nothing, etching those discussions in my memory.

"In the conversation I am telling you about, there was a difference. My mother's voice had piqued my interest because she punctuated her words with sniffles; she must have been weeping. She sounded sad, not angry, and I had rarely seen this. My father's voice was also different, not the low bass that he used when talking to his ministers, but a voice that pleaded, almost a whine in the beginning, then transitioning to the bass as he became more confident and assertive. He had mentioned my name, Devavrata, and I took that as a cue to enter."

DEVAVRATA IS PUZZLED

Devavrata said, "I ran in breathing a bit heavily as though I had come running from further away. I look back in wonder at my ability, even at that age, for deception. I used to mimic my father talking to his ministers, my audience being the driver and the cook, and it was only a short stretch from an act to a pretense to a lie. I stood there breathing heavily and said, 'Father! You called for me! Does that mean you will play with me now?'

"My father did what he always said when he wanted to distract attention – talk. 'Yes, glorious youth!' he began. You and your generation, Yudhishthira, are used to this kind of speech, but it is a new thing, a style that the Panchnad immigrants brought to Hastinapura. Complimentary adjectives that meant little but added little flowers of grace to conversation. I had not yet been taught to speak formally, using the language of the court, but already in my father's time, the fashionable speech had evolved to this elaborate decorative form. My father could never use it with a straight face; so when he addressed me formally, I felt I was being mocked. It made me want to squirm, to scratch an itch that could not be reached. I had to keep still as he was the King even though he was my father.

"He bowed and smirked, 'Yes, glorious youth! And what is your wish this time?' I wanted the fight to stop, and the best way would be to draw him away from my mother's quarters. We used to play a game in which I would shoot magic arrows, *astras*, like the ones in the stories of the gods and demons that were performed on festival days. I would shoot Agni's *agneyastra*, and father pretended to put out the fire. I would fire Indra's *indreyastra*, which casts a web of illusion on its targets, and father would pretend to be snared in an illusory world. When I wanted to stop playing the game, I would shoot Brahma's *brahmastra*, the weapon that would destroy all of Brahma's creation, not just the material world of the senses, but the immaterial world of consciousness as well. Yudhishthira, you are smiling, but when I was a child, I wanted to believe though I knew these weapons were fantasy.

"I said to my father, 'You will be the target, and I'll shoot a *brahmastra* at you! What will happen this time?' I was concerned that this was a transparent attempt to distract him, but my mother intervened.

"My mother said, 'Dev, go outside and play!'

"That made the decision for my father.

"Father said, 'Let him be!' Then, to me, 'I'll fall to the ground and gibber like a monkey.'

"Mother's face was set in a frown. She said, 'This is what you do when I talk about my concerns. You can do what you wish to your clan. Why kill my sons?'

"Father said, 'Dev, go outside and play.' He took my hand and led me into the back garden. He pointed to a tree, 'See if you can hit it at fifty paces with your arrow.' He went back inside.

"I waited a vighati or so, hoping he would return, then sat down on the stoop by the closed door and rested my chin on my fist. That was what Sanghamitra, the cook, did when he was thinking about a recipe or contemplating a taste. He looked as if he was in deep thought, lost in an ocean of self-realization. It seemed an appropriate pose. I contemplated the *tulsi* bush and listened.

"My father's voice came through clearly. 'We have sacrificed a hundred children like them. Do I only kill the daughters of the immigrants? That was the Kavi Sangha's recommendation! I rejected that option. What was I supposed to say to the people, that we should apply such laws only to the immigrants? Are we Yavanas with one law for visitors and a different one for residents? Are we Mlecchas who enslave captured women for their own entertainment? Are we like the Sumerians who say that boys are better than girls? Are we? Are we?'

"That day I did not understand anything. Now I understand everything. What is the use of hearing if one cannot understand what is heard? Once something has been said, it can never be repeated with the same meaning. Ah! That startled you,

Yudhishthira. Isn't that a thought to contemplate? That even though the pupil is first taught to memorise, even though the crowd is displeased if a bard changes a story by as much as a word, even though our word for knowledge is memory,[25] we cannot reproduce the past even in speech – it is truly lost time.

"My boy, you are impatient with my digressions. I can see that. The point of a story is its interpretation, isn't it? You shake your head. No matter. I will get on with the story.

"What did I understand? That the Kavi Sangha wanted to kill all the children? They were talking about Uncle Vyaasa! He wanted to kill all the children. How could something so frightening be true?

"My mother said, 'You counter criticism with this story you made up, about these dead children being your nomadic forefathers, the Vasus, re-incarnated to bless your enterprise. Your poets spread this ridiculous story that every dead child, boy and girl, is a god or a goddess.'

"She continued, 'I have to do something. The banks of the river are dotted with small mounds of dirt commemorating these dead children. When this is over, we will know exactly what it has cost us. I know what it cost me. I would have been happy just to hold them for a few days. My arms longed to cradle them, my breasts longed for their lips, my eyes longed to smile back into their eyes.'

"My father replied, 'Shall I change the laws and make it apply only to daughters?'

"My mother said, 'No. What if my next two children are girls? I'll kill myself if you change the laws again. I would look forward to my next baby. But not with you for a husband…'

"My mother was going to kill herself? Why? Because of laws that my father had enforced on the advice of the Kavi Sangha. That did not make sense. What did she mean? The distracted

---

[25] *Shruti* means both "knowledge that has been revealed by hearing" and "memory of orally revealed knowledge." (Revelation was considered to be more like hearing than like seeing.) Such a concept of knowledge would characterise an oral, pre-literate culture (like Panchnad in 2000 B.C.E.).

thoughts would have made me miss the rest of the conversation, but my autonomic training helped.

"My father asked, 'Are you expecting?'

"Mother replied, 'Yes.'

"He said, 'Let's hope that it's a girl.'

"At that, my mother stayed silent. Their voices went low, and I could not hear them anymore. After some time, it became obvious that my father had forgotten his promise and was not coming out to play with me. I did not want to go in, so I left through the outhouse gate and wandered down to the river where I often spent my time."

Yudhishthira said, "Grandsire, so the law was that each family could have one son?"

Devavrata said, "Yes, and one daughter. More to the point, each person could have one child of his or her own gender to replace himself or herself."

"I see. That will keep the population constant over many years."

"Yes. Yudhishthira, I am telling this to you in the hope that you understand. My earliest memories are colored by this crisis. All our subsequent solutions to the crisis have been traumatic."

"May we not create our own solutions?" said Yudhishthira.

Devavrata reflected on his grandnephew's words. Yes. Every generation demands the right to repeat the previous generations' mistakes. It was a fruitless debate.

"You say you have a solution. You are shaking your head. You disagree with me? I don't claim to have a solution anymore, but your solutions will be no better."

He could feel frustration build up. He had to be careful that he did not gesticulate and move the arrow. That would kill him. *I'll finish the story I have started.*

"Days passed," Devavrata said. "I could not talk to anybody about this. Not Bakakula, the cart and carriage driver, however close he might have become to my father after his many years of service. Not Sanghamitra, the cook, he would withdraw at the first sign of criticism directed at Father or Mother. I could not see any way to talk to my parents about this. They would be upset that I had overheard them. I fretted for a few days, watching Mother carefully for signs that she might kill herself. Nothing happened. What signs was I looking for anyway, and how would I recognize them when they showed up? Mother was as cheerful with me as ever, nor did Father change. The words did not increase in meaning when I rehearsed them; rather they began to look more ordinary and forgettable. One of the hazards of the bard's profession, as I told you, is that too much private rehearsal of memorized oral events can result in forgetting.

"My education continued along the same two streams – physical training to be a warrior and mental training in memorizing, calculation, and reporting observations, to work as a trader. The increased emphasis on the military training was Guru Vasishtha's contribution. He had taken a trading clan and created warriors out of them, a clan ever prepared for battle. The physical training focused on the use of weapons, the effective use of armor, and accuracy with the bow and arrow. We are no longer traders, neither you nor Suyodhana have been trained to trade."

Devavrata paused in his telling. Lomaharshana leaned toward him and held a small jar of water to his mouth. Devavrata took a sip; the cool water felt sweet on his tongue. Even so, it did not wash away the bitter taste of the memories he was dredging up. *This is another slice of history you do not know, Yudhishthira. Your father is to blame for the appalling way he educated you, failing to understand why the Kauravas bear arms while the rest of the civilized world hires mercenaries.*

Devavrata said, "My mother then became ill and was confined to her quarters. I know now that she was pregnant, but I did not know it then as I was kept in ignorance of her pregnancies. She wanted the child to be a girl. I've learned that the general belief is that if a woman does not see a man during her confinement, the baby will be a girl. It does not always work that way, but the failures can be explained away. If the baby is a boy, the mother must have encountered a man during confinement, and if the baby is a girl, the mother did not encounter any men. If some man did visit, she must not have seen him. If a man visited and she saw him, maybe some as-yet-unknown factor prevented the man's inherent influence. Please note, the proof of what the mother saw is the gender of the child! That is no way to think. There is a mystery worth solving: How can one determine the gender of a child in the womb?"

Yudhishthira frowned. Devavrata looked at him and smiled. Yes, yes, I see that you do not care about this particular puzzle. Maybe, it will intrigue you later. Devavrata continued:

"Days passed and became months; by and by, the emotions faded, except for the memorized conversation that I could reproduce if asked. Nobody did. My life continued. My mother came out of her confinement, but without a child. She acted as if nothing was amiss; my father did likewise, so I did not see anything amiss."

Devavrata paused. Lomaharshana moistened his lips again. "A little more water," he said. Lomaharshana looked to the nurse who shook his head. Devavrata said, "I've barely eaten anything. A sip of water won't make me sick." Lomaharshana let him sip the water for a short time, about half a vighati. Then he took the cup away. Devavrata's eye lingered on the cup as it was handed to the nurse.

"I'll continue," he said.

TRAGEDY ON THE RIVER

Devavrata said, "Years passed. Over the next three years my mother must have become pregnant, gone into confinement, and come out without a baby. I realized only later that something was wrong. I was over eleven years old – almost twelve. I had gone into Mother's garden with some sweets that the cook had made. I wanted to surprise my mother. She was sitting by the side of the garden that faced the river, a winding path sloping gently down, flanked by jasmine and *tulsi* bushes along the edge, *ashoka* trees providing shade with their densely packed leaves, their shade keeping at bay the shadows of depression, and further away from the path, mango trees planted for their shade as well as their fruit. Mother was looking down at a small pool that had been constructed by the gardener and his staff. He had built an underground canal that brought water from a rainwater-storage tank. The rainy season had just ended, and the world was a glistening green, the scent of jasmine blown in by the breeze from the river. Mother's pose and the cast of her face and lips were incongruous with that setting.

"'Why are you crying?' I asked her. I am not sure exactly what I said. I find it very difficult to memorize my own words in a conversation. I could either talk or memorize, but I could not do both at the same time with any competence.

"She shook her head. 'You look hurt,' I said, 'Should I bring Father over?'

"Mother shook her head again. 'No, please, Dev, don't do anything. I am not feeling well.' Those were her exact words. I've played this one over in my mind many times.

"I said, 'You've been sick for a couple of months. Does Father know? Has the doctor been in to see you?'

"Mother replied, 'I saw the doctor a few days ago, Dev. This problem... she cannot help me. Your Father is busy. I must decide on my own.'

"I asked, 'What did the doctor say?'

"Mother's eyes glistened and her voice was calm and low. 'She cannot help me, Dev.'

"I was at a loss – this was the first time I had seen her like this.

"I turned to her attendant, who had just come out with a small cup. 'Chaya, did the doctor prescribe anything for my mother?'

"Chaya said, 'Yes, Prince. She suggested that the Queen eat only yoghurt made from fresh goat's milk, for three days. I've just brought her some.'

"I cried out in exasperation, 'Mother! How will that help? The doctor prescribes goat's milk yoghurt for everything. Maybe Father should call another doctor, a better one with more experience. If Father is not doing it, I will.'

"My mother said, 'No, don't call anybody. Come, let me look at you.'

"She did not say anything more, but she pulled me close. Her eyes looked steadily into my eyes, then above them, then the rest of my face. I looked back at her, unblinking. Then she looked at my eyes again, and her gaze was soft but of such intensity that I thought she would weep. I saw unwept tears shimmering in her eyes; I felt tears well up in mine. 'Don't cry, son!' she said, her arms around me in a tight hug that loosened as she slowly let me go. I did not want her to let go.

"She said, 'You are not like him at all. You look like my father.'

"I don't know what I was expecting, but that was not it. I blurted out the first thing that came to my mind. 'Mother! Father says I look like his father.'

"She looked away and faced the pool. 'It doesn't matter. Go play with your bows and arrows. Goodbye.'

"'Go, play.' That was what she said. It was a strange thing to say. I would have done as she said, but my legs had turned cold and solid like the ice that we see in the northern mountains, and those petrified legs would not move.

"'Why did you say goodbye? Are you going someplace? When? Where? Can I come too?'

"Questions tumbled out of me as my mind raced while my body stood still I must have dropped the sweets I had brought to surprise my mother.

"My mother smiled faintly, 'Don't worry, darling. I'll be with you no matter where I go. Tell your father that. He knows how to take care of you. You should take care of him too. Go, play!' and she put her hand to my back and gently pushed me away.

"Those were her last words to me. Yudhishthira, she said, 'Go, play', and with that my childhood ended. I left the garden and went to find the cook to get some more sweets to give Mother when she was in better spirits. Sanghamitra heard me out.

"He said, 'You go and fetch the doctor right away. Don't worry; she is one of the best doctors here. I would go, but I have to prepare the afternoon meal. Take the doctor directly to the Queen.'

"Two ghatis later I was back at the mansion, this time with the doctor. The garden was empty. I could hear the chatter of my mother's maidservants down by the riverbank. The curtain closing the entrance to Mother's chamber was pulled open. We went in, and I looked around the unlit room. There was nobody there. I came out.

"'Mother! Mother!' I called. 'Chaya! Anybody! Where's the queen? Mother was here just a short time ago! Mother! I've brought the doctor.'

"There was no reply. Chaya came in from the garden. She said Mother had gone out to the river.

"I was puzzled. 'To the river? Why?' I asked, but Chaya only shrugged. I went out of the garden gate, gesturing to the doctor, 'Come, let's go to the river.'

"We went down the path. The slope was such that, at some turns, one could see the riverbank where the path ended. Mother was at the edge of the water. I was excited. 'There she is! By the edge of the water!'

"'Mother! I've brought the doctor,' I shouted.

"I cannot say that she heard me. I was only twelve, and my voice was yet to break. My mother seemed about to do something. I was too far to see what she was doing, but I had stopped at a point in the path that gave a clear view and was trying to figure it out. Meanwhile, Mother finished whatever she was doing and walked into the river.

"I stood uncomprehending. Then I turned to the doctor who was squinting at the river.

"'Do you see that? Do you see that?' I said. The doctor stepped back at my vehemence but remained quiet. I do not know what, if anything, she made of the situation, but I knew what I wanted her to think.

"'She can't be going for a bath at this time of day. Something is wrong. Doctor, you must come with me.'

"The doctor stayed silent. The she said, 'Prince, the Queen might not be happy to see me. I'll wait here.'

"I was not going to put up with that kind of behavior. 'You come with me right now. Do you see what my mother is doing? She's walking deeper into the water. It gets dangerous there.' The doctor followed me, hesitating at every step. I could not bear to go that slowly. I ran.

"'Mother! What are you doing?' I shouted as I ran down the path. The workers in the garden looked at me, puzzled. Then the Queen's maidservants tried to stop me – it was the women's area of the river and men were not allowed – but I was considered a boy even if on the verge of becoming a man, so they did not try very hard. I ignored their entreaties and kept running. They followed me.

"By the time I got to the river bank, my mother had walked out about a hundred steps. The river bed sloped gently, but at that distance from the bank, the water was deeper than her height. I thought I saw her head bobbing up and down, which meant that she was trying to keep her nose above water. I shouted again, 'Mother! Mother! Come back. Somebody help her. Bring her back.'

"At that point I understood only one thing. My mother's last words came back to me – she had said 'goodbye' and evaded my questions. It hit me now, what she had meant. She had intended to kill herself! I was not going to let that happen. I screamed, 'She's going to die! Go bring her back! Now! Bring her back!'

"Their faces were blank. They did not move. *Had they not seen the Queen?* Even now, this distant memory brings a lump to my throat. If it weren't for this arrow, I would face away from you. What is the worth of an old man's tears? You do not need to see my eyes flooded."

Yudhishthira looked away. *Am I asking too much?* he wondered. Granduncle could die from remembered grief. Memory was a double-edged weapon.

Devavrata continued, ""The inactivity of the attendants aroused my fury, and I exploded with a burst of energy. I ran back up the path to the garden and returned with my bow and quiver of arrows. Nobody seemed to have moved, further feeding my frenzy. To the left of the beach, the kitchen staff had been constructing a fish weir along the curve of a bend in the river. Rope made from *sisal* was wrapped around a roller. This was the rope used to make nets in the fish-trap. I grabbed one end of the rope and tied it to an arrow. I pulled free a long length of rope. It looked long enough. I shot the arrow out over the water, but the weight of the rope held it back, and it only reached halfway to where I had last seen my mother.

"I had failed my mother. The memory of that conversation from many years ago tumbled out and my mother's words, *I'll kill myself,* echoed in my head and heart. I had known of this threat for so many years and done nothing. I looked around, and nobody was moving. Nobody. It was up to me and only me. I had to keep trying, nobody else was.

"I beckoned to one of the maidservants who were standing around paralyzed, 'You. Help me with the rope. I must get it to my mother.'

"The maidservant, a young girl named Usha, said, 'Sir, are you sure you saw the Lady go in?'

"If I had been the Great God Shiva, she would have been ash. My forehead throbbed. 'Yes, I did. Believe me! It was the Queen!' I was surrounded by fools.

"'I don't know, sir.'

"*Why was she so cool about it?* Her lack of urgency enraged me. I raved, I ranted, I pleaded. I cursed.

"'Please. I need a boat. Help me find one.'

"Nobody moved. I turned to the doctor. 'Did you see my mother enter the water?'

"She said, 'I am not sure, Prince. My eyesight is not as keen as yours. If you saw her, it must have been the lady of the house who entered the water.'

"'I'll swim,' I said. 'I can save her.'

"'Son,' said the doctor, 'I know you can swim. That is not enough. Your mother is a grown woman. Unless you are an expert swimmer practiced in saving people, you couldn't bring her back to the shore. That is assuming you find her floating rather than sunk to the bottom of the river. Let us do our duty post-haste.'

"She was right. I could barely swim. I told myself that I could have learned to swim earlier, that I could have practiced saving drowning people, that I was to blame if my mother died. I should have been able to save her. I knew, rationally, that this was not a reasonable belief, but this was how I felt. Now you understand why I made sure that your cousins learned to swim. If your father had not taken you away, you too would have learned to swim.

"I looked around for support. There was none. All the maidservants shook their heads. The palace guard had come on hearing the commotion, but he did not enter the women's area of the beach, and, watching from afar, he looked blank. Where did they imagine my mother would be? The doctor had made her best effort to pacify me: if I said it was so, it must be so. If I wanted any more action from them, I would have to order it.

"'Go fetch a boat to find my mother.' I told the guard. I faced the maidservants. 'If you find her somewhere else, let me know. If you want to stay here, get me a boat. Otherwise, get out.'

"The guard left. The maidservants gathered together and muttered to one another and then they left. The doctor shook her head and said, 'Prince, you should not have threatened them. They work for your father. You will need their help.'

"I was not mollified. 'Don't talk to me about helping. You were supposed to help her, and all you did was give her weak tea. Along with a scoop of yoghurt.'

"'She was pregnant. The baby was born, a boy. By the orders of the Kaurava, it was taken away.'

"This was news to me. I was oblivious to some things. However, it was irrelevant. There was nothing I could do about what had already happened. Right now, I had to try to rescue my mother. That was it; nothing else was more important. I stared downstream in the direction the guard had gone. I stamped my feet. I did not know why it was taking so long. Finally, a boat appeared around the bend; one of the two rowers was the guard. He said, 'Sir, where did you last see your mother?'

"I started to get into the boat, but the doctor and the guard spoke together, 'Sir, you cannot be on this boat while we conduct this search. If you too have an accident, your father would have our heads.'

"I asked, 'Who will revive my mother when she is found?'

"The doctor said, 'We will. I'll go with the guardsman. Point us to where you believe your mother disappeared. If she is there, we will find her.'

"I watched the boat carrying the doctor reach the spot I had pointed to. They were a little too far to the left, and I signaled with my hands. They seemed to understand. I heard a footfall behind me and turned. It was my father's Chief Minister, Sashidhara. A well-fed man with a smooth, oily brow who listened carefully to my father but did whatever he thought expedient. He bowed very low; you could tell the rank of any person by the depth of Sashidhara's bow.

"He said, 'Prince, salutations. I was told that you were angry and distressed. I came right away for the gardeners were incoherent and could not explain what had made you so angry.'

"I answered, 'With my own eyes, I saw my mother walk into the deepest part of the water and disappear. Nobody else was paying attention to her, as though she were invisible.'

"He bowed again. 'I will investigate promptly and report to you. Surely, the Queen is safe somewhere else.'

"I answered, 'You do not need to investigate anything. What I need from you is an explanation. The doctor tells me that my mother delivered a baby boy and my father had it taken away?'

"I expected some response, but Sashidhara's face and eyes did not change. He waited a moment as if to understand my question and then said, 'Yes, the baby was subject to the laws of our city. I am sure the King and Queen intended to tell you soon. I regret that the news came to you from the doctor. She will be chastised. Where is she now?'

"I said, 'The doctor has gone out in the boat to look for my mother. There! Look the boat has stopped, and they are waving their hands.'

"He peered. 'They seem to be shouting. I cannot hear them clearly. My eyes do not see well. What do you see?'

"I said, 'They are pulling something out of the water.'

"We continued watching. Time crawled by. The boat headed back. I walked back and forth in front of the Chief Minister, pausing to look at the boat, and then continuing. As the boat approached the shore, the watchman shouted to me.

"'Prince, it is the Queen. We were too late.'

"That was not the answer I wanted or could accept. 'Why isn't the doctor doing something?'

"The Chief Minister became solicitous. 'Son of Shantanu, please do not blame the doctor.'

"The boat reached the shore. Some of the maidservants had heard the shouting and had come to the riverside. They collected around my mother's body. It was limp, with her wet robe wrapped around her upper body. They lifted Mother and carried her ashore. We heard a commotion behind us. It was my father, with the maidservants clearing a path for him.

"He saw the body being lifted and rushed towards it. When he recognized Mother, he stopped. The group brought her gently and laid her down near his feet. The doctor could barely speak; she was shivering with the wet and the cold. The fear that she would be held accountable for failing to revive the Queen may have paralyzed her tongue.

"My father stood unmoving. When nobody else said anything, he spoke. 'Devavrata! What have you done? Why? Why?'

"I tensed at the strangeness of his charge and replied with equal vehemence.

"'You mad King! See what you've done to my mother. She died because of you.'

"My father turned to his Chief Minister. 'Sashidhara, arrest my son! He will explain himself, even if I have to drag it out of his throat.'

"Sashidhara shouted, 'Everybody! Leave, now! Take the Queen to her bedroom. Leave me with the King and the Prince.'

"In retrospect, I admire the Chief Minister's skill at being slow in following direct commands while doing something else that seemed like action. The bustle of activity satisfied my father's urge to do something immediately. In a short time, the riverbank was cleared. Then the Chief Minister addressed both of us.

"He said to my father, 'Sir, do not act hastily. The Prince is not responsible for the Queen's death.' He then turned to me. 'Prince, it is not appropriate to address your father in this manner.'

"My father said, 'The guards told me that the watchman had seen the prince go mad and drown his mother.'

"I said, 'The guard saw nothing. Nobody believed me when I said that Mother had walked into the water. He jumped to a conclusion.' Nobody was obliged to believe me, an eleven-year-old child.

"I attacked my father with words that day. He, pained that he had wrongly accused me, said little when I said he had gone mad. I attacked the Chief Minister as a liar who would say anything on my father's behalf. I attacked the Kavi Sangha as a criminal gang. I attacked the culture of the Kauravas as a bankrupt one that made its members bow to immoral laws. The Chief Minister heard me out patiently. I do not think my father heard me at all, for all he did was stare at the river shaking his head while I ranted and raved. The Chief Minister responded to my attacks with soft words, pointing out that my father was grieving and in shock; that the city needed to see its King and his heir together in their grieving; and, finally, that my mother would have wanted my father to take care of me. The words meant little to me, but his voice, soft and low, gradually doused my anger. Then he put his arms around my father's shoulder, almost as if my father was his son or a favored nephew and whispered to him until he, too, relaxed. The Chief Minister then went over to the huddled maidservants and held a quiet, almost a whispered, conversation with them. He came back and, with his arm around my father's shoulders, led him away. I stayed there, staring across the river at the spot where I had last seen my mother. My mother's helpers hung about, hesitant to come near me. Nobody spoke. As the evening came, the breeze from the river got cooler and cooler until it was uncomfortably cold. I got up to leave, and the maids followed me, keeping me within sight until I retired for the night."

Devavrata sighed and grew silent as though he had reached the end of a chapter in his life.

MANAGING A CRISIS

Yudhishthira waited silently. A vighati passed. Then another, and another. Devavrata continued to be silent as worry lines gradually furrowed the brow of the usually quiet, usually tolerant, usually patient King.

"You are sad that your mother died when you were a young boy?" said Yudhishthira. "Is that all there is to this story? Why tell it to me? Did you try to change your father's policies? Did you oppose the Kavi Sangha? Are you looking for sympathy? I have no time for that. I understand that, even after all these years, you are not reconciled to the manner of your mother's death and blame your father. So what? I too have a story of loss, as do my brothers. We lost my father when I was fourteen – you exiled him when I was born. Do I blame you? My father invited people — all people: Nagas, Hastinapuris, immigrants, even Rakshasas — to join Indraprastha, the settlement he established on the banks of the Yamuna, along one of its many branches before it had formed a permanent river-bed. When Bhima and I were toddlers running through his settlement, Father barely found the time to hug us; he was away dealing with crises every day. Then Arjuna was born and miraculously, the next three years saw a flowering of the settlement as trade along the Yamuna with the Nagas and the Yadavas flourished. Arjuna played at our father's knees. He knew him as a father, but by that time, Bhima was too big and I was too old to know him in the same way. When Nakula and Sahadeva were four years old, cracks appeared in the settlement. The relaxed founder and leader vanished; so did the unworried father. Four troubled years followed when father tried to keep Indraprastha together. The circumstances of his death were unclear ... suspicious, even. Arjuna walked around in a mute daze for days afterwards. Do I blame you for that death? The mother of the twins, Nakula and Sahadeva, died soon after. The settlement broke up with a flood of claims and accusations. Mother Kunti, convinced of a conspiracy, took us and fled to Hastinapura, to your shelter. I am, we all are, grateful that you took us in.

"However, the story of our childhood does not explain the principles we hold dear. Why was this story of your mother's death relevant to the policies you've followed?"

"Yudhishthira," Devavrata said, "When the Kavi Sangha helped Samvarana, the ancestor of the Kuru family, become the dominant power in Hastinapura, they also established the precedent that the King's laws were the final law of the land. Hastinapura was a trading town and Nagas and Panchnadis had lived alongside peacefully for they needed each other. Disputes used to be negotiated. But after the Panchala invaders were expelled, the Kauravas enforced the King's laws on both the Nagas and the Panchnadis living in Hastinapura territory. It was easy to do this within the city, but outside the city boundaries, they were often ignored. The immigrant Panchnadis accepted that law-making was the prerogative of their host state, so the opposition outside the city bemused them. The city residents, ever-conscious of hostile Panchala, needed the protection of the king's army. So they accepted the constant presence of the army grudgingly, as a short-term option, but became increasingly unhappy as time went by. The Nagas in the city were often the ones who had gone rogue in their own community. Becoming traders in Hastinapura gave them a new and prestigious role in their own culture, and so they too, obeyed the King's laws as an interim solution to the threat.

"The death of my baby brothers scarcely caused a ripple; there were so many other deaths. I am not seeking sympathy as you think. We were raised in different eras. As I grew older, I realize that even if I could not accept the law like an immigrant, I could not react like a city dweller. I was going to be the king and the sole law-maker in a new political framework. I had to suppress my anguished reaction, just as my father had suppressed his."

Devavrata continued: "The law that my mother died to protest was not repealed, but its enforcement weakened. When my father married again, his wife demanded changes. These changes crippled the law and, over time, ended it."

Yudhishthira said, "I see. Let me tell you how my father explained it to me all those years ago. The traditional, consensus-based framework under which families policed themselves in Panchnad no longer held in Hastinapura. Vasishtha and the Kavi Sangha thus created a military state, the first in this region, to ensure Kuru hegemony. This old political framework was replaced with one in which the King had absolute power. The clan became powerless and citizens had to directly petition the King. The King received too many to consider carefully. The only way to get a petition addressed was to draw attention to it by organizing public support to express outrage. That brought the King's standing army out to maintain order. The army's violence, state-sponsored violence, became an easy option to keep order. This is exactly why my father wanted change – wanted to create a form of government that was closer to the old Panchnad form. Unlike the Panchnadi towns, your government was established and maintained by the army.

"I have one question, though. You've mentioned that your brothers were killed to satisfy a law that the Kavi Sangha proposed. My father never told me what it was. He refused to tell me, saying that the law was not important. Exactly what law was this?"

"The region around Hastinapura is not as easy to cultivate as Panchnad had been," Devavrata said. "The Nagas engaged in agriculture while the city dwellers were manufacturers and traders. The standing army established after Samvarana's return was a drain on resources. When the immigrants started coming, we had to grow more food or import food. The standing army also grew in response to the increase in the population. Importing food was out of the question for the whole world was suffering a drought. We asked the Nagas to increase the forest areas they cleared for planting, even for the coming season. We assured them that it was only for a short time until the immigrants could return to their former homes. That was easier said than done. A

Naga band typically managed one plot of a size right for the number of people in the band and the effort it could muster. There was no simple way to change these age-old practices. We made other attempts to improve the production of food – both grains and cattle – but failed in the face of the Nagas' inflexibility and the immigrants' reluctance to become full-time farmers.

"A few years later, the Kavi Sangha noted that many tracts of land surrounding Hastinapura were over-tilled. Some forest land had become denuded and arid because of the smelting furnaces nearby. The Sangha projected that in a mere two hundred years, all the arable land would become unusable. There were more and more immigrants from Panchnad, and the birth rate had increased. If this continued, the land would become unproductive in sixty years, not two hundred. If the birth rate could be controlled, they would have a hundred and twenty years to repair the damage. If immigration could be controlled, it would help.

"To address this, the Kavi Sangha proposed a rule that a family of a husband and a wife could only have one girl child. There were no such limitations on boys. Female children after the first would be handed over at birth to the state. The Kavi Sangha argued that controlling the number of girls was the most effective way to controlling population growth. Restricting the number of boys would only limit population in one generation. But restricting the number of girls would limit population growth well into the next generation.

"This form of the law was difficult for Shantanu to accept. Most Panchnad cities were still matriarchies, and blatant discrimination against female babies would be opposed. As a trading center, Hastinapura maintained good relations with all settlements as a matter of policy. Shantanu did not want the remaining Panchnad cities, however weak, to consider him an enemy. To forestall that opposition, the rule was extended to both boy and girl babies. Every person could have one child of the same sex as himself or herself and no more. This was cruel but fair.

"After I was born, my parents wanted a girl, but my mother delivered baby boys. Shantanu set an example by obeying his own law. Oftentimes, he had to use the military police to enforce it in Hastinapura. The children were taken away and handed to the Kavi Sangha."

Yudhishthira said, "What did..." and stopped. Devavrata looked at him. Yudhishthira's face had frozen.

How could he explain to Yudhishthira that Shantanu was not a monster? Devavrata felt an urge to defend his father, but he did not see how.

"They took great care to put the babies to sleep by feeding them sweetened milk mixed with essence of *datura*[26]. Death would follow. Then, once a month, they would hold a memorial service for all the babies."

"My father used to say that the Kavi Sangha was the only organization he knew that was determined in its actions, whether ruthless and cruel or merciful and kind."

Devavrata said, "The Kavi Sangha is the only organization that could have done it. The Sangha is not a monolith. It consists of two parts – the bards who perform at festivals and the archivists who save the memories of a reign. They maintain histories, both financial and of events, provide witnesses for contracts, and perform other such functions. The bards keep the Kavi Sangha popular. Even in the best of times, performing at festivals may not pay well, for the

Annals of the Kavi Sangha Appendix A.6: An Archive Saved

When Devavrata realized that the Kavi Sangha had an archivist with the Pandava forces, he wondered if the Kavi Sangha had been playing on both side. The Vyaasa Shukla explained how this had come about. From the perspective of the writers of the Annals, twelve hundred years later, it was a miracle.

---

[26] *Datura* is the Indian thorn apple (*Datura metel*), first documented in ancient Sanskrit literature and traditionally used as a painkiller, a narcotic, and a poison.

bard's compensation is at the mercy of the *yajaman*[27], the sponsor of the festivities, or of the audience. The archivists bring in wealth, for the contract archiving business is critical to running the economy. The result is that the archivists run the Kavi Sangha, and it was the archivists who performed the culling. The bards could never have done it, but they went along. Laws were enforced by archivists. The bards made life bearable with their stories that explained everything."

"I did not know of this aspect of the Kavi Sangha," said Yudhishthira. "Perhaps this explains my father's opposition to the Kavi Sangha. I understood his other reasons for opposing you, but his opposition to the Kavi Sangha puzzled me. King Shantanu tried to be fair by expanding the law to apply to everybody, not just the immigrants?"

"Yes. That attempt at fairness did not make him any friends. The people watched as he applied the laws to his own family. While the immigrants accepted it, the residents did not. Unrest grew slowly; along with that, the size of the standing army increased."

"I understand. I thought you were digressing when you told of your mother's suicide. But the deeper story was the role of the Kavi Sangha. Yet, today, you are seen as the foremost supporter of the Kavi Sangha."

"Yudhishthira, my son, it is not so simple. At one time, the Kavi Sangha and I were united on all policy issues. Our interests meshed. I was their foremost supporter; they have been the bulwark of my regency."

"How did that come about? For after your mother's suicide, you must have been completely opposed to your father and to the Kavi Sangha. What changed? I am surprised at your father's behavior, not befitting a ruler. How did great-grandmother

---

[27] The *Yajaman* was the sponsor of a ritual sacrifice (*yagna*) – he paid for it, received the *prasad*, and distributed the *prasad* among friends, their families, and other attendees. *Prasad* is the sacrificial items placed on the sacrificial altar and blessed by the ritual. The priest conducting the ritual would give the prasad to the *yajaman*

Satyavati get him to repeal the law? What was the Kavi Sangha's reaction?"

Talking about his stepmother had never been easy for Devavrata. A direct question about her role made him choke, broke his voice. He moved his arm to indicate disagreement. That moved the arrowhead, and a wave of pinpricks swept over him, a hundred long needles plunging deep into his body. He felt faint and closed his eyes. Yudhishthira became solicitous.

"Are you tired?" he asked. "Would you like to rest now?"

Devavrata nodded. He couldn't speak. The pain had eased but it had left him in a mental fog that slowed his thinking. Speech was impossible. He closed his eyes, hoping the pain would go away.

"I'll come back later," Yudhishthira said. He carefully adjusted the position of his granduncle's arms and turned his head and shoulders a little so that the pressure on the arrow was relieved. Devavrata's eyes fell on the mattress that had held Shikhandin's body, and the memory pulled the corners of his mouth down, making him look like a mourner at a funeral.

Yudhishthira noted the change of expression and the loss of color and said, "I'll make sure that that bed is moved out of here. There is no reason for you to see where your enemy lay."

You do not have to do that! Devavrata commanded his mouth to speak, but it refused. He struggled to get the words out and failed. *I am like a lake after a dam has collapsed.* All his power had drained out like so much water.

Yudhishthira waited for a few vighatis. Devavrata did not want to sleep but the effort to stay awake was exhausting. His eyes closed and his breathing became steady. He was only dimly aware when Yudhishthira got up and left the tent.

DEVAVRATA REFUSES TO SPEAK

When Devavrata woke up the next day, he found that he had been moved. He could no longer see the opening of the tent. He looked around. *Where was Shikhandin? Shikhandin was gone.* Everything else in the tent was as it had been. Only Shikhandin was absent. The last traces of his presence were gone. Yudhishthira had done as he promised. *My fate,* Devavrata thought. He felt a constriction in his chest that tightened and squeezed his heart. He couldn't breathe and tears flooded his eyes. *Self-pity! I thought I had conquered this emotion years ago.* He turned his head the other way but gasped at the blast of pain that caused his stomach and neck and legs to spasm and his heart to thud in his chest. That reminded him of the arrow still stuck in him. He turned and a bolt of lightning slashed from his armpit through his heart to his left abdomen. *I am fainting.* When he opened his eyes, Yudhishthira was leaning over him.

"Grandsire! Wake up! Wake up! Ah, good!"

Yudhishthira and his brothers had been raised in exile and had not known what to call him when they were brought home. The memory of that return made him smile. They had called him "grandfather" which had made Satyavati's courtiers giggle nervously, then look around to see if Satyavati was around before admonishing them not to do so. He was their granduncle not their grandfather. Satyavati wanted to make sure they knew that. Over time, they learned to call him grandsire or granduncle like everybody else.

Yudhishthira must have been waiting for me to wake up. That was one more difference between him and his cousin Suyodhana. Yudhishthira behaved as if he cared. Suyodhana behaved as if he was the King and was above caring.

The Archivist was sitting a short distance away. Yudhishthira gestured towards him and said to Devavrata, "You've met Lomaharshana, the Archivist."

"Yes," said Devavrata.

"You're feeling rested? Have you had a morning meal?"

"Not yet," Devavrata said. "I am not hungry."

Yudhishthira frowned at the Archivist. Lomaharshana said, "I'll get him something, sir," and left.

Yudhishthira said, "What I learned from yesterday's narration was that your disagreements with your father began very early. Were these disagreements the cause of your father's decision to disinherit you? Why did you agree to his outrageous request? What role did Satyavati play in it – she was young, a girl, barely a woman. How did she manage to convince Shantanu to disinherit you and make her son the *Yuvaraja?*"

The flap that covered the door was blowing in the wind creating a steady beat. The season of cold winds from the Himalayas had begun. The sound of the flap merged with the beat of his heart. *Why do I have to tell this story?*

"Yudhishthira. There was no estrangement between my father and me on policy. The policy I implemented in later years was the policy that my father and I agreed on."

"He still demoted you and denied you the kingdom. Why?"

"It wasn't over policy."

"Then, why?"

"I don't want to talk about it."

"Your father's action was the most controversial of his reign. Some people still talk about it – the injustice your father did you. They even claim that it is the cause of Hastinapura's downfall. We are being punished for the injustice done to you."

"Yudhishthira! I do not want to talk about it."

"It is possible your father had good reason for it, and I just do not know. I cannot believe that it was mere whim. Why not tell the world your side of the story?"

Devavrata could feel his heart beating faster, much faster than the fluttering of the door-flap. *Why was Yudhishthira persisting in these questions? There was only one thing to do.* He tried to turn his face away, but his shoulders would not move, and the wound protested with sharp jabs. He closed his eyes.

"If it wasn't policy, what could it be?" Yudhishthira said to the silent Devavrata.

Devavrata's eyes remained closed.

The Archivist returned with a ceramic bowl of soup and a small plate of seasoned rice with yoghurt. He looked at Devavrata who had his eyes closed. Yudhishthira was frowning.

The Archivist asked, "What happened, sir?"

"He just stopped talking and closed his eyes. He did not want to answer my question."

"What question?"

"Why he gave up the kingdom to Satyavati's children."

"Hmm..." Lomaharshana put the food down near Devavrata. He walked out of the tent, gesturing to Yudhishthira to follow him. When they were both outside, he whispered, "The Vyaasa is coming this afternoon. Ask him."

"The Vyaasa? Why haven't I been told of his visit?"

"It is not a public visit. He does not want the news broadcast. I don't know if he would know the answer to your question, but I hope so."

Yudhishthira squinted in the sunlight. "Hmm... I must have angered the Regent. You are right; the Vyaasa should know if anybody does. I would be unhappy if the Regent stops talking because of me."

"I'll see what I can do, sir."

"When the Vyaasa comes, he may be able to talk to him as a friend."

Yudhishthira left, and Lomaharshana went back into the tent.

Devavrata looked away when the door-flap opened. He did not give Lomaharshana a chance to speak.

"I am tired today. Leave me alone."

"The Vyaasa will be visiting us today. He expressed a desire to see you."

Shukla and Devavrata were old friends, but communication between them had become infrequent. As Shukla became more influential in the Kavi Sangha, finally becoming its head, it became harder to meet as they used to. Every meeting was fraught with meaning to the people around them. *It will be good to meet without all that.* There was a hitch. What was Shukla doing here in the enemy camp? The Kavi Sangha supported Devavrata's plan. *Or had that changed? Were they double-dealing? Why?*

"Shukla? Here?"

"Yes, sir."

"It will be good to see him. Wake me up if he wishes to see me."

"Yes, sir." Lomaharshana stood up and bowed with joined palms. "By your leave, sir," he said, as he left.

SHUKLA'S VISIT

SHUKLA'S REASSURANCES

Lomaharshana could not sit still. He stood in the shade of the banyan tree at the north end of the camp. The entrance at that end was formed by parting the roots hanging from the branches. It was mid-afternoon and he had been waiting for the Vyaasa since morning. The Regent had shut up, for the day as he said, and had refused to listen or to talk. The guards occasionally glanced at Lomaharshana as he paced around the tree. They knew who he was, knew that he was harmless, and so they left him alone.

What he was planning to do was a break in protocol. The King would expect to be the first person to meet the Vyaasa. The Vyaasa was not just another head of a guild. As the head of the Kavi Sangha, he wielded tremendous influence in the marketplace, and as the intellectual descendant of Vasishtha, he was the chief advisor to the rulers of Hastinapura. The Vyaasa was close to the Regent, believed to be a close, even only, friend. The capture of the Regent could change many things. *Why had the Vyaasa sent word to cooperate with the King?* It was the first time that the Vyaasa had used the renegade group of kavis in the Pandava camp, and that could be interpreted as approval. From that point of view, the Regent's refusal to talk was a disaster. *Did I make a mistake in leaving the King alone with the Regent? What had happened while I was gone? The Vyaasa will hold me responsible. He could withdraw his tentative approval of our work.* Lomaharshana decided he had to talk to him first.

There was a flurry of movement as the guards came out and opened the small gate. The Vyaasa came in. Lomaharshana expected the usual entourage of helpers and onagers[28] drawing carts. There would be a circus performance of the guards inspecting everything and chatting with the driver and the cook. That would give Lomaharshana the opportunity to talk with the Vyaasa without interruption. But the Vyaasa appeared to have come by himself. *Had he walked?* Lomaharshana wondered. *All the way from Hastinapura? So no circus. He would not have much time to present his problem.*

Lomaharshana went up to the Vyaasa and bowed, his palms joined, "Welcome, sir!"

"Ah, Lomaharshana. It is a pleasure to be welcomed by you at the gate. Is the King not well?"

Lomaharshana looked towards the leader's tent, and his face darkened. The King himself was coming towards them. There was no time to explain.

The Vyaasa interpreted Lomaharshana's quick look, "Difficulties with the King?"

Lomaharshana nodded. The Vyaasa smiled as Yudhishthira came up to him.

Yudhishthira said, "Welcome, sir. You visit here after a long time. We are grateful for your years of advice, even support. The Council waits for you."

"Thank you for the welcome, my boy. I would like a quiet visit without any public acknowledgement. I will meet only the very few. I want no ceremonies."

---

[28] The onager is the Asian wild ass, of the equid family, larger than a donkey and smaller than a horse. Its range extends from West Asia to India. It was one of the first equids domesticated for hauling and may have been the preferred mode of transport from 3000 BCE to about 1500 BCE after which it was largely replaced by horses and oxen. The Indian onager is a subspecies that is easier to tame than the other members of the family

Yudhishthira sighed and then pursed his lips. Worry lines crossed his forehead. He said. "I'll give instructions right away, sir. We'll not hold any public meetings; none have been announced as we did not know that you were coming."

"Thank you, that is excellent," said the Vyaasa, squelching any hopes that Yudhishthira might have had that he would change his mind. "I heard that the Regent might be a prisoner here."

"Yes, sir."

"Is he alright? Has he been injured?"

"The doctors say it is a fatal wound that they can do very little to heal. In any case, he cannot move. I'll take you to him right away, sir."

"It is late today. I'll see him tomorrow morning."

"Yes, sir. We have prepared a tent and a bed for you." Yudhishthira led the Vyaasa to a large tent, unusually large for just one occupant. The floor sloped slightly from east to west, and the entrance therefore was at the western end. A rectangular trench about ten hastas[29] across and eight hastas deep had been dug. Three rows of poles were embedded into the ground, the outer row in the trench and the two inner rows on slightly higher ground. Crossbars were placed at the top and tied to the poles forming a roof that sloped to the back. In addition, ropes of sisal from the middle row of poles to the outer one and cross ropes created a web. The web was overlaid with large felted cotton squares that were tied to the ropes. The walls of the tent were formed of cloth or felt hanging from the ropes. The floor was rammed earth, a luxury made possible by the fact that this camp had been occupied for many weeks; a temporary tent that was broken up every night would not have such a floor.

The tent was covered with felt, a luxury offered to the Vyaasa. The trench was a traditional feature of permanent structures, also

---

[29] *Hasta* is the same as the cubit, the length of the arm from the elbow to the tip of the middle finger, which is approximately eighteen inches. A more exact definition is needed when the term is used as a standard unit of measurement because each person has a "personal hasta" measure.

The Vyaasa's Tent

The details of the Vyaasa's tent are based on examples of housing from the Sarasvati-Sindhu Culture as well as other Bronze Age cultures. Permanent settlements often follow the layout of temporary housing used by nomads, so the design of Vyaasa's luxury tent has been re-constructed from the design of housing in the Sarasvati-Sindhu Culture in places like Harappa, Lothal, and Kalibangan. The walls would have been cotton felt for short-term camps and wattle-and-daub for more permanent camps; the floor would have been rammed earth, and the ceiling would have been cotton felt. Cotton and cotton felt was used extensively in the SSC as it is cheaper than woven cloth. The toilet and the sewage trench are based on the permanent structures of SSC housing. Rain except during the monsoon months is rare in South Asia, and nobody went to war during the rains, so tents often did not have ceilings and drainage ditches did not have to double as storm drains. Seats would have been constructed from tree trunks before the invention of multi-legged chairs, and pillows would have consisted of pieces of waste cotton and felt rolled up inside a larger piece of felt and the corners tied off. Tables would have been made from tree-trunks. A raised bed with a mattress would have been an expensive luxury. The mattress itself may have been constructed by tying pillows into a "raft," or coiled like a snake (possibly the source of the image of the god Vishnu lounging or resting on the coils of the Naga Adisesha).

put in for his convenience. The brick houses in Panchnad had a similar trench for sewage. It could deal with the rare rainstorm. The trench was not intended to be rainproof; it didn't have to be. It was customary not to go to war during the rainy season. One corner of the tent served as the toilet. A hole had been dug in the ground and a ceramic pot with a number of drainage holes in its bottom placed in the hole. The dug out soil was mounded to the side, with a small wooden paddle stuck in it, used as a scoop to cover sewage and other trash. A small bucket of water stood nearby with a large flat round paving stone to wash the face, hands, and feet. The water drained from the stone into the trench. Another luxury prepared for the Vyaasa was a low bench with a tile top that covered the hole. This was short-term accommodation. If they broke camp in an orderly manner, the pot would be removed and emptied into a field trench, and the hole filled. The trench around the tent would also be filled.

The tent contained a sleeping area along the side furthest from the toilet area. The sleeping area had a few more pieces of felt. A roll made of cotton cloth sewn along the long edge and stuffed with cotton served as a pillow. The Vyaasa's tent had a wooden slab cut from the trunk of a tree of approximately two cubits in diameter polished on both sides – this served multiple purposes for it could be a seat for a visitor, a table to eat off or to plan a campaign. The Vyaasa took in all this, the effort made for him. He washed his face and hands and feet at the stone and lay down for a brief rest. Yudhishthira would want to talk during the late afternoon break.

Rest eluded him. He had heard that Devavrata Bhishma had been wounded badly and was dead. Then he heard that he was alive but on his deathbed. And then again, that he was dead. In his mind, he was not a single person but two. He had come here in the hope that he could confirm that Devavrata was alive. But he could not shake off the feeling that Bhishma's death would be convenient. In his heart, he wanted Devavrata alive. What of Bhishma? Did he want Bhishma dead? Bhishma's death would free the Vyaasa of the debts he owed Devavrata, debts he could not ignore. Now, he found Devavrata to be still alive but fatally wounded and not likely to last more than a few days. That Devavrata was still alive meant the Vyaasa could see him one last time. In recent years, their interactions had become formal, and he missed the informality they had enjoyed as young men. He could share this feeling with Devavrata, however much he may have become Bhishma.

It was not as though they did not have strategic issues to discuss. His last interaction with Suyodhana and Karna had been wasted effort – the two behaved like a pack of hunting dogs that had cornered an injured doe and would not be pulled away. If

Devavrata was no longer around, Shukla would feel less of an obligation to Hastinapura. Right now, he owed a lot to the Regent of Hastinapura and little to Indraprastha and its allies.

Lomaharshana, the chief Archivist for Indraprastha and leader of the small group of bards in the Pandavas' camp, had broken protocol to find some time to talk to him. Lomaharshana was worried and needed reassurance, some guidance, and if possible, better direction. That group of kavis was an unexpected treasure that was paying strategic dividends at no cost. If Hastinapura lost this unnecessary war, the Kavi Sangha would survive as the advisor to the Pandavas. If the Kavi Sangha survived this war, it would need leaders like Lomaharshana. All they had to do was survive.

Sleep was fitful, and Shukla felt barely rested when he woke to the sound of the bells ringing outside his tent, but as was usual with him, he sat up fully awake. The bells had announced Yudhishthira.

"Come in, my son. Come in," Shukla said.

Yudhishthira came in with joined palms, "Jaya! We seek your blessings, honored Guru."

"Live long, my son! You have them a thousand-fold."

"Are you comfortable, sir? Is there anything I can do for you?"

"You've done very well, Yudhishthira. I am comfortable. There is nothing that should concern you. I have not had a chance to see your brothers. Are they doing well? What news of your wife, the Queen of Panchala? How is she?"

"Honored Guru, your concern for my brothers and wife is much appreciated. My brothers are doing well; they wish to see you if possible. Panchali, of course, has her responsibilities in Panchala. We send messages to Kampilya[30] past Suyodhana's troops and Sushasana's spies. They patrol all the paths leading from the old city towards us. Please share your news with us, sir. How is it with you and your sister, my grandmother Queen Satyavati? Tell

---

[30] Kampilya was the capital of Panchala.

me how my mother fares? My uncles Dhritarashtra and Dharmateja Vidura – are they well?"

"I am glad to hear that all of you are well. Come closer, Yudhishthira; do not stand so far away. Sit here near me, so that I need not speak so loudly. I will talk to you as an advisor, not as your master. I am not the King, you are."

Yudhishthira moved closer and sat facing the Vyaasa, who sat up to look at him.

The Vyaasa said, "Now tell me what this is about."

"It's regarding Granduncle Devavrata. He agreed to work with the Archivist to record his story. Then, when I asked him about something, he stopped and has refused to speak since."

"What did you ask him?"

"To explain how Satyavati, his stepmother, convinced his father to disinherit him. Why did he accept the decision? Were there differences over policy? He said there were no such differences. He refused to explain any further. His answers were terse, and his attitude was brusque. Finally, he refused to answer any questions. When I insisted, he stopped and told the Archivist to come back the next day."

"Hmm... why did you insist?"

"There are so many questions to which only he can provide answers. What was Shantanu's plan, and how did it differ from Devavrata's actions? Did the crown make a difference? If Devavrata had become the King, would he have followed different policies? What was my father's disagreement with the Regent that he gave up the crown and exiled himself? These differences and what they meant – we must understand them."

Yudhishthira stopped.

Shukla said, "Do you want answers to these questions? Those I can give you."

"Answers without context are useless, sir."

Annals of the Kavi Sangha

The future King asked the Vyaasa a number of questions about the details of the events that led to Devavrata's vow. Shukla's answer is recorded in the Annals.

Appendix A.7: The Disaster

Yudhishthira wanted to know why and how the Disaster happened. The Annals only know what happened and how the people made it worse!

Appendix A.8: The Panchnad Migration

The Annals describe how the Migration proceeded – who went where, who was displaced, and what were the consequences.

Appendix A.9: The Refugees in Hastinapura

The Annals answer Yudhishthira's questions about what the refugees from Panchnad expected when they came to Hastinapura.

Appendix A.10: Panchnad Fails to Come Together

The Annals explain how and why the cooperation that the Panchnad settlements had been famous for broke down in the period after the Disaster.

"You are right. Your father's differences with Devavrata were many and deep, but that occurred before I became the Vyaasa. I spent much of that time in Takshashila. But between King Shantanu and Prince Devavrata, I can assure you, there were no differences on policy matters. Not even when Devavrata became Regent after Shantanu died."

"How do you know, Gurudeva?

"I was there. Satyavati is, after all, my sister. Devavrata became my friend when Satyavati married Shantanu. I know why he declined the crown. I had a small if unfortunate part in it. I could have kept aloof. Instead, I stirred the pot and made complex what might have been simple and uncomplicated. I am not proud of my role."

"The reason or reasons he declined the crown – how did they influence policy, if they did?"

"They did, but not in the way you would expect. My advice to you is to avoid raising this matter with the Regent."

"Skip the story of his disinheritance completely?"

"No, you do not have to do that. Just do not ask Devavrata. I will tell you, and the Archivist can listen and include it in his archive. Let me get ready. Ask the Archivist to come here. I would like to speak to him."

Yudhishthira sent a guard to bring Lomaharshana to the Vyaasa and then took his leave. Lomaharshana arrived in half a ghati.

The Vyaasa came directly to the point. "The Regent Devavrata will not willingly tell of what led to his vow and of Queen Satyavati's marriage to his father. I played a small part, so I am familiar with it," the Vyaasa said. "It would have been best if the Regent's story had been told in his own words, but I do not expect that he will do so. You will supplement the Regent's narrative with this story that I will narrate."

"Where does it fit, sir?" asked the Archivist.

"It is about the marriage of Satyavati and Shantanu and of Devavrata's vow."

"I am ready, sir. When should we start?"

"Shortly. I will attend a meeting with the King's closest councilors. The King is eager to start that meeting. I expect it will last most of the afternoon. Most likely, we will have two ghatis before the evening meal."

Lomaharshana bowed and turned to the door. As he was stepping out of the tent, the Vyaasa said, "You have done very well, Lomaharshana. Your team, too."

Lomaharshana turned, bowed again and left. *Praise from the Vyaasa was a rare thing.* He felt lighter as though a burden had lifted.

When the Vyaasa returned from the meeting, he found Lomaharshana waiting for him. It was past time for the late-afternoon snack. A bowl of fruit lightly mashed with mead, lime, and water from the camp kitchen was sitting untouched by his bed. Lomaharshana waited as the Vyaasa carefully picked out the bobbing crab apples and placed them to the side.

"Lomaharshana, you will get real apples when you are sent to Takshashila. That's if this war ever ends. Those apples almost rival the mango in taste, though they are very different experiences. For now, enjoy these small tart cousins."

The evening meal was announced. Even as the Vyaasa got ready to go to the kitchen, a meal was brought to him and Lomaharshana. "The King's order, sir," said the bearer. It was a traditional light meal of rice and salty buttermilk. They sat outside the Vyaasa's tent as the sky turned dark. A bright band of stars spanned the sky. It was the eleventh day after the full moon, and the moon would rise closer to daybreak. It would be a dark night, one for reflecting on the stars. An attendant came by and lit a small fire in a pit a few feet from the entrance of the tent. A few sprinkles of citrus oil would keep insects away.

Soon, Yudhishthira, the King, came by.

"Lomaharshana tells me that you will be narrating the story of Devavrata's renunciation. I would like to hear it first-hand."

"Yes, you shall" said the Vyaasa Shukla.

THE RENUNCIATION

"Devavrata said, 'I renounce my rights to Kingship...I will not marry, I will not have children, I will not make love to any woman.' "

The Vyaasa Shukla said, "With those words Devavrata created this world; he set in motion a chain of events that led to this war."

"The fires of Devavrata's anger were stoked by a woman and a king. The king was his father Shantanu. The woman was his stepmother-to-be Satyavati. The public cause was the King's willingness to circumvent his own laws to satisfy his desire for Satyavati. Of private causes, there were many. It is likely that if the King had not made those laws in the first place, none of these consequences would have come about."

"Gurudeva, I do not understand," Yudhishthira said. "What did the King's laws have to do with this renunciation?"

"Everything," Shukla said. "That is what I will explain."

"If the laws were responsible for everything, I must know what they were and why they were made in the first place. Without that, the narrative is incomplete."

Shukla nodded slowly. "I was hoping to finish in a couple of ghatis. But the story of the laws is long, for it is the story of the Disaster. We will need most of the day tomorrow to satisfy your request."

"That is acceptable. Begin with the story of the Disaster."

Thus, in answering the King's question, Shukla narrated the history of the Disaster and the resulting Migration.

SHUKLA'S WORLD

Shukla took a deep breath and exhaled slowly. Then he began: "Satyavati and I come from a family of Meena-Nagas, called 'Matsya' by the Panchnadis.[31] Hah! You look surprised. Yes, I am a Naga and so is Satyavati. Lomaharshana, you are a Naga, but

---

[31] *Meena* was the Naga word for "fish", while *Matsya* was the Panchnadi word.

not a Meena-Naga. We Meenas are different from you, even though we are Nagas. The last fifty years have seen much change, for the Nagas as well as for the Meenas. I will describe the world my sister and I came from.

"My father's sister was the matriarch of our small band of five families. My father, the matriarch's eldest brother, was the head of the band's fighters. That made us part of the ruling family, but with no expectation of ever being the chief or matriarch. Unlike Panchnad, we had no guilds. We do share with the Panchnadis an obsession with the number five. You've seen often enough how Nagas like to see groups of five. Five is considered a lucky number. The size of a band like ours can vary, but the number of families in a band is a multiple of five; large bands are often composed of five smaller bands which may be similarly structured. We have had bands with over a hundred families.

"Unlike other Nagas, the Meenas do not migrate for land – we migrate for water. We establish our settlements on the edge of the river at a place where a small pond or lake can be formed. Such lakes are often created naturally at a bend in a river. But if the downstream channel silts up, followed by the upstream channel, the depression is cut off from the river and the lake dries up. The Meena-Nagas specialized in restoring such lakes. The depression had to be suitably small, but not too small. It had to be large enough and not too far from the changed course of the river. A number of Meena-Naga bands would get together to dig a new short channel from the river to the depression and a longer straight channel downstream back to the main flow. The channels were designed to cut the speed of the swiftly flowing river, which reduced soil erosion. It was hard work, but finally, when ready, such a lake would support many Naga bands.

"The Meena bands could not settle down immediately after digging the channels. It would take a few years for grasses and other plants to begin to grow near the lake, followed by the appearance of insects and tadpoles. The next season, small fish would appear, followed by bigger fish. Lastly, the river dolphins would enter the lake. They are the vehicles of the Goddess, signaling plenty and giving us permission to settle on the lake. The calm lake provided a home for fish, including river dolphin and trout. The construction of such a lake was a major investment and we did not easily abandon a lake. A fish weir could be constructed, though we only did that in preparation for hosting the clan's *potlatch*[32]. The houses by the water might be on platforms held up by stilts, while the houses further back would be on the ground. Once a band settled down, it could establish a garden for root vegetables and herbs close by.

"Our band had settled on the banks of such a lake, near the southern border of Hastinapura. The city-dwellers had occupied land that the Nagas had left fallow and used it for their ceramic and metal furnaces. The Naga bands had grumbled at this, but as no bands were occupying that land, there was nobody willing to protest. In those years, the Nagas avoided conflict by moving elsewhere. They did that for many, many years. The Naga chiefs were sensitive to the changed balance of power created by Samvarana's return. Hastinapura had become a militarized capital city, not just a trading entrepôt. The Hastinapuris abandoned their foundries when the chaos of the immigration crisis cut the eastern trade for ore. The land to the north was a sorry, blighted stretch. But we assumed that this was how the city-dwellers left land fallow and that they would return to use it when it was productive again.

"I was fascinated by the Hastinapuris and spent much time with them. Noticing my interest, Parashara adopted me as his protégé. This was before he became the Vyaasa. He had come to our settlement to assess how the city-dwellers and the Nagas could cooperate rather than fight each other. Refugees were coming in from the west in steadily increasing numbers. The Kavi Sangha hoped to help them establish new settlements rather than overwhelm Hastinapura. The Nagas' cooperation was essential. The immigrants could learn from the Nagas and the Meenas how to live off the land and river.

"Parashara spent a lot of time with us. He was freely available to me as a teacher. I did not know then the reason for his frequent visits, but at that time, I was excited about city life. My life by the

---

[32] The word "potlatch" comes from the name of a redistributive feast held by the Trobriand Islanders of New Guinea.

lake seemed monotonous and boring, and I felt useless. Parashara sponsored me into the Kavi Sangha and enrolled me in the school of bards even though, at ten, I was much older than the six-year-olds around me. I was excited and engaged. I did very well, so much so that in less than two years I caught up and was counted among bards of my age who were the most skilled at memorization and storytelling. In those skills, I was the equal of Devavrata, who had established extraordinary performance records when he had studied with the Kavi Sangha apprentices.

"In the meantime, my sister Satyavati, a few years older than me, became pregnant. A pregnancy unacknowledged by a father was not considered remarkable among Nagas. The same held true in ancient Panchnad, the matriarchal Panchnad. When Samvarana regained Hastinapura, it should have become a matriarchal settlement like the others in Panchnad, but it did not. It was ruled by a head trader, and succession was to the trader's son. Fatherhood became more important. The Kavi Sangha thought it knew everything about fatherhood. They had rationalized the change as being in line with local hegemony enforced by a standing army. In recent years, the focus on fatherhood has become more intense. I do not know why. Suyodhana and his brothers are particularly obsessed with establishing paternity, and, as they call it, 'the purity of the mother.'

"The situation was not so extreme when Satyavati delivered Parashara's child. Parashara asked us to be circumspect among city-folk. We were puzzled but followed his advice. That year, he became the Vyaasa. His visits stopped. Unfortunately for Parashara, the leaders of the Kavi Sangha learned that Parashara had fathered a child with a Naga woman. I should mention that, in ordinary times, this would have barely caused a ripple. But these were not ordinary times. The Vyaasa's credibility as an observer and memorizer of Naga customs and an advisor on policy towards the Nagas was compromised. His secretiveness made his behavior seem deceitful and unwise. That the woman's father was the chief of the Naga band raised more questions – the immigrants did not trust the Nagas, and every action by Shantanu had to appear fair to both groups. The senior members of the Kavi

Sangha, its governing body, determined that Parashara should be penalized.

"Parashara realized that he had compromised his role as an advisor to Hastinapura, the Nagas and the Panchnadi refugees. From that point of view, his actions had been either wrong or unwise. He agreed to a penalty. The Kavi Sangha determined that he should take a two-year vow of silence, a particularly harsh sentence for a bard. Parashara decided to spend his two years of silence on an island near our lake. In Panchnad, his responsibility to his child would have been to ensure acceptance into a guild. I do not know what he thought was right in this situation, but he chose to stay close to us. The mother, my sister Satyavati, was also upset, first about the secrecy that she had been asked to maintain, then about any public disapproval. Faced with the stance of the Kavi Sangha, Parashara's questionable judgment, and Parashara's fickleness, she decided to raise the boy herself and refused to allow Parashara any significant role. Thus, Parashara's efforts to be near his child came to naught, but he was still my Guru and my mentor within the Kavi Sangha."

Lomaharshana said, "The great Parashara was penalized? While he was the Vyaasa?"

The Vyaasa Shukla said, "Yes."

"But... but... such a punishment is not mentioned in any of our archives."

"The entire episode was kept within the highest circles of the Kavi Sangha," Shukla said. "Hastinapuris were given the impression that this was a vow taken by Parashara for personal spiritual reasons. Even Shantanu was not told. It was felt that his trust in the Sangha would be tested. He was not inquisitive by nature, and he accepted Parashara's story.

"My sister named her child Dvaipaayana[33] to acknowledge his obscure parentage. His skin color led to the nickname Krishna[34], partly in contrast to my name Shukla because I was so light-

---

[33] *Dvaipaayana* means "born on an island."
[34] *Krishna* means "dark," while *Shukla* means "light." In this case, the names described the color of their skin.

skinned. He looked like his mother and had the family hallmark, the full upper lip that curved down. He was a chubby, playful boy whose presence cheered my father.

"Mine was a peaceful world that had been peaceful for many years. But it was turned upside down by the events I am about to describe. I was not present at the beginning, but my father and sister were. I picked up bits and pieces of information that I have woven into a narrative. Even in those days, long before I heard of the Kavi Sangha, I delighted in creating and telling stories. I would have been a natural candidate for membership to the bards' guild at a young age if I had lived in the city. I have thought over these events so many times, in the hope that I can discover a prefigured destiny that would give meaning to the rest of my life. This is what happened one day in the life of my father and sister, and what I did that day."

SATYAVATI

THE KING COMES A-COURTING

Shukla continued: "It was about a hundred moons[35] after Devavrata's mother had killed herself. One day, my father was outside his house playing with Krishna Dvaipaayana, who was then forty moons[36] old. Satyavati was sitting on the steps of our house watching them play. I was away collecting wood in the forest and heard about what happened much later from my father.

A stag burst out of the forest to the east of the clearing and stood panting by the riverbank. It continued along the river and entered the forest to the west. "My father was quick. 'Hunters!' he called out the warning, 'Satyavati, go in.' She did so, leaving my father by himself when, a few *vighatis* later, four men came out of the forest from where the stag had appeared. They were armed with bows and were following the stag's trail. They stopped when they saw my father. One of the men walked towards him. After some hesitation, two other men followed while the fourth held back. My father knew the first man – he was Shantanu, the King of Hastinapura. He came up to my father, held out his arms, and embraced him.

---

[35] Almost eight solar years.
[36] About three years.

"Shantanu said, 'Rajah! I rejoice to see you. How is your land here? Does your family flourish? Does this mighty river provide enough for you?'

"My father was relieved but taken aback by the friendliness. He tried to respond with the same enthusiasm.

"'You are welcome, brother, to my small home! The goddess has treated us well. We flourish, too, in the shadow of your protection. What cause for worry could we have? It has been many years since you came this way. How are your Queens and your children?'

"'My dear wife passed away many years ago. This is my only son, Devavrata.'

"Shantanu gestured at the man who had not come forward, who still did not respond. He was the youngest and slightest of build and was engrossed in shining his bowstring with a piece of leather. One of the other men went up to him and nudged him. He looked up, flushed, and stepped forward. He struck my father as much younger than the others, but his bow was strung more tightly than theirs, and he had more arrows in his quiver.

"Devavrata bowed to my father who raised his hands in blessing.

"Shantanu said to my father, 'How are your children? You had two, as I recall, when we last met. Are they still with you or have they joined other families?'

"'My children, Satyavati and Shukla, are still with me.'

"Meanwhile Satyavati had put down baby Krishna inside the house and had started rolling up the pads we slept on. Krishna did not like being put down and showed his displeasure by crying. Without thinking, Satyavati went to the door and said, 'Appa, can you …'

"She froze when she saw the men. Her eyes scanned all four; they stopped when she saw the fourth man. After a moment's hesitation, she looked towards my father and finished her sentence: '…give me his toy elephant?' even though her voice had dropped until it was almost inaudible.

"At the sound of a woman's voice, the men looked up. Devavrata, who had returned to working on his bow, put it down and looked at her. All the men stared at Satyavati, as if they had been frozen by a spell. My father picked up the toy and handed it to her, and she went back into the cottage. My father watched as the group slowly unfroze. Devavrata was the last one, but the King had already asked my father a question:

"'Is that charming lady your daughter?'

A thousand thoughts went through my father's mind. Ever since Hastinapura had established itself as the dominant power on the strength of a standing army, Nagas had learned to be cautious around the city dwellers, especially the armed fighters. Some, like Parashara, were friendly, but there was the occasional arrogant one around whom caution was warranted. He hesitated – he appeared to be making up his mind about something.

My father said, "'Yes, sir. That is my daughter, Satyavati. She is taking care of Guru Parashara's son. As you know, he has retired to a nearby rest house while observing his vow of silence, but his wisdom shines through. Please come in and grace my home. Stay for a meal.'

"My father hoped that by mentioning Guru Parashara, he would mitigate the risk posed by the arrogance of the Hastinapuris. The invitation to a meal was a calculated risk. It was not yet time for a meal, and hunters usually did not abandon their prey unless they were hungry. These men did not look as if they had ever been hungry.

"Shantanu looked at his men. They seemed ready to leave. He said, 'Thank you, but not now. We will resume our hunt. Some other time, perhaps. You did see a stag come this way?'

"'Yes, sir. The stag passed by a short time before you arrived. It went that way,' said my father pointing west.

"Some days later, the King's messenger came with presents from the King. The messenger explained that the King wanted my father to consider a future for his daughter in the Kuru family.

"My father thought they meant Devavrata. The boy was young and malleable, and my father was amenable to the notion of his courting Satyavati. The city-dwellers did not have the same customs as the Nagas, and the city women were less forthcoming than Naga women. But in matters of love, all men and women were similar. He recalled the wandering soma-peddler from a few years ago, the one who consumed as much of his drug as he sold and was always in a semi-trance. The peddler had claimed that he had gained spiritual powers from the spirits in the Himalayas. On seeing Satyavati, he proclaimed that she would be a great matriarch and her progeny would rule the greatest empire in the land. Everybody had laughed – she had five cousins who were in line to be matriarch – for they all knew that Satyavati was an unlikely matriarch. The only way my sister could become a matriarch was by spinning off a daughter band – and our band was itself newly formed and too small for offshoots. The prophecy would make perfect sense if Satyavati married Hastinapura's King and became matriarch of Hastinapura. Why, Hastinapura was the only candidate for any kind of empire within a hundred yojanas.

"My father's response to the request from Shantanu was, 'The boy can come himself and persuade her. Naga women make their own choices.'

"Later that day, Devavrata approached my father asking permission to court his daughter. 'I am the King's son and heir. I will be King after him. The people of the city will treat your daughter with the greatest respect. You need have no fears about her wellbeing.'

My father encouraged Devavrata to court Satyavati himself. He said, 'Naga families do not arrange marriages. Feel free to approach her directly. However, remember, she is as free as you. Any Naga woman would be delighted to be invited to be the matriarch of a band.' My father did not fully understand Kuru customs, and he tried to make sense of them in the light of Naga practices. He thought that marrying the King's son would elevate Satyavati to the status of a future matriarch.

"With that, Devavrata left to find Satyavati.

"In the meantime, the messenger came back and clarified that the King wanted to marry Satyavati himself. My father realized that there could be trouble, and his family would be in the middle of it. He rushed to prevent Devavrata and Satyavati being attracted to each other. He managed to cut short the first meeting between Devavrata and Satyavati; they only managed to speak a few words. Unfortunately, I was again away that day. If I had known all that was happening, who knows if I would have acted as I did. Things might have turned out differently. As it happened, I returned just before Satyavati.

"When Satyavati came home, she said, 'Why did you call for me, Father?'

"My father looked at me. I thought he was going to ask me something, but then he turned away. He said, 'I have something important to discuss with you.'

"Satyavati said, 'I'll listen.'

"'Satyavati! The King visited us today. He wants something from me that is not mine to give. What am I to say? I am troubled by strange dreams and visions. I do not know how to express what I am feeling and thinking.'

"Satyavati said, 'Don't worry, father. I know what he wants.'

"'You do?'

"'Yes. I hope you told him that among us, the boy takes the lead,' She smiled as she said this.

"I found out afterwards from her friends what had happened. Devavrata had met her when she was with her friends. He had been tongue-tied and awkward, while her friends teased him. He had made hurried excuses and left. It had been, she told her friends, very sweet of him. The 'boy' she referred to was Devavrata.

"That got my father's attention. 'What did you say?'

"'I know why he came.'

"'I cannot tell the King how to behave; a King does not behave like a commoner. He does not know our customs. It is dangerous to run afoul of the Kauravas, especially a powerful chief like Shantanu.'

"I did not know what my father was talking about. Nor did my sister.

"'What's the danger? What are you worried about? It is not up to you to say no! I am the one to decide. As should be the case right now. I see no reason to say no. You've raised me from childhood, father, and you know me well enough. You cannot decide for me.'

"My father continued his puzzling behavior.

"'Satyavati, my dear. This had gone beyond my simple powers of explanation and understanding. I will let the Kaurava do what he will and you what you must.'

"What did he mean by Kaurava? Why was he talking about 'the Kaurava' as though there was only one such person?

"Satyavati said, 'What is the matter with you father? I've not seen you behave so before. You worry needlessly. We haven't heard anything bad about him, the King, or the King's men. I am sure he is an honest, caring, and earnest boy, and there is nothing to be afraid of.'

"My father mumbles when he is confused. 'If only your mother were here. Oh, what am I saying, even she could not have helped me. How do I explain this?'

"Satyavati tried again. 'It would be nice to have a father for Krishna. You've told me so yourself. We are fisher-folk, not city-dwellers with their ridiculous laws. Following our custom, the boy approaches me. That is as it should be. Why should I worry?'

"'The Kauravas are not Nagas. You cannot stay here; they will expect you to go with them.'

"I listened silently to my father and Satyavati. I was excited to hear that if Satyavati married a city-dweller, she would live in the city. It would mean that I would have a safe place in the city to achieve my ambition. This is where I joined the conversation.

"I said 'Father! Satya! Your friend Gauri told me that the King came here! You should have called me! You know I want to move to the city permanently. I could have asked him.'

"They ignored me. They stood, looking sad and unhappy; Satyavati sniffling, with her mouth set in a pout, while my father was walking back and forth, mumbling inaudibly. I persisted; this was not an opportunity to be missed.

"'Isn't that what you are talking about – Satya going to Hastinapura? I can go with her. Will they let me stay in the palace?'

"Satyavati eyes narrowed. She said, 'Oh, Shukla! Is that all you think about – your future in the city? Maybe you'll be jester in the King's court.'

"'I'd like that. Dad! What is going on? Why are you both looking so upset?'

"My father said, 'The King wants to marry Satyavati and take her to Hastinapura.'

"Satyavati said, 'Father is against it. So he says. Only, he won't explain why…' and then she stopped when she realized what our father had said.

"We both said, simultaneously, 'What?'"

WHO IS THE GROOM?

Shukla paused, reliving the moment. He emphasized each word as he continued, "Satyavati and I had frozen when my father's words registered. Then, we both said, simultaneously, 'What?'

"My father said, 'No, no! I made a mistake, I was just mumbling. It's nothing, nothing at all.'

"It made no difference to me as long as I made it to the city. I said, 'Great! You won't be lonely; I'll go to the city with you! This is great!'

"But Satyavati gave a shudder. I sometimes imagine that she must have felt an ice-cold breeze from the Northern mountains suck the joy out of her life.

"'The King! Marry the King? I won't, Father, please, tell him no! Why should I not marry Devavrata? I'll kill myself. How can I be the King's wife?'

"It took my father some time to register what Satyavati had just said. 'That's why I don't know what to do! ...what did you say? How do you know about Devavrata? Did you meet him?'

"'We exchanged a couple of words. He seemed charming and shy. I just thought...'

"My father interrupted her. 'What did he say?'

"'I know he came to see me – my friends told me that. We hadn't said much. Then you were shouting for me, and he ran away. Maybe the King is coming on his behalf?'

"I finally understood what Satyavati's objection was. She did not want to marry the King. She wanted to marry somebody else, somebody named Devavrata. That I could not understand.

"'You don't want to marry the King? What kind of silly idea is that? Are you worried about your baby? The King can certainly be his father. Who is Devavrata, anyway? Sounds like a citified name, not a Naga.'

"My father said, 'The King will have my head!'

"Satyavati said, 'What did you tell him?'

"I had to make my concerns known. I said, 'I hope you said yes right away.'

"Satyavati looked at me, her eyes wide, nose flared, and lips pinched together. I did not know what she was accusing me of. Her voice rose to a higher pitch.

"'I hope you told him no, right away.'

"My father and I were familiar with that higher pitch, which brooked no opposition. We both spoke up.

"'Please, Satyavati, don't start now.'

"My father said, 'We are not a wealthy or powerful band. The King courteously calls me Rajah; he is being polite, for it is merely a courtesy. If I say no, he can destroy us.'

"I said, with the conviction of youth, 'This is my only chance to enter the city as an equal and not a supplicant.'

"Satyavati said, 'I don't care. If my life is to be destroyed, why should I care about you? Father, you must stop this. It is my life.'

"My father held his head in his hands. He was the nominal chief of the band because his sister was the ruling matriarch, but life had been peaceful and avoiding conflict had been his metiér. 'Satyavati! The matter is beyond my control. If you refuse, the Kaurava will destroy us and you will be his property. If not, you will reign as the Queen, and we will survive.'

"I added to the objections. 'I will have a glorious career as the councilor to the great King Shantanu.'

"Satyavati said, 'If he knew that I love his son, he might change his mind.'

"That was when I finally got it. She loved this boy Devavrata. But he was not just anybody. Devavrata was the King's son. The King's son. My voice joined hers in an upper register.

"I said, 'His son?'

"'My father said, 'I cannot do that. Suppose he does not accept that. As far as he knows, you've never met his son.'

"I got my voice under control. My mind was still flailing to understand.

"'His son! Oh…'

"Satyavati said, 'Father, tell the King to ask his son.'

"I was in two minds. There were two options. Either option sounded fine to me.

"I said, 'Why would you want to marry the son when you can be Queen with his father? Fine, all right. You love the son, you don't love the father, whatever… You get what you want. And that's what you want… you can be Crown Princess and I'll be famous as the advisor to the glorious Samraat Devavrata.'

"Satyavati went and held our father's hands. 'Yes, that is what I want. Don't tell him about his son. Tell him that I will not be

Queen. That I am not trained for it. That I will disgrace him in public and his people will be ashamed to see me.'

"'Satyavati, I'll do as you ask. I expect he will answer those objections. You can be trained. You won't disgrace him. What if he says all this and accepts whatever demands you make? Will you marry him and forget the son?'

"'Never. Tell him something else. Help me. Shukla, stop thinking about yourself. Help me.'

"The problem was intriguing. I look back at myself and wonder at my insensibility. I said, 'Hmm... King Devavrata. I wonder what he will do if you marry his father?'

"'I don't know. Don't ask me these questions. He'll run away. Maybe kill himself. How do I know?'

"'You're sure?'

"'Yes.'

"'I don't think so. Let me tell you how they do it in the West, in Sumer and Parsaka. Traders from there tell stories of heirs who rebel against their fathers. Their father orders them to debase themselves in apology for some insult to him, under pain of death. The desperate heir refuses but does not allow himself to be killed. He is angry, not with the king, but with the person he blames for the falling out, oftentimes a stepmother, a brother or a sister, even someone who may have been trying to help him. He will exile himself and bide his time. When the king's named successor tries to occupy the throne, the exile returns to fight. If he wins, he kills his rival and anybody else whom he blames for his falling out with his father. Most court officials desist from taking sides between father and son, as it is a risky business.

"'Devavrata will follow that example. He will go into exile. When the King dies, he will return and become the Chief. Then, he'll kill you. That's how they do it in the West.'

"My father said, 'Shukla! Are you mad? Don't come up with these grotesque scenarios. Help us come up with a plan. What do we do?'"

SHUKLA'S CONFESSION

"My answer to my father's question had many consequences. One shameful act by an ambitious young boy made me what I am. It led to Devavrata's renunciation. It led to my sister's unhappy life. It brought us here."

Lomaharshana frowned. The Vyaasa had made this announcement as though they were unquestionable conclusions.

"What do you mean, sir? What ambitious young boy?"

"I was that foolish boy. This is my confession, meant only for your ears, for Yudhishthira, and the archives of the Kavi Sangha," said Shukla.

"Sir, am I the right person to whom such a confession should be made?" said Lomaharshana.

"Yes, you are the right person, Archivist. I have lived long and do not have much longer. I may not have the time to submit this confession to other senior members of our Sangha, to be judged as my predecessor Parashara was. I do not have the courage to accept that kind of punishment if I live much longer."

Lomaharshana said, "Sir, you are the head of our Sangha. I am merely a fledgling, a child. I ask you once again: Is it appropriate that you confess this to me?"

Shukla said, "My confession must stay secret; my punishment would have to be at least as rigorous as Guru Parashara. I cannot risk it. After the war, perhaps..."

SHUKLA'S PLOT

Lomaharshana said, "Sir, let us return to the narrative and postpone completing your confession. My task as Archivist takes precedence. We can rest now and continue later if you wish."

Shukla shook his head. He could feel anger building up in him against his younger self. *How arrogant, how thoughtless he had been.* Another thought struck him. *If I stop now, I will not have the resolution to complete this part of the story.* There was no alternative.

Shukla said, "Lomaharshana, you are right, we should continue with the narration of the events. No, I do not need to rest.

"I said, 'Father, this is my proposed plan. Demand that your daughter be crowned the matriarch of Hastinapura, with her husband as the King. A husband as king would be unorthodox for a Panchnad city, but Hastinapura is not a Panchnad city and only the King rules. It would be unorthodox for Hastinapura to have a matriarch. Demand that this new practice will continue for future generations. The matriarch's eldest daughter will be the next matriarch, and that daughter's husband will be the King. While the matriarch is unmarried, a regent chosen from the qualified nobles may perform the King's rituals. Secondly, demand that the King's laws about the number of children you can have do not apply to Satyavati; her children cannot be killed by the King.'

"Satyavati said, 'What are you talking about? I do not want children by the King.'

"I was ready for that. 'Look, Satya! The king cannot have any more sons because of his own laws. That's why his first queen committed suicide. This plan does not require that he break his own laws. His daughter will inherit. However, Devavrata is a danger to this plan, and he cannot simply exile or kill Devavrata. That would lead to civil war because the Crown Prince is popular. The plan puts pressure on him to do something against the son he loves. The King will have to give you up. Later, after the dust has settled, and he comes to his senses, for you are so much younger than him, his son can marry you.'

"'Why won't he just kill us and take her?' said the father.

"'Make the demand in public. Tell him that an astrologer foretold at her birth that her descendants would be monarchs.'

"'You think he'll believe that nonsense? How does that allow me to marry Devavrata?'

"I had come up with the idea in an instant. It was so obvious that I could not see any problems with it. I knew how it would work. I knew why it would work. I said, 'The King will give up the idea of marrying you. In a few years, Devavrata will ask to marry you and it will be seen as fulfilling the prediction. The King will have forgotten this instant infatuation. He will realize how much more suitable you are as a daughter-in-law.'

"My father said, 'I don't like this. What will Guru Parashara say about this?'

"'Don't worry. He has been observing a vow of silence. I am the only student who understands his signals. I'll provide his advice.'

"My father's fear of retribution was far greater than his worries about making up a story about a prophecy."

Lomaharshana said: "Sir, were you not afraid of Guru Parashara exposing you?"

Shukla said, "I do not know, Lomaharshana, where I got the gall and the deviousness to plan this trick. This is the first I have talked of it."

For a few vighatis, they were silent. Shukla's shoulders slumped and his eyes were downcast. His hands began to tremble. He brought them together and interlaced the fingers tightly. Shukla glanced briefly at Lomaharshana's face but it looked blank, almost as though he were practicing the *nishkamkarnarpana* discipline. *Does he not judge me?* Shukla found that he could not guess what Lomaharshana was thinking.

Lomaharshana's mind had been whirling. How am I going to keep this a secret? Why is the Vyaasa confessing at this time? Why to me? I cannot forgive him; his Guru must. He tried to keep his emotions from showing on his face, but the effort made him involuntarily enter the *nishkamkarnarpana* trance state.

Shukla continued: "We waited half a day for a reply from Shantanu. My father did not attend to his routine tasks. The fish line was not pulled up nor the fish harvested. He did not go to the men's hut where he was expected. Satyavati also hung around doing nothing, her eyes listless, a face thin and drawn. Nobody ate. I asked my father to explain what had happened, and that is how I learned all the details. Of course, I am a storyteller, and I have added the necessary rhetorical elements to make a story out of a collection of events.

"Shantanu's messenger returned about eight ghatis later. I went up to him and offered him some lunch. 'I am in a hurry,' he said,

'King Shantanu is waiting for a reply. Do you have a message for me?'

"I said, 'Yes, I do. This is what my father says, these are his own words: To my brother and great King, Shantanu, greetings. You can be assured of my deepest respect and regard for you. Your offer does my daughter a great honor. It does me and my family a great honor. We are greatly indebted to you. That my daughter Satyavati came to your attention is surely a sign of a great and good future. However, she is concerned, as am I, about the rift, the abyss that yawns between our customs and yours. We are different people who live different lives. Far be it from me to judge what is best for your people, your family, or for yourself, O King. My daughter is born to be a great queen, so said Guru Parashara when he first beheld Satyavati. Among the Meenas, she might become a great matriarch of an influential band. What would she be among your people? There is no matriarch in Hastinapura. Will she be another one of your wives? Will that fulfil her destiny to be a great queen? Further, the fortune-tellers say that from her womb will be born a dynasty of great rulers. How can that come about when, by Hastinapura custom, your older children will take precedence over hers? Your son, Prince Devavrata, is the *Yuvaraja* and next in line to be King. Lastly, your law limits every family to one boy and one girl. You already have a son. Any sons born to Satyavati would be surrendered and killed. Only one daughter will be allowed to live. If she does not have daughters and is not permitted to have sons, she cannot establish a dynasty with you. She cannot accept marriage under these conditions.'

"The message continued, 'As Satyavati's father, I do not intend to bar the fulfilment of your mutual desire. These are my conditions: Satyavati will be your only wife and Matriarch of Hastinapura. All of Satyavati's children must be allowed to live. Her eldest daughter, if she has any, and only her daughter must be the next Matriarch of Hastinapura. The matriarchy shall continue through that daughter. If Satyavati only has sons, one of them or their progeny, and no others, must be crowned King of Hastinapura. The King's wife shall be the matriarch, and their daughter will continue the matriarchy. Neither Devavrata, nor any of his descendants, nor any other descendant of yours who is not also descended from Satyavati can be King. Satyavati's dynasty cannot be allowed to die with her. Satyavati's promised future must come to be. These are all my conditions, there will be no others.'

"Shantanu's messenger took this response back to his master."

THE CHIEF MINISTER RECONSTRUCTS A MEMORY

"'This is preposterous. I can't be expected to comply. I cannot disinherit my son.'"

"The Chief Minister said, 'Shantanu's response was immediate. His smile had become a grimace and his face had darkened to a deep brown. He then walked away.'"

Shukla said, "That is how Shantanu's Chief Minister Sashidhara described Shantanu's reaction to the message. I got the story from him when I paid him a visit after his retirement.

"Sashidhara retired when he became ill with a disease that was robbing him of his energy and the doctors had given up on him. He piqued my interest during a visit. He said, 'Everybody gave in to Shantanu's demands. So did I. He charmed us. The only time it mattered though was when I helped him exploit Devavrata's generosity.'

"'What do you mean?' I asked.

"His eyes lit up. Then he said, 'It's a long story. I tire easily and I don't know that I can tell it all in one sitting.'

"I love stories, always have. Sashidhara was getting bored in retirement. I said, 'If you will tell me the story, I'll visit every week.'

"My duties to the Kavi Sangha were not onerous then. My position as the brother of the Queen meant that my movements were not questioned or subject to review. I paid many visits to the Chief Minister, which enabled me to reconstruct the events that took place after Shantanu received the message from our father.

"Sashidhara, the Chief Minister, was an extraordinary story-teller and actor. It is a curious act of fortune that the Chief Minister for Hastinapura came from the guild of performers. This goes back to Hastin's time, when Nagapura was founded as a caravan site. Caravans go on trips lasting months. Even though every day requires work, the tedium can be extreme. All caravans carry one or more performers who provide entertainment. Sometimes, a performer might become a close friend of the head trader. The guild of performers had always been one of the core guilds in Hastinapura.

"Shantanu had not been trained to be King. He had two older brothers, Devapi and Bahlika, and even if one died the other would succeed. When Shantanu became King, he was not ready to play the role. Shantanu had rejected the advisors suggested as Chief Minister. They were much older than him, closer to his brothers, and he felt patronized. Sashidhara was a friend he trusted, and he trusted the performer's ability to read people's faces. He insisted that Sashidhara attend all meetings and all events alongside him. His friend's presence increased his confidence. Later, Shantanu insisted that Sashidhara be his Chief Minister. But the situation was not a happy one as Sashidhara lacked essential knowledge of statecraft. Finally, Pratipa's old minister decided that it was best to accommodate the King. He took charge of Sashidhara's training and made a chief minister out of the actor.

"Sashidhara had been present when Devavrata renounced his inheritance. Despite the passage of time and his illness, Sashidhara had never forgotten the events that had led Devavrata to renounce his inheritance. He was able to recall those events with exceptional clarity, and portrayed, with his *abhinaya* skills, the participants' feelings as revealed in their posture, their behavior, their actions, and their words.

"Sashidhara was a skilled actor. He performed for me Shantanu's reaction when he heard the messenger. Then, as he narrated other events, he performed other parts. It was a tour de force of the craft of *naatya*. Sashidhara told the story to make the listener feel as though he was an invisible spectator watching a play. What I will tell you now is Sashidhara's version of the events of that day as he narrated them to me.

"When the messenger came up to Shantanu and announced that he had come from the fisher chief, Shantanu began to smile.

The messenger asked for forgiveness if his message caused consternation. This prologue was unexpected, and Shantanu's smile became strained and his face darkened. When the messenger had finished delivering the message, Shantanu's hands were shaking. There was no smile on his face when he said to Sashidhara, 'This is preposterous. I can't be expected to comply. I cannot disinherit my son. Nor can I change the law just for my own sake, for I will be rightly condemned as a hypocrite. Send an answer to the fisher chief that his message hurts me.'

"Having said that the king walked out of the council chamber and entered his own quarters in the mansion. He did not come out for the next several days.

"Over the next few days, the council did not meet at all as the king was absent. He would send a messenger after the morning meal to announce that he, Shantanu, was not well and did not wish to leave his quarters.

"Sashidhara did not send the fisher chief the message that Shantanu had given. After a few days, he came to the King's private quarters. He said, 'Sire, you do not need to make yourself ill. These requests from Satyavati's father can be addressed without changing anything.'

"'You are doing it again,' said the King. 'Trying to cheer me up by being optimistic. You can stop it. Or else...' He stopped as the meaning of the second sentence sank in.

"The King continued, 'How?'

"'Thank you, my lord, for listening to me. I do not offer a foolish optimism. All of Satyavati's requests can be accommodated, at least for the immediate future. First, you will announce that people can transfer their rights to a child to another person. Some transactions like these have already been reported, we would just be permitting something that people already do. I will then arrange for a number of volunteers, both men and women, who are willing to give up their rights for your sake.'

"'Surely that is not enough. What about my son Devavrata? What of his right to inherit the rule of this city?'

"'Sire, it is your prerogative to name Devavrata your heir, not his to claim it by right. You can promise Satyavati that when a son is born, you will simply make Devavrata's rights subordinate to those of your new son.'

"'That does not change anything. I will still deprive Devavrata of his birthright.'

"'Yes, sir. That path is strewn with conditions. Satyavati must first give birth to a son. Maybe sons. Those sons must then grow up to be crowned. For that matter, Prince Devavrata himself must survive until you die. This issue may never need to be settled.'

"'I will not lie,' said the King.

"'There is no need for you to lie. Nor will the Prince. I will talk to him about this.'

"Then Sashidhara approached Devavrata with a request. He said, 'Dear Yuvaraja, the King, your father, wishes to make a request of you.'

"'My father is always welcome to ask, for his request is a command,' said Devavrata.

"'King Shantanu would like you to relinquish the title of heir apparent.'

"Devavrata said, 'Relinquish my title as *heir apparent*? Have I done something? Or not done something? I fail to understand. Is this a punishment? If so, why request it? The King has the right to withdraw this boon at any time. It is not a request; it is a command. I will comply. Tell me one thing, if you can... Why?'

"Sashidhara said, 'Your father, the King loves a woman and wishes to marry again. His wife-to-be has demanded that her son should be the next King. Only a descendant of both the King and the new Queen can ever be the ruler.'

Lomaharshana was jolted out of his trance state; he could not understand this proposal.

Lomaharshana said, "Sir! Please stop. I am confused. Satyavati had not demanded that."

Shukla said, "Good! Good! You get the point. Sashidhara understood the patrilineal mode of inheritance and re-interpreted Satyavati's request, *my request*, in those terms. In his mind, the rule about who became the Chief was more important than the rule about who became the Matriarch. But any Naga would have focused on the matrilineal descent requirements.

"I had asked for Satyavati's daughter to be Matriarch and for her son to be the next King. Sashidhara and the patrilineal Hastinapuris focused on the second part of this demand, that Satyavati's son must be the King. They ignored the first part. They also ignored the modification that if my sister had sons but no daughters, her son's children would inherit with the daughters coming first. The sons' rights would always be subordinate to the daughter's rights.

"If Satyavati did not have any sons, any other son of Shantanu could be King. That was unchanged.

"The two modes of inheritance could then be reconciled by requiring that the matriarch marry her half-brother the King, or any other male descendant of Shantanu and crown him King."[37]

Lomaharshana said, "I understand the intent. What happened?"

"I thought I was being clear," said Shukla, "Unfortunately, I was not understood. There was much confusion. I had not intended that at all. Some of that confusion has undoubtedly played a part in the disputes of today."

Shukla continued with the story he had been told. "Sashidhara had conveyed the request to Devavrata, and Devavrata had fallen silent. It was a long silence. As the vighatis flowed by, Sashidhara wondered if he should have taken a subtler approach. Then Devavrata said, 'This is good news! My father has been lonely and needs a Queen by his side. She would be my mother, and my life is hers to command. A title is a little thing; I can easily give it up. Is that all she wants? Is there anything else I should give up?'

---

[37] The Pharaohs of Egypt followed a rule of inheritance that could have developed from matrilineal succession along similar lines.

"Sashidhara said, 'That is a true observation, and wise, *Yuvaraja*. This is all she asks. Your father will appreciate your generosity and greatness of heart.'

"'Nothing else?'

"'Yes. Nothing else from you.'

"'Who is she? How long has my father kept his wish a secret?'

"'He has not known her long. He has asked that this desire to marry again, as well as her identity, stay a secret for some more time.'

"'If he wishes that, I will certainly obey him.'

Shukla paused and took a sip of water.

Lomaharshana said, "Sir, may I venture an opinion?"

The Vyaasa smiled and said, "That is not expected of an archivist. The best archives contain facts, not opinion."

"Sir, it is a Kavi Sangha principle that one person's fact is another's opinion."

"Tell me," said the Vyaasa. "What opinion would you venture?"

"The events you have described an emotional mess. How can I convert it into a coherent story?"

The Vyaasa stared at Lomaharshana. Neither of them spoke. As the silence lengthened, the fear that he had overstepped his boundaries overpowered Lomaharshana and he started shivering. Suddenly the Vyaasa laughed.

"Lomaharshana, courage is another attribute of a good Archivist, for falsehood must be confronted. You have done well. I agree. The Chief Minister's story is difficult to understand. Simplify it if you can."

"I'll try."

The Vyaasa said, "Now, let's get back to Sashidhara's narration. My age makes me lose the thread. What was I saying?"

"Sashidhara had been telling you the events of that day. He had just informed Prince Devavrata that his stepmother-to-be wanted her sons to inherit the throne, and the Prince had agreed to it with barely a moment's thought."

"Ah, yes. Sashidhara continued narrating the events following that conversation.

"The next day Prince Devavrata heard a proclamation in the center of Hastinapura. I made the mistake of asking Sashidhara the question that popped into my mind. 'How did you know that Devavrata heard this?'

"Sashidhara's eyebrows went up, and he stopped talking. It was a silly question. Sashidhara had spies reporting on the public actions of the Prince and the rest of the ruling family.

"The King's herald proclaimed, 'Attention! Attention! O People of Hastinapura! Attention! The King has issued a proclamation!'

"Devavrata was in a class at the Kavi Sangha when the announcement was made. The class was conducted under a banyan tree in a small garden off the central square of Hastinapura, and the town crier's voice could be heard in the class loud and clear. One of Sashidhara's spies following Devavrata reported that, at first, Devavrata turned towards the source of the cry and there was a smile on his face.

"The crier continued: 'The King has decided to heed the call of his people. A market in which men and women can buy and sell their right to have a child will be established. His son, Prince Devavrata will be the arbiter. The Prince will deal with all questions. He will be personally responsible to the King for his decision on every purchase.'

"The spy did not expect what followed. The spies had not been given any specific directions other than to note the Prince's activities, but they were expected to keep the Prince from coming to harm. This time, the Prince's behavior was inexplicable. As the announcement ended and its meaning sank in, the Prince jumped up and shouted, 'No!' It was apparent that the announcement was a surprise for the Prince. The other students and the teacher had turned to him, but he was oblivious to their stares. He looked around as though he was lost, as if he wanted to run away. When he began to walk away, the other students parted to clear a path for him. He sat down hunkered against a tree, his knees drawn against his chest and his head bowed down. Everybody was silent.

"Later, the Chief Minister met the teacher and the students to persuade them to remain silent about the Prince's reaction. The teacher, a kavi who had a fondness for simile and metaphor, described the Prince as a man who had walked off a cliff and was desperately flailing his arms and legs seeking support. The teacher and students cooperated, and news of the episode never spread.

"Back in the class, ten vighatis passed. Devavrata's head came up. His eyes were dull and seemed to be focused far away. He stood up and without looking at anybody or even acknowledging the teacher, he walked out of the class. The spy followed him. Devavrata went to the council chamber where his father was in a meeting with the Chief Minister.

"He said, 'Father! Chief Minister! I just heard your town crier announcing the new market for buying child rights. What is this? When did you decide this? When did you decide to name me as the arbiter?'

"Sashidhara said, '*Yuvaraja*! Were you not informed? This plan was discussed at an emergency meeting this morning. Your servants told us that you were away by the river.'

"Devavrata's eyes were cold and distant as he turned and stared at the Chief Minister, as though his presence was an unfortunate accident. Devavrata said, 'Please do not explain why you did not tell me. I know why you did not tell me. I want to know why you are creating a market for these rights at this time.'

"The Chief Minister said, 'Yuvaraja, you know yourself that the law we have created is a harsh law. We need it because of the crisis. The Kavi Sangha expected that the law would discourage the refugees from coming to Hastinapura. We hoped that those who did, would go on to the newer settlements further south along the Ganga where the law would not apply. Within Hastinapura, the law has fallen most heavily on people who are poor and do not have the resources to adjust to the crisis. This has been a source of unrest.'

"'We have known this for a long time,' said Devavrata. 'What is the difference now?'

"Sashidhara continued, 'In celebration of the King's wedding, we thought that we could soften the law. Every year, some people try to circumvent the law and the result is unhappiness. We could address that problem, for every year a number of childless persons die, forfeiting their right to a child. They could transfer their rights. Some of these people die of illnesses that require special care or for which the only cure is in a foreign land, Takshashila, for instance. If they had some property or other wherewithal, they could arrange with a merchant or trader to take them there in exchange for this right. Their right to have a child is the only valuable property they possess.'

"The Prince was not mollified. He said, 'Your spy service needs to be re-trained, if they cannot track all the pregnant women in Hastinapura at any one time.'

"'I will certainly deal with that deficiency, Yuvaraja. Your advice is most welcome. Meanwhile, some residents of Hastinapura desire another child. We asked the Kavi Sangha whether it was wise to let such people buy the child-right of another. Initially, the Kavi Sangha opposed such changes. Softening the law would gut it, they felt. During the morning's discussion that you missed, Yuvaraja, the question that came up repeatedly was the seller's reasons for selling the child-right. The Kavi Sangha representative suggested the reasons we came up with. For my part, it felt less than legitimate. One sold one's child-right at the risk of injuring one's ancestors, whose spirits rely for sustenance on the food we eat. The ancestor with no descendant is doomed to starve in the world of ancestral spirits. However, I did not wish to oppose the Vyaasa's counsel.

"'The Kavi Sangha added one minor condition. They wanted Shantanu to encourage the seller to migrate to one of the frontier settlements where the right to children would be restored. This would encourage younger, more flexible men and women to be pioneers while the older immigrants tried to make their living in the city.'

"Devavrata said, 'Kavi Sangha proposals have never been adopted hastily. How was this proposal approved in one short meeting? Was the Vyaasa consulted?'

"The Chief Minister said, 'Yuvaraja, you know that Guru Parashara has taken a vow of silence. He does not speak. It had to be this way.'"

The Vyaasa Shukla said to Lomaharshana, "The Chief Minister would recall his faux pas vividly in later years. The only decisions that were described as 'it had to be this way' were ones that the King had already made, ones for which the council approval was *pro forma*. As the head of the Kuru family became increasingly regal, his expressed wishes had become commandments. What followed was a direct consequence."

Shukla continued, "The Chief Minister reported this as one of the most dramatic confrontations he had seen between Devavrata and his father. Devavrata turned to his father, 'Why now?'

"Shantanu could not meet his son's gaze. He looked away, then down. His hands shook and a slight flush crept up his face. 'It had to be now.'

"Devavrata said, 'Your new wife wants children and does not want to be bound by your laws!'

"The King's voice was a whisper. 'Yes.'

"'You've already asked me to give up my right to the crown. Why did you not ask me to give up my right to a son so that you and the Queen can have a boy as well as a girl child?'

"Shantanu's eyes scrutinized a spot on the ground. He said, 'Err... I am sure we would not want that...'

"The Chief Minister said, 'We know, *Yuvaraja*, how devoted you are to your father. I advised the King to be cautious. There are so many problems. The new Queen may be barren. She may only have daughters. Who but you could be King?'

"Devavrata looked at his father and then at the Chief Minister. As the implications of the Chief Minister's statements dawned on him, his face changed. Anger had turned it red; shock drained it of color. His eyes had sparkled with rage but now became hooded and dull. His full cheeks lost their tone and turned grey like unpolished granite."

The Vyaasa Shukla said, "Recalling how Devavrata changed color, the old Chief Minister's voice shook and became a whisper. I had to lean very close to hear him.

"The Chief Minister told me, 'That was one of the times that I watched the Prince closely, and I felt I was looking into a soul in pain. He resembled his father in so many ways, except this one – the King never seemed to have suffered any kind of deep hurt. The manner in which Devavrata conducted himself was also revealing. He was a young man with a well-toned physique and was impressive when he held himself straight. His father had looked like that when he was twenty. Devavrata's neck turned pink and if his *angavastram* had not covered his upper body, we would have seen it spreading down his chest. I watched as his face regained its color. His fingers were shaking. If he was anything like his father, he was going to explode with anger. I signed to the guard, for prince or no prince, he could not be allowed to injure the King. Devavrata finally spoke, in a low bass voice from lips curled in bitterness, with the nose flaring with every word.' I was struck at the vividness of the old man's memory and applied all my skills to memorize his exact words. He continued with his narrative:

"Then the Prince said, 'Is this how you begin your new marriage – with a lie and a promise? You tell her that her children will be King, that she can have as many as she pleases. My mother died for your plans. My brothers were killed as babies. Now you want me to arrange the buying and selling of child-rights for your new love?'

"The King looked up briefly and was about to say something. Sashidhara thought it would not be wise, no matter what the King said. So he made downward motions with his palm, signaling the need for patience. Fortunately, he said, the King saw the gesture and remained quiet, not saying whatever he had intended to say. He let his eyes drift back to the ground. Devavrata did not stop his rant and the words poured out.

"'You did not want to ask me to offer the logical sacrifice now. If there are no sons, there would be no need to deliver on the promise you would have demanded of me. You even created a new role for me – chief broker for buying and selling children.'

"Sashidhara tried to intervene – he said, '*Yuvaraja*...'

"Devavrata turned to him, his face livid, 'Don't call me *Yuvaraja*! I am done with that title. You chose this... this is your solution.'

"That was the last time the Chief Minister called him by that title. He said, 'You make it sound complicated.'

"Shantanu's face sagged and looked grey. He said, 'Son, please do not be angry. I want her to be my Queen. I think of her constantly, and I am unable to do anything else until I have her.'

"Devavrata's voice did not change. 'Take me to this paragon. I will renounce my rights to the crown before her.'"

RENOUNCING THE CROWN

"I will renounce my rights to the crown in front of the future Queen."

Shukla continued with Sashidhara's story, "Devavrata said that in a flat unwavering voice, neither warm nor cold. But it froze the King and the Chief Minister. They stood unmoving like blocks of ice cut from the eternally white heights of the Himalayas. Sashidhara wanted to suggest a quiet meeting in a private location, but Devavrata forestalled him. He did not wish to wait. Sashidhara often wondered what would have happened if he had succeeded in preventing the ensuing drama. The world might have been a different place today.

"Devavrata called out in a louder voice to the doorman, 'Call Bakakula, right away.'

"Sashidhara heard the King say, 'Stop! Don't do this,' but the words came out as a gruff mumble. Sashidhara did not want to go either, but when the cart came, they followed Devavrata into it silently.

"Devavrata said to the Chief Minister, 'Tell him where to go.'

"The Chief Minister looked at the King, but there was no help there. The King seemed to have been struck dumb, almost as if bewitched. Devavrata made a sound, a groan that sounded as if he was about to rant again. The Chief Minister said to Bakakula, 'Take us to the fishing village. You know the house.'

"Bakakula nodded, and they set off. Nobody spoke during the ride. They rode past the village, and that is when I saw them. The way they sat in the cart struck me as strange; I did not know what to make of it. I thought it might have to do with my sister, so I followed right behind them. As I expected, they went to my father's house. Sashidhara looked at me, but at that time, I was just another Naga boy, and he did not even recall it later.

"Devavrata had sat unmoving in the cart, as though completely oblivious to everything around him. When the cart stopped, his forehead furrowed. I heard him ask the driver, 'What are we doing here?'

"The driver said, 'This is the lady's house, sir.'

"Devavrata shook his head as though he did not believe him, but he did not move.

"My father must have heard them, for he came out of the house. I could see that he was nervous. He rushed down the steps and stood before the cart. He was prepared for an assault, if it came to that. He saw me and waved at me – he wanted me to go away. But I did not obey his signal. He was not smiling, but his mouth was set in a grimace instead of the usual welcoming smile. In all my life, I had never seen him act as strangely as he did that day. The Chief Minister whispered something to the King, but the King's countenance did not change and he showed no sign that he had heard or understood what Sashidhara said. Later, the Chief Minister told me what he had said. *Be careful; he looks like a frightened man and in his fear, he may go berserk. We should act to reassure him.*

"I think the Chief Minister's reading of my father was wrong. My father glanced at me again and frowned. He really wanted me to leave. I did not. He made a sign with his hands. It was the *reversed pataka* sign, used to warn people of the presence of a deadly predator, like a tiger. I rejected it; I did not leave. He frowned but had to attend to his visitors. Later, he would tell me that he was concerned that the King might kidnap Satyavati and kill anybody who tried to stop him. He was worried when I did not leave.

"My father said, 'Welcome, sirs. We are overjoyed at your visit to this humble house. We cannot compare to your palaces and mansions, but please accept our hospitality.'

"The King and the Prince were silent, gazing into the distance. The Chief Minister said, 'The King and his son wish to see your daughter Satyavati.'

"Devavrata turned sharply when he heard the name. A glow returned to his eyes even as his brow furrowed.

"'My dear daughter is inside. She will be delighted, I am sure, to see you. Please come in.'

"The King and Chief Minister climbed out of the cart. Devavrata did not move. The Chief Minister made a gesture. Devavrata remained motionless for a vighati or so before dismounting. They went into the cottage, and I followed despite another frown from my father. The baby was in a hammock hanging from the ceiling a short distance from the door. Satyavati was rocking the baby in his hammock. Inside, clean banana leaves had been laid in front of seating pads; they were preparing to eat lunch.

"When the visitors entered through the door, Satyavati rose and spoke, palms joined. 'We are honored that you have come to our simple house. Please come in. Please sit here,' she said, pointing to a low seat next to her.

The Chief Minister spoke while both the King and Devavrata stayed silent.

"'Namaskar, Satyavati! The King will speak to you.'

"Satyavati's eyes were wide, and she smiled. She looked perfectly composed. I knew there was turmoil in her mind. How she managed that smile, I do not know. Despite his anger, I could see Devavrata respond. The lines of anger in his face disappeared as he drank in her soft brown eyes and a reflected smile began to form in his eyes and on his lips. Satyavati had been looking at him, but she then turned to the Chief Minister. I think that was when the significance of the Chief Minister's words must have hit him, for the smile vanished. The strangeness of the situation, his father's presence, and the exchanges he had had with the Chief Minister all conspired to drag that smile away. His eyes became slits and his forehead wrinkled. I could see his throat move as he swallowed.

"Satyavati said, 'Speak to me?'

"The King seemed to be having second thoughts. Then he asked a strange question. 'Is it true that an astrologer has predicted a bright future for your descendants?'

"Both Sashidhara and Devavrata's faces were studies in puzzlement, eyes moving, brows furrowed.

"'I don't know, sir, but that is what some people say.'

"Her father said, 'Sir, forgive a foolish man's credulity. I should have known better than to tell people of the astrologer's ravings.'

"'No matter,' said the King. Their words had given him the time to compose himself. This time, he spoke plainly. 'You have demanded that I marry only one wife, namely yourself. That I will assent to. You also said that you would only marry me if my laws did not kill your children and if your sons would be King after my death. These are difficult demands. Tell me, are these your wishes?'

"Devavrata was standing aloof from his father. His head snapped round at his father's words. I watched Devavrata all the while. His eyes had a faraway look. He was swaying slightly. He must have been feeling the ground disappear beneath his feet.

"I had not anticipated this path. I did not know where it would lead. My sister was on her own and would have to navigate by herself.

"Satyavati said, 'Yes, sir. Those are my conditions.'

"*Don't say that!* I wanted to say, but 'No' led into a fog of uncertainty.

"Shantanu said, 'Your demands have created a storm in my family.'

"Satyavati glanced at Devavrata, looked away, and fell silent. When Sashidhara was describing this to me, I told him of what had transpired between Devavrata and my sister. It was the first time he had learned of their mutual infatuation. He now believes she was waiting for Devavrata to say something. I was too inexperienced to make that deduction, so I do not know that I could have done anything. Neither Devavrata nor Satyavati said anything. I regret that they did not – if only they had... if only they had...I regret that I did not do something, anything, that could have stopped what happened. My father had spent the whole day worrying over what he should do and what he could say. Faced with the King, he shelved all those plans and stayed silent."

Shukla stopped. He turned his face away from Lomaharshana and stared into the far corner of the tent. The wrinkles on his forehead deepened and his eyes retreated into the shadow of his brow. Lomaharshana waited. *There is no hurry*, he thought. *This story has been simmering for a long time, and we can wait a little longer.*

Shukla turned his head and stared at the Archivist. I hope he survives this test of faith. The war between the Pandavas and the Kauravas has done much damage to the Kavi Sangha. Now, I've laid out my contribution, my corruption, and my regrets. If only that were all. But there is more.

Lomaharshana said, "Are you feeling ill, sir? We can continue later."

Shukla said, "Thank you for your patience. I have much to atone for. I don't want to stop. I would much rather finish the story."

"As you wish, sir. I am ready if you want to continue."

Shukla said, "After that exchange between the King and my sister, everybody was quiet. The King, Devavrata, Satyavati, my father, and Sashidhara stood still as statues. Nobody paid attention to me. The silence went on and on. I glanced at Devavrata, whose eyes were glazed. Satyavati did not turn to look at his face. Devavrata's head must have been spinning. Two vighatis felt like an eternity. Then Satyavati said, 'My conditions are just and honorable. My children would not be subject to death if I were to marry someone in my band or even in other Naga bands. Why should they be subject to your arbitrary culling because of our marriage? As a mother, I shall want my children to prosper and not be subject to Hastinapura laws. My descendants will be free if they rule. It would not be honorable to plan such a succession after we are married, so I make this condition clear beforehand.'

"Shantanu said, 'I accept your conditions.'

"Then he pointed to Devavrata. He said, 'This is my one and only son, Devavrata.'

"When he said that, Satyavati's head snapped around to look at Devavrata, who was now looking at the ground as if wishing that it would open and swallow him.

"Shantanu continued, 'He has been my heir since he came of age and was expected to rule after me. Today, he renounced this inheritance. As a condition, he desired to see you and to hear your conditions directly from you.'

"My memory of this moment is of unmoving statues. Sashidhara's version was dramatic, especially after he learned of Devavrata's nascent feelings for Satyavati. The walls imprisoning Devavrata could have collapsed at the King's words, but Devavrata did nothing to breach them. He raised his head to look at Satyavati, but he could not meet her eyes. I think in these last minutes, he lost hope that she might prefer him to his father and that doubt held him back from speaking. He hung his head and looked at her feet. His eyes were dull, like the eyes of a recently released prisoner. Devavrata would only have seen boundaries and restrictions no matter where he looked.

"Then, breaking all the rules that Sashidhara believed governed human behavior, Devavrata raised his head and stared directly at Satyavati. Satyavati flushed at the implied challenge, and her own anger at the world that was being constructed around her flared up.

"I looked at my father, waiting for him to say something. He had been still as a statue, the King's words flying past him but not ever touching him. He had been looking at Satyavati and he turned to face the King and he started to say something, but he was cut off.

"Satyavati said, 'I am touched by your son's desire to satisfy his father at the cost of his own interests. The Prince is always welcome to visit me and to ask me any question.'

My father turned back towards Satyavati. His face had lost all colour and his eyes had the look of a mouse transfixed by a swaying cobra. I thought he was going to fall.

"The King glanced at Devavrata, trying to understand his son. Devavrata stared at Satyavati as if he wanted to read her innermost thoughts. This time, Satyavati looked away, her eyes dull and blank. Sashidhara enacted their looks for me, a look that showed a man who feels betrayed to the core, and the look of a woman who had lost faith that her life could be salvaged, that somebody could do something to stop a runaway cart. They were silent. The silence stretched for one vighati, then another, then a third. The Chief Minister coughed.

"Devavrata stirred. His eyes were looking at something far in the distance. He said, 'My father has announced that I will manage a market in which people can buy and sell their rights to have children. He expects that he will be able to buy as many child-rights for you as you desire. I am no longer his heir. I am the supervisor of the barter of children.'

"Satyavati said, 'That is not what I asked for–'

"She could not finish the sentence for Devavrata went on.

"'I will not be party to such trades. My father desires you, and you want your children to rule. Your demands...'

"'But...'

"'Rather, your wishes shall come true. I hereby renounce all my rights to have children, and give them to my father.'

"'Prince, but...'

"Shantanu interrupted, 'Devavrata, what are you saying?'

"Devavrata bowed deeply to his father, palms joined, 'Father, our ancestor Yayati demanded a year of youth from his son Puru.

With the help of the gods that was possible. As it was for Yayati, so must it be for you. Your desires too must be satisfied, by me if not the gods. To you, I yield my birthright. Lady, I see a woman mad with the desire to be mother to kings. My mother asked me to promise that I would take care of my father. I see no way to stop this lunacy without violating that promise and causing pain to you, my living father. You will not need a market for the trading of children, and I do not have to create one. This is my vow: I will not marry; I will not have children; I will not make love to any woman. O King, my father, my right to father a male child is yours. Welcome, O Queen, to the Kaurava family.'

"Tears came unbidden to my sister's eyes. She said, 'But...' and stopped, for Devavrata had turned away and was walking to the door.

"Shantanu followed his son, and the Chief Minister followed the King. Satyavati too followed them, and I was close behind her. Shantanu said, 'Son! Why did you do that? You don't need to swear an oath. Not such a terrible one. Chief Minister, say something to stop him. Bring him back. What a terrible vow.'

"The Chief Minister said, 'Do not worry, my dear friend. This storm will pass. You have what you came for.'

"He repeated this last piece of advice, appealing to the King as his lifelong friend, his voice a whisper. Meanwhile the King mumbled his plea to Devavrata, his voice slowly losing strength. They did this repeatedly. Finally, Shantanu stopped, turned to Sashidhara, and the whisper was heard.

"The King turned back to Satyavati and said, 'Satyavati! Your demands have been met. I assure you that I will do whatever it takes to ensure that your children will live. Your son will be King after me.'

"Satyavati stared at Devavrata who continued to walk away towards the hunting trail. She was still trying to say something, but only managed to get out 'But...' and was interrupted again. This time it was the Chief Minister.

"'Great lady, I take your leave! Let your father know that he should prepare for the wedding.'

"With those words he left, following the King, who was following Devavrata."

"My father had come back to life just as the King, the prince, and the Chief Minister had left the room.

"He said, 'Satyavati, what have you …?'

"Satyavati said, 'I am lost.'

"I heard these words and when I recall them my throat chokes up. But that day, my reactions were unforgivable to this old man."

Shukla said, "That was the end of that climactic scene as the King, the Chief Minister, got into the cart and Devavrata walked off into the forest."

Lomaharshana said, "So the most dramatic moments in this story are the imaginings of an actor?"

Shukla smiled and said, "Shush, boy! I was there, and what happened differs only in emphasis from Sashidhara's description. His memory of the conversation matches mine exactly. I had some training in the Kavi Sangha schools, so I think I can be confident that I remember it as it happened."

Shukla continued, "I kept quiet as the visitors left our house and the cart with the Chief Minister and the King drove towards the forest. As soon as they disappeared from view, I ran to my sister and hugged her. I said, 'You did it! You did it!' repeatedly, while she stood stiff like a tree trunk. Even now, after all these years, I can feel the smile that broke out on my face.

"I said, 'You are to be the Queen of Hastinapura! That's marvelous! That's the best thing that could happen.' I looked at my father who had frozen up again. I remember thinking, *What's the matter? Why aren't they happy?*

"Satyavati said, 'I am lost. I will kill myself.'

"My father said, 'Shukla! See what your mad plan has done. The King agreed to all her demands. Now she must marry Shantanu.'

"I had watched the Prince earlier when he approached my sister. Now, I had seen his extraordinary reaction to the King's acceptance of the demands. *What kind of man gave up so easily? He is a weakling, not one who would create an empire. If there is any truth to the fortune teller's predictions, he is not fit to be her husband.* I occasionally recall that judgement, and how wrong it was, how ignorant and arrogant. The memory serves to curb my own sudden groundless enthusiasms.

"I said, 'This is the best outcome. The Prince is a young man who does not know his own mind. He loves her now, but that can change with the next beautiful woman he sees. Now she is destined to be the Queen, and our band will gain protection from the city.'

"'I'll be the Queen, the dead Queen.'

"Our father said, 'Satyavati! Please do not speak like that.'

"'It doesn't matter,' she said. 'I might as well be dead.'

"'If you kill yourself, our band and other Meena bands will suffer at the hands of the King. You cannot do this.'

"'I might as well be dead.'"

Lomaharshana had been looking confused. It seemed to Shukla that he looked increasingly uncomfortable.

The Vyaasa said, 'What's the matter, my son?'

Lomaharshana said, 'Sir, excuse me, I understand the Queen Mother's reaction. The Chief Minister's story, ending with the King leaving in a cart and the Prince walking off into the forest, makes no sense. What happens next?'

The Vyaasa grimaced and said, "Lomaharshana, I am reporting the Chief Minister's memory of an old conversation. I was there, and all I remember are the words but not the feelings. I did not know Devavrata those days, and even though we became friends later, there were certain subjects that were never talked about. I don't think he knew that I knew of his loss. I did not know then why and how his mother died or what he had been through. He should have hated his father, but he was in his late teens and I was a few years younger. When we were together, we were occupied with other things; I was not privy to his innermost thoughts."

SATYAVATI'S DECISION

"I might as well be dead."

Satyavati's announcement resounded like a gong made of lead.

The Vyaasa Shukla continued his narration of Satyavati's desperate response to the sudden turn of events.

Shukla said, "My sister thus announced her indifference to life. My father and I were familiar with Satyavati's passionate proclamations, but there had never been anything as unusual as this situation or an announcement as extreme as this one. *I might as well be dead.*

"I recall thinking, Yes, the situation is extreme. You could say it has got out of hand. However, she was going to be a Queen. Why did it matter who she married? I look back at the young Shukla and am appalled at his insensitivity and selfishness. Was that me? Are all children like that at that age? I could not imagine why my sister would wish herself dead over a marriage. After all, there had been no drama when, at the age of fifteen, she had welcomed Parashara to her bed. He was handsome, clever, fit, and devoted to her. I was barely ten years old and did not pay attention to most of the social interactions that went on around me, whether romantic or otherwise. Unfortunately, he was even more devoted to the Kavi Sangha. When he asked us to keep his parentage of Krishna Dvaipaayana a secret, she had gone along and asked us to honor that request. There had been no drama, no morbid resignation. She finally told him that he was not welcome at our home, but it had been a calm and reasoned decision.

"Parashara's request shows how different we Nagas were from the Hastinapuris. Parashara's belief that the baby Krishna Dvaipaayana was his son and not another man's child seemed to us a peculiar fixation. Satyavati went along in the beginning. She was unhappy when he told her that he had to stop visiting her for he was going to be the Vyaasa, but she accepted his decision. The Nagas allowed both men and women the right to make such decisions. When he returned as the leader of the Kavi Sangha but punished with a vow of silence, she found that he was no longer the man she wanted but a stranger and she did not receive him again.

"After her startling statement, my father and I were worried about what she might be capable of and we tiptoed around her. Fortunately, my sister did not commit suicide. She did not even make an attempt."

PARASHARA'S BLESSING

Shukla said, "There is one additional vignette to narrate. Following Kaurava practice, Shantanu visited Parashara, the head of the Kavi Sangha, to get his blessings for the marriage. My father had kept away saying that he was not well. My sister pleaded the malady of women, the monthly period of rest and seclusion. I went along as the only person in the village who could interpret for the Vyaasa. Sashidhara did not know of this expedition. I suspect he would not have been as easily deceived as the King.

"Shantanu did not know that the baby in the house was Satyavati's son by Parashara. Young children in Naga bands had many caretakers, and he had assumed that the baby Krishna was just some child in the band. He did not know that Parashara had once been my sister's lover.

"Shantanu informed Parashara of the proposed wedding and asked for the Kavi Sangha's blessing. I could see conflict in Parashara's eyes but Shantanu did not. Parashara

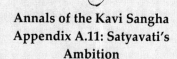

**Annals of the Kavi Sangha
Appendix A.11: Satyavati's
Ambition**

The Annals of the Kavi Sangha do not provide good answers to the questions about Satyavati's ambitions. What did she want and how did she try to get it? Despite her brother Shukla's rise to the role of Vyaasa, it is generally believed that he was too close to her to be objective.

controlled his feelings and gave his blessing. If only Shantanu had stopped there, I would not have guilt hanging over me.

"Shantanu saw fit to ask about the prediction that Satyavati would be the mother of great kings ruling an empire. Over many years, and despite my father's feeble attempts to correct it, the prediction by a wandering traveler became ascribed to Parashara just before he had stopped speaking. Shantanu chose to ask Parashara about the prediction.

"Parashara signed that he knew nothing of a prediction. I kept my voice low as I translated for the King that the prediction was real. Parashara had taken a vow of silence, but his hearing was acute. He signed some more, demanding that I tell the truth. I translated these new signs, constructing a revised version of the prediction. Parashara became increasingly disturbed and tried once more. I continued my dissimulation.

"Lomaharshana, you might wonder at my younger self's actions. I was playing a dangerous game, one hanging by gossamer threads. I hoped Parashara would not break his oath for I had seen him hold his tongue when my sister exiled him. I also relied on Shantanu's love for my sister. The King would be angry with me if I were exposed, but he would stay his hand. For a few moments, Parashara hesitated, then stopped signing. To my relief, he did nothing. He sat still for a few vighatis, signed again, and then left abruptly.

"'What did he say?' asked the King.

"I had to say something. 'He warned me to stay close to my sister for she would need my protection as well as yours.'

"In this manner, I assured myself a permanent place in the entourage of the ruling family."

DEVAVRATA'S LIFE

Shukla said, "Devavrata disappeared. First he secluded himself, and then one day, before the wedding, he left Hastinapura and walked to the site of the first settlement he had created – Varanavata, named after his ancestor, Samvarana. He did not attend the royal wedding. Shantanu took this to mean that his son was not reconciled to the loss of his princely ambitions. The rumor mills of the city churned with the news of an imminent rebellion. It came as a surprise to most people when Devavrata returned to Hastinapura a few months later. Only three people knew the nature of his loss – my father, Satyavati, and I.

"Do not judge Satyavati by the standards of Hastinapura. The Kauravas had already started down the path of walling women away from power. Satyavati was and is a Naga woman. If she had stayed with the Nagas, she would have eventually founded a band as a matriarch. She would have been a powerful mother-ruler, caring and terrifying to her children. She did not know the system she was marrying into when she married Shantanu. For that matter, I did not either. We did not understand how patriarchy worked and how it had changed the Kauravas. When the trader Samvarana returned to Hastinapura as a king leading an army, the core leadership of the kingdom passed to warriors. Kuru, who came immediately after Samvarana, was a hybrid – a trader and a warrior. But he was still a trader first and a warrior second. That changed. Even though the city was renamed after Hastin, a trader, and the ruling family took Kuru as their dynast, the later generations trained to be warriors first and traders second. This was the society Satyavati entered.

"Devavrata's vow became publicly known in a modified form. His mother's suicide was believed to have been a protest against the one-child-per-person law, and she was revered as the goddess Ganga to whom the culled children had been consigned. Devavrata's renunciation of his birthright on the occasion of his father's marriage gave notice that his mother was not forgotten and that her pain was his pain. Some people called him *Gangaputra*[38]. When Shantanu finally repealed the law as a failed enterprise, Devavrata was credited with making the change, though it was Satyavati's demands that were instrumental in persuading Shantanu.

"I discovered that life in the palace was mostly tedious and only the Kavi Sangha's meeting halls provided a stimulating environment. Devavrata would also be there, and I was only a little younger than he was.

"I think that Devavrata welcomed the loss of kingship. In those early meetings at the Kavi Sangha, Devavrata questioned the Kavi Sangha's wisdom, which he had not been free to do as Crown

---

[38] Gangaputra means "Son of Ganga."

Prince. He was still a prince, and he was not a guild member. That meant that he could not be pressured into agreement.

"There are two parts to the puzzle of Yuvaraja Devavrata as he was then known. Only he knows what happened between him and his father Shantanu in the years following his mother's death. He had blamed his father and the Kavi Sangha for that death. The Chief Minister, reminiscing all those years later, said that he took the young Devavrata under his wing. The Chief Minister was empathetic and allowed Devavrata great latitude to express his feelings about his mother's death and find his own way to deal with it. He pointed out how dependent his father was on the Kavi Sangha and how the Kavi Sangha used the King to execute its plans. In the ordinary scheme of things, the guild of bards was a useful organization. It had acquired great power with great potential for evil, and the Vyaasa was directly responsible for using this power.

"The young Devavrata was convinced that his father was weak and a powerful Vyaasa had manipulated him. The Kavi Sangha archives reveal how often this had happened, from Samvarana onwards. Yes, Vyaasas sometimes bite off more than they can chew. Even the founder, Vasishtha, could be said to have overplayed his hand when he established a standing army. The Vyaasa Bharadvaja[39], who proposed the one-child-per-person law and was the Vyaasa when his mother Ganga died, passed away a few years later. Parashara became the next Vyaasa. One of Parashara's first acts as Vyaasa was to come to Devavrata and express sorrow at the death of his mother. He also promised to work at changing the law, but before he could do that, he was surrounded by controversy and sentenced to a vow of silence. Parashara's intervention enabled Devavrata to grudgingly accept that his father was not responsible for his mother's death, and he recollected the many conversations in which his father had expressed sorrow and contrition at what had to be done. Bharadvaja, inclined to be manipulative, could be blamed for

---

[39] I have imagined *Bharadvaja* as a complete rationalist and pragmatist, taking this assessment from Kauṭilya's *Arthashāstra* in which many amoral, if pragmatic and rational, policies are ascribed to a predecessor named Bharadvaja.

some of these extreme policies. The Chief Minister considered the reconciliation between Devavrata and Shantanu his own greatest achievement.

"Sashidhara was in a nostalgic mood. The floodgates of reminiscence opened when I told him of Devavrata's feelings for Satyavati. It explained so much that had puzzled him. In his opinion, Devavrata could forgive his father for falling in love with Satyavati – it was human nature. Satyavati was beautiful. His father was weak, one who gave in easily to his desires. Devavrata did not extend that forgiveness to Satyavati herself. Her actions were not a result of a Kavi Sangha plot gone awry, but those of a deceitful and dishonest person. She had deceived him, if not with her words, then with her eyes. The demands she had made of the King showed her for the ambitious woman she was – one determined to be Queen and Matriarch of a dynasty. He would have suspected even the Chief Minister, Sashidhara thought. As Chief Minister he had displayed his chicanery. He had played a trick to persuade Devavrata to give up the throne. The Kaurava family had become rotten at its core. The thought of a market for the right to have a child — and being in charge of it — must have made Devavrata feel as if he was sinking in sewage and putrefying matter, as Sashidhara put it using his actor's felicity with words. Devavrata would have felt relieved that he had forestalled the rot by vowing celibacy. If Satyavati suffered because of his vow, she deserved it. Everybody around him was flawed, and only Devavrata had held to the truth. He would gladly give up the throne if it would make his father happy. He would be happiest if his father obtained release from the deadly embrace of the Kavi Sangha.

"I questioned the Chief Minister closely about this interpretation of events. 'Experience is the mother of all knowledge,' he said. He pointed to his belly. 'I understood Devavrata here, in my gut,' he said. 'Devavrata was quick to judge, quick to act, and quick to forgive.'

"Whether accurate or not, this assessment of Devavrata did not describe his actions with respect to Satyavati. She was judged in the blink of an eye; the vows made in the next instant; but there was no forgiveness for my sister.

"Satyavati became the cup-bearer of all Devavrata's anger at his mother's death, at the Kavi Sangha's wrongdoings, and his disdain for my sister's ambition as he saw it. I could not tell him of my role in devising the disastrous strategy. Nor could she, for he so clearly lusted for her, perhaps even loved her, but could never have her.

"I observed him closely during the days immediately after that dramatic vow. If he was angry about it, he did not show it. He avoided the subject of Satyavati, his new stepmother. He avoided her. If she was in the palace, he would be out of it. If she was in the city, he would go hunting in the forest.

"The only subject he seemed to care about was the refugee crisis and how it could be managed."

SHUKLA'S LIFE

Shukla said, "I visited my sister often. I was a few years younger than Satyavati and was still considered a boy. My time with Parashara had made me eager to live in the city, and I was ready to abandon any Naga constraints. I was already studying with the Kavi Sangha and that, along with my sister's place in the ruling family of Hastinapura, would let me enter the most powerful cliques. I also knew that I would never be chief of my own band even if I wanted to (my father's sister was the matriarch, so her daughter would be the next matriarch and her son, if any, would be the next chief). I now regret that I had not completed the adult initiation ceremony to join the fraternity of Naga men. Without that, I cannot be considered a 'real' Naga man.

"Occasionally, if a Naga matriarch had no brothers, a band would look for a chief directly related to her, such as male cousins born of her mother's sisters. If the chief died, his brothers were next in line. If he had no brothers and no acceptable cousins, the band would look for a trusted chief outside the band and not directly related to anyone in the band. This was rare. If Satyavati had founded a Naga band, I would have been her obvious choice for chief, but she left to go with the Hastinapuris. She expected me to accompany her. I wanted to, so it was an easy decision.

"I was in constant terror that Parashara would denounce me when he returned at the end of his penal term. I could not tolerate the thought and one day went to Parashara and apologized profusely. I do not know what I was looking for, but Parashara's countenance did not change. I cried. I demanded to be punished. I vowed that, like Devavrata, I would give up all pleasures. But Parashara maintained a stony visage. A few months later Parashara died, still observing his vow of silence. That is when I understood what he had intended to convey with that stony face. He must have known that he was going to die and no longer cared about the success or failure of the activities of the Sangha.

"The court that I had so longed to join was a meaningless façade for power games. I was a mere spectator, its inner workings unknown to me. Daily, there were reports of disorder in the refugee camps, rumors about Panchala. Where was the imagined heart of the kingdom where powerful individuals congregated for animated discussions over important issues? The most excitement was generated when a caravan arrived with news of the western world. The news evoked memories of the stories that Parashara told the children of our Naga band, stories of the grand courts of the Kings of Parsaka and Sumer. These were the stories that had fired my imagination. I also realized that at least some of the stories were made up. One of the more amazing stories was that Sumerians claimed to be the inheritors of an ancient world with a single culture and language that had perished when they constructed a giant brass tower or needle to pierce the veil of heaven.[40] Why would such a greatly advanced people have bothered to import the tiny bronze figurines from Panchnad or the cotton textiles that the Yadavas specialized in? Other stories, which mentioned gigantic buildings that rose high and from whose top the Great Father[41] could survey his whole empire and command obedience, underlined the difference between us and the rest of the known world. Nobody in Panchnad would construct such a thing.

---

[40] I've imagined what a Panchnadi might make of the story of the Tower of Babel.
[41] *Great Father was* one of the titles of the ruler of *Pitr-vihaara-naadu* (Land of the Temple of the Ancestors, i.e., Egypt), the greatest of the western lands.

"I began spending more and more time with the Kavi Sangha. As a Naga, I was not raised to be a member of any of the Panchnad guilds. I did not have to join one, but I participated in all the lessons of the guild of bards. Despite my late start, I did well. That is how my life became entwined with Devavrata's life, for he too, had begun to spend more and more time with the Kavi Sangha.

"In Devavrata's case, he was avoiding Satyavati. He avoided the areas of the palace she used. By not joining the court, he avoided seeing her sit next to his father. Just like me, he found his vocation in the Kavi Sangha.

"In the beginning, this made Satyavati unhappy and angry. Matriarchs of Naga bands learn a style of speech, a commanding voice, that is used to control and manage the men who enter the band, whether they were born in the band or received as adults who visit the women of the band. The men learn to obey a matriarch's command voice. It did not work that way in Hastinapura. She expected me to obey her and I did. It was a habit for both of us, and to this day she commands me to do trivial chores. 'Bring me that pillow,' she says, and I do it. It is only the complex demands that are deliberated over. She expected that others would obey her, and they did, but not because of her command voice. They obeyed her husband with greater alacrity.

"Satyavati also found that, unlike Naga matriarchs who worked just like other women except when in a formal role, she had very little to do as Queen of Hastinapura. When she tried to do something, one maidservant or another would jump up to do it. Her role in court was to sit next to Shantanu on formal occasions. Shantanu tried to dissuade her from attending private meetings with him. When he finally relented, Satyavati found that Hastinapura was, all said and done, still a trading town and much of the private discussions were about shares in caravans, dangers avoided during trips to Laghu Nagapura, the dramatic drop in trade since the refugee crisis began, and other such matters. This contrasted with the life of a Naga matriarch – in daily life treated as any other member of the band, but the ritual head of the twelve festival days of the year. The twelve festivals were the first day of spring, the feast of the mango, the feast of the burnt sacrifice, the ceremony of planting, the blessing of the waters, the day of waiting, the ceremony of the first harvest, the ceremony of closing the harvest, the day of decorating the earth, the return of the sun, the hunting ceremony, and the gleaner's day. For four of these, the matriarch was the focus of celebration. The Kuru traders had nothing like this. Their observances were centered on the safety of the caravan. In a ritual sense, Hastinapura was still a caravan led by men and women had only a small part in it.

"Satyavati found a mission that she could lead, the establishment of community festivals and traditions that would make Hastinapura a city of people rather than traders and warriors. It was a gallant effort and, over many years, she created a meaningful way of life for the community, a cycle of annual celebrations that gave meaning to daily life. This war has brought ordinary life to a halt and threatens to undo all that she has done."

Shukla stopped. For a few vighatis, he was silent with eyes closed. Lomaharshana extended a small bowl of water to Shukla. Shukla drank, almost absent-mindedly. Lomaharshana pursed his lips and frowned. *Has he fallen asleep? Dare I interrupt his train of thought?*

Shukla stirred and focused on Lomaharshana. He said, "I wanted forgiveness from Parashara but did not receive it, for he despised me. I wanted forgiveness from Devavrata but never asked for it. I wanted my sister's forgiveness, but she refused to think back on the events of that day. My father, who died of a broken heart soon after Satyavati left our house, forgave me on condition that I stay around to take care of my sister. That condition has constrained my choices; I still did my best to take care of my sister.

"Lomaharshana, Satyavati's actions and achievements, both good and evil, deserve their own separate treatment. The changes introduced by Satyavati made her ubiquitous and Devavrata felt haunted by that presence. He wished to leave the town, but Shantanu would not hear of it. Shantanu was cautious – this happens to all kings who have adult heirs. Even though Devavrata seemed to be loyal, he could change and might regret his sacrifice.

"Our activities in the Kavi Sangha had proceeded in parallel and we were companions through much of our education. Devavrata appeared uninterested in Satyavati. Maybe he was, but he would always ask to see me after my visits to my sister, but he never asked about her. We became friends. Together, we came to understand the Kavi Sangha and its projects and appreciate its way of thinking. Despite this improved understanding, in his heart, he could not reconcile the logic of empire-building and the sacrifice of his infant brothers.

"After Parashara died, Devavrata persuaded the next Vyaasa that the one-child-per-person policy had been ill-advised. It had not taken into account the response of the common people, and Shantanu's small modifications had not made it any better.

"This is the story that Devavrata has never revealed to anybody. I know it because I witnessed the events and saw what happened to him. He did not know of my shame and regret over the advice I gave Satyavati that caused so much unhappiness. We never talked about those days, no matter how deep our friendship."

The bell at the entrance to the tent rang to announce Yudhishthira. He came in and said, "Gurudeva, how is the narration proceeding? I am finally free to listen to you, if only for a couple of days. But I must urgently talk to the grandsire. I am concerned that his strength is fading fast."

The Vyaasa said, "Yudhishthira, my son! Lomaharshana can narrate his composition to you. It will answer your question about

Annals of the Kavi Sangha Appendix A.12: Policy Changes

The Annals of the Kavi Sangha are incomplete when discussing the changes of policy under Shantanu. The Kavi Sangha went through some difficult leadership transitions and failed to record the archives completely.

the policies of the Kavi Sangha and how they changed as a result of the events leading to the marriage of Shantanu and Satyavati. When you feel you have understood your grandsire, you can speak to him. If he is not pressed on this matter, he should answer your questions.

"I will visit Devavrata tomorrow before I leave. We shall see."

Yudhishthira said, "Gurudeva, I am deeply indebted to you. I will come by tomorrow."

SWAPPING TALES

The next day, the Vyaasa Shukla was up early. He stepped out of his tent and looked east. The sun had not yet risen and a slight fog had crept up overnight from the river to the campsite. The camp was on a slight rise in the ground north of the Yamuna. As Shukla gazed out over the river, dawn appeared to the east. As it grew lighter and the fog dissipated, the river emerged out of the haze. It moved swiftly past the camp, slight eddies of white marking the place where it flowed over rocks near the bank. He felt at home. It was nothing like the placid lake of his childhood, nor was it the Ganga. *Hastinapura is never like this,* he thought. *Despite the many years I've spent there, I did not feel at peace like this.* Telling the story of his sister's unfortunate demands had made him think of her as he went to sleep. He had woken up still thinking of her. She had been an unintended victim of his own ambition. Now he would have to convince Devavrata, another victim of that same ambition, to plunge into that past to retrieve... *Retrieve what? What will he find in that desolate land of lost time?*

The camp had been up for some time. As Shukla prepared himself for the day, a bearer from the kitchen brought a warm cup of almond milk, yellow with turmeric, and a few slices of guava sprinkled lightly with salt and pepper. The light meal satisfied him, and as he finished it, Yudhishthira and Lomaharshana arrived to escort him to Devavrata's tent.

Yudhishthira said, "Gurudeva, we will stay outside until you ask us to come in. My ears will be closed to anything said inside until then."

Shukla nodded his assent and rang the small bell before he stepped inside the tent.

"Devavrata, my friend."

The familiar voice cut through the fog that Devavrata had wrapped around himself. *It was a bad dream,* he thought, and opened his eyes. He was still in a tent and his legs and one arm were tied to support poles. *Did they think he would attempt escape?* It was as he had imagined in the dream. It was not a dream, and he was not free. His shoulder was sore and hurt. There might well be an arrowhead in there. Then he remembered that he was mortally injured. The voice was Shukla's voice. *What was Shukla doing here? He had left him back in Hastinapura.* Maybe he was on the brink of death. Maybe it was still a dream and he was imagining a visit from an old friend. *Is this how I will die? With all my friends flashing in front of my eyes?* He was lucky he had so few friends; he would die quickly. But not if, like these conjured-up memories of friends, they talked so much.

He turned his head but stopped when the flashes of pain in his shoulder became continuous. He was determined to control the pain and not let it control him. He closed his eyes, but then his face set in a grimace that betrayed him, and he opened his eyes again to look at his friend.

"Shukla, my brother," he said. "What are you doing in the enemy camp?"

It had been over a year since Devavrata had been able to meet the Vyaasa in private. Public meetings in Suyodhana's court had become exercises in formality once war broke out with the Pandavas. Suyodhana did not trust the Kavi Sangha. Though the Kavi Sangha supported Hastinapura and had done so for many generations, though the Vyaasa had called for the Pandavas to make peace on Suyodhana's terms, though there was no reason for the Kavi Sangha to change its mind, Suyodhana remained suspicious of Kavi Sangha activities. The Kavi Sangha had told him that he should be gentle with the Pandavas if they surrendered.

Shukla said, "I, too, am a prisoner at home."

"Are you? I've met the Archivist here. He says your whereabouts are secret."

"Ah. Yes."

"He predicted yesterday that you would come today. You must keep him. He seems to know when you are not in your prison."

Shukla laughed. "There's no need for sarcasm. The Kavi Sangha has its ways to communicate. An army, Devavrata, does not imprison me. More than anything, my body betrays me and holds me captive."

"As does mine. I have an arrowhead in my lungs. I am to die of it."

"I, too, will die very soon. My doctor says it will happen, he just cannot say when. Soon."

"What does the doctor know, Shukla?"

"He says my urine is a sweet dish for ants. My waning eyesight is a warning sign. The aches and pains in my arms and legs are a prelude to the final days."

"Is this why you came here? To join me on the deathbed?"

"No. I came for many reasons. I had hoped to archive your memoirs in Hastinapura under more pleasant circumstances. Now, that will not be possible. So I ask you to work with the Archivist here. Before your capture, a Hastinapura victory in this unfortunate war was inevitable; now it is not. Suyodhana and Karna are impetuous, strong-willed, and wrong-headed. Only you could have restrained them and focused their efforts. You knew that, too. I was not in Hastinapura when you decided on this expedition. You are the most senior commander. What could have possibly tempted you down this foolhardy path?"

Devavrata grimaced. "Shikhandin offered us a chance…"

"Shikhandin? Of Panchala?"

"Yes. You know of him? He came to Hastinapura on a secret mission, a proposal from the disaffected leaders of clans within Panchala."

"He convinced you?"

"Yes."

"How did he do that?"

"I know now what I did not know then. I was inclined to believe him. He revived old memories."

"Amba?" Shukla said, his voice low.

"You knew?"

"Did I suspect it? Yes. Not with any certainty, though. Some Kavi Sangha members visiting Panchala returned with disquieting news. I had asked them to assess Panchala's preparation for war. You recall how the chief Drupada used to issue challenges to Hastinapura every few years to meet Panchala on the field of blood. The Kavi Sangha members reported that nobody was preparing for war. The spear and arrow makers were idle, and the smiths were preparing for the harvest festival. The challenges were just fuss and bluster.

"I see. Does it mean that you've suspected all these years that Amba was alive?"

"All these years? No. I learned this just a few years ago."

Devavrata tried to raise himself on his elbows and fell back. He said, "You must tell me more."

"I will. I want to trade though. You must help us with your memories."

"Why now?"

"I told you. I am old. I will not have many more chances to reconcile warring factions. Consider it a plea from my deathbed."

"You know what they want me to tell them."

"Yes. I have relieved you of a painful narration. I told Yudhishthira and the Archivist of your first meeting with Satyavati. I have told them all about it. You do not need to recount it. Go beyond it. Start with the death of Shantanu."

"Why is this memory a part of your archives? You tell me that it is a part of your story. I am not convinced that what I felt or what happened to me matters. Is it not enough to describe what happened and let my sorrow be private and forgotten? You already know how the world has changed. Make that your story."

"Let the Kavi Sangha be the judge of that, Devavrata. There is more to a culture than dynastic family trees and an inventory of monuments or even the stories of victory."

Devavrata sighed. Why did it have to be the story of my life that he wants to add to the history of our culture?

"You think that that the 'more' is the story of my life?"

"Among others. I plan to interview Dhritarashtra, Kutaja Drona, Kunti, even Suyodhana and Yudhishthira, young though they are. They have to stay alive and stay healthy. I'll wait for them just as I wait for you. Why, if I can get to them, I will even listen to the Queen of Panchala, Krishna the Yadava, and others."

Devavrata said, "Good luck to you and your wait."

Devavrata was silent. A few vighatis passed in silence. Then Shukla closed his eyes.

"How long will you wait here?" Devavrata said.

Shukla opened his eyes. "Until you agree," he said.

"Hmm… what if I refuse?"

"That is not an alternative."

"I could choose to die."

"Then you will not know what happened to Amba."

Amba's story. That was the only story he yearned to hear. *Shukla's words implied a threat – 'agree now to tell us what you know or we will let you die unsatisfied'?* He did not understand the sinking feeling of despair that engulfed him when he thought of Amba. He had failed her, and he was desperate to know the extent of her suffering. He wanted to mourn that lost life, he needed absolution. He had been responsible for Amba's pain. She had raised Shikhandin on her own. Shikhandin had died in his arms. He wanted to tell Amba that her son had felt his father's touch at least once in his short life. How could he tell Amba that he understood her pain if he did not know what it had been? Her suffering was his suffering, but for that to be true, he had to know what the rest of her life had been like. Even the bare bones of her story would be better than nothing.

What was Shukla offering? He wanted to take their story and make it public. It would become another story used to titillate the public, stories of the clay feet of great men.

"The Kavi Sangha performs historical story-telling every year at festivals here and in Panchnad. Will this memoir be part of every recital?"

Shukla smiled. "Don't worry. There will be no performances based on this archive for many years. The Kavi Sangha will recite archival histories only after seven generations have passed. All persons in these histories will be dead before the stories are made public. Not every story makes it to a recital. The stories that do are always more than entertainment."

Devavrata considered that assertion. Was it good enough? I do not want to be reassured; I want a commitment I can believe.

"What about him?" Devavrata indicated with a glance the Archivist standing quietly.

"You know the rules of Kavi Sangha," Shukla said. "You considered becoming an archivist yourself when your position in the city seemed precarious and you thought it possible that your brother, the King, would imprison you if not kill you. Joining the Kavi Sangha would have saved your life."

"The King? You mean Chitrangada, Shantanu's and Satyavati's son," Devavrata's voice fell.

"Tell me about him," Shukla said. "Tell me how he died. Satyavati says a gandharva killed him, that you were there when he was killed, and you were too cowardly to bring his body back. Did you tell her that? If so, what was the truth? Gandharvas, magical beings who sing as they fly, do not exist."

Devavrata had made up a story that would save Satyavati grief, but the lie had not satisfied her, and now it had caught up with him. It had been a hastily conceived lie, built on memories of the stories an imaginative twelve-year-old Chitrangada told his five-year-old brother Vichitravirya, stories of a king with magical powers named Chitrangada. Now Satyavati's brother was asking for the truth. *Can I trust him?* The answer would have been clear if Satyavati had been anybody but Shukla's sister. As it was, the question was not easily answered. Shukla was neither a trader, nor a warrior. A trader habitually keeps secrets; a warrior learns not to obsess over scenes from a battlefield. *Is the value of telling the truth of Chitrangada's death greater than the value of letting it die with me?* Such questions clouded Devavrata's mind.

It is a good thing that I am dying, Devavrata thought. He had never bothered to find out Satyavati's side of the story. He did not want to know it either. We have stayed aloof for so long, what was the point of cutting open an old wound to see if it was healing?

The story of his life after Shantanu and Satyavati married was a story that had been told and retold in public. Devavrata had devoted himself to projects that took him away from Hastinapura. Two years passed. Satyavati had a son, Chitrangada. When Chitrangada was seven, his brother Vichitravirya was born. Whenever Devavrata came to Hastinapura, he saw Shantanu playing with Chitrangada. The toddler looked like his father, a miniature Shantanu, except for his eyes and the pouting mouth, which opened in a broad smile when he saw his older brother. *Anna,* he would scream and run to Devavrata. Shantanu was almost fifty years old then and not inclined to play on the floor with his son, but Devavrata could. Chitrangada would mimic Devavrata. He would run when Devavrata pretended to be angry and chased him round and round the room without catching him. Chitrangada would climb up Devavrata's body onto his shoulders and then jump off into the arms Devavrata held out. As Vichitravirya grew older, he too joined in their games, but the first and strongest tie was between Devavrata and Chitrangada. Despite the hint of Satyavati in Chitrangada's features, or maybe because of them, Devavrata grew to love his brothers.

The bond between Chitrangada and Devavrata did not repair the relationship between Satyavati and Devavrata. Occasionally, Devavrata noticed his father's puzzlement at some complex interaction between his son and his wife. But he was mostly oblivious to the tension between them. It was possible that he sensed some of the truth but chose to ignore it. It took many years. But Devavrata and Satyavati slowly settled into a routine that allowed them to appear next to Shantanu in public. In private, they avoided each other.

Shortly after Shantanu's death, Shukla had persuaded Satyavati and Devavrata to meet in his presence to resolve a conflict. It had been an awkward and disastrous meeting in which both proved incapable of initiating a discussion or following up on Shukla's leads. *It was good advice, maybe just premature,* Devavrata thought. They were both unwilling to try again and never did.

Then Chitrangada went on a fateful expedition. Devavrata was too late to save Chitrangada from death. Lies had been made up to spare Satyavati the details of her son's end.

Devavrata was silent again. *Everything I love turns to dust. Such old memories and they still make me sad.* A few vighatis passed. Shukla looked at Devavrata with concern, "Are you alright?"

"Yes."

"You were silent, and your eyes looked far away."

"I was thinking about Chitrangada's life and his coronation."

"His coronation?"

"Yes. A lot started with that coronation."

"I want to know about his death."

I am a trader and here I am, freely giving away this story. Devavrata laughed at the thought of payment. He stopped as the shoulder shot its message across his chest. *I can get stories out of Shukla! A bard habitually tells stories.* He returned to his earlier questions.

"Do you really know what happened to Amba?"

Shukla slowly turned his head away, but not before Devavrata saw his eyes lose focus. He waited for almost three vighatis and then tapped the tent pole with his feet to get Shukla's attention. The tent shook, but it did not seem to affect Shukla. A short time later, Shukla turned back to him.

"Are you alright?" Devavrata asked. "Am I not allowed to ask you questions?"

Shukla smiled. "You would want to know about Amba, wouldn't you? Here, let's play your game; let's trade. You tell me about Chitrangada's death, and I will tell you about the events that followed Vichitravirya's death."

He does not want to talk about Amba. Why? Every reason for secrecy has disappeared in the last few days? Was there more? Devavrata found his own questions multiplying.

"Can the Archivist memorize all that?"

"Oh, much more than that."

"Amba's story has three parts," Devavrata said. "The first part I know and will tell you. It's the story of how I met Amba. The second part I do not know: why she left and what she did afterward. Do you know that part? The third part, I think you know: What happened to her, how she ended up in Panchala, and how she raised Shikhandin as a warrior?"

"I don't know everything. Yes, how you met her, how you bonded with her is still a mystery. If you tell that story, I will have the boy recite how and why Amba escaped Hastinapura and hid from you. I'll tell you what I know of Shikhandin and how he was raised. I still do not know exactly how Amba ended up in Panchala."

Devavrata was struck by the words. Once again, he had said that Amba escaped! Escaped from what? From a person, perhaps. Who could it be? Shukla's offer seemed to be a fair exchange. Devavrata felt exhausted and needed rest. *Not now. I cannot take this in now.*

"I am tired. After the midday meal," Devavrata said. "I will start with Shantanu's death and how Satyavati and I became co-regents. Then, the story of Chitrangada's northern misadventure. Finally, I will tell you the truth about Amba. You will then tell me of Vichitravirya's death and what happened to Amba after she disappeared from Hastinapura."

"Yes. Only what I know."

"No drama then. Good. Now, go away. Let me rest."

Shukla said, "Stay strong, old friend," and left silently.

Devavrata fell asleep after Shukla left. The narration was not physically tiring. But with every word that he uttered, he felt he was losing a piece of his soul. That was emotionally exhausting. Some memories rang with joy but many were dark monsoon clouds obscuring the sun inducing gloom. Some memories he had worked hard to forget were returning, an alarming occurrence for one trained to remember and trained to forget. He woke up later that morning with Satyavati's words *He is going to kill me and then my children*, echoing in his mind. *It's only a dream*, he comforted himself; almost immediately, he realized that it was a true memory and not a dream. Shantanu had died, and Satyavati had barely waited for the funeral ceremonies to be completed before she rushed off with the children to Varanavata. This was what he had to tell Shukla and Yudhishthira. His father's death, his stepmother's panic, his own deep conviction that he should not be the ruler, the co-Regency and how it worked. This was not a dream, it had happened, and Shukla was coming with Yudhishthira to hear his version of the events.

The sounds of the camp grew during the midday meal. A nurse had to take care of his every need, and Devavrata found that uncomfortable. In any case, he had lost his appetite and only ate a small amount under the nurse's urging. He still needed the occasional drink of water, just to wet his mouth as he talked. With the water came gurgling sounds from his empty stomach. Hunger in itself was not a problem. Every trader and every warrior encounters a time when meals are irregular. A day or two may pass with no meals because of an error of judgement – taking the wrong turn at a fork in the road or hastily shooting off an unsteady bow and missing the quarry. Hunger wasn't the problem. Thinking about it and thinking about food made him queasy. He waited uneasily for the meal-time sounds to cease.

Shukla came in with Yudhishthira and the Archivist. They complimented him on his ability to look powerful and healthy despite his injuries. *Did they have to be so unrelentingly positive?* It only reminded him of the pain that he was trying hard to ignore. But his visitors insisted on pointing to that elephant in the room.

Shukla said, "Devavrata, let's get started."

Yudhishthira and Shukla sat cross-legged facing Devavrata while the Archivist took his place behind his head so that Devavrata could not see him. *That was a good idea.* Devavrata considered asking Yudhishthira to position himself similarly, out of sight, but... a reasonable request to make of a host but not of a jailer, however considerate. *It might be easier talking about these events if Yudhishthira were not here.* What could the story of Amba, of Chitrangada's death, or a host of other Kuru family secrets mean to Yudhishthira, who had been a stranger to that family for much of his life.

Yudhishthira spoke first.

"The Vyaasa tells me that you have much to talk about. There is much I want to know. If my duties call, I will have to leave. But the Vyaasa assures me that the Archivist will reproduce all that you say without any error, and I can listen to him. You will not have to do this again. Meanwhile, I am available."

Shukla felt cheerful. He enjoyed the rare experience of listening to fresh stories, anecdotes that he did not already know. Most often, he was expected to be the originator of narratives. The other source of pleasure was the private meeting with Devavrata. It had been difficult to meet Devavrata in private in Hastinapura. A meeting between Devavrata the Regent and the Vyaasa of the Kavi Sangha was a political event, fraught with consequences. Suyodhana would come by with questions and not accept the answers. Under that tension, his friendship with Devavrata threatened to disintegrate, the bond as frail as a spider's web holding a hummingbird – a bird small enough to be caught, too big to be eaten. A meeting between them was long overdue; it was a pity that they had waited until Devavrata was dying.

Devavrata continued his narration to his friend Shukla and the Archivist Lomaharshana.

SHANTANU'S SUNSET

SHANTANU'S DEATH

Devavrata said, "Satyavati said, '*He is going to kill me, and then my children.*' With these words, she gathered her sons and made her way overnight to the town of Varanavata."

Shukla said, "I was absent when Shantanu died. What led to Shantanu's death, so soon after the birth of his sons?"

Devavrata said, "A few years after the birth of Vichitravirya, my father fell ill. The right side of his body was paralyzed. Then his organs failed. He had complained of a headache, mild at first, but increasing every day despite the doctor's ministrations. Then one morning, he could not get out of bed. I was visiting Hastinapura from the extended waterworks projects that kept me busy and kept me out of town. I had asked to meet my father and the Vyaasa Jaimini about problems posed by the Meena-Nagas, Satyavati's people, who were expanding their range up the Yamuna into the land called Khandavaprastha. The king's illness precluded this discussion, and at the Vyaasa's insistence, I stayed on in Hastinapura.

"I spent my time playing with my brothers. There was nobody else in the court I wanted to meet, and nobody wanted to be seen with me, for that might arouse Satyavati's wrath. My father was young, in his early fifties. Chitrangada was eleven, and Vichitravirya was about four. I was in my early thirties. Nobody expected Shantanu to die, but he grew weaker and weaker. Some days he was delirious or seemed to be living a different life in some other world. He talked to his first wife, my mother, calling her 'Gangu' as he had many years ago. He would be animated whenever I went to his sickbed and spoke to him. He would recognize my voice and try to sit up and respond. He spoke clearly and did not mumble, but his words made little sense.

"If there was a theme to the delirious rambling, it was guilt and sorrow. One of the more comprehensible statements was about the one-child-per-person policy. *They welcomed me into their midst. 'Who are you?' I asked. 'The children you killed,' they said. 'Now we are immortal. Come join us.' There were so many.* If I were asked to explain that, I would have said that he was describing a nightmare in which he was surrounded by dead children.

"Another discernible guilt-ridden statement was that he had deprived me of something. *I failed you – Gangu was supposed to kill all of you.* This was strange indeed, given that the order to kill the babies had come from him and my mother had nothing to do with it. He went on to say that I could have been in heaven like my dead brothers, but had to suffer here. He offered to release me from mortal suffering so that I could join them. *I can make you immortal, just like me. From heaven, all is possible.* Of what he had truly deprived me, there was not a word. So this was another nightmare, not a message from an afterworld of dead persons' spirits.

"He conversed with his absent brother Bahlika. He said to his oldest brother Bahlika, 'Come back to Hastinapura. We will honor and welcome you.'

"Bahlika had left with his family long before Shantanu became King, intending to go as far west as he could. Shantanu seemed to believe that Bahlika's children had died. It is said that men who died without living progeny suffer eternal hunger. He may have believed that his brother was in torment, which added to his hallucinations.

"He dreamt that his second brother Devapi was dead. *Devapi, my brother! Forgive me for making you leave. I should have stopped you that day.* Devapi had left his royal clothes at the end of the forest and was believed to have entered the woods leaving behind a wife, but no children. *Shantanu had seen Devapi leave?* This was the first time I had heard that my father could have stopped Devapi. The dead Devapi had other concerns in my father's imaginings. *'Where are my children?'* he asked.

"If Devapi had children they would have been the rulers of Hastinapura. But Devapi had had no children; his wife had been barren. She continued to live in Hastinapura, a sad and invisible ghost, until she died. Shantanu dreamt that he had been very clever and had convinced his brother that he was cursed, could not have children, and should abdicate. He had not expected Devapi to go away – maybe Devapi had killed himself. Now Shantanu felt guilty that he had not tried to find Devapi. At first, he had not wanted to find Devapi; later, he thought it would make relations with Satyavati even more fraught if his brother were to return. It was news to me that he and Satyavati were unhappy with each other. He called it his *karma* – Shantanu thought that his actions in depriving Devapi of his birthright were the cause of Satyavati forcing him to deprive his son of his. Shantanu was sorry that he had made me give up my birthright. He had a boon for me. *You can choose the time of your death.* A strange boon. My father was delirious when he talked to me. His idea that Devapi had children was disconcerting. If it was not a delirium-induced nightmare, it would only make the chaos around us worse. I took the possibility seriously. I sent trained searchers to look for Devapi in all the likely places, all the way to Laghu Nagapura, but they found nothing.

"Shantanu ignored most visitors but some visitors could arouse him. Satyavati would come with Chitrangada and Vichitravirya. I would leave when I was informed of her coming. So I never learned what was spoken between them.

"After a few days, I thought he was getting better and said so to the doctor. The doctor shook her head saying, 'He smells sour, and I cannot change that. This disease mimics health shortly before the patient's death. I have seen it often – caregivers are often fooled.'

"That kind of pronouncement left me unmoved. What did the doctor mean? The patient smelled sour? Why would his smell, probably caused by drinking spoilt milk, indicate any disease?

The doctor had no explanation; rather, the one she produced in public mentioned mystical influences entering through the mouth. It was nonsense, but I let her continue. In private, she would explain that the smell was an indication that the body was consuming itself and that indicated a disease without a cure. She did not have a name for it. There would be periods when the patient appeared to get better, but this was a side-effect of the body cannibalizing itself. The king daily appeared more active and the delirium stopped. He was more in control of his mind if not his body. One side was still paralyzed, but his mind seemed to function normally.

"Of course, the doctor was proved right. One morning, I went to consult Shantanu about the Vyaasa Jaimini's proposal to stop using the army for civil construction. Jaimini had become the Vyaasa just before Chitrangada was born and had worked at creating alternatives to the plan developed when Bharadvaja was the Vyaasa.

"Bharadvaja's plan entailed the use of the army to suppress opposition. Lakes and waterworks were to be constructed and would be owned by the state. Immigrants would settle newly irrigated lands. Nagas would not be allowed to return with their slash-and-burn practices. With the immigrants leading as the advance guard, the empire would expand south by a sequence of waterworks defining the boundary, creeping south every generation, and slowly eliminating the Nagas from their current range. When Parashara became the Vyaasa, he wished to change the emphasis from exclusion to inclusion. His penalty cost him influence and subsequently, death cut short his tenure. His inclusive policy was not put into effect. Jaimini, who followed Parashara, was not a revolutionary, nor was he enamored of Bharadvaja's imperial solutions. He could not support a waterworks empire that catered to one group and destroyed another. I agreed with him, but thought that he lacked pragmatism. In his search for the best and fairest solution, he ignored what was happening on the ground with the help of the army. Slowly but steadily, the boundary between Hastinapura-irrigated land and Naga territory moved south.

"We were in the King's room discussing the Vyaasa Jaimini's proposal to withdraw the army from frontier construction projects that Shantanu had been directing. The King was walking around; he felt the need to keep his legs healthy with some form of exercise. At one point, he stopped pacing around. He closed his eyes and bent his head; then, he complained of excruciating pain in his left arm. He sat down, his mouth set in a grimace. Even as Shukla and I considered calling for the doctor, Shantanu said that his chest hurt and collapsed. We picked him up, but he had lost consciousness and felt limp in our arms. We laid him out on the bed. As we waited for the doctor, I listened for a heartbeat but could not find one. Just as the doctor entered, the smell of urine and waste filled the room. The King was dead.

"A messenger was sent to Satyavati immediately. She came back with him, her children in tow. I could not bear to meet and commiserate with her. I left the room and retired to my quarters.

"The Chief Minister came to see me that night. He said, 'You must take charge, Prince Devavrata. There is much confusion all over the city.'

"'Why?' I said. 'The Queen is in charge. I will support whatever action she wants to take.'

"'She has left with the princes for Varanavata.'

"'What happened?'

"'She was heard to say, *He is going to kill me and then my children.* It appears that she is uncertain of your intentions.'

"I did not want to rule. I had said so, but the statement had seemed mere talk to others. Even the Chief Minister, Sashidhara, seemed uncertain of what I would do. *He has known me since I was a child. Despite that, he, too, is skeptical. What can I do if, after all these years, I am not trusted? Nor am I understood.* In the few days before my father's death, I had begun to imagine that he would agree with me about the imperial plan. *Was that also a delusion?*

"Why did I think that the Chief Minister did not understand my intentions? I thought that he did not respond appropriately to Satyavati's fears. A loyal, knowledgeable minister concerned about the succession would have reassured her that I had no intention to harm her or her children. It is only if he himself were uncertain of my intentions that he would hold back.'

"I know now that I was naïve. In Panchnad, the Queen's council made decisions jointly. In Hastinapura, the King made the final decision. That decision is based on many streams of information and can appear opaque, even surprising, to the observer who only sees a part of the information. This was normal. This was why, even when following the policy suggested by the Kavi Sangha, Shantanu looked unpredictable to some of the participants in the process.

"Looking back, I think that the Chief Minister was being properly cautious in not responding to Satyavati's fears. If I intended to get rid of my brothers, his loyalty to the princes would make him suspect, and if I intended to support my brothers, then his encouraging Satyavati's fears would also make him suspect. However, the caution made me unsure of his intentions. As it was, I decided that my father had left the task of implementing the policy concerning the immigrants to me, and I had no major disagreements with my dead father and King on that policy.

"From then on, I was treated as the King. I found myself receiving the information that usually only went to my father. It helped me understand how much he had walled off his differences from me. My father could partition off the implementation of this policy from his personal life, and I could not. After the trauma of my mother's death, Shantanu maintained a strict separation between his own wishes or desires and the Kavi Sangha policies that he implemented. I could not do that. When I gave up the kingdom, it had been with the expectation that I would never rule and therefore never face the dilemmas that my father encountered. Unfortunately, this was not to be. I have had to shoulder the King's burden often. As I waited for the flurry of activity caused by my father's death to subside, I had a nebulous idea of withdrawing from public life and leaving it to my brother, Chitrangada, to implement the long-term agenda of Shantanu and the Kavi Sangha. My brothers were too young to understand why I would do such a thing, so I had to reassure Satyavati. I would have to meet her, and it could not be a public discussion. Yet, I did not want to meet her in private either."

Yudhishthira came in silently – the Vyaasa and the Archivist were in the *nishkamkarnarpana* state. The Archivist did not move. The Vyaasa formed the *jalam purayatu* mudra with his right palm and paused. The King picked up a small clay pot with water that was by the side of bed and held it to Devavrata's lips. Devavrata drank and wet his lips. Yudhishthira put the cup aside and sat down. They waited for Devavrata to continue with his narration.

SATYAVATI'S RETURN

Devavrata continued, "Rather than follow and face Satyavati, I postponed meeting with her. Instead, I arranged to meet the King's council in her absence. When I entered the council chamber, I could feel the excitement ripple through the room, like the warm summer breeze blowing in from the river in the late afternoon. The members of the council and the attending citizens were standing. They bowed low to me as if my face was too bright to behold. The Chief Minister seemed to have lost his luster. The smiling group that usually clustered around him stood just a little away from him and they were not smiling. The Chief Minister himself stood, his upper body erect and tense, a pose I had never seen him take in council.

"I realized they were expecting me to declare myself King. I walked slowly, glancing at every one of them as I walked by. Nobody met my gaze but looked at the ground and bowed. I wanted to scream at them, to admonish them, but did nothing as I walked past them. The throne was on a stage reached by three steps. It consisted of a section of a ficus tree trunk about four feet in diameter and about a *hasta* tall, its top covered with cotton padding. On top of that was a cushion. My usual place was on the floor to the left of the throne, marked by a single pillow. To the right of the throne was a place similarly marked by a pillow. Satyavati sat there. I sat down at my usual place. I felt a sigh make a second ripple through the room.

"In the past, when the King was absent, Satyavati would call the meeting to order. That day, I initiated the meeting, even though I did not want to do so. The people present acted as if this was perfectly normal and as if it was merely a matter of time before I moved over to the throne. I asked the ministers to summarize the state of their departments and report on what had been done that year and what else needed to be done. They responded with much alacrity and little substance. They made no attempt at providing the summary I had asked for or describing the state of their responsibilities. Instead, they devoted their time to extolling my virtues. *They had always been impressed by my deep understanding of discussions. I had brought reasoned thought and a keen intellect to the discussions. They were awed by the wisdom I had shown even as a young boy.* Unfortunately, in the past, they looked to Shantanu and Satyavati for direction and my ideas only received the respect that my father bestowed on them in public. *'Now we see how right you have been, sir,'* they said. I wondered if my father had felt as repelled by this false praise as I did. I wished I had not called the meeting.

"After half a dozen hagiographic reports, I stopped the speaker and said, 'The next speaker who avoids reporting and uses the time to praise me will be expelled from the council and from his post.' The room became very quiet. All the little sounds, the ripples if you will, that mark a group of living people, died. The unfortunate councilor who had begun his report, a polished and sophisticated urbanite, an early immigrant from Panchnad, stumbled through the rest of his very short presentation and returned to his seat. The session moved very quickly after that. Then it was my turn and by now, some life had returned to the group, for I had not yet punished anybody.

"I said, 'My brother Chitrangada was anointed as the Yuvaraja by my respected father when he lived. My father's wishes were clear, and we proclaim that, in accordance with his wishes, Chitrangada will be crowned King when he comes of age. In the meantime, his mother, the Queen Mother Satyavati, will be Regent.' I then announced that I would go to Varanavata to bring the Queen Mother and Regent, along with my brothers, to Hastinapura for the formal investiture.

"The silence that followed this announcement was quieter than the earlier quiet. Nobody moved. I could almost read their minds: *Is this a trick?* I wanted to shout from the highest mound: *This is what I want.* Unfortunately, I don't think that anything I said would have been credible. The last part of the surprise was that some of the listeners smiled and glanced at each other and bowed even deeper than before when I passed by. *Had they expected this?* The announcement should have been a surprise, but they acted as though it was routine. They had interpreted my statements looking for deeper meaning and had found what they were looking for. I wondered what I could have said that would not be twisted on reinterpretation.

"Satyavati received reports of this meeting. I received reports of these reports. Your stepson Devavrata has pretended to obey his father's wishes. His speech was a transparent attempt to convince the councilors of his intentions, but nobody was fooled. The report inserted an implied threat into every sentence that I had used. When I went to Varanavata and requested a private meeting, she refused. Her reply was: Come to my public hall ten ghatis after sunrise. There will be others asking for an audience. There, in public, I will certainly listen to you. I will hold you to your oaths.

"I had decided that I would do as she wanted no matter what it was. I had promised that I would ensure that Satyavati's children would inherit the kingdom. When that oath was demanded, my first impulse had been to refuse. If I had refused, my father would have been humiliated in public. To avoid further conflict, I would have left Hastinapura.

"It does not take much to insult a king. A king cannot swallow insults, either. This is one more difference between the old Panchnad cities and Hastinapura. A matriarch's rule is not threatened if somebody refuses to obey. A king's rule cannot survive if such disobedience is tolerated. At that point, I felt a deep empathy for my uncle Devapi's decision to abdicate and disappear. My vow prevented me from doing that. The vows demanded that I stay and create the institutions that would keep the country under the control of Hastinapura. If I walked away, I would allow some usurper to eliminate my weak young brother and my father's wife. *That* would be breaking my promise."

Shukla said, "I was there and recall your actions distinctly. Satyavati left for Varanavata without waiting for me to come to

Hastinapura. When I found out, I followed her to Varanavata. Things happened there when I couldn't be present."

Devavrata said, "I did exactly as Satyavati asked me to. I went to her public hall as a supplicant. I was surprised to see you in the audience. In the public court, I beseeched her to return to Hastinapura as the Queen Mother and Regent for the future King Chitrangada. I don't believe Satyavati expected this. Her eyes gave away her apprehension that this was a trap. I saw fear in her eyes when I looked up. *She is driven by fear. I must reassure her now, otherwise this fear of me will continue forever.*"

Shukla said, "Satyavati described this meeting to me in her own style, one that she had developed during those years with Shantanu. She said, 'I looked in Devavrata's eyes and saw the cold, hard calculation of a man plotting the best time to take revenge.'"

Devavrata smiled.

Shukla said, "My sister has a talent for dramatic expression."

Devavrata said, "You, Shukla, who was not then the Vyaasa, advised Satyavati. I was grateful for that. At your suggestion, Satyavati made a counter-offer. She and I would be joint Regents. She would keep control of the city and any part of the army within the city, and I would administer the rest of Kururashtra. Her first entry into the city would be after I left it. She would announce that she had invited me to be co-Regent. It would be my reward for my loyalty to my father and to her. She had rules that I was required to follow. I could only return to the city after she had taken control of the army. She would make any other rules as and when they became necessary and would tell me of those. She named her purpose. She was doing this for the safety of her son, the true heir to Shantanu. She wanted me to repeat my oath that one of my brothers would become the future ruler of Hastinapura. Thus, she and I would bring peace to a city that was on the brink of civil war between her supporters and the malcontents who were against her because she was a Naga.

"I accepted her proposal. I would have accepted anything that would erase her fear, the fear that I had finally recognized. Satyavati was afraid of me, but she was even more afraid that the people of Hastinapura would not accept a Regent of Naga origin. There were still a few who were angry with her conditions at the time of her marriage. If they rebelled, I might be forced to make common cause with them. In sharing power, she had made a calculated decision to ensure that I would support her.

"Satyavati did not return immediately to Hastinapura. Her absence, coupled with disbelief in my announcements, began to weigh on the various families that had settled in Hastinapura along with the Kauravas. A second public embassy led by Shukla was sent to invite her to return. She returned to a grand welcome that I organized, even as I left the city before the event.

"This was the problem: My avoidance of Satyavati was not conducive to building trust. Satyavati had feared me, and even though I had abased myself and begged her to return, she continued to fear and distrust me. Our agreement that I would stay outside the city while she stayed inside was unworkable. She needed to go out of the city, if only for pleasure, and I had to enter it for meetings with administrative officials and their ministers. We modified the agreement, but it continued to be difficult to manage. It was stressful and irritating to me that I had to constantly monitor my actions so as not to violate some element of the agreement. The core of the agreement held. Satyavati became co-Regent and Queen Mother, and took care of her children, Chitrangada and Vichitravirya. I was co-Regent and managed all the internal affairs of Kururashtra. We shared responsibility for collecting taxes and authorizing expenditures. The Panchnad model that mandated standard taxes and standard expenditures was already in place and did not change. Monarchies spend to glorify the ruler. In the absence of a ruler, the revenues could support minor luxuries for a principal family.

"Satyavati raised the boys by not denying them anything. They were self-willed and stubborn, and nobody chided them. Left to their mother, they would have learned nothing. I worked with the Kavi Sangha to arrange teachers for them in history, economics, trade, martial arts, and strategy.

"Meanwhile, the Kavi Sangha and the Vyaasa Jaimini worked to create a state that maintained order in the face of chaos, while preserving what had been best in the abandoned cities of

Panchnad. The Kavi Sangha could preserve knowledge as long as the rest of the world functioned well enough – destruction of knowledge was threatened in every riot, every clash between immigrant and Naga, and every conflict over scarce resources.

Knowledge in an Urban Culture

The Vyaasa Bharadvaja convinced Shantanu to allow Panchnadis into Hastinapura in order to preserve their advanced knowledge. Chaos destroyed knowledge even when it did not kill the bearer. *'Knowledge,'* he said, *'in an urban civilisation like Panchnad did not just reside in the minds and bodies of individuals – it also resided in the relationships between people that characterised urban life. Knowledge was lost when the smith who knew how to smelt metals went south while the craftsman who knew how to construct the moulds for a graded sequence of cast weights went north – the system of standard weights that supported an honest oral trading infrastructure would be lost. Similarly, if the last brick-maker who could make high-quality bricks of a fixed shape, size, and strength was lost, the engineer who knew how to make buildings with those bricks would no longer make solid structures. The bricklayer would struggle to lay irregularly shaped bricks and would create a pastiche wall, ugly to view. In an urban civilisation, knowledge nestled in all kinds of niches, waiting to be exploited.*

"Chaos was unavoidable; it streamed in steadily from outside. The solution was to channel its energies. During the last years of Shantanu's reign, I had begun building dams to create small lakes and ponds along the paths of the Ganga and the Yamuna. The Kavi Sangha suggested — and I agreed with their assessment — that the settlement of Varanavata should be the model for new settlements. Varanavata was the camp where Samvarana had spent his years of exile. It was on the banks of a constructed lake on the Yamuna, and over the years, it had become a prosperous agricultural community. Canals and irrigation channels brought water to the fields. The plan was to create more agricultural settlements in the land between the two rivers north of the ridge where the Yamuna had changed direction. The Nagas had only expanded slightly in that direction, and there were only a few bands to deal with. Immigrants could settle this land. Rainfall was meager, and water had to come from the two rivers."

"By the time of my father's death, we had stopped enforcing the limits on the number of children in a family. A limit on the number of children is easier to enforce in an urban setting, not so in a rural setting. The need for limits did not go away. We were left with only two ways of managing the growth – not let in any more immigrants or make them move to the outskirts of the land we controlled. We were not prepared to turn back the refugees, at least not yet. We would have to settle new refugees near the border. They would have to farm the land. The massive dislocation of people had made the trading network unreliable, so they would first aim to produce the food they needed before producing for export. The fine pottery and ceramics for which Panchnad had been famous could no longer be made and exports to the West collapsed. In Panchnad, the land to the south had been extremely fertile while the land to the north was good for crops only in narrow strips on either bank of the river. As a result, Panchnad had two kinds of towns – the northern towns that specialized in manufacture and the southern ones that produced food. This model could not be reproduced in the new border settlements. Among immigrants, there were many northerners and few southerners because most of the southerners of Panchnad had moved into the unknown territory of the Southern Peninsula. Because the border settlements needed farmers, we tried to make the Nagas our 'southerners,' but that was misconceived. Every lesson that we learned consumed our best efforts, but worse, it took us years to absorb. Meanwhile we were sending the refugees to these half-built and half-baked northern settlements."

Devavrata paused. Yudhishthira brought water in a clay mug and Devavrata took a sip. It was almost a ghati after the sun had disappeared, and dusk was falling fast. Shukla and Lomaharshana relaxed, dropping their listening pose.

Yudhishthira said, "We must continue tomorrow with the story."

With those words, they adjourned.

KING CHITRANGADA

The next day after the morning meal, King Yudhishthira, the Vyaasa Shukla, and the Archivist Lomaharshana arrived together at Devavrata's tent. The entrance was closed with a curtain of felted cotton. The nurse came out and said, "Excuse the delay, sir. The Regent is not yet ready."

After about a ghati, the nurse invited them in. Devavrata was lying on his side, his eyes closed and his mouth set in a thin line. As they entered, he opened his eyes and said, "Come in. I regret to say that I can no longer control my body. Give me death."

The King said, "Grandsire! We regret to trouble you in this manner. We cannot heal your wound, nor are we ready to kill you in your present state."

Devavrata said, "Should I attack somebody or strive to escape? Then you will kill me?"

Yudhishthira said, "Sire! I value your life and everybody in this camp knows that. In any case, we would not kill a wounded soldier without cause."

Devavrata said, "Then you do not hold out any hope for me. Am I to continue in this undignified manner?"

"I've asked everyone here to treat you with respect. They will do so."

"You are here for your purposes. Why should I care what you want?"

"Because we have the same goals –to create a kingdom that benefits its people. The Kavi Sangha wants to record your life. We both seek to honor your life and your work. You have done much, and even if I do not agree with all that you have done, I still wish to understand it — if only to avoid repeating your mistakes."

"Is that the consolation you offer me? That you will remember me for my errors?"

Shukla intervened. He said, "Devavrata, my friend. We have known each other for a long time. You will die soon. I will die soon after. You can be remembered for all you have done, both successes and failures — errors, if you will. Alternatively, you can be forgotten completely. Which would you prefer? That choice I can offer you as the Vyaasa. Forgive Yudhishthira. The ghost of his father, your nephew, drives him. Tell him what he wants to hear, so that your brother's son may rest in peace."

The three of them contemplated one another in silence. Devavrata considered what had been said. He had given up so much in his life. Was this to be the ultimate fruit of his sacrifices? He had killed his own son; Amba had attempted to kill him; the people he had sworn to protect had died, his brother Chitrangada, his nephew Mahendra Pandu, many others who had opposed him. Shukla offered him oblivion or fame – Shukla did not realize that he cared for neither. The only person who had expressed sorrow at his present condition was Yudhishthira, who had little reason to be kind to him. If he owed anything to anybody, it was to Yudhishthira, who empathized with him when no one had for many years. It would be an act of kindness to satisfy his request, and it was the only one within his power to grant.

"Yudhishthira, my child! I'll do as you wish. Come, Archivist, sit near me and listen to me talk. Yudhishthira, is there any question you want me to answer?"

Yudhishthira said, "Lomaharshana ended yesterday saying that refugees were directed south into hastily made homes in territory that the Nagas had left fallow. What was the reason for that?"

Devavrata was silent in response to Yudhishthira's question and stared at the ceiling of the tent. He looked about to say something, but then stopped and continued staring. They waited for ten vighatis. Then he closed his eyes. Yudhishthira did not move. Lomaharshana could not wait.

Lomaharshana said, "Forgive me, Lord. Could you continue with your narrative?"

Devavrata's eyes opened, and he looked at Lomaharshana. So did Yudhishthira and the Vyaasa, causing the young man to cringe.

"Yes, I will," said Devavrata. He gazed at Yudhishthira. Shantanu used to have the same stubborn look of conviction. *Memories are lost in time, and we lose ourselves in memories.* Yudhishthira did not appear to have changed and was looking at him with the same concern that he had shown the day before and the day before that.

Devavrata said, "Yudhishthira, I will answer your questions when the time comes. At this time, I will speak of Hastinapura after my father married Satyavati.

"As I said yesterday, Satyavati and I established a co-regency. A few years passed; Chitrangada came of age and was crowned King. He died fighting Shakas in the north."

Shukla said, "This is a point that has created much debate. My sister was told that a gandharva, also named Chitrangada, challenged him. Well... we know that gandharvas are imaginary beings and do not exist. Whoever told Satyavati that had not told the truth. Now you say Shakas killed him?"

Yudhishthira asked, "What exactly was the Queen Mother told?"

The Vyaasa continued: "I learned from her that Chitrangada had set out on an expedition to the northern border and that Devavrata followed him to stop him. Devavrata's men came back with a story of a gandharva killing Chitrangada. At that time, I investigated on behalf of Queen Satyavati. I questioned Devavrata's soldiers and they all had the same story. Chitrangada was already dead by the time they arrived. The gandharvas had vanished leaving behind a small contingent of their allies, the Shakas. The ensuing battle with the Shakas lasted longer than expected, and there were more casualties than expected, but Devavrata's army had finally prevailed. Many Shakas were captured and following their own practice, they were enslaved. The Panchnad settlements do not have slaves, but they could be easily sold to the western countries that clamored for them. The Shaka prisoners were shipped to the port of Tripura on the

Sindhu delta from where they were taken to the West for sale. You cremated Chitrangada's body because, in a few days, the body had begun to decompose and could not be carried to Hastinapura safely."

Devavrata said, "Yes, gandharvas do not exist. I made up that story to spare Satyavati the details of her son's death. I also wanted to spare the people of Hastinapura those details."

Shukla said, "The bard reciting the story knows what to include and what to exclude, for the audience dictates the telling. However, the bard must know the whole story so that he can make the choice at the time of the telling. You've already told us of the death of your father and the co-Regency that you set up with Queen Mother Satyavati. What happened after that? What led to your brother's death and to another co-Regency?"

Devavrata said, "That I will cover. Recall that my second step-brother, your grandfather, had become king after the death of Chitrangada. He died some years later, leaving two Queens pregnant with Mahendra Pandu and Dhritarashtra. That was the third co-Regency. Later, when Mahendra exiled himself, he left behind his blind half-brother Dhritarashtra. A blind person cannot be crowned King, so Satyavati, Dhritarashtra, and I formed the fourth co-Regency. For whom were we holding the seat? When your father died, one faction wanted you, Yudhishthira, son of King Mahendra, to be crowned King. Dhritarashtra remained quiet when Satyavati objected, but it was clear that the suggestion to overlook him because he was blind had offended him. He supported a second faction that wanted to make his son Suyodhana the King. This was considered radical and against custom. The custom among caravan masters was that a son could supplant his father as Master only if his father died or was mentally incapable. This was intended to prevent a caravan from being hijacked by a coup. Hastinapura had never been a matrilineal matriarchy – the Master was called King. Suyodhana could not become King while his father was alive and in his senses. Yudhishthira, your father was dead – you could be made King, if we agreed. A compromise was reached. Dhritarashtra gifted your father's forest back to you. When you accepted the offer, you gave up your legitimate claim to be the King of

Hastinapura. We mutually agreed to call Dhritarashtra the King, for it pleased him and did not change anything.

"Sending you away did not resolve Suyodhana's problem. He could still not become King. He could not kill his father because that would not sit well with Queen Satyavati, or, for that matter, with me. He could declare his father incompetent and prove it by a public demonstration of his father's dementia. Satyavati would not countenance such an act nor could I. However, Suyodhana's faction dominates the councils and the city. So Suyodhana now rules in the name of his father, the co-Regent. I am the other co-Regent, along with Queen Satyavati, but almost everybody obeys Suyodhana's dictates as though he were already the King."

Yudhishthira said, "You have been co-Regent for Hastinapura many times. Tell us about these co-Regencies and what you accomplished during that period."

Devavrata said, "I have talked about the death of my father and the establishment of the first co-Regency with the Queen-Mother Satyavati. I will now tell you about the short reign of my brother Chitrangada, his northern misadventure, his death, and..."

Yudhishthira said, "Excuse me, Grandsire! At another time, I would have urged you to tell me all about my granduncles. Today, I want to know about the forces that motivated your imperial decisions. Granduncle Chitrangada ruled for a very short time. I've heard that Grandfather Vichitravirya showed little interest in governing. Neither of them could have affected policy in any significant manner. As co-Regent, you ran the country. What does the foolhardy death of my granduncle Chitrangada matter if it did not affect your imperial plans?"

Devavrata pursed his lips and nodded. His brother's death by itself meant nothing; the chain of consequences from that death was significant. Chitrangada had been suspicious about the Kavi Sangha, a suspicion he derived from Satyavati, who considered the Kavi Sangha evil, even as she used its volunteers to do things that she wanted done. Chitrangada had suspended all cooperation with the Kavi Sangha. His death had restored the Regency and reinstated the agenda of the Kavi Sangha.

Devavrata said, "My son, Chitrangada's reign and his death forced the Kavi Sangha and me to change, to expand substantially the scope of our imperial plans. His younger brother Vichitravirya was too young and had not been raised to rule. He showed no desire to act as King and ruled only because he had to and because his mother wanted him to. Vichitravirya enjoyed life with his two wives and neglected the office of the king. His unexpected death and the subsequent late birth of his children allowed us, the Kavi Sangha and me, to collaborate with Satyavati and put in place many irreversible changes. The events leading to and after Chitrangada's death changed many things – that death was a turning point. The co-Regency after Vichitravirya's death lasted eighteen years until Mahendra Pandu ascended to the throne."

Devavrata paused. *Only I know how my brother died. Amba does, too. That's how I met Amba.* These thoughts added to his melancholy.

He continued, "Shukla, my friend. I have one wish."

Shukla nodded.

Devavrata said, "You must tell me what you know. You said that you knew how Amba reached Panchala and her life there and of her son Shikhandin. That is all I wish to know. You must tell me of Amba's life."

Yudhishthira said, "Does this need to be a part of this archive?"

Shukla was silent as he considered his answer. *Why was Yudhishthira, who had been so solicitous earlier, showing signs of impatience?* His father Mahendra Pandu had disagreed with Devavrata over policies, as a result of which Mahendra Pandu deliberately withdrew into self-exile. Telling the story of Devavrata's life in such detail postponed the explanation of that decision. Given Devavrata's condition, he might never get to that point in the story. Devavrata's life outlined the framework on which Hastinapura had tried to address the crisis created by the refugees from Panchnad. Some key events in Devavrata's life corresponded to shifts in policy. Devavrata's mother's death resulted from Shantanu's first attempt to limit the population of Hastinapura. Shantanu's marriage to Satyavati heralded a change in policy that was given to Devavrata to develop. Shantanu's death and the terms of the co-Regency took Devavrata outside the city. Chitrangada's death led to an alliance against the Shakas. Vichitravirya's death gave Devavrata sole control of policy. It was not until Yudhishthira's father came of age that Devavrata's power began to diminish. Yudhishthira must think that the story of Amba and Shikhandin was a distraction that postponed the discussion of the differences between his father and Devavrata.

When the silence had continued for many vighatis, Devavrata said, "I don't care whether Amba's story is included in the archive. But if you do not tell me what happened to her, I have nothing more to say to you."

Shukla said, "Yudhishthira, the archive is not solely a repository of how the city was governed. By creating stories that can be recited and will hold an audience's attention, we keep alive the history of the city. Perhaps you wish to get to the causes of your father's self-exile. I promise that we will get there."

It was Yudhishthira's turn to ponder. Finally, he said, "So be it. I shall be patient."

The bell at the entrance to the tent rang. A Panchalan soldier came in and bowed to the King. He said, "Sir! The night's reconnaissance teams have just come in. They have requested a meeting with you and your brothers."

Yudhishthira grimaced. They had successfully executed the ambush and captured the Regent, but the war would not end so easily. If the night patrol had seen a troop movement by Hastinapura, it would be valuable to get the Vyaasa's opinion as well. Meanwhile, Devavrata was working well with the Archivist, recounting what Yudhishthira wanted to know, and that had to continue.

Shukla interrupted, "Yudhishthira! Lomaharshana is a master of memorization and archiving. He will do a perfectly good job even without our presence."

"Gurudeva, I am not concerned about Lomaharshana's skills. The Regent wants to narrate the events that led to the deaths of my grandfather Vichitravirya and his brother Chitrangada. Your presence and mine are the only guarantee that the Regent will narrate the histories we wish to know. You and I are the ones who can decide if a digression should be pursued or should be dropped. How can Lomaharshana make that decision?"

"You are right," Shukla said, "You are the best person to elicit the knowledge you seek from the Regent. However, we both know that you cannot be here all the time. You have the opportunity to tell Lomaharshana what you are looking for. I will have Lomaharshana summarize for you this evening and he can get any missing details the next day, while the memories are still fresh."

Yudhishthira hesitated. I am the King, he thought. I should... but I am the King, and there are many other matters to be addressed. He knew what he had to do.

Yudhishthira said, "Lomaharshana, listen! Grandsire, this is what I seek. My granduncle Chitrangada and my grandfather Vichitravirya ruled for a very short time. Yet, you seem to place great importance on their short lives. Why? Battles were rare in those times. It was over two thousand moons[42] since Samvarana was restored by violence. Yet, Chitrangada died in battle. My grandfather Vichitravirya became the ruler at a young age and died young. I am told he died before his sons were born; their births were described as miracles. I am eager to hear of them, even though my mind is pre-occupied with this war. What was grandfather's life like? What did he accomplish? His death must have been a shock to the Queen Mother Satyavati."

Devavrata said, "Yudhishthira, your granduncle, my half-brother Chitrangada, was eager to show off his skills as a warrior. I had trained him, and I believe he wanted to impress me even as he charged me with treason for not handing over full command of the army. His mother had handed over the control of the troops stationed in the city to him, but Chitrangada wanted to command all the troops including the ones protecting all the things I had been building – dams, canals, roads, and settlements."

"Why did you not give him complete command of the army?"

---

[42] About one hundred and sixty years.

"He was impetuous and inclined to quick action without thinking through its consequences. I asked him to command the army through me, but he soon realized that I was slow to respond to demands for urgent action. He could not see how often a looming crisis would pass without requiring any response. Unfortunately, he did not learn the futility of hurried action from these episodes.

"I also kept control of the secret service. I told him that this was the traditional practice, so that the King's reputation and character were not sullied by contact with low and despicable persons who were only fit to be spies and provocateurs. After that bit of dissimulation, it was a relief that he never found out about his mother's secret agents; he might have confined her to her home to prevent further damage to her reputation!

"Despite my best efforts, I had to hand over control of the army to the King. I retained my personal guard, almost a hundred men, but I did not use them to guard me. They guarded the projects I had in progress throughout the region. I also created a border police force to augment the guards used inside the city. They would help manage the flow of immigrants and keep them from conflicting with the Nagas."

Yudhishthira said, "You told us earlier that the official story of Chitrangada's death was false. Do you know the real story?"

"To the best of my knowledge, there are no gandharvas – they are mythical beings. I do know the manner of his death – I've kept that secret for so many years. I used to think, *when I die, it will die with me*. Even the Kavi Sangha's archives do not contain that truth."

"It is not appropriate that nobody in the family knows the truth about his death. As long as you were alive, you could reassure yourself that somebody knew the truth. It is incumbent on you to tell the story to somebody. If there is cause to keep it secret, let the burden be mine. Lomaharshana, do you understand what I would like to know?"

The Archivist replied, "Sir, the best test is, as Gurudeva said, for me to memorize and compose a narrative, then give you the chance to review it. I am open to correction."

Both Shukla and Yudhishthira stood up. As they were leaving, Shukla said, "Good luck, my boy! You must now take the King's place."

Lomaharshana nodded. He turned to the Regent Devavrata and said, "Sir, please continue."

THE FIRST CO-REGENCY

CHITRANGADA'S WAR

Lomaharshana said, "Sir, you heard the guidelines I have been asked to establish in your narrative. Will you be able to tell me everything without tiring yourself?"

Devavrata said, "It is not easy to tell you this story. It does not deviate from your directions. What it does, though... even thinking of it creates a knot deep in my chest. As recently as three days ago, I would have claimed that this reaction has nothing to do with history. My encounter with Shikhandin has altered that belief. The knot in my chest is a complex one. It has three strands of which one leads unerringly to the man I just killed.

"Killing Shikhandin completed the story of my killing of Chitrangada. Yes, I will not hide it any more. I killed Chitrangada. Believe me, it had to be done. Killing him created that first strand of the knot that now threatens to choke me. That strand earned me my name, *Bhishma*, the Terrible. Not even *Devavrata, the Terrible*. *Devavrata, the Terrible* would have been fine. But just *The Terrible*? Am I *adhvaya*, sui generis, one of a kind? The *Terrible* kind?

"Killing Chitrangada brought Amba into my life. When I lost her, the second strand of the knot was created. I had given her up for dead. Shukla says that she left me for Drupada. Drupada? The bombastic hothead from Panchala? No, that makes no sense. Shukla says that she has lived in hiding all these years. That does not make any sense, either. Her actions created the third strand that was hidden from me until revealed by Shikhandin. These three strands, let me call them *Chitrangada-Amba-Shikhandin*, independent though they may seem, are entwined tightly, each born of the previous one.

"Why did I kill Chitrangada? The easy answer is that I saved him from a terrible fate. When I decided to kill him, my mind was clear and without any doubt. But even as I acted on that decision, my thoughts whirled and became muddled, and the purity of the initial intention was compromised. For I always wonder how things would have been different if I had been the King.

"When Chitrangada became the ruler of Hastinapura, many citizens of Hastinapura rejoiced that they were no longer subject to the rule of a Regent. The boy was just sixteen years old, and under Satyavati's encouragement, had become confident of his own ability to rule. I had trained him to be a warrior. He was good at the business of war; he would have made an excellent commander of a battalion or even a division. That was not good enough for him. He considered himself a warrior in the tradition of Samvarana, father of the dynast Kuru. Shukla, who knew Chitrangada well, can tell you how ridiculous that was. My ancestor Samvarana had become a warrior under the personal tutelage of the great Vasishtha, founder of the Kavi Sangha, so that he could regain Hastinapura. In the emptying cities of the west, the leaders hired mercenaries. They were the guards for trading caravans that went west. Now they guarded the leaders and maintained order; they prevented riots when the poorest felt unfairly treated. Mercenaries were the only ones who trained to fight.

"Since the time of Samvarana and Kuru, Hastinapura had defended itself from the Nagas of Panchala and had defended Laghu Nagapura from the attacks of Rakshasas[43]. We do not use

---

[43] The Rakshasas ("protectors" in the Naga language) occupied much of the Southern Peninsula of South Asia, the plateau south of Laghu Nagapura, and both sides of the Ganga to the east of Laghu Nagapura.

mercenaries but fight to protect ourselves. We keep our trade secrets. My father and I established an internal security force to manage the influx of immigrants and the resulting conflicts with the Nagas. That force became a police force and enforced his laws about children. The Kavi Sangha supported him fully. Mercenaries do not make a good standing army. They only know how to make war and enforce martial law. They do not know how to enforce civil laws. They could not take a child away from its parents without killing the parents.

"My army was not made up of great warriors. If we had ever faced a mercenary army, we would have lost. Luckily, the mercenaries are no more; the guild of mercenaries has vanished. The mercenaries have no jobs because the caravans no longer travel west through dangerous lands. The Panchnad cities do not exist anymore and so do not need champions to fight on their behalf. And finally, there are better opportunities for guards in the west. So the east has been abandoned.

"After my father's death, it was a simple step for me to create an armed militia. I needed them to protect the dams I had built upstream from the northern boundary of Panchala. The Panchalas could easily destroy them. South and west of the Ganga, the wayward Yamuna had made the watershed unstable, and new waterworks had to be built to control the old monsoon-fed rivers. The army came in useful to coordinate the design between towns and villages and to direct the construction of dams, canals, and ponds by local workgroups. By the time Chitrangada was crowned, we had a small construction corps that could be used for projects.

"A ruler with an army will itch to fight. Chitrangada's first wish after being crowned was to use our army – *my* army, my *small* army – to attack Panchala and avenge Samvarana's humiliation. *Samvarana had re-taken Hastinapura, but the Panchalas had to be taught a lesson.* Satyavati and I rarely agreed, but that time, we dissuaded Chitrangada by pointing to the difficulty of launching an attack across the river. Unfortunately, I also raised the possibility that we might not have the full support of the Nagas. Once this sank in, it colored Chitrangada's attitude to the Nagas; he in turn influenced Vichitravirya, and the brothers distrusted the Nagas ever after. This distrust was a disease difficult to cure. Even though the Queen-Mother Satyavati was a Naga, both Dhritarashtra and Suyodhana were infected with it.

"Chitrangada wanted recognition as a warrior. We had checked that ambition, but it never went away. The result was tragedy.

"I had continued my project of creating dams and canals wherever it was feasible. One of my greatest successes was restoring Varanavata, Samvarana's old abode of exile, located on the edge of Khandavaprastha at a point where the recently diverted Yamuna exited the forest. A monsoon stream ran through the shallow valley, its channel now overflowed with the waters of the Yamuna. My engineers had designed a series of crescent-shaped ponds that channeled the river, making it flow faster and deepen its median channel. The result was a river that flooded less. Canals led from the crescent ponds to Varanavata's fields much further away. Thereby, the town had prospered and was slowly filling up with immigrants.

"I was visiting Varanavata when an urgent message came from Hastinapura. Chitrangada had received news of an incursion into Hastinapura territory at its northern extremity close to one of the branches of the Sindhu. I had not anticipated Chitrangada's reaction. I had learned of the incursion some weeks ago and had decided not to do anything about it. The Panchnad people claimed suzerainty over Jambudvipa, but it was a formulaic suzerainty. Nobody enforced it. The incursions had become an annual event over the last twenty years. Some Naga bands had settled near there, and I expected the intruders to go back as they usually did.

"*Who were these intruders*, you ask. The intruders were from an uncivilized nomadic collection of tribes that called themselves 'Shaka[44],' and they came from the open plains northeast of the plateau of the Parsakas. The mountainous and forested lands that we inhabited were useless for them, and they usually left after a few weeks. *Why did they come?* They came to trade. They came

---

[44] *Shaka* refers to Scythians (as named by the Greeks) who roamed over much of the steppes of Eurasia.

with lapis and agate, both polished and rough. They brought partially tanned skins of many animals large and small. Occasionally, they would have a small collection of yellow nuggets of pure gold. In the days before the disaster, Hastinapura would have viewed them as competition.

"*How did they come?* This was the most interesting aspect of their visit and the reason I did not try to eject them post-haste. They were in carts pulled by small horses. Not onagers like we had, but horses. They did not behave like most traders. For instance, they did not bring their goods directly to the market. Instead, they would set up a camp in a secluded defensible place and come to the market with their goods on their backs or in small handcarts. Thus, they would never bring their horses to the trading site. Once I invited them to come on their horses for dinner. They refused to do so. They cited cultural prohibitions that prevented them from eating with a non-Shaka. What I did not realize until much later was that they had started coming only after I built a dam across the Yamuna ravine, well within the mountains. Previously, it had been difficult to cross with carts and supplies. Now, the dam provided the path. I would pay for failing to anticipate that.

"I had sent some spies to keep track of the intruders and received a message regularly. When I was not in Hastinapura, the messenger would be re-directed to me. The last messenger had gone to King Chitrangada's council-room. He tried to withdraw when he realized that I was not present. But before he could retreat, the King saw him and commanded him to deliver his message. Chitrangada then expressed to his mother his dissatisfaction with my decisions and his shock that I had put the country at risk. He decided to take our army – *my* army – and teach these intruders a lesson.

"I received a confused message from Satyavati about the matter and rushed to Hastinapura. But it still took a few days. Satyavati was agitated by the time I reached. First, she urged me to leave immediately to help Chitrangada. Then, she fretted that I would steal from her son the credit for repelling the invaders and wanted me to stay out of it. Then again, she wondered if my people would protect the King or if it was a plot against the King. I kept quiet during these crying fits. What could I say? *It's my army he has taken with him, the five hundred trained fighters that I gave up to him, leaving only a small force of a hundred boys-in-training to protect the city!* Such a statement would only have made her angrier and more suspicious. I left as soon as I could with about fifty of my personal band. Chitrangada had left me with only a hundred men, and I left half of them behind to supplement the hundred men of his army protecting Hastinapura.

"There was not much we could do to go fast. Not with our onagers. The Shaka are trained horsemen; they use horses in their land for everything. It is a mystery to us how the Shaka can ride them in such a carefree manner. I have seen a horse, and when it is angered, it is a terrifying sight. Many years ago, a trader had brought a wild horse in a cage. He showed us how it would refuse to submit to a yoke, and even if a yoke was somehow placed on its shoulders, it proved to be an uncontrollable power. Only the Shakas have mastered the secret of taming the horse. They do not part with that secret for anybody.

"Anyway, using onagers for transport, I travelled as soon as I could."

DEVAVRATA TO THE RESCUE

Devavrata continued, "We loaded our supplies onto a dozen carts pulled by onagers. Onagers are stubborn willful creatures, but when harnessed with other onagers, they could pull carts. We needed to make speed, so we had two animals pulling one cart while two spare ones walked alongside. The crowd listening to a bard's stories does not always realize that it takes an army to move an army. My squad of fifty fighters needed sixty onagers and fifteen carts for transport. Forty-five of the fifty men were divided into three squads that were responsible for driving the carts.

"The day began with a meal followed by harnessing the onagers and travelling for twelve ghatis. There was a break for a midday meal of flatbread and salted meat. In a more traditional campaign, we would have stopped to hunt for meat if the game looked promising, and we would have bartered our salted meat for hot cooked meals from local towns and villages. But we were in a hurry and we ate what we carried. After the meal break, we could change the onagers and go for another twelve ghatis or until the sun began to set. Then we would settle down for the night after a light meal, the same flatbread and salted meat.

"Our fifteen carts were loaded with three or four men each, their arms and armor, their food, as well as forage for the draft animals. Each cart selected one man to stay awake the first half of the night and a second man to keep watch during the second half. My primary worry was wild animals – for instance, a tiger tempted by the easy prey that an onager seemed to be. In a small squad like this, the onagers of the carts on the outside might be attacked by wolf packs if they looked vulnerable. The tiger and the wolves were the most dangerous as they were not easily frightened away.

"My second worry was the *kapi*[45] that roamed in bands and made trouble everywhere. I've been told that these monkeys can be used as spies. That certainly seems possible, but I've only found them to be nuisances. If a cart were not constantly protected, it would be ransacked. The onagers were tied to each cart on opposite sides so that, if they were startled in the night and panicked, they would pull in opposite directions and so not be able to run away with the carts and be lost. Far more destruction has been caused in camps by distraught onagers than by even the fiercest enemy.

"If the destination was far away and speed was essential, each onager would be spelled by a second onager that walked unburdened. That would double the distance we could go in a day. Our haste added to the problems. We had to carry twice the hay and grain for feeding the relief onagers while cutting the number of soldiers and including one or more handlers for the additional onagers. The point is that moving an army, even a small army, is not an easy task. I knew that Chitrangada had left in a hurry without enough draft animals and would have had to slow down to a sustainable pace.

---

[45] *Kapi* refers to the Indian rhesus monkey.

"Chitrangada had a lead of seven days over us but he would have moved slowly, with almost five hundred men and a couple of hundred followers who provided support. Instead of the four days we would take, he would have needed six or seven to reach the intrusion point. We had had some experience of unexpected confrontations with the Nagas of Panchala. It usually took a few days of maneuvering and observation before it became clear who had the upper hand. Against a Panchala corps, the smaller group would configure itself in a defensive formation and send for reinforcements. The bigger group would assess its chances of total victory before those reinforcements came and configure in an offensive formation. We inherited these forms of maneuvering, called *vyuhadyuta*[46], from Panchnad. It was rare for such a procedure to guarantee victory for the larger group; so, much of the time, nothing happened. A great superiority in numbers was needed before the larger group attacked. When reinforcements arrived, the forces might be equal or the relative strength might be reversed. The strategic implications of their relative strength would lead to reconfigured formations. Unless there was an overwhelming advantage for one group over the other, these maneuvers would end in a stalemate. Both groups could withdraw, and sometimes both declared victory. Sometimes, the groups might engage in battle. This could happen for various reasons – the personalities of the leaders, or an error of judgement by one side or the other, or even a momentary lapse in attention that allowed one side to get an advantage over the other.

"As I mentioned earlier, in the past, I would arrange to monitor the Shaka 'visitors' but not engage them in battle. The pattern was that after a few weeks, they would leave. They were not used to the never-ending forest and were a noisy bunch, especially when they rode their horses. I had a spy once who followed the Shaka back to their homeland and spent a few years with them. He returned in bad shape – a nervous wreck, voice pitched higher than before, slurring words as though he might lose them if he slowed down, eyes staring down and constantly moving. When he delivered the report of his two years on the road, he spoke quickly and I had to slow him down, but he was constantly

---

[46] *Vyuhadyuta* means a shadow duel of opposing battle formations.

speeding up as he spoke. He gave me useful information about the Shaka. Unlike their peaceful behavior when they visit us, they are extremely warlike in their own land. Every would-be warrior has a horse; the team of horse and warrior can be terrifying when confronted on an open field.

"My spy described a battle he had seen when a Shaka band had attacked a caravan on their border with Parsaka. The guards protecting the caravan had formed a defensive perimeter when the Shakas were sighted. A Shaka warrior would gallop past the line, close enough so that they were within the range of his arrows, firing constantly. Arrows shot and spears thrown at the Shaka missed as they moved unpredictably on their horses. If the line of guards wavered, the horseman might go in closer. Once, an injury to a captain had distracted the soldiers near him and a horseman managed to get in among the defenders. He had inflicted terrible damage with a heavy sword while the guards struggled to organize. As soon as the guards regrouped, the horseman rode away with barely a scratch. The Shaka strategy was to make the defenders use up their arrows and lose spears thrown in haste.

"After a few days of this, the defenders became desperate and made overtures, offering tribute. The Shaka accepted the offer and came to collect it. Once in the camp, they rampaged through it on their horses, attacking the lightly armed guards and the defenseless traders and workers. It had been a terrifying sight – a man on a horse charging down a narrow path, slicing the walkers as they scattered left and right. They then proceeded to ransack the camp and kill most of the fighters. The few women in the caravan were taken as captives. They tortured the men for amusement, killing most of them in the process and leaving the rest maimed and injured.

"My spy had been one of the tortured ones who survived. He shook uncontrollably as he tried to describe what had happened to him but became incoherent when I pressed him for details. I learned later that castration was a part of the torture. I retired him to a home where he was taken care of for the rest of his life. His return to me to report had been an act of perseverance and loyalty. I wish I could have done more, but the doctors shook their heads and could do little for him.

"I understood then that as long as the Shakas were far from their own land and faced with a land or by a people they could not conquer, they would be peaceful. If they sensed an opportunity to deploy their preferred mode of warfare, on open fields mounted on horses and dominated by the use of the bow and arrow, they would win every encounter against foot soldiers. Our Shaka traders had been peaceful because the Nagas lived in forested areas and the traders had come over the mountain passes. They had come with only a few horses pulling carts. Something had changed, and this time they were behaving differently.

"As I said before, we have tried using horses to pull carts with no success. In recent years, we have managed to use some young female horses to pull light chariots, but it is a difficult task. These young horses are fragile, temperamental creatures that need a lot of care. Maybe Shaka horses are more docile. The hooves of our horses become tender and inflamed, the horses become lame, and they are easily startled. Unlike our onagers. Onagers are placid. They will do nothing that will damage their hooves, like gallop. Only the most fearsome predator will startle an onager. The only problem is that it is not possible to ride an onager. I know, for I have tried.

"The Shakas use horses to make war. We have no experience of such wars. In the world of the Panchnad cities, war was rare and conducted by mercenaries as a game. Samvarana's eviction from Hastinapura and return to it was the only real war in our recent history. A smaller force was trapped by a siege and lost. An onager could not race past a line of infantry like a horse, the very idea is a farce.

"Horses are not useful everywhere. A forest is no place to ride an animal like a horse. We cut paths and create trails for people and carts, not animals with a man sitting on top. The trails cut by Nagas in the forest will not even support an onager-drawn cart. A small horse could probably make its way through the forest. But a bigger one or one with a man on it would be blocked by branches that have to be pushed aside, a slow and noisy procession. A troop of horses would have to go single file, which makes them vulnerable to attack by an enemy. That thought made me confident. I felt that we had nothing to fear from the Shakas. In case of conflict, we would deal with them in the forests and not on a battlefield. I had instructed my observers to avoid confronting the Shakas as much as possible. Everything had worked out well. I did not want to fight the Shakas. There is no predicting what would happen in a battle, and the stakes were too small to risk it."

THE SHAKA ATTACK

Devavrata continued: "Two days after we left Hastinapura, we were met by one of my observers returning with a message and a head in his cart. The head was that of one of my captains. The news stunned me. The King was missing. The Shakas had attacked us.

"My spy gave me some of the details. Chitrangada had planned to camp near the village of Seshanagaram, a Naga village that was a few yojanas from the Shaka camp. The village of Gandhanagaram was much closer, less than a yojana, and would be an observation post for his scouts. Just as they began the tedious task of setting up tents and lean-tos, a small group of women and children came streaming out of the forest.

"Gandhanagaram had been attacked. Many of the adult men had been killed. It was the season for planting seed. As was Naga practice, the women had gone into the forest with their children to gather firewood and gather fruits. The able-bodied men were preparing the fields for planting, which involved dragging a large wooden wedge to create a furrow. They would make the furrows of one crop at right angles to the furrows of the previous crop, so that the soil was evenly used. This practice made it harder to drag the wedge. The job required more strength, and only the men were considered suitable for it. That left a few older men and women not working at anything but relaxing in the central quadrangle of the living area of the village.

"The Shaka horsemen had come along the trail that led to the river. It was a narrow trail and it must have been rough going, as the trail was not cut for horses. That had not deterred them. As they emerged from the trail, the horsemen had spread out along the perimeter of the field. They were quiet, but it was the middle of the day and they were quite visible. There were about twenty Shakas. They did not make a sound, did not announce their intention, but they did not have to. The Nagas were not familiar with the use of a horse in warfare, but the armor and weapons told of what the Shakas planned. The men in the fields began to run towards the center to get to their weapons. The women who had not gone to the forest ran into their huts. The old men and women went into the central hut. As soon as the running started, the horses started in towards the center. They speeded up and quickly caught up with the fleeing men who were closest. The Nagas had no chance. The riders wielded bronze swords that they used expertly to kill or disable the men.

"It was fate, or perhaps ill luck, that Chitrangada had just arrived at the campsite south of the Naga village when the Naga women who had seen the assault from the forest had run for help. Quick response is what I had trained my men for and within a half-ghati a squad of twenty men were ready for battle. One ghati later, the Shakas watched the armored and armed band make its way into the village clearing. Following the same tactic that they had used with the Nagas, the horsemen charged the soldiers who were armed with spears and carried leather shields.

"Riding bare back, the Shaka warrior looked like a part of his horse, a second torso with a human head rising above the horse's shoulders. The horse came at our soldiers with terrifying speed. Chitrangada's men (*my* soldiers) were unfamiliar with such attacks. To the first soldiers to face the horses, it appeared that they would be trampled. They sidestepped the horses. As the horses flashed by, the riders slashed at them with swords. My men's spears protected them from the first assault. But the passing of the horse unbalanced them and many of them fell to the ground. The horse stopped and turned around to run at them, but much slower. Some of my soldiers had time to retrieve their spears and succeeded in wounding the Shakas as they returned. Some Shakas fell off their horses and, though they landed nimbly, a few were killed – maybe five or six. Ten of our soldiers were killed and two were wounded. In the meantime, a second squad of soldiers had come into the opening. The Shakas realized that they were outnumbered and that they could not afford to lose so many fighters. One of the Shakas shouted and all the others still on horses wheeled them around and galloped back onto the trail they had come by. The other Shakas fought to the death. There were no captives.

"The reinforced squad of soldiers did not chase the horse-riding Shakas. This may have been a tactical error for they would have had the advantage, with the horses slowed by the narrow trail. Such possibilities reveal themselves only in hindsight. Instead, our soldiers stopped and helped move the wounded and the dead to Chitrangada's camp. All the Naga men who had been preparing the field for planting were dead. With the departure of the Shakas, the women came out of the forest. The old men and women of the Naga village were found hiding in the innermost hut. They had been saved only because the soldiers had arrived so promptly. A number of Naga women were missing. The missing women had been foraging in the forest in the direction of the Shaka camp or along the trail to the Shaka camp.

"Chitrangada was furious. No Shaka had been captured; they had fought to the death. More of his men were dead than Shakas. There was no live captive Shaka to be questioned. Chitrangada questioned the competence of the troops I had trained. The captains tried to calm him down. Finally, Chitrangada called the officers into a quickly erected tent to decide on strategy.

"That was when Chitrangada decided that more information had to be obtained about the Shakas. It was a fateful decision. The villagers knew nothing. Nobody knew how many Shakas had come, how many were warriors. *Were there any traders among them, or was this a raid presaging more raids?* There was no answer! One of the spies said that he had seen women and children in the camp, but that report never reached the King. His captains were cautious. I had trained them well. Until they knew more about the enemy, they wanted to take a defensive posture. The King was furious. *How would they get this information?* They replied: *slowly. Spies will observe from hiding.* That was what I would have done. The King had disagreed. *Just capture one, and we will wring the information out of that one.* The captains demurred politely. *We would have to send a squad and that would attract attention. Until we know more, we should avoid exposing our warriors. We only have sixty trained soldiers; the rest are fresh recruits in training.* The King was livid. *Cowards,* he shouted and stormed out of the tent.

"The captains conferred among themselves and proposed a compromise to satisfy the King. A small squad would go out that night while the Shakas were still tending their wounds. They would proceed silently. The goal was to capture one of the enemy and bring him back. As far as possible, they would not engage with the Shakas in any other way. It was an unwise plan made to appease the King because nobody could oppose his wishes.

"When the captains' proposal was put to Chitrangada, he assented with a qualification; he himself would lead the squad. There was no changing his mind. The squad led by the King had left the previous night and were expected back by daybreak. They had not returned when expected.

"Late that evening, a second team consisting of two Naga members of the army, was sent to find out what had happened. They were to return before nightfall. Moving quickly through the forest, they arrived near the Shaka encampment with no sign of passage of the King's squad though many signs of Shakas on horses. The Shaka were not silent. The observers were about to turn back and report failure when they came across signs of fighting in a small clearing. Some of the trees still had arrows stuck in them. Other trees showed signs of damage from swords. Freshly broken branches lay around. There they had found the head of the squad's captain. It seemed obvious that the Shaka had fought their squad. The spies could not spend much time looking as night was falling and the forest would be completely dark until the moon rose. They could not wait that long. It appeared that the King had lost the battle, and it was not known whether the King was dead or was a prisoner.

"The news of the King's capture or death created turmoil in the camp. The captains could not agree on a course of action. Unlike my usual practice, the King had not included them as councilors and consequently they knew very little of what he wanted to accomplish and how they were expected to support him.

"Where was the King? Where were the soldiers who had gone with him? Another squad of spies was sent at moonrise more or less around midnight. They could not go far as the Shakas were more active that morning and had been working on rearranging their campsite, strengthening its defenses. The squad returned and reported no signs of the King or the squad. The officers in charge could not agree on a course of action. They were too few to defeat the Shakas on horses, but they had to provide the Naga villages with some feeling of security. They had learned this much from our past encounters with Panchala. I would guarantee the safety of Naga villages or towns that we passed through and was rewarded with help and loyalty.

"The captains needed reinforcements if they were to get the King back. So they sent me a messenger with the head they had found as a way of impressing on Hastinapura the urgency of the matter. Then they deployed the troops in a defensive formation around the Naga village and waited for events to unfold. They did not know what to expect. The normal practice among the mercenaries of Panchnad was to propose exchanges of equivalent prisoners or a demand for ransom. This was usually simple except when a leading officer was captured. That required more bargaining. The released men promised not to participate in the war. They would also exchange the bodies of the dead enemy for their own dead. My men knew that as the usual practice, and so they waited for a message from the Shakas. And waited. There was no overture. Nothing happened.

"With a sinking feeling in the pit of my stomach, I roused my group and we set out as fast as we could. Without a leader, and missing a captain or maybe more, my five hundred would be massacred. We got to the campsite that night. At first, I was pleased. A defensive perimeter had been set up. Inside it, though, was chaos. There were areas of furious activity and completely calm areas where soldiers were lounging around. There was a commotion at the eastern end of the campsite, where we usually placed a gate. People were rushing back and forth, looking for something. A few were carrying buckets of water. Nobody recognized me until I was well inside and saw one of my captains who took one look at me and shouted, 'It's the Regent! Regent Devavrata has arrived!'

"The news of my coming spread like a ripple created by a stone thrown into a pond. Very soon I had my captains and a collection of soldiers and helpers around me. The source of the commotion was a group of unfamiliar people – Nagas, mostly old men and women and children. They looked like they had been through a forest of thorns – they had blood on their clothing and clotted blood on their arms, legs, and faces. Some had hands hanging useless by their sides, barely connected to the arm. There were a few younger men, but they seemed to have suffered battle injuries. One man had his right eye covered with a cloth that looked freshly bloodied. Another had been laid on the ground, his legs covered in blood.

"There were two doctors with the Hastinapura army, and the Naga villages had their herbalist and physician. I could do nothing for these victims of the Shaka attack. The captains had given up hope of a negotiation and expected an attack in the morning. My first concern was that the camp would be targeted as it could defend the villages. My second concern was to get news of the King. Had he been killed? Why had the Shakas attacked this Naga village? There was no precedent from the many years of Shaka visits. That was meaningless. There must be a first time for everything. I would have to ensure that it was the last.

"The Nagas from the village that the Shakas had attacked decided to make a formal appeal for my help. You know how unusual that is. Nagas help each other unasked if there is a family connection and only if there is a family connection. Any other request must be made formally. Some Nagas in frequent contact with us in Hastinapura are not such sticklers about that custom and have become more like us. There are frequent misunderstandings, situations in which a Hastinapura Naga expected to get help from a bystander unasked, as well as situations where a bystander intervenes and is vilified by all sides to the dispute. Here, away from Hastinapura's cultural influence, old Naga practices were still observed. The Nagas appointed a representative, one of the older men who had escaped injury by hiding in the community hut. He asked to see me and said, 'Sir, we, the Nagas of the northern hills, need your help. I am assured that my cousins in the south by the Great River are allied with you. If that is true, I invoke your help.'

"I replied 'Yes, indeed! I will help you. That would help me as well, for I come in search of my brother, the ruler of my city, who may be a captive of the Shakas. You must tell me more about these Shakas. Did you meet any of the traders?'

"This was not the first time the villagers had traded with Shakas. The Naga band that populated this village had moved here fifteen years ago. As usual, they burnt a section of the grove, cleared it of trees and shrubs, and offered sacrifices at the four corners of the clearing to the mother Goddess. They sowed the first seeds, shortly after the spring festival. They then used the trees and branches to build permanent homes – wattle-and-daub cabins with roofs made of crossed branches covered with thatch that would keep them dry during the coming rainy season. This was their age-old practice.

"The Naga band encountered the Shakas some months after the rains. They were clearly visitors for they had not been there before the spring planting season and occupied makeshift homes consisting of conical frames covered with leather. The band consisted of about ten men and women with their children. They came in covered carts pulled by horses and carried merchandise for trade. The Shakas had been peaceful. The Nagas and Shakas did not have a common language, but the Shakas had useful and decorative objects that they would barter for grain and vegetables. They wanted bronze but would accept copper.

"When the Nagas took the Shaka items to Hastinapura, the merchants, Kuru as well as those from Panchnad and points further west, were impressed by the size of the gemstones. They were awed by the thickness and nap of the bearskins and even the deerskin, so much larger than the native black bear and sambhar deer. They positively bubbled with excitement at the yellow nuggets. They wanted to know where these were from, but the Nagas kept the Shaka source a secret while the Shakas did not tell the Nagas anything. It was also made clear that the Shakas did not want the Nagas to find out. The Shakas would usually leave when the weather turned warm and the sun began its northward course across the winter sky. Well before winter ended, they would be gone.

"This pattern had held for almost fifteen years. The ash layer created in the grove from the old burn was almost drained of its fertility and in another year or two, would have to be abandoned. It was time to move on and the band had started the process of finding a new grove to burn and settle in. In the typical case, it would take a year or two to complete such a move. The Naga band did not want to lose their exclusive access to the Shakas by moving further away, so they had moved closer to the place where the Shaka usually camped.

"Something had changed this time. The Shaka group was much larger. More than forty or fifty men had been seen, a larger number of children, many more horses and carts. They were too many for their old campsite and had instead occupied a cul-de-sac in the side of a small hill, and constructed a thorn fence with a gateway. They worked on their settlement and did not try to contact the Nagas immediately. The Nagas took the initiative and sent a small group to welcome the traders. The Shakas met them at the gate; they were formal and correct, but would not let them in.

"After a couple of weeks, the Shakas sent a small group with a cart loaded with goods for barter. This was as expected, and the Nagas eagerly welcomed them to their new settlement. It did not take long for disappointment to set in. The Shakas had brought little worthy of barter. Most of the skins would be unsaleable as they were old and worn, nothing like the large, furry, and well-cured skins from previous years. These skins showed signs of many years of use. In exchange, they asked for the same products – grains and vegetables, copper and bronze – as in previous years. The Nagas were disappointed and refused to take what was offered. The Shakas were insistent. The request to barter became demands, which the Nagas rejected. The demands became unmistakable threats, at which point the Nagas stopped all talk and sat quietly. The Shakas were equally patient or apparently so. They sat for most of that day. The Nagas even offered them meals. In the evening, all the Shaka got up and left silently.

"The refusal to barter was unprecedented among Nagas. It was commonly the case that every place they occupied, every time they moved, new traditions would be created and some old ones dropped. Bartering with the Shaka was now a tradition here. They had been bartering with Shakas ever since the first year of the settlement. Some of the older Nagas had muttered about the bad luck that breaking with tradition would bring. Others pointed out that what the Shakas had brought was itself a break with a much more ancient tradition. The Nagas did not want the Shaka skins and gold for themselves but for trade with other groups, and the products offered could not be traded. Accepting the trade in the name of a tradition here would cause a break in tradition later. The Shakas were upset. They spoke among themselves, glared at the Nagas, and left with their offerings.

"This attack, then, was their response to the Naga refusal to accept substandard products. This was not how a trader would act. Even in the most difficult encounters, traders try to keep the peace. Peace had brought prosperity to the people of Panchnad. The violence of these Shakas showed that they had not come in peace to trade, but to raid or to colonize. In either case, they planned to terrorize the local population. *Were the Shakas ever traders? Maybe we were imposing a category we understood on the behavior of strangers.*

"'The traders who came to our tents were old men,' the old Naga man formally requesting my help said. 'They did not come riding on horses but carried their meagre products by in a cart drawn by two of their oldest horses. They looked impoverished and appeared to be hungry.'

"'Does that mean that nobody knows anything about their camp?'

"'Sir, our chief visited them the first day to make them welcome. He wanted to assure them that we would, as always, engage in fair bartering. He knew that they would want grain, for their land did not produce any. In the meantime, if they needed grain while they were visiting they should ask, for we would not refuse. He thought this would tell them that they were welcome, even if trading was not possible. Our chief's visit is part of the tradition; it is one of the ways we assess the people we trade with.'

"This aspect of Naga tradition surprised me. It indicated a level of sophistication in managing trade with strangers that I had not been aware of.

"'I need to talk to the chief, then.'

"'He is dead, sir.'

"A dark shadow crossed over my heart – not a monsoon cloud promising rain, but the occasional burst that presaged a raging flood. *Was it going to be a lost cause to find my brother?* I turned away.

"'Sir! Please listen!' the Naga continued. I turned back to him.

"'The chief went with a small entourage – all men except for his oldest daughter.'

"'Where are his men?'

"'Dead, sir. They all died in the raid. His daughter is still with us.'

"The Nagas have some strange customs – at least, strange to us Kauravas who grew up with Panchnad customs. Among the Nagas, men and women played different roles in daily life. By contrast, in urban Panchnad, there was no cause for differences in roles. Of course, only women gave birth to children. Both cultures required women to care for the infants. The Naga women foraged for fruits and nuts and edibles that grew wild and could not be cultivated. The men were farmers and fishermen. They tilled the fields or fished – they called it giving birth to their food. In Panchnad, a guild, one of seven (not counting the mercenaries), determined the daily life and labor of its members. The only task that was reserved for men was trading. Few women became traders or participated in years-long caravan trips. War was not one of the duties divided between the men and the women; both were equally unprepared to defend themselves or their village. The task of such protection was assigned to the guild of mercenaries. That guild consists mostly of men, though a few extraordinary women have been members, too. In recent years, Kuru women have been sequestered out of the public eye. This had started when Samvarana sojourned in the forest with Vasishtha and rebuilt his army. Vasishtha had been insistent that there would be no women fighters. It was a new rule previously unheard of. Vasishtha was exploiting the small strength advantage that a trained man has over a woman of equal training or skill. That rule continues to the present day.

"'How old is the chief's daughter? Is she here?' I asked the Naga man.

"'She is an adult, sir. Her name is Amba. She is here in the camp.'

"I said, 'I wish to speak to her. Please ask her to come here.'

AMBA

Devavrata paused. His eyes opened wider and for the first time smiled, a smile that seemed to brighten the darkened tent. It appeared to Lomaharshana as though the memory of Amba had blown away dark monsoon clouds, the ground sparkling with raindrops in the light of the sun.

Then Devavrata resumed, his voice clearer and louder. He said, "That was how Amba came into my life. She was – dare I say it – beautiful. My mind struggled for control over my body – my face wanted to turn to her, my lips wanted to smile, my feet wanted to dance, despite the seriousness of the situation. When I first saw her, she was wearing a plain wrap that had once been white – now it was bloody and torn along the hem. I learned later that she had been attending to the injured. Her dusky complexion made her smile glow – *how many times have I felt a rush of joy at that sight and smiled in response?* – her face was oval with almond-shaped eyes. She wore a necklace with a single strand of beads – this revealed her age, for older Naga women would have more necklaces with precious beads, reflecting their wealth. To say that I was smitten is to understate it. It had happened once before, when I had first met Satyavati. My heart raced, and it felt as if everybody could hear its drumbeats. I stood still, looking at her, afraid that any movement would betray my feelings.

"'You called me, sir?' she was polite. Her eyes caught mine, and I felt warmed by her smile. She looked away but not before I saw the hint of acknowledgment. *She knows the effect she has had on me.*

"My voice died – it came out husky and low-pitched.

"'You are the chief's daughter?' I was inaudible.

"'Excuse me, sir?' her voice was neutral but her eyes glowed.

"'You are the chief's daughter?' I said, louder than I intended, and immediately berated myself for asking such an inane question. The glint vanished from her eyes. Her face fell and she became sombre. Her father was dead, and I had reminded her of it.

"'Y-yes, sir.'

"The smile was gone from her face and like a *soma* addict, I wanted it back. I regretted that I had reminded her of her father. I adopted a matter-of-fact tone that I could barely manage.

"'They tell me that you went to the Shaka camp with your father.'

"'Yes, sir.'

"'What did you see?'

"'They must have come down south along the river bank. It is barren rocky ground that opens out into a flat, grass-covered grove. The soil there is not deep enough for planting, so we do not use the grove. It was their first campsite. The gate faces the trail from the village. The two sides are dense forest and difficult to move through. The back is protected by a rocky ridge and at one corner the trail continues uphill. Their tents face inwards in a circle and block any other entrance to the grove, so you can only go through the gateway they've established. The river runs white over rocks, but between the rocks it can be deeper than two onager-drawn carts. Inside, they have a central tent. Their wagons are behind that tent. Their horses are corralled further back, so they cannot wander away.'

"'Is it a defensible encampment?'

"'Yes. The village trail opens out into their grove. They have built a wall across the width of the grove with trees and branches. There is a small entrance, about five or six hands wide – their horses can come through. You cannot attack from the front. The river is difficult to cross, and on the other side is a steep hill. In the back, a rocky path goes uphill to a ridge that runs along the river bank.'

"'There is a trail to your village?'

"'Yes. The children used to play there.'

"She turned to leave. I grasped at a straw. Something. Anything. So that I could be with her a while longer.

"'Can you guide me and my troops?'

"'Yes.'

"'At night? Silently? Without any light?'

"'Yes, even a half-moon is enough. But noise will travel – you must be silent.'

"'My troops will not make any noise. We will be ready a little after midnight. The half-moon should be rising.'

"She took that as dismissal and walked away. My heart was thumping. I looked around – the camp seemed unreal. It was as if I had spoken to Amba is another world.

"We gathered late that night just as the moon appeared in the east. We prepared fire arrows, with tips wrapped in cotton soaked in pine-oil, and one of my men carried embers covered with ash in a small clay bucket.

"Amba led the way. She began at the village where the trail began. The moon's light was just enough for us to walk carefully through the forest. I was proud of how silently my men made the trip from the village. It took us almost five ghatis at a normal walking pace. Running would have been too noisy and too risky on a forest path in the dark. Amba walked carefully but without hesitation, glancing at me from time to time. Her proximity was heady. I wanted to show her all that I could do, but that went beyond the needs of the expedition. When she talked, I became tongue-tied. We skirted the Naga village. Amba pointed out some landmarks in the village – the central hut in which the seniors had hidden and so survived, the granary, and the communal space around which the huts were clustered.

"We reached the place in the forest that the Shaka had come through on their horses.

"'How much further from here?' I asked.

"'About three ghatis at the pace we are going.'

"The moon was nearing the zenith; we had about eight ghatis before sunrise. Maybe a little less if the dawn was clear.

"'We have to move a little faster.'

"Amba looked at me. I looked back, not as a challenge but because her eyes held mine. Maybe mine held hers. We trapped each other in that glance.

"'We should keep to this pace to prevent accidents,' she said as we both looked away simultaneously.

"I grunted. I glanced sideways to see her smile – her teeth and eyes reflected the moonlight.

"We continued walking carefully along the path that Amba showed us. About one ghati later, we heard a rustling in the bushes. I looked at Amba. She understood my question.

"'There are no large wild animals here. A lone wolf, perhaps.'

"I took my knife out of its scabbard and signaled the men to stop. I wanted to investigate the sound myself. I moved silently towards the sound. My men knew what I wanted from them – they stopped and waited. Amba followed me. I hesitated, then made a fateful decision. I let her accompany me.

"We came to a small clearing. There were a number of bodies lying on the ground. I could not make out the faces in the moonlight, but some clothes were easily recognizable. These were the King's troops. Chitrangada had followed my example and created uniforms for his men – not the unimpressive grey of my troops, but red and gold. A few ornaments glittered reflecting the moon. Nothing was moving. Then something rustled on the opposite edge of the clearing. I went across; Amba followed.

"There was a body stirring there. He was not dead – he responded to the sounds of our talking by getting up on his hands and knees and then tried to stand up, but his feet could not support him. I recognized the injury; he had been hamstrung, the tendons in both knees cut. From his hands and knees, he looked up at us. Amba gasped and her hand grasped my upper arm. I don't know if I showed any emotion, but I was overcome by despair and sorrow for now I knew what the Shakas had done to this man. His eye sockets were empty, and in the light of the moon, they were dark blobs reflecting nothing. He moaned, and I could not understand him. That sound would later resonate in my memories and become familiar; it was the sound made by a mouth from which the tongue has been ripped out. The man's body folded on itself and collapsed.

"I took out my knife and stepped up to him, pulled back his head and sliced the throat from one ear to the other in a single stroke. I held the thrashing body as warm blood spurted onto my arms and flowed down his chest to the ground. Slowly, the thrashing stopped. Amba made a sound. I looked up at her. She stood still and looked at me, her eyes shining in the moonlight. I dropped my eyes. I could not bear to link those glistening eyes to this act. *What could I tell her?*

"Her words came to my rescue.

"'You are a kind man,' she said, 'Was he one of your men?'

"'He was my brother.' I hugged the dead body of my brother, Satyavati's son, Chitrangada, King of Hastinapura. Then I gently lowered to the ground. I turned him so that he faced the earth. There was no reason for our men to see his mutilation. I got up and wiped the blade of my knife clean."

DEATH OF A BROTHER

After he said those words, the Regent looked at Lomaharshana. For a brief moment, Lomaharshana felt like he had been thrown into the coldest Himalayan stream in the depth winter. He could not meet the Regent's eyes – to do so would have been to leap into the vast empty chasm that is said to lie between this world of humans and the heaven of the gods. He turned his head and heard a long sigh from the Regent.

Then there was silence. Lomaharshana felt powerless to pierce that silence. *Was that even his task?* It was a silence filled with a uniform noise, a cosmic noise that, like a god, had frozen its listeners in a single moment of time. It was the primal silence that preceded the primal scream when the universe was born of the body of Brahma. Whatever it was, Lomaharshana was relieved when the Regent finally stirred.

The Regent broke his silence and said, "Despite all our problems, Chitrangada was my brother and I cared about him. He was born when I was twenty years old. My father continued to be infatuated with Satyavati. After the day's necessary duties were done, he spent his time with Satyavati. She left the rearing of her children to her maids and wet-nurses. I, too, had withdrawn from all but the most necessary of official duties. I did not see my half-brother when he was born and not for many years after.

"The monsoons had been good for a few years. For a brief period, the Sarasvati had flowed with water again. The refugee stream stopped as people of Panchnad considered their future in their homeland. We always knew it was blind chance that the river flowed. But hope overwhelmed calculations of chance and the refugee crisis in Hastinapura seemed to abate. Some Panchnad refugees even made plans to return. Those were the good years.

"The rains come with their own crises. Once, heavy rains eroded the soil under a boulder that then rolled off and damaged the levee near the women's quarters in Hastinapura, the place I had avoided ever since Satyavati moved there. I now had to inspect the levee with my inspectors to assess the damage. Chitrangada was playing in the courtyard with the women. He must have been about four or five years old. I had not expected it – I thought that all the women and children had moved somewhere else. I look sufficiently like Shantanu that Chitrangada thought it was his father. He came running up to me. Some children are unafraid of strangers; that would describe Chitrangada. He paused when he realized that I was not his father, but he came up to me anyway and asked me my name. When he learned I was Devavrata, he said, 'The aunts here say that I have a brother by that name.'

"'I am that brother,' I said.

"Delighted, he shouted, "My brother! My brother!" and ran around me while I stood unsure of what to do. Then he stopped and said, 'Why are you so big? I have another brother and he is tiny. I am not allowed to play with him. Can I play with you?'

"It is hard to describe my feelings at that moment. I realized that if I had married Satyavati, this would be my son. I could not take out my anger at Satyavati on my half-brother. I told him that I was busy then but would certainly play with him later.

"I continued to avoid Satyavati. My anger and resentment against her did not go away. But I would go to the women's quarters to play with Chitrangada. Later, when Vichitravirya was old enough, all three of us would play together."

At this point, the Regent Devavrata stopped. Lomaharshana was listening and memorizing Devavrata's words mechanically.

"He was only a child," the Regent said. The words seemed to force themselves out of his mouth. Then he stopped and closed his eyes. Silence again. A few vighatis passed. He leaned back for a moment, forgetting the arrowhead in his chest, and his eyes opened wide in pain. He gasped and jerked forward; then his body relaxed in a faint. His eyes were closed and he had turned over onto his stomach.

Lomaharshana moved forward and raised the Regent. He was surprisingly light – the Archivist had expected a greater weight. *He is old. For an old man, he is holding up pretty well.*

Lomaharshana called for the nurse, who came in right away. The nurse took one look at the body in Lomaharshana's arms and moved quickly to take over from him. He asked the Archivist to move the bolster and the stuffed mat and laid the Regent down again, making sure that the arrowhead did not move. He held the Regent's wrist with thumb and forefinger, and closed his eyes for a vighati.

The nurse said, "There is a pulse, a bit slow. He will live, at least for now. He is a hardy man. What happened?"

"He recalled something that surprised him, and he leaned back against the arrow. I think he forgot it was there."

The nurse left. The Archivist called in a passing messenger and gave him a message for the King, asking him to visit after lunch if possible.

After lunch, Yudhishthira came, with the Vyaasa in tow. The Archivist took his place at the foot of Devavrata's bed. Devavrata was sleeping. The Vyaasa said, "He must have been exhausted."

The Archivist said, "Yes and no. He talked all morning."

"Where did he stop?"

"Just after he killed King Chitrangada. He then began explaining how he had first met Chitrangada and... I don't think he wanted to go on."

The Vyaasa stared at the Archivist. "Did he say that he killed the King himself?"

"Yes, sir. That is exactly what he said. His last words were 'That was my brother. He was only a child.'"

"That was not the story he told Satyavati. That was not what he told anybody."

"Is the official story already recorded in the archives?"

"Yes. Here is a quick summary. When Devavrata came back, he said that gandharva allies of the Shakas killed Chitrangada. That did not make any sense, for the gandharvas, even if they exist, have not been known to ally with human. I questioned the men who had been left behind in the camp, but they did not know how the King died. The man who found the King's body said that he had been ordered not to speak of what he had found. Did Devavrata speak of it? Did he tell everything?"

"Enough, sir."

"I can guess. The Shakas are known for their practices. When Devavrata returned, some of his troops were calling him Bhishma. That was an unusual name to call the commander of an army, but he did not stop them. He said very little about that expedition to me or to anybody else."

The Archivist was quiet. The Vyaasa made a gesture of dismissal. "Don't worry, you may go now. Come back after you've had lunch and rested. You can come back if he wakes up and is ready to talk some more."

The Archivist left.

The King said, "Gurudeva, I will rely on you to keep me informed. I must leave."

The King too left. Shukla was now alone with his sleeping friend.

He sat down by Devavrata's side. These were memories from a long time ago. He had to reconstruct them as much as recall them. Devavrata had come back with the news of Chitrangada's death, but long before he arrived, a new name for the Regent had spread among the people – Bhishma. The story was that the captured Shakas, men and women and children, had been tortured in public. This had changed the people's perception of the Regent. He was no longer the young disinherited heir who had remained loyal to the King despite being pushed aside by the ambitious new wife, but a fearsome and bloodthirsty army chief to be feared and despised. The young man who had vowed celibacy on impulse had been a friend if not a kindred spirit. The ambition that had driven the Vyaasa Shukla from the fisherman's hut to the leadership of the Kavi Sangha, an often quarrelsome and contentious group, was lacking in Devavrata. He had sublimated his passion in the most down-to-earth projects – building dams, ponds, and canals; taking on the problem of feeding the refugees; dealing with runaway rivers; maintaining the trade route for which Hastinapura was entrepôt; expanding relations with the Nagas around Hastinapura. There were failures as well. He could not establish peace with Panchala; all his overtures to the Rakshasas east of Laghu Nagapura were ignored.

The man who had come back from the encounter with the Shakas was a silent man. The memories of his return were lost in the upheaval attendant on the death of the King. *It was before I was the Vyaasa. I was just Shukla, the queen's brother, just another rising star in the Kavi Sangha.* The old Devavrata would have paid him a visit to describe the events of the encounter and to consider future actions. The new one barely acknowledged his old friend. Shortly thereafter, he, Shukla, had left for the great learning center of

Takshashila in the northwest. His being sent there was the recognition of his potential to climb up the Kavi Sangha hierarchy. When he came back a year and a half later, he had expected a joyous reunion with Devavrata. Instead, he found a man who had adapted to the new name, *Bhishma*, the Terrible. This man Bhishma had barely returned his hug and then suggested that Shukla should describe his experiences at Takshashila in open court. What had happened to the Devavrata who would have demanded a detailed narration, in private between two friends, of all that Shukla had experienced? His request for a private meeting had been met with a non-committal *Yes, we should meet,* and not followed by any action.

Shukla had questioned his sister. Satyavati was still in mourning for her son Chitrangada. She had been told the official story – that gandharvas had killed Chitrangada. Devavrata's behavior that had led to the title *Bhishma* was inexplicable. Why did he torture the Shakas? Shukla had thought then that it was a lie spread by the Regent's enemies.

"Sir," a voice interrupted the Vyaasa's reverie. The Archivist had returned. Devavrata was still asleep. The Vyaasa motioned for silence and moved outside the tent.

The Vyaasa said, "Continue with him after he has had a meal. There is more to come."

"He said he killed his brother. What greater secret could there be?"

The Archivist stopped. The Vyaasa was staring at him.

The Archivist continued, "I beg your forgiveness, sir. I will arrange to make him comfortable when he wakes up. If he wishes to continue, we will. Later, I will come to you."

The Vyaasa smiled. Had he been like this as a youngster? How irritating he must have been. *I know exactly how irritating I was!* That was why he had been sent away to Takshashila to study.

"You'll do fine, Lomaharshana. Continue. Get as much of the story as you can."

Lomaharshana the Archivist watched the Vyaasa leave. He breathed a sigh – that had been close. He, Lomaharshana, at the threshold of his career in the Kavi Sangha, had expressed an opinion and talked back to the Vyaasa, the senior-most member. Yes, he was the Archivist, and Archivists like him with a prodigious memory and native skill came by only once or twice a generation. But still, he was lucky that there was nobody else around. It would surely have been the end of his career if a good candidate had been available to take his place. He breathed a sigh of relief.

The Archivist went to the cook's tent and arranged for the Regent's afternoon meal to be delivered. A soup made of salted roast mutton, rice, and herbs was the most the Regent could eat. When he returned, Devavrata's eyes were open and staring at the door of the tent. It seemed to the Archivist that Devavrata was waiting for him.

"There you are," said Devavrata, "Why did you leave when I was just resting my voice?"

"You fell asleep, sir. It has been a few ghatis. Do you feel rested?"

"Rested? With this arrow in me?" Though it was a rebuke, his eyes were bright almost as though he was free of pain.

"My apologies, sir. I must have judged incorrectly. It has been almost five ghatis, and it is time for a small meal recommended by the doctor. After the meal, we can continue if you wish."

"Of course, I do. I can accomplish little else here. Let me satisfy your master, the Vyaasa."

The Archivist smiled. Making the record was his assigned task, and he was happiest when it made progress.

"Where did I stop? What did I tell you before my nap?"

"You were with a Naga girl, Amba, and you had found your brother maimed by the Shaka and killed him."

Devavrata closed his eyes and took a deep breath. It was as though a monsoon cloud had moved in front of the sun. When he re-opened his eyes, they looked weary and not bright any more.

"Must I continue? No, that was a silly question; I must continue. Let me tell you what happened after I put down my brother's body."

REVENGE

Devavrata said, "I faced Amba. I could not read her face in the moonlight. Her eyes were wide and with her right hand she held her throat.

"'You are a kind man,' she said, 'Was he one of your men?'

"'That was my brother.' She turned her face away from me. I laid down his body and stood up.

"I could not bear to see her turn away from me. Without much thought I grasped her upper arm. Her head jerked back to look at me. Her hand came up and stroked my cheek wet with the tears that were flowing freely. She kept her hand there for a short time and then started to withdraw it. She did not, for I took her hand in mine and held it to my face. She stood still for some time as my tears flowed onto her fingers.

"A brief moment later, she said, 'Sir, you must continue.'

"She was right. I squeezed her hand lightly and let her take it back. We re-joined the squad.

"What is left to report of this expedition is already known. We reached the camp well before sunrise. The Shaka had become careless after two encounters in which they had overwhelmed the Nagas and our troops – they had not posted any look-outs. Otherwise, we could not have done what we did. While the fire-throwers stayed back, the rest of us crawled to the wall of branches that hid the first row of tents that backed up against the fence they had put up. When we were ready, we signaled with the bark of a fox. The fire-arrows hit the first row of tents. The alarmed sleepers rushed out creating a commotion. That let us scale the wall and move into the tents from the back. We waited. When the Shakas realized that the fire was not an accident and that they were under attack, they went to their tents for their weapons. We slaughtered them in their tents. By that time, the people in the second row of tents had realized the camp was under attack. As they struggled to pick up their weapons, their tents also caught fire.

"Without their horses, and with hastily grabbed weapons, the Shaka were less formidable as enemies. Within two ghatis, we had complete control of the campsite, except for the central tent. We surrounded it, and I asked the people inside to surrender.

"A young boy came out, hands held out in front. 'We will surrender. Please do not kill us.'

"'Who is in there?' asked Amba.

"'My aunts and sisters, my cousins, and my grandfather and two of his friends.'

"'Tell them to come out slowly and throw their weapons to the side.' I indicated a spot well away from my troops. I kept the boy to my side.

"When they all came out, we counted sixteen prisoners. Two men were fighters who were supposed to protect the others but had decided that it was better to live as slaves than to die as warriors.

"That was not to be. On the way back, I made a detour with a chosen few of my men to the clearing where the King and his squad lay.

"We brought their bodies back to the camp. The next day, we went with the Naga villagers to the site of the Naga massacre. The Naga villagers gathered around us in a big circle. My soldiers formed a barrier to prevent them from coming closer. I lined up the captive Shakas – women, children, and the old men. Then I brought the two fighters to the front.

"'I am looking for the King,' I said to the fighters. 'Can you tell us what happened to him?'

"One man stood still. The other replied in the language of the Nagas. 'We don't know of any king.' He then whispered to his friend who nodded his head.

"I described Chitrangada – young, haughty, skin the color of the elephant grass that grew by the banks of the Ganga, a small moustache, and a stubble of a beard.

"The quiet one nodded. He whispered to the other, who spoke.

"'Yes, we know the prisoner. He was a tough one.'

"'What happened to him?' I asked.

"They whispered some more in their own language. Then the speaker turned to me.

"'Nothing. We just kept him as a prisoner. We did not know he was the King.' He seemed to shrug as he said this. My eyes narrowed, and I felt the upwelling of bile souring my mouth.

"'Nothing?'

"They conferred some more.

"'Nothing unusual.' That shrug again. My hands trembled. I struggled to control them.

"'Was he tortured?' I asked.

"More whispers. The quiet one turned his head away from me but not before he had caught my eyes and then averted his gaze. The speaker looked down as he spoke. I thought he too was avoiding my eyes.

"'No.' he said. No shrug that time. The quiet one was now looking straight at me. A sneer lurked at the corner of his lips.

"'You must tell me the truth,' I said, 'else, I will punish you.'

"The speaker looked away to my right and said, 'He was not tortured.'

"I got up and looked away and then sighed. They relaxed a bit – I had accepted their information.

"'Do you have a wife? Any children?' I asked.

"The speaker shook his head. 'No.'

"'What about your friend here? Are one of these prisoners married to him?'

"He hesitated. 'No.'

"I turned to him, my face livid. I came close and my voice fell. 'You are lying. Both of you were standing next to women. You had two girls by your side, and he had one boy. Tell me the truth. Now.'

"The speaker backed away from me. I must have looked insane. He then pointed to one of the women. His friend looked at him and shook his head, but the speaker was not looking at him. 'That's his wife.'

"I had my soldiers bring the woman over. A boy about eleven years old grabbed her hand and pulled. My soldiers held on to the woman who held on to the crying boy.

"'Bring him instead.' I said.

"They separated the boy from the woman and brought him over. The woman now screamed. More soldiers were needed. It was hard to control the boy who shouted for his mother. The quiet one looked away; there was nothing he could have done. The boy was not easily controlled."

Devavrata paused. "I can't go on," he said.

The Archivist said. "Why, sir? Are you tired? Hungry? Look, the soup has just come."

"No, no, I am not tired. I am... I... how can I tell this story? My gut refuses to rest. Come, Lomaharshana, pour me some soup. A few sips might soothe my heart and calm me."

The Archivist poured out two small bowls of soup. He brought one to Devavrata's lips. The soup was lukewarm. Devavrata took as few sips, then waved it away.

"I cannot drink it. Why don't you have some?"

The Archivist had not intended to drink his soup, but Devavrata's eyes watched him carefully as he emptied his own bowl.

"Good," said Devavrata.

The Archivist stood attentively, waiting for the Regent to say something. The Regent lay motionless and silent, his eyes unfocused. Lomaharshana waited. Half a ghati passed and the Regent had not moved. *What should I do?* Lomaharshana thought. His voice low, Lomaharshana said, "Sir. Should I come back at a later time?" There was no response. Lomaharshana tried again, louder this time, "Sir!"

Devavrata's eyes focused on him. "Oh! Yes, you are waiting for me. I... I... was recalling what happened. Yes, let me continue from where I stopped."

Devavrata continued, "There was nobody there who could have stopped me. Instead, I was obeyed as I proceeded to do the indefensible. The boy was uncontrollable. I took out my sword and with the flat hit him on the side of his head. He collapsed in a faint and was as quiet as his father.

"How can I continue with this narration? Whatever I did that day, I did not plan it. That day, I earned the name *Bhishma*, the Terrible. I had intended to punish only the two men – torture *them* the way they had tortured my brother. It was not hard to contemplate making them suffer. What I wanted I did not get. I wanted one thing – I wanted them to admit that they had tortured the King. I wanted them to acknowledge the justice of the punishment I planned to inflict. That was not to be. In extenuation, I point to those almost invisible shrugs – they goaded me. These are excuses for my commands that day. They are pathetic excuses. I gave the commands, and maybe somebody objected. Maybe somebody objected, and I still did not listen. My men bear no blame. I hope they tried to stop me, and I refused to listen. I do not know why my men followed my orders, but they did. They too had seen the King's body, and perhaps the same demon that had gained ascendance over me ruled them.

"By the time I was done, three children and two women lay dead on the ground, hamstrung, blind, and mute. *I have been kind.* I told the two men. *Kinder than you were to the King. They were not tortured.* I pointed to the bodies with my foot and turned one over. *See, no signs of torture. They died before they suffered much. Am I not kind? Can you acknowledge my mercy and ask for more?* The lurking smile and uncaring shrugs had vanished, but the stony faces and fixed eyes did not change. My captains' whispered pleas finally got through to me; my actions might turn the local Nagas against me.

"I had my men drag the two captives over to me. With careful deliberation, I did what I had to do. I did it myself, making sure that each could see what was happening to the other one. They were not dead when I was done, and I laid them next to their families to await death.

"The local Nagas watched unmoving from the perimeter where I had placed them. There was no sound from that group. Not then, not later. Amba was present and watched unmoving. I tell myself that Amba's presence had nothing to do with my actions. She had taken part in that night's battle in the Shaka encampment. I thought that the carnage should have satisfied her. She would not have moderated my rage. Her father and mother were dead – her father's head almost severed from his body. Her mother had run towards her husband. They had not found her body in the field, but they had found her mutilated remains in the Shaka camp. These two would have been among her torturers. Amba had seen the King alive, a young man who cut an impressive figure. She and the Nagas must have put their faith in him. And then she saw his mutilated body, saw why he had to be killed. People like us, raised in a city, are overwhelmed by death. Amba was a Naga who lived in the forest. She saw death every day, but the manner of death that the Shaka had inflicted on her parents would have left her angry. I wanted to show her that my anger equaled hers and that my resolution equaled hers. She had seen me cry and might think me weak. I wanted to show her that I was strong. But was she among the Nagas who thought that I had been wrong to order the killing of women and children? If so, she would turn against me.

"I tell myself that I was angry and confused and did the unthinkable because I was not myself that day.

"That day, only Amba and the group that had attacked the Shaka encampment knew what I knew – that the King had been tortured the way I tortured the prisoners. The King's men, the other men from Hastinapura who had come with me, and the surviving Naga villagers saw a side of me that had never before been seen, maybe had never before existed. As a result, I became *Bhishma*, the Terrible. My men took up the name, and over time, *Devavrata Bhishma* became just *Bhishma*.

"I look back and imagine myself not doing what I did. Could that have been a different Devavrata who returned from the campaign, not the Devavrata Bhishma that I had become? Maybe I would have become somebody who could be liked and not feared. Loved and not just respected. I became Bhishma, a person to inspire terror. When does the thirst for revenge edge over into insanity? I was insane that day. Later that day, we reconnoitered the route by which the Shakas had come, and I discovered that they had brought their vehicles and horses over a dam that I had arranged to construct some years earlier. I did not say anything. In hindsight lies wisdom, I thought, as the sour taste of victory returned to my mouth. We followed the road and found another Shaka encampment, larger but with mostly older men and women and children, mostly non-warriors. We attacked and killed the ones who resisted. We left a few wounded survivors to return to their homeland with the message – we do not want you. The uninjured we enslaved.

"On our return, we prepared the bodies of the King and his squad so they looked presentable and cremated them *en masse*. The bodies were already stinking, and I did not see the point of taking them home. Satyavati would chasten me later about my haste in cremating her son, but I did not want her to see what had happened to him. Nor did I want to tell her that the King's captains had let him leave on a spying expedition with a very small force; heads would have rolled. With the connivance of my troops, I invented a story of a pitched battle with an intruding army from Gandhara. This changed in the telling and retelling to the *gandharva* of popular imagination, magical creatures invented by a teller of tales we both know well."

The Archivist frowned. "Do you mean the current Vyaasa?"

"Yes," Devavrata said, and continued, "I saw Amba later that day, the day I killed women and children. We were by ourselves, and I certainly was mad that day. That night, I was subject to no oath. The oath that Satyavati so relied on had lost its hold over me that night. I was not Devavrata, bound by Devavrata's oath. I told Amba to come with me that night. She too must have been insane. Her father and brothers had been killed; her mother was dead. She had tasted revenge, but this blood did not quench the heat of the inferno raging within her. I must have been insane to think that I could keep my relationship with Amba secret from Satyavati. She must have found out quite soon after we returned to Hastinapura but said nothing. Why did she keep quiet? Maybe by becoming *Bhishma*, I had terrified her. Maybe somebody had told her the truth behind the name. The old Devavrata had kept the vow for long years and had proved his fealty to the part of the vow that she cared about – support her descendants as the rulers of Hastinapura. If she had made a fuss, she might have aroused the demon that was Bhishma; Devavrata, the dutiful son of his father, might have disappeared completely. Civil war between my supporters and hers, she knew, was unthinkable for the old Devavrata, for it would have ended his imperial plans. That day, after the death of Chitrangada, it was not something Satyavati wanted to threaten."

LOVE

"That night I broke my vow of celibacy. That night I freed myself of Satyavati."

Devavrata continued:

"Amba came to me willingly. I had enough of Devavrata in me that I told her of my vow. She did not understand such a vow. To her, it was worse than the monogamy that the Shakas required of their women. I could not explain the self-imposed restrictions I had lived with all these years. I abandoned the effort to explain, but she accepted the need for secrecy. We entered the woods silently. There was nothing gentle about our lovemaking. Memories of my brother's dying moments intruded. She responded in kind, possibly driven by what she had seen of her dead father and mother. Our rage found its outlet in sex. It was many weeks before our encounters became tender and loving."

Devavrata paused. He was barely whispering. The Archivist moved closer to hear him. Devavrata shook his head and put out a hand to motion him back. Then he winced and withdrew his hand. His voice grew stronger as he continued.

"The next day I mulled over the problem of what to do about the Naga village. The surviving Nagas – women, some older men, and children of both sexes – could not be a self-sustaining community. Without the men, who would till the gardens and fields? Without champions who could challenge other bands, their band would lack standing in the six seasonal festivals of the year. Locally related bands, clans related through sisters and mothers, vied for the right to host a festival for it was a source of prestige and respect for the band. The women formed the heart of a Naga band – the matriarch and her friends who stayed in the band and took care of the children were its heart and soul. The women managed the band. The relationship between bands could be competitive. This was displayed at the festival get-togethers.

"The men played an important role in these festivals. In most bands, the men were charged with organizing the food and other supplies for the festival. The leader convinced the men to help him using a mix of persuasion, charisma, and social pressure. The men used their skills to organize and host events that made their band an attractive one to join. The success of a hosted festival did not accrue just to the men – it also accrued to the band and was useful during negotiations.

"If a community lost a few men, it could replace them at the next festival by pleading with and persuading others to join. The politics of these festivals was a sensitive matter – a band with men born and brought up in other bands could garner support from their parent bands in times of need. A band with a group of men who knew how to build dams could lend these men's services in exchange for other benefits. It was through the medium of festivals that each band displayed its capabilities.

"A band whose men were all dead stood alone. This was the state of Amba's band after the Shaka attack. Such a band had nothing to offer and would be asking for a lot. It would command little political status or power. To compound the situation, a band that did not have enough men might become prey to wild rogue Nagas – boys and men who had never had a home band or who had been expelled from their communities for some reason, usually an inability to control rage. They lived on the fringes of the Naga world, alone or in small groups. They did not form larger groups, for such men did not know how to cooperate with each other, either. Sometimes, rarely, an unlikely leader would emerge who coalesced a few small groups and individuals into a larger gang that would become a source of danger to the Naga bands of the region. Such gangs were dealt with harshly when they were captured, with the leader and most of the older members being killed. Even if the women were strong enough to repel one attack by such a gang, the knowledge that a weak, poorly defended band existed would attract more violent gangs.

"As a result, on losing all or most of its men, a band would usually disband unless the matriarch and her women could attract good men from other bands, sometimes by bartering with the other bands.

"Hastinapura had no place for potlach festivals, and the festivals of Panchnad did not include communal feasts. Nor did Panchnad settlements exchange men. I could accept these as Naga customs. You see much less of these festivals because free Naga tribes are disappearing as they succumb to Panchala or come under the protection of Hastinapura.

"We stayed in the Naga village for a few weeks after the attack on the second Shaka camp near the dam. We stayed to both prevent and hold off any more Shakas attacks that autumn and to help the band collect what they could from their settlement and move to another site. Nobody wanted to stay where a massacre had just taken place. The move turned out well, I thought. Some of the Nagas in my army, who had been trained by me and were trusted soldiers, took the opportunity to return to the Naga way of life. They would have been considered wild, for many of them had left their bands at a young age and, failing to find a band, had come to me. Now they could return with the credibility of having worked with me. It meant that I lost a few good men, though they would prove useful later. Their skill in war and organization, and their loyalty to me, provided Hastinapura with a solid bulwark and buffer against further Shaka attacks. The Naga bands they joined are still some of Hastinapura's most faithful Northern allies despite King Suyodhana's disdain for the Nagas. *How do I know that?* Yudhishthira had sent emissaries offering an alliance. They were treated politely but sent back empty-handed. Of course, this was reported to me. All the Nagas in the Hastinapura army come from these bands, collateral descendants of Amba and her sisters.

"Amba's aunt, the matriarch of the band, was not happy with our relationship. The Naga band was grateful for what I had done for them, and they were grateful for the men who were leaving my army to join them. But my killing of the Shaka prisoners had terrified the peaceable Nagas. Even the matriarch, otherwise cold-blooded and calculating, who had sent the first emissary asking for my help, shied away from me. The stain rubbed off on Amba – there were no secrets among the Nagas – and her people avoided her. They saw nothing wrong in Amba's taking a sexual partner, just that the partner was a monster. That exclusion from her band is the reason Amba decided to leave with me for Hastinapura. With the death of her mother and father, Amba's response to rejection was further withdrawal. I did not know how this would turn out. Repeatedly, I went over the need to maintain appearances, to keep Satyavati and others from finding out about our relationship. Every time I did that, the discussion led to angry words that ended in the urgency of sex.

"Amba's sisters – ten-year-old twins named Ambika and Ambalika – made a fateful decision to go to Hastinapura just for that winter. They had nothing to do with me and were under no pressure to leave. We Kauravas would have called them 'orphans' and looked for relatives who could take care of them. But in a Naga band, aunts and cousins took care of each other. Later, my enemies would accuse me of kidnapping the three sisters, hoping to drive a wedge between my nephews and me. Ambika and Ambalika were excited that their sister was going to the city and wanted to go with her. Amba said that she would bring back her sisters, and I believe that was truly her intent.

"A sad procession returned to Hastinapura. Two months had passed. The city had been in mourning for the King, and very little government business had gone on while they waited for us. We received daily demands for information from the Queen, along with implied accusations of treachery. I kept her informed with the requested daily reports, but after the first few confusing days, there was nothing to report. I told her nothing of my crazed revenge, but she heard that I was now called Bhishma and that I had terrified the Nagas. She did not care to find out why I was called so, but she found it useful to broadcast my new name. A confused mélange of rumors were also reported in the town. I had kidnapped three Shaka princesses for my brother to marry. I had been rejected by a Shaka woman and had taken a terrible revenge. Among the few people close to the ruling family who knew of my vow, the rumor was that the unnatural celibacy had caused a mental breakdown. Sometimes this breakdown was attributed to rejection by Amba. It was also said that I was regretting my pledge to protect Hastinapura and support Satyavati's sons in their claim to the throne. Satyavati and I agreed to suppress the story of the Shaka invasion to avoid panic. My dam-building project had made our northern border porous, and I did not want that to be widely known.

"I learned later that an extended period of drought in Shaka-desa (the land of the Shakas well to the north of the Snow Mountains) had occasioned a great migration of the Shakas into Parsaka and Mleccha-desa. My massacre proved to be politically useful in deterring further invasions. I made sure that traders going towards Parsaka and Mleccha-desa were told a lurid and bloody version of the massacre. It has been forty years since the massacre. The sleepless nights, and there have been many of those, are spent replaying the events that led to it. That I was insane with fury is no excuse. But it is possible that the story of the bloodthirsty ruler of Hastinapura kept away many subsequent invaders. When the invasion comes, as surely it must, it will not be by a small band, but a large and well-equipped army.

"I introduced Amba and her sisters as daughters of the chief of the northern Nagas. I think the Naga residents of Hastinapura understood this exaggeration, but others did not. As the daughters of a chief, they were welcomed and treated with respect. Satyavati took them under her wing and would have asked the younger girls to stay with her. But Amba insisted on keeping them with her in separate quarters. Thus began a winter of subtle gestures, meetings in dark places, sneaking out of my home and sneaking into Amba's. Ambika and Ambalika often slept through these assignations. We explained the need for secrecy and they kept our secret."

THE SECOND CO-REGENCY

LIFE WITH AMBA

Devavrata had woken up from a dream still lurking at the edge of his consciousness – a full moon shining over the lake in Varanavata formed by the dam he had built. It was his first and favorite project, and it had been completed on the same day that Vichitravirya died. He recalled gazing into that clear and cold night with the simple thought – *how fortunate he was that he could not be King*. It was a serene time remembered in the dream, and the calm carried over into his waking in which the sensation of pain in his shoulder was a tolerable anomaly. The King, the Vyaasa and the Archivist were sitting by the entrance to his tent. They moved closer to him and the Vyaasa had said, "Good! You woke up. That was a long sleep. It is almost ten ghatis after sunrise. Are you feeling unwell? Is this effort too tiring?"

Devavrata's mind was clear and, but for the pain, he felt as rested as the Regent of Hastinapura could ever be. He said, "That is indeed late. I feel fine, though. If not for the arrow, I would jump out of the bed to face the day."

"The nurse has brought you fruit mash to eat."

"I don't need it; I do not feel hungry. I cannot do anything lying here, so why don't we just continue with the record of the past,"

Devavrata said. The nurse extended a small bowl of copper containing the slightly fermented mash, and Devavrata slurped it. The smell of the fermenting fruit revived memories of his mother – fermented honey had been her favorite drink, but she would never let him drink it. He had stolen a sip once and spent the rest of the day trying to wash the taste off his tongue. The memory made him smile. After one more slurp, he said, "That's enough. I am not hungry. Tell me a story."

The Vyaasa said, "On the death of Chitrangada, Vichitravirya did not become the King right away as he was underage. You became Regent once more. Tell us about Vichitravirya's life in that period."

Devavrata eyes dropped and he pursed his lips. He said, "That isn't a story. It is a question asking me to tell you more. Haven't I given you enough? Will you now tell me what happened to Amba?"

"I will do that, but I do not know much. I would have liked to talk to her first," said the Vyaasa.

"Amba is in custody in this camp," said Yudhishthira.

"She's here?" said Devavrata. "I assumed that she left the camp when I did not hear anything about her."

Yudhishthira said, "We detained her because she was not in her right mind. We intend to send her back to Panchala under guard. But other events have taken precedence, and she is still here."

Shukla said, "That is good! It gives me my first chance to talk to her. My friend, can you wait a little longer? Distract yourself with our questions. You were the only one here who knew Vichitravirya as a brother. Tell us about him."

Devavrata considered this new postponement of his request. Would Amba talk to Shukla? She knew him from a long time ago, from a time that was less warlike even if not less tense. *She would certainly not speak to me,* he thought. That decided him to give in.

Devavrata said, "Vichitravirya? There is nothing much to say about him. Vichitravirya was twelve when Chitrangada died, too young to be made King. The co-Regency of Devavrata and

Satyavati was revived for another three years. Vichitravirya lived, loved, and died before he could do any damage as King."

Shukla said, "He had children. That should have been good enough. Particularly as you stayed faithful to your vow to Satyavati."

"Yes. The one thing that Vichitravirya did right was to get his wives pregnant before he died. If he hadn't done that, I would have become the King I never wanted to be. But I wish that was enough. My old friend, I needed your advice then, but you were not there. You are right about one thing. My vow allowed me to be the ruler I wanted to be and let Satyavati's spawn be the Kings she wanted them to be. I had no desire for children."

"You could have sent for me, if you had needed my advice. When I arrived, you had already become Bhishma, the unreachable."

"You do not understand."

"I understand only too well," said the Vyaasa. "I am only sorry that I did not tell you Amba's secret sooner."

Amba's secret. What was it? The Vyaasa had mentioned this earlier. What difference would it make? But ...

"Archivist," Devavrata said. "Come here – I'll tell the rest of what I know."

"Vichitravirya was twelve when his world was changed by Chitrangada's death. He had been raised to believe that he would never be King, and the responsibilities slid off his shoulders like water off a turtle's back. He met Ambika and Ambalika at a young age when he was not interested in them. They were in shock after the Shaka attack and in awe of the city. Amba protected them, and as the months passed, they adjusted to their new situation. Amba was much older and had always been like a mother to them, so her role continued naturally. They were aware of their sister's liaison with me, but as Nagas, they were not surprised. They were surprised that we wanted to keep it a secret, but accepted the argument that we needed to be careful. City people, after all, were different.

"If Amba was considered beautiful – I am biased and perhaps my memory has faded, but she was very beautiful – her sisters were set to be even more so. Satyavati, being a Naga herself, felt they would form a bond. She grumbled that Amba had refused her hospitality. Satyavati spoiled the twins as though they were the daughters she never had. Amba could do nothing to stop this. Then Amba disappeared and against their wishes, I attempted to send the younger sisters back to their Naga band. The attempt failed, and they lost any trust in me."

Shukla said, "Tell me about the disappearance of Amba. I've known about what happened later, but the period leading up to her disappearance has been obscure. How and when did it happen?"

Devavrata said, "I've always wondered if keeping our relationship secret was the cause of her troubles. What if I had simply acted as though there were no vow? I still do not know why she left. Do you?"

Shukla said, "I will surely tell you what I know, but later, after I have talked to Amba."

AMBA DISAPPEARS

Devavrata said, "Great happiness is followed by great sorrow – that may be inevitable, and it has been so for me. Hastinapura returned to normal. That was the winter of my happiness. I did not know that, come spring, Amba would disappear. Every year during the spring thaw, the snow-fed rivers rose and, somewhere or the other, a flood occurred. I had built dams on the Ganga, so Hastinapura was safe. We could do nothing about the Yamuna. It was a crazy river in the spring, especially the new stream going to the east of the Aravalli range. My job every spring was to find a

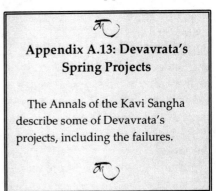

Appendix A.13: Devavrata's Spring Projects

The Annals of the Kavi Sangha describe some of Devavrata's projects, including the failures.

way to keep the flooding rivers from destroying the new settlements along their banks and along the canals.

"I was away for two months, almost all of that time just north of the wasteland we call Khandavaprastha. I left six days before the full moon, that being the best time to travel (the moon makes the nights safe for resting), and came back two days before the second full moon after that. When I came back, Amba was not in Hastinapura, and nobody seemed to know where she had gone. Nobody had looked for her. Amba's house, the one I had prepared for her, was empty. It had been cleaned out after she disappeared. I could not ask Satyavati directly for that might reveal my interest, the relationship I had been keeping secret. In any case, Satyavati never told me the truth when we worked together. So my search for Amba was low-key, the questions I asked were indirect, and the answers I received seemed to be evasive.

"Her sisters Ambika and Ambalika were useless in this search. They had been moved in with Satyavati. At their age, they were too young to live by themselves. They also did not volunteer any information. I was sure they knew something, and as I listened to their lies – *lying to my face!* – my face turned red and my hands shook. The girls began crying, and their sobs attracted the attention of the servants. Most of the servants were my agents assigned to Amba, but I had had to include a few provided by Satyavati. Amba was well-spied on with these two groups. The attendants came in and surrounded the girls and consoled them. Satyavati appeared and chided me. The appearance of these women moderated my anger. I now knew that I was capable of torture – and I was grateful for that knowledge. I stormed out and found my men standing around in two groups. Both groups had drawn their swords and were prepared to act on my command. They turned when they saw me come out by myself. That was one day that my training with the Kavi Sangha, brief as it was, helped me. I sensed the tension in my men's disposition, calmed myself, and projected calmness. Seeing me relax calmed the men. Their captains came to me. They did not say anything. I was Bhishma, my actions unpredictable. Some of my men considered me capable of torturing the girls. I do not know if I would have tortured them to find out what they knew of Amba's disappearance if my women and men had not stopped me.

"So, I sent the girls back to their home with the northern Nagas, protected by a small armed party. This was against their will, but I made it clear to all that I had made a promise to their aunts and I could not break that promise. Satyavati understood me, I think, and did not object. The girls were terrified of me. The entourage came back with the girls and with disquieting news. The matriarch had died. she had been older than the other women but not that old, so her death had precipitated a crisis. Her sons had died in the Shaka attack. There was no one to inherit the role of chief. Her daughter had not partnered with a man who wanted to stay with this band; he would have been a viable candidate for the role. Now, the daughter was unable to find a man who would take on the role of defense chief. A rumour had spread among other Naga clans that this band was cursed. Without a credible defending force, the band's crops were at risk of being looted by wild Nagas or, sometimes, other hostile or opportunistic Naga bands. Even the Naga soldiers I had left behind were losing hope that the band would survive. Ambika and Ambalika had become accustomed to living in Hastinapura and did not want to help re-establish their band. Their refusal to return to the band, even as matriarchs, was a catalyst. Most of the men walked away; the women were unable to agree on a matriarch. There were not enough people left to form even one band with a good mix of older and wiser seniors and younger and more flexible youngsters. It would be a long time before such a band could provide a protective home for the girls.

"My men whom I had left behind had formed a band that offered to help Naga bands in trouble. This was how they ended up as a specialized band of Naga mercenaries. The sisters asked about Amba, but she was not with the band, had never gone there. I wanted to question Ambika and Ambalika again, for I could not believe that Amba would have gone away without her sisters."

"When the girls returned to Hastinapura, Satyavati took them completely under her control, and I did not have Amba to provide counterweight. I had to ask Satyavati's permission to interview them and she agreed with conditions – her guards would be within sight and I had to stay at least ten hastas away from them. My new name was beginning to influence people and make them fear me."

THE INTERVIEW

Devavrata continued: "Satyavati may not have cooperated, but she did not want to oppose me at that point. She sent Ambika and Ambalika, escorted by women from her entourage. I asked to talk to them in private, and the women assented with ill grace. Satyavati later chastised me as though my request had been improper. As usual, she overlooked my rights as the guardian of the girls. I had frightened them when I sent them back to their band. They felt they could not trust me anymore. When Amba was in Hastinapura, we had used my guardianship of the twins as a cover for my visits to Amba. Now I wanted to ask them about Amba's disappearance. The girls and I went to my chambers accompanied by one of Satyavati's women and another woman who was married to one of my men. Informal seats had been arranged for us. There were three large stuffed cushions arranged around a low table. In the middle was a large plate with dried fruits, rice cakes made with puffed rice and honey, and a bowl of honey with a number of dipping sticks. I indicated the cushion for them and waited for them to choose. Ambika chose the cushion furthest from the fruits. Ambalika moved towards the fruit and would have sat down next to them, but looked to Ambika who was glaring. She sat down by the other pillow, leaving me closest to the fruits. Ambika looked straight ahead, avoiding my eyes.

"'It has been a long time since I've seen you. Are you satisfied with my mother's hospitality? Have you made friends? Do the attendants treat you with respect?'

"Ambika replied, 'Yes, sir. We are well. You too have been well, we trust?' Ambalika looked at her sister and nodded.

"This was not good. *Why was she being formal?* I could not understand.

"'Yes, my dears. Thank you for asking. You know that I am concerned about your welfare. I promised your clan's matriarch that I would be responsible for your health and safety.'

"'Yes, sir. Thank you for your concern,' Ambika said, as Ambalika nodded again.

"'With your sister missing, I have not been able to take care of you as I promised.'

"'Oh, you do not need to worry. We are doing fine in the care of your Matriarch, the lady Satyavati.'

"Matriarch Satyavati? What had my stepmother been telling them? In retrospect, it was obvious what Satyavati had done, but at that time, I was befuddled.

"'I sent people to many Naga bands in search of your sister but did not find her. Your aunt, the new matriarch, was not pleased to hear of her disappearance. She expressly asks after you and I have to reply. Would you like to return there?'

"Ambika looked away. 'Tell our band's matriarch that we are in good health. We are safe in the protection of the Hastinapura matriarch. We do not wish to return.'

"'Ambika, Ambalika,' I said. 'Please tell me – do you know what has happened to Amba?'

"'You do not know?' Ambalika said, and her sister frowned.

"'No, I do not know.'

"Ambika's eyes narrowed and she looked at me directly. I stared straight back without blinking. She looked away, and I knew that she was not going to tell me. That time, Ambalika came to my aid.

"'Why don't you know? You had asked her to come and meet you. She left in a hurry with a few of your...'

"Her sister stopped her by squeezing her upper arm.

"'My men?'

"'Yes, your men. We saw them – they were dressed in an off-white half-panchagacham and brown angavastram padded with cotton. Your uniform.'

"I don't need to state the obvious to you, Lomaharshana. I had not called for Amba nor had I sent an escort to bring her to me.

But somebody had done it. *An enemy?* I could not think of anybody who was my enemy. Would Satyavati have the gall to do this? To what end? To kill Amba, for I was sure that if she was still alive, she would have contacted me. The men were dressed up as my troops. Why make me the culprit? What was the message that convinced Amba to go with the men? *Was she dead?* What had she told the girls before she left, or what had Satyavati told them about Amba?

"Amba's disappearance was my fault. I had not protected her. Was she still alive? I could not believe that Satyavati would have had her killed. The fact that the sisters trusted Satyavati meant that they must have received some reassurance from Satyavati, something that convinced them that she had been helping Amba. This was some devious plot by Satyavati. I did not know what she might have arranged and why the girls no longer trusted me.

"'When was this?' I asked the girls.

"'The very day you left. You sent your men for Amba. We have not seen her since.'

"'So, when I came back without Amba, why didn't you ask me?'

"They were silent.

"'Did she send you a message?'

"It looked like Ambalika might speak, but then she held her tongue. Ambika spoke, 'Sir, we will not discuss Amba with you. If there is anything else you wish to ask us, please do so. Please do not ask about Amba, we cannot and will not talk.'

"I was the Regent, one of the most powerful men in the city. They were mere slips of girls. Yet, with the backing of Satyavati, they felt that they could refuse me.

"This was the story I began with. Men dressed in my troop's uniform had taken Amba away and later the girls had been told, or received a message – *from Satyavati?* – that had led them to suspect me and to seek Satyavati's protection. I stood up and gazed through the open door at the garden that Amba had planted. Before Amba came, it had been choked with weeds and grasses. It was on the way to the outhouse, and no one saw a need to decorate the path. Amba said that the garden reminded her of her Naga clear-cut fields. *Give me full rein over that piece of land,* she said. *I will set fire to it to clear the ground and prepare it for planting.* When she said that, she laughed to see the shock on the face of the old gardener who took care of the front of the house. He appealed to me, as he was terrified that Amba would set fire to all of Hastinapura, and I had to reassure him. Amba had not yet understood the obligations a master or mistress had to their employees, and she treated them as though they were the almost-equal members of a Naga band.

"I could not see how to reassure the girls that I had nothing to do with Amba's disappearance.

"'I had nothing to do with Amba leaving,' I said. 'Those were not my men. I know nothing of this. Can you believe that?'

"They kept quiet. I watched them to see if there was any inclination to talk. They looked away and stayed silent.

"'I need to find Amba. She was my life. I would never harm her.'

"There was a little flutter when I said that Amba was my life. It did not last long but died in an exchange of glances. Nothing I said after that had any effect. My heart began to race, and I felt that I was losing control over my breathing. I needed to calm down. I signed for them to leave. They bowed, and I blessed them.

Devavrata paused and closed his eyes. His recital had slowed down. The Archivist did not mind; the slower Devavrata spoke, the easier it was to rehearse and memorize. Devavrata's voice, already low, had become rough, his breathing ragged.

It was late in the evening in autumn. Some trees were shedding their leaves, and some were now bare. Every year when the Archivist saw a tree bare of leaves, he would worry that it would die, and every spring when it came to life again, he worried that it would be less full or less green than it had been. It was so much easier to memorize and recall, to versify and enact, he thought, than to be a farmer and worry about the rain, about floods and droughts, about planting and harvesting. His life was so much simpler than Devavrata's, without never-completed goals of peace, without subterfuge, and without plots.

If Devavrata had simply given it all up, he could have gone away with Amba. Lomaharshana sighed and looked at Devavrata, who had fallen asleep. How strange that he could sleep like this even though he had an arrowhead piercing his lung. *It's time to join the Vyaasa and the other Kavi Sangha members for the evening rituals.* Followed by five ghatis in the dark of rehearsing the material he had just heard, then sleep, which would inevitably consist of dreams about what he had just heard. Refreshed, he would then return tomorrow with his teacher.

THE MARRIAGE PROPOSAL

Devavrata said, "Vichitravirya was twelve when his brother died; he could be crowned King at sixteen at the earliest. He had not expected to become the ruler. The country had been at peace, and his brother had inherited all the martial ambitions of his ancestors. As a result, Vichitravirya's princely training had been mostly ignored and his education neglected. Now, he would be the King. He needed to be trained in military matters, and he should have been trained in command. His education was my responsibility. I was limited in what I could do, for if I came down hard on the boy, I would get complaints from Satyavati. He had to be educated in a hurry, so being soft would not do. With Chitrangada, I had had the time and opportunity to develop rapport, but I did not have this luxury with Vichitravirya. Did this have anything to do with what happened next? Perhaps, for in hindsight, I see a connection.

"I rarely saw Ambika and Ambalika. To all appearances, the girls had forgotten their clan and the events in their village. They never brought up the subject of Amba. Was Amba in touch with them? I don't know, and I did not try to find out.

"Satyavati took the girls under her wing. They were always in the house when Vichitravirya visited his mother. As the years passed, Vichitravirya began to notice them. They were beautiful girls close to his own age, and they fascinated him. Satyavati must have been happy to see this, for she had been worried that he would find brides who might not look up to their mother-in-law. Worse, he might get a wife who aspired to power. Satyavati was confident that Ambika and Ambalika, as her protégées, would align with her and never turn on her.

"The day came when Satyavati raised the matter in open court. 'Elders of Hastinapura!' she said. 'It has been three years since my dear son, your King Chitrangada, passed away. Soon, we will crown my son, Vichitravirya, as the heir apparent. A city without a ruler cannot prosper, without a governor it will disintegrate, without a judge it will not survive. He will be all of these, a far-seeing ruler, a stern governor, and a wise judge. He will be a great king.'

"Considering that Satyavati had been an ambitious Naga girl who knew nothing of Hastinapura when she married my father, she had mastered well the council language of the Kauravas. 'Yes, Mother!' I said. She frowned at my form of address. 'He is certainly of age. Let him take the charge he is born to. Let an appropriate and auspicious day be selected.'

"She smiled. The court erupted in applause and shouts of joy. My supporters could never match the ebullience of Satyavati's courtiers. Her courtiers' actions always matched her moods – a deathly silence when she was angry, an excess of bonhomie when she smiled. Satyavati's smile was smug. She had a surprise for me.

"'We have already suffered through the childless death of one Kaurava king,' she said.

"This was her revenge for my calling her 'mother.' I was the senior Kaurava prince here, and if not for my oath to my father, I would have been the Kaurava king.

"She continued, 'My son Vichitravirya is of a marriageable age. For the sake of the Kuru family, he must marry soon.'

"A chorus of agreement came from the council. I had not anticipated this proposal, and my supporters in the room stayed quiet, waiting for a signal from me. On the one hand, a crowned Vichitravirya might be an interfering monarch like his brother who wanted to display his authority and ability. In this matter, I had no say. He would be crowned when his mother considered him ready, and that was now. On the other hand, a married Vichitravirya would have interests other than public displays of authority and ability. That would let me return to executing my plans."

Yudhishthira said, "What plans had you formulated at that point? What role did you expect the King to play in these?"

Lomaharshana said, "Gurudeva, should I include details of these plans at this point in the narrative?"

Shukla said, "Lomaharshana, you are correct to be concerned. The plans are already part of the archives and you can arrange with the King to provide that further detail on those early plans later this evening. Devavrata my friend, for now, please tell us what you did about Satyavati's plans?"

Devavrata said, "Even the Kavi Sangha supported my efforts. When Shukla came back from Takshashila, he supported me and counselled his sister not to interfere with my plans. Now that he is the Vyaasa, he is too powerful and that is boring. She won't listen to him anymore, and so he comes to squeeze stories out of me."

Lomaharshana glanced at the Vyaasa, who was smiling.

Shukla said, "My friend, it is good to see your spirit restored. If I had known that telling stories would cure you of your melancholy, I would have insisted on it from the first day that you came back with Amba. I would have been squeezing these stories out of you for a decade at least, instead of in a hurry today."

Devavrata said, "I like it this way, Shukla. It gives me something to do while I wait for an accident that will kill me."

"True. We both wait to die, you in your way and I in mine. I prefer to squeeze stories out of you."

The Vyaasa continued, "Where you find these metaphors I do not know!"

Devavrata nodded. "I must disagree – the stories of my regency would dampen any listener's spirits."

The Vyaasa and the Regent looked at each other and smiled. It seemed to Lomaharshana that their talk surpassed language, that they were engaged in a conversation that he could hear but not comprehend. It was one of the more dubious pleasures of being a memorizer – occasionally a contract would be incomprehensible, containing encoded or cryptic references, where the word 'fish' might refer to a diamond, and 'pig' might refer to a coat of armor. Lomaharshana took the opportunity to yawn. Then he rotated his upper body to stretch his abdominal muscles, and the movement broke the tension.

Devavrata continued where he had left off. "When Chitrangada was alive, he was suspicious of my motives. He insisted that the cadre of armed farmers that I was training vow loyalty to him. Though the Kauravas had begun to use the words 'king', 'queen', 'prince', and 'princess' for the ruling family, they had not yet begun professing personal loyalty. That is Suyodhana's innovation. He is rigid and unswerving in his demand that all his people vow personal loyalty to him. Though I do not like to acknowledge it, that demand for personal loyalty will make the difference and ensure Suyodhana's victory over Yudhishthira. In those times, the old Kuru residents viewed us as senior chiefs and me as the leading representative of the ruling clan. There was much confusion over my oath to my father. Even my ideas about uniting for defense felt like a claim on people's loyalty and they resisted it. Chitrangada's demand of an explicit pledge of loyalty did not sit well with the people at all. With Chitrangada dead, there was no demand for a vow of loyalty, and as long as Satyavati and Vichitravirya did not ask for it, I could go back to creating a buffer region populated by armed allies who had not vowed loyalty, but worked with Hastinapura out of mutual interest.

Appendix A.14: Devavrata's Early Plans for Empire

Yudhishthira said, "Grandsire, you've mentioned plans for creating an empire as early as Chitrangada's reign. What were these plans?"

Devavrata's reply in The Annals of the Kavi Sangha are in his own words.

"By creating an empire I would fulfil my promise to my father that I would protect the Kuru family and his descendants through

Satyavati. This goal was yet to be achieved, and I would not be able to accomplish it if Vichitravirya or Satyavati interfered. All in all, the idea of Vichitravirya marrying appealed to me. Both he and his mother would be distracted and not inclined to interfere with me as long as I did not interfere with them. He should marry anybody other than an ambitious princess who would question the sincerity with which I had accepted the loss of my birthright.

"I was surprised when Satyavati announced in the open court that she had found the perfect match but that she was not ready to announce it. The assembled court cajoled and pleaded with her, and then she added a second surprise. She said that I was the reason she was keeping it secret – I had not yet given my permission. I let surprise reflect in my face – whatever she was doing, I would go along.

"Such surprises were the way Satyavati exercised her power in those days when she was young and certain of herself. She is too old for this kind of melodrama now. In any case, Suyodhana does not allow her to leave her quarters. She has no say in his court. He would certainly not have put up with any drama that did not come with his blessing. Seeing my surprise led her supporters to exchange knowing glances. More cajoling followed, along with an erudite discussion on the merits and demerits of marrying a local girl as opposed to one from another city. *Of course, they hoped that the great Regent Devavrata would bless the event.*

"Then Satyavati said, 'They are not local girls,' and I knew whom she meant and understood her reasons for this rigmarole. Not local girls, indeed! I had not seen Ambika and Ambalika for weeks after they had entered Satyavati's clique. My attempts to arrange a second meeting or to have them visit me had been rebuffed. That was certainly Satyavati's doing.

"Satyavati continued, 'Ambika and Ambalika, the Naga princesses, have shown us their grace and elegance since they came here. My son knows them, and they know him. They are well-matched.' Then she turned to me and stated the obvious, 'Ah! Devavrata, you look surprised. Sometimes the warden is the last person to learn what his wards are up to.' The court dutifully followed her in laughing at my apparent humiliation.

"'You are right,' I said. 'I am surprised. As their guardian, I should know more about their thinking. Please arrange to send them to my house.'

"There was silence in the court. A hint of a frown showed in Satyavati's perfect visage. She said, 'Of course, my son. They have been willful girls not to visit you more often.'

"The court hummed and twittered at the overt condescension. I thanked her and left to await the arrival of the girls."

THE SECOND INTERVIEW

Devavrata said, "This interview played out like the previous one. My staff arranged the room and its decorations to be beautiful. The room smelled of sandalwood and jasmine. They hoped it would please the girls and perhaps they would answer my questions.

"I asked Ambika and Ambalika about the proposal that they marry Vichitravirya. They told me that the room was much more inviting now than it had been the last time. Ambalika and Ambika acted as if marriage was a game – their attitude was the Naga attitude. Marriage among Nagas was not taken as seriously as among Hastinapuris. They talked willingly about marriage or pairing customs among the Nagas. The Nagas only celebrated the matriarch's marriage, which occurred on the same day every year, at the full moon before the spring equinox, one month before the spring sowing season. Other couples might decide to pair up that day as a couple and take part in the celebrations. The Hastinapura Nagas did not follow that practice, for they had moved away from many Naga traditions. I've gathered from the Nagas that Panchala follows the old customs.

"Ambika and Ambalika were going to be disappointed when they found that Satyavati was not going to take another spouse the same day, and I did nothing to explain. They chattered but avoided any subjects I might be interested in. They were polite and uncommunicative. My occasional attempts to ask about Amba continued to fail. I let them go back to Satyavati's care. There was no reason to block the wedding; the sooner

Vichitravirya fathered children the sooner I would be relieved of the worry that I would be made King!

"The announcement was made, and the city prepared to celebrate a coronation and a wedding."

Devavrata paused in the telling of the story. "Shukla, my friend," he said to the Vyaasa. "I've told you all that happened from the day Amba disappeared to the day my brother was crowned and wedded. Come, Shukla, tell me about Amba. Yes, yes, I know what you think, that I may be dying, but still I grasp at straws. Laugh at me, but tell me what I want to know."

The Vyaasa smiled, "I am not laughing at you, my friend. I smile to see that you still remember the parable of the man suspended by a straw over a snake pit. Lend me your indulgence, for if you tell us your old memories leading up to the birth of Dhritarashtra and Mahendra Pandu, the Archivist will have enough to work on, and then we can exchange these stories."

"There is little to add," said Devavrata. "Vichitravirya was not cut out to be a ruler, but he represented all of Satyavati's hopes and ambitions."

THE DEATH OF VICHITRAVIRYA

Devavrata continued, "Vichitravirya was sixteen when he was crowned King. He had to be educated in a hurry, so being soft was not an option for the teacher. After all that, he was still not ready to be a King when he was crowned.

"I rarely saw Ambika and Ambalika. To all appearances, the girls had forgotten their clan and the events in their village and they never brought up the subject of Amba. Was Amba in touch with them? I don't know and I did not try to find out.

"The tedium of governance weighed heavily on Vichitravirya. He was expected to lead the council in making decisions, but the meetings bored him. All that education compressed into a tight schedule had soured any desire to rule and left only the desire to be indulged. He enjoyed the time he spent with his wives and their women and complained about the time that the official meetings took. Slowly, more and more of the administration reverted to me, and the councilors turned to me for guidance and direction, while the King spent time with his two wives in picnics and parties. Satyavati was not pleased, but he was still young and willing enough to practice martial arts in front of his wives.

"Seven years passed. The promise that Satyavati had extracted from Shantanu that she would mother a dynasty of rulers, would only be fulfilled if she had great-grandchildren. Satyavati was looking forward to that day – the day she could stop worrying. There was reason to worry, and she voiced it to me – *why were there no children? Was there something wrong with Vichitravirya, or with Ambika and Ambalika?* Some of her women would try to assuage her worry – *he was still young. Seven years without a pregnancy between the two girls was a bit unexpected, but such cases did happen.* I don't think Satyavati ever stopped worrying.

"I was out of the city inspecting a dam we had built prematurely on the Yamuna. Premature because, after keeping to one path for many years, an onrush of water down the river had broken a new path upstream, and now the old channel was dry and the dam useless. We had spent much effort on planning and constructing the dam, so the settlers I had sent there were working to send the river back into its old channel. The Yamuna had not yet found a permanent path to the sea – maintenance of this type was almost a routine task. However, I wanted to see the damage and talk to the engineers about the design so that we did not repeat old mistakes. That was where I was when I received word that Vichitravirya was dead.

"I needed a day to assign to others the power and responsibilities that I had kept under my control. Then I left for Hastinapura, reaching it as the thirteenth day ceremonies were ending. There is one reason I envy the Shakas' ability to ride horses, quickly getting from one place to another. If I rode a horse, I could have reached Hastinapura in four or five days following the treeless bank of the Ganga.

"At the dam site, the messenger had little to tell – he had been sent to fetch me as soon as the King died, so he had not had a chance to hear gossip. The news of the King's death changed everything. *The King was dead, long live the... who?* As I prepared to go to Hastinapura, the foremost thought in my mind was of the succession. I was reconciled to not being King, but it felt like Shani[47], the Lord of Destiny and Arbiter of Fate, demanded that I be the King, was telling me in so many ways, *You will be King*, and worked matters so I would have to assume the crown that I had surrendered so many years ago. I did not want the crown, but the rule passing out of Kuru hands was not acceptable."

The Vyaasa said, "At that point, you thought that Vichitravirya had died without children. When did you learn that Ambalika and Ambika were with child?"

"Quite soon. For seven years I had kept my expectations to myself. I left immediately on hearing of the death, fearing the worst, but I was far from the city. As I've mentioned before, you cannot make an onager go faster than it wants to go. It took me a week. By the time I reached Hastinapura, almost two weeks had passed since his death. The city was, of course, still in mourning – white and saffron flags were raised at every corner and the colorful gates of the city were draped in white. Preparations for the ceremony of bidding farewell to the departing soul and wishing it a pleasant welcome at the home of the ancestors were in progress, the ceremony itself having been postponed. I wondered at that – these rituals should not have been held at all – my brother had died childless. But I assumed that nobody had dared to correct whatever command had come from the palace. It was a minor matter, and if it helped my stepmother feel better, I was for it.

"I could only imagine what Satyavati's state of mind must have been. She had no more sons to raise to the throne, and her sons had given her no grandsons. I think she would have liked to establish a matriarchy, but she had no daughters either. When I reached Hastinapura, the city was in turmoil. The guards, some of them my agents, reported that Satyavati had been issuing commands and threats of revenge if poison were discovered. The funerary rituals usually required the body to be cremated on the third day, but at Satyavati's insistence, the body had not been

---

[47] *Shani*, pronounced "shun-ye", was believed to control a person's fate. The god could also afflict a person with the condition we call "depression." In modern times, Shani has been identified with the planet Saturn.

cremated – it was believed that poison would prevent it from decaying – and stank. The poison tester had tasted all the food in the kitchen and any fruits, nuts and even leaves growing near the house; he was still alive. It did not satisfy Satyavati, who was not prepared to believe that Vichitravirya had died of some disease or other natural cause. She wanted results – the killer who had poisoned her son must be found, or else... Her guards had demanded access to the homes of people she thought were in the plot. No evidence had been found, but that was taken as proof that the conspiracy pervaded the entire city. They were against her because she was a Naga.

"I found out very soon that my worry was misplaced. I went straight to the palace to express my condolences to Satyavati and to the queens Ambika and Ambalika. The queens were nowhere to be found. Their attendants told me that they had gone into seclusion, almost immediately after Vichitravirya's death. Satyavati was in the council chamber. As I expected, everybody was busy with administrative trivia – there is no better task to take one's mind off distressing news.

"I left my cart with my men and went directly to the council chamber. Satyavati was there, sitting on her throne. The councilors were standing. She did not see me at first for I did not announce myself as I usually did. The caretaker of the Treasury, an old man who had fulfilled this thankless role for the city for many years, stood in front of her trembling. Satyavati was scolding him.

"'What do you mean, you can't account for twenty-five copper seals? They could have been used to pay an assassin.'

"The man was trembling and his voice had a slight quaver. 'Madam, this discrepancy has existed in the treasury since before your husband died.'

"He was right. Satyavati was constantly finding errors and omissions, many of which represented transactions that were not completed. Once, Shantanu had arranged to "steal" twenty-five copper seals to see if the loss was reported. The minister had reported with such an abject look of fear that Shantanu could not bear to tell him that it had been a test. Nor could he return it without making the minister suspect something. Instead Shantanu 'forgave' the minister for having committed such an error, but the minister had kept the loss on the memorized accounts as a reminder. Satyavati had not known about the test. Subsequently, in the complete audit of the treasury conducted every seven years, when the treasurer completed the inventory of gold, silver, copper, and tin, he would discover the discrepancy and assume that the caretaker was trying to hide it. The error would be announced, and Satyavati would berate the minister for his incompetence. At the end of it, he would be ordered to maintain the discrepancy in the archives. Satyavati was berating the minister once again, but this time the threat of punishment might be real, and everyone trembled.

"I could not bear to see this continue, and I moved so that Satyavati saw me. 'Devavrata! You have come just in time. I was beginning to fear for my life. Nobody here is competent to protect the Queens as they need to be protected.' Then, to the minister, 'You! Go back!'

"Satyavati had never welcomed me in this fashion. I was not comfortable, for as a rule we stayed apart. I took my seat. She burst into tears – *What a miserable being I am – I have suffered the loss of my husband and my children.* It was an old lament of hers, her misfortunes and her bad choices – and for a moment, I felt a knot of sympathy in my gut. Only for a moment, for this lament was usually followed by a demand for some extra consideration from the King. I tensed, waiting for the description of a problem only I could fix.

"I walked up to her seat and sat to her right – she was seated in the Queen's seat on the right of the King's seat. The seat to the right of that was for the chief councilor, and I intended taking it as a signal that I preferred not to rule. She stood up and, as I sat down, she said in a quiet voice, 'I have some fortunate news to announce.'

"She turned to all the other people in the room and asked them to leave for she would be discussing family matters with me. They left. Her maids stayed. She asked me to sit closer. Practices of over twenty years were being abandoned in summary fashion. She whispered even though only her maids – and my spies – were in the room. This was all very unusual. I felt certain that some unusual, perhaps bizarre, demand was going to follow.

"Satyavati said, 'My poor son. Fate is cruel, indeed.'

"She stopped, waiting for me to respond. I nodded. She then continued. 'For seven years, he waited anxiously for a child. The day he died, that very morning, Ambalika had missed her period, for the second time. You know how she has never missed; this time she had missed two.'

"She stopped again. I nodded again, in acknowledgement, even if I did not understand why I was being told this. I had never known when any of the women were bleeding. For that matter, I did not know that Ambalika had missed any periods. *Why was she telling me this?* Satyavati's words added to my confusion. Daksha, the lord of the moon, we are told fills every woman once a cycle, afflicts them with pain or tension at that time. Daksha, it seems, is not satisfied with the twenty-seven star-brides that he dallies with in that cycle. The explanation is a bit fantastic, but that is typical of doctors, seeking the cause of illness in things invisible and unknowable.

"Satyavati said, 'The doctor could only come that afternoon. She held Ambalika's hand and listened to her chest. She tasted her spit and smelled her urine and afterwards told me that Ambalika was pregnant. I had not told Ambalika or Vichitravirya – I waited for them to come in for dinner.'

"Satyavati said, 'Instead of my delivering the good news to the girls, they reported bad news to me. Ambika and Ambalika were in the garden as the sun was setting. The rains were almost over, signaling the beginning of the harvest season. My son had come into their garden and Ambika and Ambalika were excited, showing him the colors limning the clouds. They said he was very happy and enjoying himself. He must have been at his poetic best, for I heard giggles and laughter. Then Vichitravirya said, *I have a headache,* and sat down. Ambalika gave a graphic report – the shine had vanished from his eyes. She had held a hand against his temple. He turned pale even as they watched, not yet comprehending; then, he shook his head and put his finger in his ear as though he were trying to dislodge something and fell back.

They rushed to pick him up, but he was already unconscious. They called to attendants, who lifted him and brought him in.

"'They called the doctor back, and she examined the comatose Vichitravirya. She detected a faint heartbeat and said he was not dead. At the same time, she held out no hope. Without a fever or other external symptom, she could not ask him whether he was in pain or where the discomfort was located, or if some part hurt when touched or pressed and so on.'

"Satyavati continued, 'I came in at that point. I was concerned that my son's spirit might be suffering from the uncertainty that he had no children and would suffer in the hell reserved for people whose sons do not fulfil their duty to their ancestors. Even if he was comatose, I felt he might be able to understand – so I informed Vichitravirya and his wives that they were going to have a child. I hope the news gave him some relief. Later that night, he was delirious and called on his brother to help with unseen opponents. The doctor thought that was a hopeful sign, but those were the last words he spoke.'

"Satyavati said, 'That was not the end of it. The next day, we discovered that Ambika too had missed a second period, and the doctor declared her pregnant, too. I informed my son, comatose or not, immediately. I could not see any difference in his condition, but in my heart, I know that he felt me mourning for him. By coincidence, one of the queen's attendants, a concubine of the King, had discovered that she was pregnant two weeks earlier. A surfeit of babies after seven barren years heralded the King's death.'

"Again, Satyavati waited for me to nod and I did. We were getting into deeper waters that I knew little of. I had no idea why Satyavati was so concerned about menstrual periods – I thought it might be a holdover from when the matriarch ran the family. The women were in charge of every detail, and the men were superfluous visitors. A woman's partner would not be allowed to approach her for a few days every month – I think they did this so that the woman could rest, a luxury that young lovers considered superfluous. Why women laid a claim to these rest periods even after their partners had grown old and less driven by *kama* I do not know.

"Satyavati said, 'My only remaining son died that afternoon. He neither spoke nor opened his eyes, but he did become delirious moments after the doctor's assessment that he would not live long. Along with his wives, I held down his hands and legs for he thrashed them about even as we told him the news. Then, he suddenly went limp. He was dead.

"'Ambika and Ambalika were stunned. I took them to our chambers and had my women stay with them and console them. A messenger was sent to ask you to return post-haste. Others took care of the body, and plans were made for cremation as soon as possible. That is when it struck me that my son could have been poisoned. If we had chosen a date and time and cremated him, it would have been impossible to discover the cause. I decided to postpone the cremation, overriding the objections of traditionalists. I pointed out to them that Panchnad had an ancient practice of burying people in earthen jars, a practice that had died out in favor of cremation. I offered to return to that practice, so they stayed silent.'

"In this manner, dear Shukla, I learned of the conception of my nephews. Satyavati decided that a King with an heir merited an elaborate funeral ceremony, equal to that of a Matriarch of Panchnad. For seventy days, I was required to perform an extravagant solemn ritual that Hastinapura had put aside. At the ceremony, I overheard one of Satyavati's maids comment that the Queen Mother had suffered much and life was sad and unfair. I was surprised to hear Satyavati say, 'My son may have passed on, but I am blessed that both queens and even a maidservant, have become pregnant at almost the same time. We will even have at least one wet nurse we trust. A triple pregnancy is uncommon; it is an omen – my line will not die. That is why I have been able to accept the deaths of both my sons.'

"After Satyavati's explanation, I realized that the prospect of grandchildren had allowed Satyavati to be reconciled to her son's death. Of course, it wasn't that simple. She still wanted revenge against a poisoner if there was one. She felt that she would only be respected if she pursued justice and achieved it. She maintained her pressure on the city's investigators.

"Satyavati seemed to become much more calm after relaying all this to me. She had no choices left – after the deaths, she could only rely on my oath; she had to rely on me. The patient hearing I gave her must have reassured her.

"It is now common knowledge that Surya, the sun, and Chandra, the moon, govern the birth of a baby. The healthy child lies in its mother's womb for at least eight moons and up to one moon beyond that. I figured that we had about thirty-two weeks to prepare for the babies' births. It was fortunate that the maidservant had become pregnant at the same time. Among the forest Nagas, the freedom of the spring ritual led to many women conceiving at the same time and giving birth at about the same time the following winter. Thus they could help one another in taking care of and feeding a baby. A baby born at any other time was rare. The Kauravas did not follow that ritual, and the city Nagas had given it up. Children were born at all times of the year, and consequently, the mother ran the risk of not being able to find a wet nurse. The Kurus of Hastinapura, like the non-matriarchal ruling families of the far West, provided the wife with a trusted maid who would become a mother at the same time. Yes, my dear friend, it was controversial. How did they find the maid, how did she become pregnant, what would happen to her child – there are many questions that I did not ask. The practice stopped because of my father's laws limiting the number of children. Satyavati herself had given birth to Chitrangada and Vichitravirya, and I remember the tense days after each birth, waiting for her milk to flow. I wondered if Satyavati had revived the practice of providing a wet-nurse, then decided that this was not an issue worth raising at that time.

"Nothing with Satyavati was simple. After poisoning had been ruled out – pieces of the King's body were fed to rats and cats that were then observed for signs of illness – I thought we were done. Satyavati wasn't done.

"The funeral rituals completed, I was called in for a meeting with the Queen-Mother. She had an urgent question."

THEY SHALL BE KAURAVAS

"'How will these children become Kauravas?'"

Devavrata recalled that he had remained silent when Satyavati posed this question. He told Lomaharshana, "After a few vighatis, Satyavati said, "Devavrata, please answer my question. If my grandsons are raised without a Kaurava father, they will never become Kauravas."

"My step-mother's question was completely unexpected. She was desperate – she had addressed me as 'Devavrata', not as 'my son' – she had never done this before. Why was she desperate?

"What did she mean? As it turned out, she was concerned about conception and childbirth. I knew very little about this, so I kept quiet.

"She continued, 'I've questioned the doctor, and she said that there must be almost daily contact between a woman and her husband while she is pregnant. Then the child will inherit the features, strength, and wisdom of her husband's family. Otherwise, some stray man passing through at a vulnerable time will imprint the child. We must have a man, a descendant of Kuru and a close relative of Shantanu, stay in this house for the entire period. He does not have to do anything, just be there.'

"I was the closest relative of Shantanu. His eldest brother had died; the second had renounced his inheritance and vanished into the forest and hadn't been heard of since. For other relatives, we would have to go further away into the abandoned Panchnad cities or even further up the ancestral hierarchy. The difficulty of finding such a person made me the easy choice. The proposal was out of the question, and my dissent must have showed in my face.

"Satyavati said, 'I told the doctor that what she was proposing was impossible. I asked her for alternatives. She consulted her archives and came up with a compromise. The Kaurava father-substitute was not required to be there for all sixty ghatis of the day. He should visit this house daily and spend the whole day-time with or near the queens.'

"The Kaurava father-substitute under consideration was, of course, me. Spending even thirty ghatis every day in this manner was out of the question. Satyavati seemed intent on this, and I could not dissuade her.

"I asked, 'Wouldn't it be equally possible for the child to be influenced by a woman of Shantanu's family?'

"Even as I said this, I realized that my father had no sisters we knew of. I could not shrug off the responsibility. Satyavati replied, 'It must be you. You see why it has to be done. If we don't, the child will not be a descendant of your father. It is Shantanu who will suffer for the sin committed by his sons.'

"'Does it have to be in the same room? Does it have to be all day?' I was grasping at straws, anything that would preserve my separation from Satyavati.

"'I don't know. I will call the doctor.'

"She gestured to a maid and asked her to fetch the doctor. We waited silently.

"To my relief, the doctor was very pragmatic. She was also expert at reading my mind through my face and eyes. The next room would be fine. The night was fine, too, perhaps even better than the daytime, as the aspect cast by the man would be purer. The complete investment, for it was not guaranteed, would take at least two to four months. In fact, two months would do, but that was an absolute minimum.

"I said, 'Send the Queens and their attendants over to my house before dusk. They can sleep in a room adjacent to my bedroom. In fact, they can take over a number of rooms. In the morning, they can return here.'

"It was an uncomfortable four months as I had become used to a solitary life. Initially, I thought it might be possible to ask the queens about Amba or even eavesdrop on their conversation. I did not stoop to these depths; it would have been a scandal if I were observed.

I had to find other ways to conduct the after-dark meetings with spies and other confidential messengers. We were at peace in those days, and I learned a lesson in moderation. The girls found it tedious, for I limited them to one attendant each. Shortly after the third month, they decided that they had had enough. It took a little longer before Satyavati was satisfied. In the sixth month, she declared that she was satisfied with their exposure to my

Kuru aura, and they were clearly showing signs of a routine pregnancy. The nightly walk to my house was getting difficult, and it made sense to stop this ritual.

"In the seventh month of their pregnancy, Satyavati announced that, in her opinion, Vichitravirya had been poisoned after all, by a slow-acting undetectable poison. Given the time at which the babies were conceived, the unborn children could also have received the poison. The Queens must rest so that the children would be healthy. Ambalika and Ambika were kept indoors out of sight. They did not complain. I was satisfied because it made it much easier to keep them safe. I did not have to sleep near the queens. I could leave Hastinapura; I could return to overseeing the progress in building water tanks and irrigation canals. I had expected Satyavati to relax as the months went by; the girls stayed healthy, and nothing bad happened. I was wrong. Satyavati was at her best contrarian self that year.

"As the weeks passed, Satyavati became increasingly tense. Lines of worry marked her face. She was constantly demanding more and different kinds of food for the mothers-to-be. At one point, I found that she had arranged to obtain live carrot plants from Takshashila, where they are a medicine for blindness. The carrot, of all things! Its leaves smell and the dirty white flowers are impossible to admire. The root is eaten, a crooked purple stalk of wood with a pungent taste that the onagers love, so the cart drivers carry them to use as a treat. How do I know of Satyavati's purchase? A month before the queens were to deliver their children, a caravan from the west arrived carrying a hundred whole plants on the verge of flowering. A hundred plants! They had been purchased by Satyavati to be sent live from Takshashila four months earlier so that when they arrived they were just flowering. The price was staggering: bronze and copper tools for five kitchens, or equivalent in gold. The order had come from Satyavati. She had told me that she wanted to order some plants. Those days, I had been struggling to fit in the day's work into the time when the sun was up so that the girls would not be disturbed at night, and I had told the accountant to obey the queen without checking with me. I guess even somebody as cautious as Satyavati can lose her sense of purpose under stress – in this case, she definitely had. I asked her in private why she had spent so much gold. *The carrots are good for pregnant mothers,* she said. If they were so good, and were so expensive when imported, why hadn't she told me? I would have arranged to buy seed and grow them in my own garden. Satyavati was not troubled by the cost – she was protecting her future descendants. The worry lines did not fade from Satyavati's brow even after this rare shipment was received.

"As the seventh month ended, Ambika and Ambalika grew slowly – by the seventh moon they were still on the small side according to Satyavati who worried every day. Finally they began to show their pregnancy. I learned a lot from observing this pregnancy. I received reports on their fluctuating moods, the vomiting over the first one hundred and eight days, their tiredness, Satyavati's worries, and so on. There was nothing I could do but observe. The seventh full moon passed with no sign of trouble but Satyavati decided that it was time to withdraw the two of them from public sight. Then halfway into the eighth moon, she announced the news – Ambika and Ambalika had given birth to sons. Ambika was first by a day. Even after nine full moons in the womb, the babies came out unready and unhealthy. They were small and sickly. Satyavati walked around moaning and cursing as though she herself had just given birth to them.

"The Vyaasa was to play a part in our lives once more. If it had not been for the Vyaasa, the children would have died."

"The Vyaasa Shukla?"

"No, no, not Shukla here, but his predecessor Jaimini. Shukla, my friend, I have wished to say this to you for a long time. I am astonished by the influence that the Vyaasa Parashara has had on this family. Along with the Vyaasa Jaimini, Satyavati had daily visits from Shukla, and Krishna Dvaipaayana Paaraasharya, to whom she was much attached, having cared for him as a baby. Only later did I realize that he was her son.

"It is not surprising that the Vyaasa Jaimini was concerned. It is surely astonishing that the birth of my nephews was also a major concern to our current Vyaasa, Shukla, and to Krishna Dvaipaayana, who is apparently a potential Vyaasa. It all begins with my father's respect for Parashara. Parashara, as the head of the Kavi Sangha, influenced my father. He was Shukla's teacher and Krishna Dvaipaayana's father. All three of them were Parashara's children, physically or intellectually. You could almost call Parashara the root of the tree of cause and effect that has led to this war."

"My friend," Shukla said, "I wish it were so. But our influence has not prevented this war, despite the best efforts of the Kavi Sangha. Of Dvaipaayana, the less said, the better. For many years, I despaired that he would remain in the Kavi Sangha, for he was a wayward young man. Vichitravirya's death shocked him and made him change his ways."

"Wayward young man? Unlike you, at his age? It reminds me that when he was six or so and had just started training with the Kavi Sangha, he would be teased by everybody. They would call him Shukla, to which he would respond with a vigorous *I am not like Uncle Shukla*, as he calls you. Then they called him not-Shukla. He did not like that, and one day he said, *why don't you call my uncle Not-Krishna*. People pointed out that they did – 'not-Krishna' is what 'Shukla' means. I observed the teasing once and was struck by the role names played in our lives. Take the name Krishna – maybe it is only a coincidence, but life is a mess of such coincidences. Shukla the Vyaasa is a not-Krishna. There is the Yadava Krishna whose support for Arjuna and the Pandavas has helped them continue this war and resulted in my capture. There is Krishnaa Agnijyotsna, the Dark Lady, the Matriarch of Panchala, whose blistering rage has not allowed this Kuru family to resolve its internal conflicts. Your nephew Krishna Dvaipaayana will find himself in good company.

"Pardon me for this digression, but I have one more observation. It is not so strange that Satyavati's family became so central to life in Hastinapura, for Satyavati spent all her efforts and influence to ensure that her descendants would rule Hastinapura in the future. That makes us no different from Panchala; we too have our own Dark Lady whose personal ambitions for her children have precluded compromise.

"As for your father's foster-child Krishna... ah! Krishna Dvaipaayana. What an impressive young man he became after Vichitravirya's death! You were absent, gone to the Kavi Sangha's university in Takshashila, and missed this part of his life. I think of him as a child, even though he is only a decade or so younger than you. He has become a major intellectual force in the Kavi Sangha, something I would not have predicted. As a young man, he was well liked, though his behaviour was irresponsible and difficult to condone. He did not like to stay in one place but would be constantly moving around. He would come once in a while and wheedle gold and silver out of Satyavati and then disappear. In the beginning, I would receive reports of his activities that somehow never ended unhappily. An abandoned girl would follow him but, after talking to him, return home with a wistful smile. An insulted bard would come to chide him and leave praising his kindness. The only exception seemed to be Satyavati: every visit ended with Satyavati getting angry and ordering him to leave. Then she would cry and ask him to promise to return. In your frequent absences, he was her sole link to your father who had raised both of them. I expect that he was rebelling against the expectations that people had for him, as the son of Parashara. As I mentioned, he changed. He visited me shortly after the birth of Vichitravirya's children. I had not seen him in many years, and I was overwhelmed by his charm. He was polite, he asked after my health, made light conversation, and left me babbling about his generosity in favoring me with a visit. I am told he has that effect on everyone.

"That was when Krishna Dvaipaayana started building a new life. Satyavati asked him to visit the babies, and he obliged. He even played with them. Satyavati stopped crying after his visits. I stopped getting reports from the places he visited. Then I heard from a proud Satyavati that he had risen fast in the Kavi Sangha. He was a skilled poet and is a rising leader in the Kavi Sangha hierarchy. As I mentioned, he is even a possible Vyaasa."

Shukla said, "Archivist, that is a long digression. I will help clean it a bit later. Devavrata, my friend, please continue with the birth of Vichitravirya's sons!"

Devavrata said, "On the Vyaasa's advice, Satyavati placed the babies in a warm room heated by a hypocaust[48] fired all through the day. To make sure that the babies came to no harm, her maids were in constant attendance on them. A piece of cotton would be dipped in goat's milk and squeezed into their mouths. For two months, they were fed like that. By that point they were healthier and ready for their mother's breasts, but Ambika and Ambalika were unable to lactate by then. It had been too long since the birth. The baby suckling at her breast is necessary for the mother to produce milk, and their babies had not done that. As a coincidence, the pregnant maidservant gave birth to her own baby just two weeks before the baby boys were ready to be switched to mother's milk. Her baby was also a healthy boy. She was a sturdy woman – she produced enough milk for all three boys, though with three feeders she no longer had the energy to attend to the queens.

"Whoever said that a pregnancy lasting nine moons would result in healthy babies should take heed. The child of the wet nurse, born late in the eleventh month, was named Dharmateja – yes, the same Dharmateja Vidura whose moralizing lectures discomfit Suyodhana in Hastinapura. Please understand, Dharmateja Vidura is probably the most ethical, the kindest, and the most far-sighted of Dhritarashtra's councilors. I would rate him as wise as you. His advice to settle this war peacefully enraged Suyodhana. Vidura was healthy at birth. Even though he was conceived a couple of weeks before the two princes, he was born well after them – he was a prodigy, born after eleven months! If only the two princes could have stayed in the womb for another two months – unnatural that might be, but maybe it would have resulted in healthy babies. The two princes were not healthy babies.

"Ambika's son was named Dhritarashtra. When he was finally ready to be shown to the public, it became clear that something was wrong with his eyes. He kept his eyes closed. If we tried to

---

[48] A system of underfloor heating, used to heat houses with hot air. The Romans used it and claim to have invented it, but there are structures like that in Mohenjo-daro and other Sarasvati-Sindhu Culture sites.

hold his eyes open by parting the lids, he would struggle violently and cry. We determined later that he could not bear to let light into his eyes. As a result, he did not look at people's faces when they looked at him or spoke to him. There was nothing wrong with his mind for he listened intently to sounds. Other than this blindness, the stay in the warm room had not hurt him at all. He was healthy and grew up to be strong. Healthy, but blind.

"Ambalika's son was named Mahendra. He had been born white as milk – later he would be nicknamed *Pandu*, "the pale". Even though he shared the heated room treatment along with his brother, Mahendra Pandu remained just as pale as he had been at birth. As the years went by, his skin color changed, but unfortunately not uniformly. He developed large patches of pink and white skin separated by areas that were tinted brown. His eyes were pink. He could not tolerate the glare of the sun, but unlike his brother, he learned to cope with it and could see. Otherwise, just like his brother, he was healthy and grew up to be physically fit."

Devavrata looked at Vyaasa, "There. I have told you of the birth of Vichitravirya's children. That is how far I will go. Now, tell me Amba's secret."

The Vyaasa smiled but only with his lips – his eyes did not and his nose flared a little. "Devavrata, in some ways you are so naïve. Yes, I shall tell you Amba's secret, but I did not imagine that Satyavati's secret, Ambika's secret, and Ambalika's secret were also hidden from you."

"What secrets? You smile. Are you mocking me? I don't care about Satyavati's secrets – she had many. The two girls, Ambika and Ambalika, were innocents who had no secrets from the world."

"No, I am not mocking you," said the Vyaasa, "I wonder... why do you want to know Amba's secret when there are so many other secrets you do not know. If you learned of a new secret, even one about Amba, what can you do with that knowledge? I fear you will not recover from your wound. You may recall the Kavi Sangha's maxim, 'that which does not lead to Action is not

Knowledge'. There is no meaningful action you could take even if you knew all their secrets."

"I don't want to do anything. My father appeared in my dreams last night. I assume everybody has occasional dreams of their parents, so this is not unusual. Dreams are creations of the mind. Who can say with authority that they know how dreams correspond to material things? In the last few days, a particular dream has become constant. In the first dream, my father appeared and told me that I had fifty-six days. I didn't understand. Fifty-six days for what? Father said no more in the dream but vanished. In the next dream, he told me I had fifty-three days. When he showed up yesterday, he said that I had forty days. That is sixteen less than before. Where did my sixteen days go? I've been in bed since I was wounded. Are these sixteen days in bed the ones that are lost and that I no longer have? What will happen when there are no days left? Perhaps I will die. It would certainly be considered a miracle if I survived another forty days. What is the meaning of such a dream? I've seen scholars debate about dreams, but they do not come to any conclusion. Perchance, in forty days, reason will have prevailed and this war will end. Maybe I will be released in forty days completely healed and will stop having these dreams. If it is my father coming to me in a dream, he must think there is something I can do. My task is to determine what that something is."

"In any case, you promised," Devavrata reminded the Vyaasa.

"I will do as I promised,"

"That is the least I expect."

"There is something only you can do in forty days," said the Vyaasa. "Only you can bring the warring parties to the negotiating table."

"I've tried."

"Oh, no! You haven't. Not in the council and not in private. In the council, Karna, Suyodhana, and the rest of that gang shouted you down. But you could have stuck to your points and insisted on an honest negotiation."

"It is over. I do not wish to debate it. Even if that is the meaning of my dreams – what my father wants me to do in forty days. I call out your promise. Tell me Amba's secret. No more diversions."

AMBA'S FLIGHT

"Tell me Amba's secret."

The Vyaasa dropped his eyes and took a deep breath. His shoulders slumped. He did not move. Ten vighatis passed as Lomaharshana and Devavrata watched him. It felt like a long time to Devavrata. Then the Vyaasa raised his head and nodded at Devavrata.

"Devavrata, why can't you see the obvious? You accuse Satyavati of all kinds of plots and dealings, but the biggest plot eludes you."

"Satyavati has plots in her blood. She had been plotting from the day I met her."

"Satyavati has been trying to make amends ever since that day. For much of what she did, she consulted me. She did not always do as I suggested, but I always knew what she would do. Once, only once, she plotted without asking me for advice – that was Amba's disappearance. I was in Takshashila. I would have stopped her, but I could not. Why didn't you, who mistrust her in everything, not think that she might have had something to do with Amba's disappearance?"

"I did consider it but did not see why Satyavati would want to get rid of Amba. Even if she knew that we were lovers and that I had broken my vow, she faced a risk only if a child was born. That possibility itself gave her power over me, for she could denounce me as an oath-breaker. Civil war would be my only option, and she knew that I was averse to that. Why, then, would she want Amba gone?"

"The obvious one. Consider this. Why did you and my sister plot against each other when it would have been so much easier to cooperate? After all, you agreed to split responsibilities after Shantanu died. She handled the internal affairs of the city within

Hastinapura, while you extended it into an empire. What did you think was going to happen when you brought Amba into the arrangement?"

"I would have kept it secret. For if Satyavati found out, she could threaten to disclose it and shame me."

"Because you broke your vow?"

"Yes."

The Vyaasa touched his fingers to his forehead and took a deep breath. Then he laughed. "My friend," he said, "you are a fool."

The Vyaasa continued, "Vows are broken all the time. The tempest caused by that charge would have lasted half a day. No ally would have left your side as a result. Satyavati did the next best thing. She made it appear that you wanted to get rid of her but were incapable of coming to a decision. That made you look weak and kept your potential supporters uncertain. She had not expected that it would be so easy to discredit you. And Amba may have believed that you would do whatever you thought needed to be done, that you would not flinch, because she knew how the name Bhishma had been earned."

Devavrata silently absorbed the revelation. Satyavati had kidnapped Amba and made it seem that the kidnappers were Devavrata's soldiers. *If they did not kill her, what did they do? She must have been pregnant with Shikhandin – how had she managed during that difficult time? Who had helped her? How did Shikhandin end up in Panchala?* The Vyaasa watched him for some time and then said, "Satyavati told me much of this when I returned from Takshashila. Your reaction, though, surprised me."

"What surprised me was that nobody else seemed to be concerned about Amba's disappearance," Devavrata protested.

"That was to be expected. Amba had kept aloof from most people during her stay in Hastinapura. She spent time with her sisters and with Satyavati. You, too, of course. She had left without fanfare saying that she would be visiting her home. It was your reaction that baffled me."

"What about my reaction?"

"You seemed preoccupied and distant. All issues that came up were dealt with efficiently. You did not even talk about Amba's disappearance. You did not do anything about it."

"What I did, I did secretly. I did not want it to be publicized. She was a gift of good fortune to me, and now, like all such gifts, it was taken away."

"I assumed you knew about her pregnancy. I was puzzled that you did not seem concerned about her health. I was puzzled that you did not mourn the child she was carrying. Your child. I was truly puzzled by you."

Devavrata's tried to turn to face the Vyaasa. He regretted it immediately; the movement pressed the arrow deeper and he stopped. He could only turn his head slightly and look sideways at the Vyaasa.

"But the truth is that I did not know."

The Vyaasa leaned closer, his voice a whisper. "You did not know that she was pregnant when she disappeared?"

Devavrata shook his head slightly, "No. I only found out a few days ago during the ambush. How did you learn of it?"

The Vyaasa's eyes narrowed. "You never knew of the pregnancy? I... I cannot believe that."

Devavrata shook his head more vigorously. "I've told you more than once – I just found out a few days ago when I killed Shikhandin. And it was confirmed when Amba tried to kill me. How did you know?"

"Amba's doctor told me. Amba had asked her not to tell Satyavati. But after Amba disappeared, the doctor felt she had to tell somebody responsible. She came to me. I told her to keep it secret until it became necessary to reveal it. I thought you must know as Amba would have told you even if she didn't tell anyone else."

Devavrata closed his eyes. "Go away," he said. "You can tell me the rest later."

The Vyaasa got up slowly. He felt his bones creaking and his joints complaining. He groaned. He gathered the folds of the upper garment and moved towards the entrance. As he stepped through the doorway, he heard a sound from the bed. He turned around a little too quickly and lost his balance. He would have fallen if the Archivist had not stepped forward to hold him up. "Did you say something?" he said.

"Come back and finish telling me what happened to Amba."

"Yes, of course, I will," said the Vyaasa as he returned to his seat.

"Should I memorize this, sir?" said the Archivist, who had been silent all along.

"Yes, yes. You have been listening, haven't you?"

"Yes, sir."

"Devavrata, my friend," said the Vyaasa. "Can I begin now?"

"Yes."

"I used to spend many months in Takshashila. I knew even then that the Kavi Sangha was going to be my life. I came back to Hastinapura once or twice a year. The trip was tedious and took too long. The organizers of caravans had no interest in the affairs of the lands they traversed. It would be some years before I realized how much they knew that was important. They knew the border guards, they knew the officials to go to for various permissions, they knew who could provide protection and who could not, they knew who was predatory and who wasn't, and they knew what could be exchanged where.

"Sorry, I digress. Let me tell you what I found when I returned to Hastinapura after Amba's disappearance.

"Satyavati was in good spirits. She had taken over the care of Amba's sisters. Amba's absence did not seem to have affected anybody. Including you. Satyavati was short when I asked about Amba – she had gone away was all she would say. I could not ask you, for you had made it impossible for anyone to see you except on official business. My status as Satyavati's brother and as someone who took care of her interests allowed me much more access to her attendants. I found that Amba had employed a weaver to help her with clothing appropriate to the city. The weaver became Satyavati's eyes and ears, and now she talked willingly enough to me. She had realized that Amba was pregnant and had reported it to Satyavati.

"I questioned Satyavati about Amba. Her first answer was that Amba had said that she was going on a trip. When I mentioned that Amba had been pregnant, she feigned shock. I then told her that I knew that she had known of the pregnancy. I reminded her that she was my sister, and I would protect her interests. She swore me to secrecy. Amba had been pregnant for maybe two moons. Satyavati had always feared that such a thing would happen. She had to act and she could not wait for my visit to discuss what to do. She had arranged for two men, dressed in the style that you, Devavrata, had established for all your soldiers, to visit Amba with a message from you. In the message, you would ask her to come to your project site, as the work was significantly delayed. To Amba, this would have been good news; it would make their relationship public. Satyavati's spy, one of Amba's maids, had reported on Amba's hope that you were preparing to acknowledge her publicly, thus ending months of secrecy. She hoped that it would include the recognition of her future child's standing in this patriarchal city. She had left the next day with the messengers. Satyavati said that Amba had asked her to take care of her sisters while she was gone. She told her sisters little, just that she was going to meet you.

"The men had been instructed to kill Amba when they were alone and make sure that her body would not be found. That was the first time my sister shocked me; I had not expected such ruthlessness. My shock showed, and she began to cry and explain that she had been afraid. I berated her, and she asked for my forgiveness. I told her that such forgiveness was not mine to give. Then she threw a *vajra*, a lightning bolt. Neither the men nor Amba had returned. Maybe Amba had managed to bribe the men or escape their custody. The men would not return if they failed or abandoned their mission. At any moment, Amba might come back and denounce Satyavati. To prepare for that eventuality, Satyavati was kind and solicitous towards Ambika and Ambalika. When Amba did not send a message that she had arrived safely, the sisters had begun to worry. Satyavati stoked their worries about your intentions. They knew what you were capable of; they had been witness to the Shaka massacre. Satyavati sowed the doubts; your apparent lack of concern convinced them.

"When you returned from the dam site and said that you had not seen Amba or sent for her, they were sure that you were lying. If you were lying, they did not want to deal with you. They avoided you. They felt powerless to denounce you; they were too young. There was no life for them in their band. You then tried to send them to their old settlement – that convinced them that you were trying to hide something. Satyavati was considerate and charming. She was kind and not brusque like you. They had not seen or heard of her torturing anybody as you had done. For the first time, they were told of your oath of celibacy, which they knew you had broken with their sister. That only made you more of a villain. Was it possible that you had arranged to get rid of Amba – maybe not kill her, but make her disappear? Over time, they became reconciled to Amba's absence, to life in the company of Vichitravirya and other children of their age, and finally to marriage.

"Satyavati had made no effort to determine what had happened to the men who had taken Amba away. Any discovery, even if by her initiative, might reveal her role. She asked me to investigate in secret.

"She was my sister, and I was concerned about her state of mind. The impulsive and ruthless plot bothered me. It seemed so unlike her that I investigated the matter personally. I went out into the forest with a Naga guide skilled in the trails and pathways in the forest. We found signs of three overnight camps, suggesting the first three nights of a journey, there was nothing further. At the point where a fourth camp would have been made, there was no evidence of habitation. We traced our way back and at one point, the guide pointed to a trail that some large animal had used that cut across the path. We followed the trail and came across bones. Hidden behind a dense thorny bush was a human skeleton. It had been scraped clean by animals, and two limbs were missing. There was no flesh, nor clothing or any sign to indicate who this had been: a man, a woman, a soldier, a fisherman, a hunter …

"I measured the skeleton carefully – the handspan, the length of the arm from elbow to the tip of the finger, the circumference of the wrist, and so on. It was not a woman. How do I know? The Kavi Sangha has collected information on the sizes of the bones of men and women. We know.

"If it was a man's body, it could not be Amba. It could be one of her guards. I was relieved. We continued to follow the trail and about a hundred hastas further, we came to the banks of the Ganga. It is a fast-flowing and wide river at this point, about ten kros[49] south of Kampilya, the capital of Panchala. The forest vegetation grows almost up to the edge of the riverbank where it gives way to water-loving plants. Elephant grass grew in clumps there. The trail from the skeleton ended at the water's edge. The water was too far below the ground level, so it was an unlikely waterhole for animals. The way the trail jutted into the water suggested a natural or artificial dock for a boat, though long abandoned. To the left, a section of elephant grass had been pulled out of a four hasta-square piece of land about one hasta above the waterline. From there, footprints made by a smallish foot went north along the riverbank. I stepped barefooted next to one of the footprints and made a larger footprint for comparison. It seemed clear that a smaller person made the old prints. If this was Amba's route, it appeared that she had passed this way some weeks ago. North of there, she would sooner or later reach a town with a ferry crossing. She could make a quick escape to the Panchala side of the river and then the road would lead her to Kampilya, the capital city of Hastinapura's enemy. There was no point in chasing Amba this way and she would be long gone, to Panchala if she was lucky. More likely, she had fallen victim to hunger, her own or that of a tiger or a pack of wild dogs.

"Some years later, shortly before I became the Vyaasa, the Kavi Sangha managed to place a few spies in Kampilya, the capital of Panchala. The spies reported to me every six months. In the second year of espionage, we received an applicant to the Kavi Sangha from Kampilya who was a fount of gossip. You know that the best bards are natural memorizers of whatever they hear. This

---

[49] *Kros* is a measure of distance, a little over two miles.

bard in training relayed rumors that the Matriarch of Panchala was unhappy with her brother Drupada because he had brought an outside woman into his palace. Unlike other men, Drupada, also called the King[50] of the Naga band, never went out of the band to find partners. As the King, he could not move to a partner's band; any permanent relationship would require the woman to move in with him, leaving her band. It was generally felt that there must be something wrong with a woman who would leave her band.

"However, that was not the Matriarch's reason for opposing this relationship. The woman's dialect marked her as one of the Nagas from the Hastinapura territories. A year earlier, a Naga band allied with Hastinapura was reported to have fought off invaders from across the Northern Mountains. The invasion had been stopped. There were hints of atrocities committed during the battle. Instead of enhancing the reputation of the band, the victory had led to its collapse when it could not recruit new members. The assumption was that the woman Drupada had taken in was one of the women scarred by that experience. The Matriarch did not want any member of such a band in her town, much less the royal palace. It was said that this woman was so beautiful that Drupada had refused to obey the Matriarch's demand to verify her antecedents. I learned a lot about Panchala and its rulers from that applicant, the gossiping bard. In a traditional Naga band, the matriarch would have the power to enforce her commands, but in Kampilya, the power relation between Matriarch and King had switched. In a deep sense, Panchala and Hastinapura were twins, twin patriarchies-to-be.

"The applicant joined the Kavi Sangha in Hastinapura but stayed in touch with the events and gossip in Kampilya – and I stayed in touch with him. He brought news of Drupada's woman giving birth to a son as well as the ebbing of the feud between the

---

[50] The title for the army chief and the brother of the Matriarch could have been "Senapati" ("Lord of the army"), but that usage mixes the two roles. He may well have been addressed as "Rajan" (meaning "resplendent one"), or "Mahanaga" ("great Naga"), or even "Nagarajan" ("Lord of the Nagas" or "King of the Nagas"). "Nagarajan" could also be interpreted as "King according to Naga practice," i.e., the brother of the matriarch. I have translated all of these possibilities as "King."

Matriarch and the King. The woman lived a quiet and secluded life and did not seem to care that the birth of her son was not recognized by the Matriarch. The Matriarch may have reconciled with the King, but she displayed her anger by not acknowledging the birth of the child. Because the mother was not part of the Matriarch's family, the birth of her son was treated as a non-event and ignored by everybody. The King did not seem particularly distressed. As usual, this was reported and recorded in the Kavi Sangha archives.

"Even then, I suspected that the woman was Amba. I could not go to Kampilya to verify this, nor could I send another senior Kavi Sangha member. I had to rely on Naga students who went home annually. When the boy grew up, he played with the other children in Drupada's palace and in the city. He was sensitive about some things. He could not bear to hear gossip about his mother and would attack the gossiper. Questions about his father made him sad and withdrawn.

"The Kavi Sangha members in Panchala, though few in number, helped me collect more detail about the mystery woman. There is no doubt that she was Amba. I do not know how she did it, but Amba found her way into the protection of the King of Panchala, Hastinapura's enemy. She raised the boy in Drupada's palace. That was Shikhandin, your son. Shikhandin. When the boy grew up, he enlisted in a select group of warriors led by the Panchalan army chief Dhristadyumna, brother of the current Matriarch and nephew of the now-retired senior chief Drupada."[51]

"Shikhandin," said Devavrata. "He behaved differently towards me. Many men feared me, but a few hated me. He was one of the few haters. Why did he attempt to kill me? I had to kill him in self-defense."

The Vyaasa was silent. *What can I possibly say?* he thought. He had wanted to protect his sister, and so he had kept Amba's child

---

[51] Dhristadyumna was the son of Panchala's Matriarch, brother of the Matriarch-to-be, and therefore, the King-to-be in Panchala. As such, he is the formally acknowledged commander of the Pandava forces in the Great War.

a secret from Devavrata. It had seemed like a small thing. But was the loss of Amba the reason that Devavrata became even more *Bhishma* than he had been after the Shaka massacre – opaque, uncommunicative, and difficult to comprehend. It became impossible for Shukla to tell him the truth. Bhishma was a hard shell from which Devavrata only dealt with the business of empire. In the meantime, he, Shukla, had become more involved in the affairs of the Kavi Sangha and embarked on the path to becoming the Vyaasa.

Devavrata also stayed silent in his bed, staring intently at the Vyaasa.

He finally broke the silence. "Tell me something. Why? Why did Shikhandin want his father dead? That is, if I am truly his father."

Shukla said, "I could not meet Amba. I relied on the aspiring Kavi Sangha student for news; his brother was married to one of Amba's maids. According to this maid, Amba expressed hate and contempt for Hastinapura. I think Amba raised Shikhandin to hate Hastinapura and to hate you. He had few friends and revealed little even to the ones closest to him. But it appears that he hated Hastinapura, too. You realize, Devavrata, that for many, many years, you were Hastinapura."

They both fell silent. For a long time, the Vyaasa sat and Devavrata lay still. After a ghati had passed, the Archivist, waiting for Shukla to continue, stood up quietly to stretch his limbs. Devavrata's eyes were closed.

"Sir," said the Archivist, "Sir, are we done for the day?"

That aroused the Vyaasa out of his reverie. "Devavrata," he said. "How were you captured?"

Devavrata did not reply, and his eyes remained closed. The Vyaasa laughed. It was indeed an opportune time to fall asleep, to avoid questions. He stood up and got ready to leave.

As he moved towards the door, Devavrata said, "Shukla, you are not done!"

"You are awake!" said the Vyaasa, "What do you mean not done? What is left to tell you?"

Devavrata said, "You promised to tell me Satyavati's secrets, Ambika and Ambalika's secret."

"It has been so many years. It isn't particularly interesting."

The Archivist said, "Don't we need to make it part of the archive?"

The Vyaasa frowned. The Archivist saw the frown and fell silent.

"Come back and finish this," said Devavrata. "It won't take long – I may know more than you think I do."

THE SECRET OF THE THREE QUEENS

The Vyaasa said, "Do you recall what you were doing when Vichitravirya died?"

"I certainly do," said Devavrata. "How could I forget? We've gone over it all in the last few days – your Archivist has recorded it all."

"Right. I want you to think back to when his sons were born. Do you recall anything odd?"

"Odd? I think the entire situation was odd. Satyavati was as she had always been – difficult and focused on her ambition. The anticipated birth of my nephews allowed me to continue postponing decisions about succession and rule. If I ever became the sole candidate, I would be forced to become King, and my stepmother and I would have to resolve whatever differences we had. Many years had passed since my father's death and the death of Chitrangada. I had ruled as co-Regent twice during those years. Vichitravirya left ruling to me and Satyavati. I had my time with Amba and now faced many more years of co-Regency. But even so, I felt a knot form in my chest when I thought about ruling Hastinapura and fathering children to rule after me. A knot that had been tied by Satyavati, the girl, and pulled tight by Satyavati, my stepmother."

The Vyaasa said, "This is all very true, my friend. But it seems to me that you do not want to know what you've demanded I tell you."

Devavrata replied, "I am afraid of what you will tell me. I must know it, but I would willingly put it off to the day that I die. That day is soon, maybe even today. Maybe it is now. I find that I am still afraid. Most of all, I fear that which you would disclose."

"I don't know how to allay your fears. You must decide for yourself. Your brother Vichitravirya is not the father of Dhritarashtra and Mahendra Pandu. When Vichitravirya died, the inheritance rules applicable to a trading post could have made a complete stranger the leader. Satyavati arranged for the queens to bear the children of a suitable man. I had at first thought she had persuaded you, but it became clear that she had found someone else."

The Vyaasa stopped to see Devavrata's reaction to the revelation. Devavrata was silent for a long time. Then he turned to gaze at his friend. "*Niyoga?* She found a surrogate father? That would have to happen after my brother was dead, wouldn't it?"

"Yes."

"But the Queens were a few weeks pregnant when Vichitravirya died. Are you telling me that it was done when Vichitravirya was still alive?"

"No. The King was dead. The children were conceived after he died."

Devavrata's head spun. He recalled Satyavati telling him that the Queens were a few weeks pregnant. She had lied. *Why had she lied?*

Appendix A.15: Carrots and Fatherhood

Devavrata was mystified by Satyavati's actions and demands when Ambika and Ambalika were pregnant – importing carrot plants, secluding the queens, and demanding that Devavrata spend time with his sisters-in-law seemed to be unreasonable and strange.

The Annals explain what Satyavati was trying to accomplish

"Was his father a descendant of Kuru or of Puru? Was he even sufficiently honorable to take the place of my brother? Can I still believe that I fulfilled the promise to my father?"

"Hmm... I'll let you be the judge of that. Do you recall that we were talking about Dvaipaayana visiting Satyavati with her father?"

"Yes. The elusive Krishna Dvaipaayana. What about him?"

"You know that he was Guru Parashara's son."

Devavrata thought back to the time he had first seen the baby with Satyavati. He said, "Yes, and Satyavati took care of him while Guru Parashara fulfilled his vow of silence."

"Do you know that he might well be a candidate to be the Vyaasa when I pass on."

"Yes, I have heard of his brilliant rise in the Kavi Sangha. Why should it matter to me now?"

"Do you know that his mother was Satyavati?"

Devavrata opened his mouth to say something and then stopped. Instead he started coughing as though his lungs had filled with fluid. The coughing would not stop and the nurse came over and held Devavrata so that the arrow would not accidentally move. Shukla waited. The coughing subsided and then stopped.

Devavrata took a deep breath. Then he said, "No, I did not know. Please do not tell me that everyone else knew. I cannot believe that."

"Don't fret, even your father did not know. Krishna Dvaipaayana may inherit many features of his father, but Parashara had not been seen for some years and people forget."

"So what about him, what about Parashara's son?"

"He took the place of the King and fathered children with the Queens."

Devavrata felt that time had slowed down, and his thoughts strained to emerge as speech. He managed to say, "What?"

Shukla said, "Krishna Dvaipaayana is the father of Dhritarashtra, Mahendra Pandu, and Dharmateja Vidura."

Devavrata said, "You mean... Krishna Dvaipaayana is the grandfather of..." His voice faltered. He continued, "...these cousins... the father of their fathers."

The Vyaasa smiled. "You are indeed a very perceptive man, my friend. You refuse to see beyond the tip of your nose. I am not implying anything, I am asserting it. Satyavati asked her son to father children with the queens Ambika and Ambalika."

"I see."

Devavrata's mind whirled. *Krishna Dvaipaayana was not the one responsible; Satyavati was.* Devavrata wanted to rise from his sick bed and confront Satyavati, who, at a single fear-induced stroke, had created this warped world. For an eternity that lasted a few vighatis, everybody was silent.

Then Devavrata said, "Dhritarashtra and Mahendra Pandu are not Kauravas, not descended from Kuru, not my father's grandchildren."

The various forms of the statement seemed to rush down a waterfall to a sea of conclusions. *They were not my nephews. Their children are not my grandnephews.*

"Yes. Those are logical inferences. They are not Kauravas."

Shukla's statement evoked more inferences. *They were Shukla's grandnephews. These children are Shukla's great-grandnephews.* He felt laughter forming in his throat, a mocking laughter that threatened to displace all thought.

Devavrata needed more time to express those thoughts. Satyavati's actions were in the past, a long time ago. Shukla's relationship was irrelevant to the war. *What should I do now?* He made up his mind.

"I repeat my question: Is their lineage worthy of Hastinapura?"

"Dhritarashtra and Mahendra Pandu are the grandchildren of Parashara."

"That is a glorious heritage, descendants of the great Vasishtha. But their mothers are Nagas of unknown descent."

"Does that matter? Must they be Panchnadis? All you asked earlier was whether their bloodline was noble? You had already approved of the mothers; only the heritage of the father could be in question."

The pieces fell in place like the fragments of a broken pot that had been re-assembled.

Shukla continued, "The Queens had become pregnant after the King's death. Both sons were born over six weeks prematurely. Only Dharmateja Vidura, born in the tenth moon after the death of the King was born at the right time. Satyavati had even arranged for the premature delivery with her shipment of carrots, the elixir of its flowers being an abortifacient. It even explained her concern over ensuring that a Kaurava should influence the babies in the womb. She had made sure that no questions would be raised, even by me, about the legitimacy of the two children!"

Devavrata struggled to focus his mind. I never bothered to find out why Satyavati was attached to the boy Krishna Dvaipaayana. *I just assumed that she was attached to him because she had taken care of him almost from birth.*

Devavrata said, "Did you know it at that time?"

Shukla said, "He is my nephew. I kept quiet when I found out. He was a charming boy, and I was also attached to him."

"I have no problem with his fathering future kings." Devavrata said, "However, I am troubled. I have failed to keep even the small promise I made to my father. Neither Mahendra Pandu nor Dhritarashtra are Kauravas by birth. The empire I have built will pass into non-Kaurava hands."

"That's not true. You have fulfilled your promise."

"No. That's nonsense."

"You recall the oath? Of course, you must. Recite it once more."

"Yes, perfectly. I said, 'I hereby renounce all my rights to have children, and give them to my father. To you, O King, I yield my birthright. O Queen, I will not marry, I will not have children, and I will not make love to any woman. O King, my father, my right to a descendant is yours.'"

"There is more to your oath than that."

THE UNRAVELLING THREAD

There was another long silence. Devavrata went over what he had just heard. Then he did it again. If Dhritarashtra and Mahendra Pandu were Dvaipaayana's children, they were Satyavati's grandchildren. They were her progeny, even if they were not Shantanu's grandchildren. The prediction that Satyavati's descendants would rule an empire had apparently come true. That long-gone day, he had sworn an oath that he would not have any children and would be celibate. Yes, he had already broken the vow of celibacy, but he had been not much more than a child when he had sworn that oath. He knew now that it had been a ridiculous vow. If Shikhandin was indeed his son, he had also broken the promise not to have children.

There was another oath. Before his marriage to Satyavati, his father had come to him. Devavrata replayed that scene in his mind as he contemplated Shukla's words.

Shantanu had said, "My dear son. To you, I owe the happiness to which I am looking forward! I asked a lot of you, and you have given me much, much more than you had to. I had hoped it would be enough, but I have one more request."

Devavrata had struggled to no show emotion in his face – he relaxed his lips, controlled his breathing, and focused his eyes on his father's face, the father who stood in front of him like a supplicant. He said, "You are my father to whom I owe my birth. You are the King, the lord of life and death in Hastinapura, to whom I owe my life. Ask and I shall give it."

Shantanu said, "I fear what will happen to Satyavati if I die prematurely. What will happen to Hastinapura, the legacy that I inherited? I need you to promise that you will take care of both."

Devavrata had closed his eyes in an effort to calm himself. The silence had dragged on for his father. Shantanu construed the science to mean that his son was angry with his stepmother for the oaths she had extracted from him. A few vighatis later, Shantanu said, "Please, son, at least promise that you will take care of Hastinapura and keep it strong and prosperous."

Devavrata had said, "I will swear whatever oaths you wish me to swear. I promise now that I will take care of your wife, my stepmother Satyavati, in case you are unable to. I promise that the prophecy she talked of will come true. As long as I live, I will do all I can to keep Hastinapura safe and its rulers powerful and respected."

That was it. His father had left him alone after that. He had made this oath with the full consciousness of what it meant and with time for deliberation. The vow of celibacy had been made in the heat of the moment; this vow was made with full consciousness, but not, as fate would have it, full understanding. The first vow was made to a weak man and a fickle woman; the second was made to his father alone and to the country that he was building, the empire that Devavrata would create.

Neither Mahendra Pandu nor Dhritarashtra were Kauravas, but they were Satyavati's progeny. By crowning them, he had fulfilled his promise to his father, to fulfil the prophecy that Satyavati would be the mother of many rulers, the only vow he could bring himself to believe in. Or had he? He had taken sides. When the disagreement over policies between Mahendra Pandu and Dhritarashtra became open conflict, he had sided with Dhritarashtra, for Mahendra's proposals threatened his own vision of an imperial city. He had chosen to be neutral between Mahendra's children and Dhritarashtra's children, at least in the beginning. He had only decided to support Suyodhana's claim when Satyavati insisted that the Pandavas, as everybody called them, were adopted or otherwise not Mahendra's own sons, and not descended from her. The evidence seemed compelling. It was commonly believed that albinism such as Mahendra Pandu's was inherited and none of the Pandavas were albino, though Arjuna, Nakula, and Sahadeva were somewhat paler than the two eldest. Yudhishthira's calm demeanor was unlike any Kuru family trait. He reminded Devavrata of Parashara, but Satyavati insisted that Yudhishthira inherited nothing from her or from Shantanu. Meanwhile, Bhīma's dark skin, broad face and nose, and broad shoulders hinted at a Rakshasa origin. If they were Satyavati's grandchildren through her son Krishna, then any Naga features were natural, but the Rakshasa features would require explanation. Was it possible that Satyavati had been justified in requiring that Devavrata provide the Kaurava influence on Ambika and Ambalika when they were pregnant? If he had known that neither branch of the family could claim direct descent from Shantanu, he might not have taken sides in their conflict. He could have refused to support Suyodhana exclusively. Or could he?

It struck him that, being anxious to meet Satyavati's conditions, his father had requested the wrong oath. His father was concerned about *his* descendants through Satyavati. For that matter, if Satyavati had been asked, she would have said the same thing. They wanted him to promise to keep the kingdom safe for *Shantanu's* children *by* Satyavati. That is what he had assumed all along. On the other hand, the words of the oath only mentioned the prophecy that Shukla had quoted. In that case, he had actually lived by his oath. He had protected Hastinapura and created an empire to be ruled by Satyavati's descendants. It was not what he had thought he was doing. Was *this* the purpose of his oaths? The meaning he had assigned to his life slipped out of his grasp every time he examined it.

The right oath would have been far more complex, covering all the contingencies that he had faced in his life. That right oath could never have been formulated for its every condition would have screamed *treachery*. Where in the oath could he have said, your children will inherit except if none of your children live, in which case my children will inherit? Where in the oath could he have said, only children by birth would inherit and not those by adoption or *niyoga*?

Such a vow had not been demanded of him – it had been his own idea. What if he had refused to make any of these vows and, instead declared his feelings for Satyavati. Would his father not have married Satyavati and allowed him to marry her? That was doubtful. Had his father ever guessed what had been sacrificed for him? That was unlikely – his father was not one to bridle his desires. *Yes, I, Devavrata, have committed a sin against my ancestors by not performing my duties to them. Nor have I performed my duties to my own soul, for I have no descendants. I will suffer for it. I expected*

to protect my father's children, and that would have protected him and
his ancestors. The only one to suffer would be me.[52]

Another thought struck him. If neither the Pandavas nor the Kauravas were descended from Shantanu, then he, Devavrata was the sole descendant of the king. Inadvertently, he had killed his son Shikhandin, who would have been his own sole descendant. Here, in this fenced camp-city of the enemies of Hastinapura, the only two legitimate heirs to the Kuru name and fortune lay dying or dead. The descendants of Satyavati and Parashara, Naga and bard, were fighting over an empire that he, a trader and a warrior, had conceived of and built. He had not ruled as king, but he had constructed an edifice that, if duly maintained, would sustain a great empire. Even Indraprastha had only become possible because he had put in place dams and created lakes that controlled the Yamuna upstream. Further downstream, the Yadavas settling down on the banks of the Yamuna were profiting from his creation. Space was being created for the immigrants from the west, from the lands formerly irrigated by the Sarasvati. They were settling in lands all the way from the delta in the south to the northernmost point at Kaalindini where the Sutudri twisted away from her innumerable children. With the aid of Hastinapura and the Kauravas, these refugees would lay claim to the triangle of land between the Ganga and the Yamuna.

The crisis was not past. Crises, he corrected himself, not just a single crisis. When you suppress one crisis, another is born elsewhere. The Pandava-Panchala-Yadava alliance would last only as long as the rivers were good fences.

Devavrata frowned – a fog was enveloping his thoughts, and he could not disperse it. This obsessive recalling of the events of his life was a foolish old man's indulgence. Dying would be preferable to this unremitting torture, but every time he moved down on the arrow, the explosive needles of pain made him choke, and his body betrayed him by shifting to relieve the

---

[52] In Hindu belief, a person who dies without descendants has committed a sin against his or her ancestors. Some variant of this belief can be seen in many religions, major ones as well as religions of small communities.

pressure. *Even on my deathbed,* he thought, *my ancestors refuse to take me back.*

The Archivist's voice cut through the fog.

THE DEATH OF SHIKHANDIN

An Error of Judgment

The Archivist said, "Sir, you've been silent for a ghati. Are you feeling well?"

Devavrata heard the urgency in the voice. It pulled him away from the emotionally draining morass of morbid thoughts. He could take pride in the empire he had created – what matter who ruled it? Rulers were all the same, whether arrogant like Suyodhana or courteous like Yudhishthira. *A ghati? Had it really been that long?*

Devavrata said, "Where's Shukla?"

The Archivist, who was the only other person present, said, "He'll be back, sir. He had to leave for a short while."

"What do you think, Lomaharshana? You've heard so much from so many different people. What do you think of all that has happened?"

The Archivist said, "Sir, I am merely the memorizer of people's stories. My opinions do not matter."

"Please. I will not insist, but I am at the end of my life. Indulge me."

"Sire, it is an honor to be asked for my opinion."

"Be truthful and nothing else.

"Certainly, sir. I must qualify my opinions, for what I have heard is complex. I have not arrived at a full understanding, the kind of deep familiarity that will allow me to reorganize it as a poem to be recited."

"That I know. At one time, I had wanted to be a memorizer like you."

"You flatter me, sir. Thank you. May I ask a question?"

"Ask away. You have earned the right to ask. I will answer if I can."

"It is a question that has bothered me for some time."

"Go ahead."

Lomaharshana the Archivist said, "Sire, you were asked a question you did not answer. I think you evaded it. It is this: How did a senior commander in the Kaurava army get captured in an ambush?"

Devavrata took a deep breath, "Overconfidence and stupidity, of course. Do you want to make it part of this story?"

"Yes, sir."

THE PLAN TO END THE WAR

Devavrata said, "A man came to Hastinapura. He said he was from Panchala. He wanted to speak to the high command of the Kaurava army.

"The man was Shi... Shi... Shikhandin... Even saying his name hurts. I did not know then what I know now, but I trusted him. He must have reminded me of Amba. That is why I think of her now. She was justified in trying to kill me. I wish she had succeeded.

"The man – he – Shi... Shi...khandin – he said he was a Krivi, the smallest clan in the Panchala confederation. He was authorized to make an offer that might end the war, and even if it did not, it would greatly weaken our enemy. The council held a meeting in secret – not in the King's court, but in a war room in my house that had no windows and walls thickened with extra branches and an extra layer of mud to protect against eavesdroppers. These were the rooms in which I met spies and secret agents. Though protected against outsiders, these rooms had hidden entrances and secret hiding places for my own eavesdroppers. I arranged for a throne to be brought in. The King must look like a King, even to a traitor like this man. Such details are important. All the servants had been sent away and only two of my trusted guards were present. Kutaja Drona, Suyodhana, Karna, Dharmateja Vidura, and Kripa[53] came. The blind Dhritarashtra came, accompanied by the bard Sanjaya, and I seated him on the throne.

"The man was explicit. His clan did not want to go down the path of war and conquest. Four of the five clans that made up the Panchala confederation did not want this war. They would prefer to trade, not make war. He had been sent by the leaders of his clan to see if peace could be negotiated. He said, 'I can set up a meeting. One senior councilor from each of the four clans will attend. Are you interested? Can you send a senior counselor who will negotiate on your behalf?'

"Dhritarashtra smiled when he heard this. 'I have nothing but goodwill for my brother's children. Are they in agreement?'

"The man looked confused. Suyodhana rolled his eyes. 'Father,' he said, 'Perhaps you should only listen and not speak. My cousins rely on the Somakas, the leading clan of Panchala. Their wife Krishnaa Agnijyotsna is the Matriarch of Panchala. Her brother Dhristadyumna commands the joint Pandava-Panchalan army. This will take away almost half their army.'

"Turning to the man he said, 'That is so, isn't it? The Somakas are the fifth clan, and they are the ones who seek war.'

"The man said, 'The Somakas are the leading clan, the *first* clan. My clan, the Krivi, along with the Srinjayas, the Turvashas, and the Keshins want this war stopped.'

---

[53] *Kripa* is Kutaja Drona's brother-in-law and skilled in martial arts. He and his sister, *Kripi*, were abandoned in the forest as babies, found by Shantanu, and raised in the palace.

"Karna said, 'If that is the case, why not just stop it? Surely, the four clans are the larger part of Panchala. You do not need to parlay with us if you wish to stop the war. Take your troops and go home.'

"The man gave a thin smile that did not change his face. 'It is not so simple, sir,' he said. 'The five clans have been allied for almost twenty generations. Begun as an alliance of equals, it changed ten generations ago to the present one in which the Somaka are the foremost. The Matriarch's family is Somaka. When she dies, the new Matriarch will not be from a different clan as was agreed upon. Instead, the Somaka imposed a new agreement that the Matriarch's daughter will be the successor. The Somaka control the army; the army controls the cities; the cities oversee the bands. It has been many years since we attempted a rebellion. The last time we did, our senior-most captains were arrested for treason and killed before they could make a single move.'

"'So, what is different now?'

"'The old king Drupada died. You know the events that led to the assault on the person of the young Matriarch Agnijyotsna, who has taken the Pandavas as husbands. Her brother, the new Somaka king, Dhristadyumna, sees an opportunity to avenge his sister and to create an empire centered on Panchala. He has taken most of his army into the field and is not in our capital city Kampilya. Our reserve forces can take over Kampilya and hold it for a couple of weeks until your forces reach there. Not much longer, for our forces are weaker than the King's. But we can hold him off just long enough. We are not as naïve as we once were. Members of our clans marching with the main army will leave it as soon as news of the takeover is announced.'

"'Kampilya will be ours?'

"'Yes.'

"'We will control both banks of the Ganga?'

"'Yes.'

"Suyodhana's eyes had lit up and he was smiling. He slapped Karna on the back.

"Suyodhana said, 'We will have the Pandavas and their wife serve us as slaves yet!'

"Dhritarashtra spoke, 'Son, I …'

"'Shut up, Father!'

"'Son, you…'

"'I said, shut up, didn't I? You have a soft spot for these supposed Pandava cousins. Last time, instead of sending them on their way as fraudulent pretenders, you gave them Indraprastha. See what chaos that caused.'

"Kutaja Drona said, 'Controlling both banks of the Ganga is a desirable goal. It can only be achieved at the cost of much blood. Capturing Kampilya by subversion is much cheaper. This proposal is worth considering.'

"Karna was infected by his friend's enthusiasm. 'Of course it is worth considering, oh great guru of strategy. We are glad that you have expressed your opinion.'

"Dharmateja Vidura spoke. Despite his low birth, I had brought him into the war council. He usually suggested a peaceful path when addressing a problem. He would have been an excellent trader. As it was, he brought the common man's sensibility to our discussions. I wish we heeded the advice he gave that day.

"'What do we have to do to get this alliance going?' Vidura asked.

"'Yes,' said Suyodhana to the Krivi man, 'What exactly are you proposing?'

"The man's face brightened.

"'Four senior leaders, one from each clan, are awaiting an emissary from you. I can take him to a meeting point, about three to four days from here. It is a crossing on the Ganga.'

"'There are a thousand crossings on the Ganga, none of them in use since the war began.'

"'I know the one where they are waiting and will lead you there.'"

"Suyodhana said, 'We can avenge the humiliation of Samvarana.'

"Samvarana had not exacted revenge for the trouble that Panchala had caused him. Avenging Samvarana was an impossible-to-scratch itch on the Kuru psyche, one that afflicted Suyodhana the most. Kampilya had to be captured and its rulers killed, its population enslaved or driven into exile.

"Suyodhana said, 'Kampilya will be delivered to us on a platter.'

"Kutaja Drona said, 'Whom can we send?'

"The man said, 'Anyone at your level would be senior enough to negotiate a peace.'

"Suyodhana's smile vanished. 'One of us? From this council.'

"The man said, 'Yes, sir. Any of the war leaders would be welcome.'

"'What kind of a joke is this?'

"'Sir, it is no joke. Whomever you send has to be able to create a workable agreement. He should be somebody who understands the strategic issues involved in making this alliance work. He should know your own military capabilities well.'

"Kutaja Drona said, 'We need to discuss this. Sanjaya, please escort him to the special guest room. Bring him back in a ghati or so. He can wait there.'

"Sanjaya took the man to the second war room located on the other side of my house. Like the first room, it was specially constructed to be secure. Back in our meeting, Devavrata, Kutaja Drona, Suyodhana, Karna, and even Dharmateja Vidura who was usually quiet, started talking at the same time. They all stopped. In Panchnad councils, there was a strict sequence in which members were expected to speak.

"Karna said, 'I like it. We can push them back into the jungle where they came from. The cost to us? Nothing.'

"Dharmateja Vidura said, 'He made a good point about trade. This war has slowed commercial activity in all the settlements.

We should never have attacked Indraprastha. Instead, we should have proposed an alliance to control the entire land from the headwaters of the Ganga and Yamuna to Laghu Nagapura.'

"Suyodhana's upper body was shaking. If we had been standing, he might have attacked Dharmateja Vidura. But we were all seated on our assigned mats, and only the King Dhritarashtra was seated on his throne, which was a stool set on a raised platform. Suyodhana's voice rose, and he stared at Dharmateja Vidura as he said, 'Will you stop telling me about trade? We are not traders! You are the son of a servant. Your mind is forever stuck in pettifogging details. I am not going to control the two banks by trade. My army will control the banks. We will show the Nagas our power; they will obey us. I will brook no talk of compromising with my so-called cousins. We've defeated them before; we'll defeat them again.' By the end of this speech, he was shouting.

"Dharmateja Vidura's face did not change. I admire his ability to give advice calmly and show no reaction whether the advice is accepted or rejected. He merits the name *Vidura* that has been bestowed on him. Somehow, through his detachment, he developed wisdom.

"The rest of us pretended to ignore the break in protocol and looked at Kutaja.

"Kutaja Drona said, 'We should consider this development. Any disaffection that the people of the enemy have with their leaders should be exploited. An independent Panchala will always be our enemy; a puppet ruler dependent on us is the best kind of ruler.'

"Now it was Suyodhana's turn, but he sat and glowered at us and said nothing. He had said all he wanted to say and we could go along with him, if we wanted to, but he had decided what he wanted to do.

"Dhritarashtra said, 'Can we help my brother's children out in a small way? My brother appeared in a dream last night and asked me to end this war.'

"Suyodhana rolled his eyes and muttered to himself. I could only make out the words 'Stupid old man.' Then he glared at his father.

"Dhritarashtra sensed his son's scorn, and the throne appeared to grow bigger around him as he cringed. He continued, 'Of course, we cannot let them hurt or exploit us in any way. Suyodhana, dear boy, you must decide that.'

"'Father, shut up!' Suyodhana said. Dhritarashtra sank into the ever-growing throne.

"Nobody said anything. I was embarrassed. I can only guess what the others thought.

"Then it was my turn, and they all turned to look at me. Vidura looked at me and nodded towards his nephew, hinting that only I could control Suyodhana now and bring the discussion back to the matter at hand. That was when I made a mistake – I made the wrong decision.

"My excuse for my error is that the last thing I expected was treachery. I can only ascribe it to Shi...Shi...Shi... the man's features must have reminded me of Amba. In my defense, I should say that nobody expected treachery, Suyodhana included.

"'This is an opportunity to win the war at little cost,' I said. 'We should follow up.'

"Now that first opinions had been expressed, the discussion began. Kutaja Drona picked up on my proposal. 'Whom can we send? It will have to be somebody who can assess these traitors. Are they serious? Are they strong enough? Will they stay committed? Will they double-cross us, either by plan or in the heat of battle?'

"Dharmateja Vidura asked the important question. He said, 'What do we want from this meeting? Do we want to end this war?'

"Suyodhana did not disguise his attitude. 'It doesn't matter what we agree to. Once we have Kampilya, the Nagas will pay for their intransigence and the insult to Samvarana.'

"Dharmateja Vidura said, 'One should not negotiate in bad faith.'

"'I do not care for your moralizing, old man. Just stop it.'

"Kutaja Drona continued pressing the issue he thought was pre-eminent, 'You still need to send somebody. Who?'

"Karna spoke up. 'Let's send our wisest. Send Dharmateja Vidura. He is expendable. And, he can prove that he is indeed wisest, by bringing us victory.'

"Suyodhana smiled. 'Yes! Dharmateja Vidura it is.'

"I objected. Dharmateja Vidura was the son of a maidservant. He was not a warrior. He was on this council because I put him here many years ago. Suyodhana did not want to confront me directly, so he had not taken his uncle off the council. Everybody knew that Dharmateja Vidura, however wise, would not be a credible negotiator in military matters.

"Suyodhana refused to consider anybody else. He turned to me. 'I want you to take this proposal to the man. Let him propose somebody else. You tell them that Dharmateja Vidura is your nominee.'

"Dhritarashtra said, 'That is an excellent idea. Yes, Uncle Devavrata, please do as King Suyodhana says.'

"I could oppose Suyodhana, but not his father, the King even if uncrowned. Especially if that father was being browbeaten by his arrogant son, I still owed him that measure of respect.

"I went to the room where the man waited and presented the proposal. He shook his head slowly when I mentioned Dharmateja Vidura. 'Sir,' he said, 'Lord Dharmateja Vidura may be the King's half-brother, but his mother was a concubine. He has never been a warrior. How can you make such a suggestion? It tells me that you are not considering our offer seriously. Are we to be treated as children playing with a ball?'

"'The King's council has asked you to counter with your own proposal if you wish.'

"'It is not my place to advise your high command. The martial arts teacher Kutaja Drona, or somebody else with his credibility, would be acceptable.'

"While I was gone, Suyodhana and Karna had revised their opinion of the offer. The successful siege of Indraprastha had emboldened Suyodhana and all his brothers. Now Karna and he thirsted for more battle and greater successes. Instead of a heroic victory over their enemies, and in particular over Panchala, this proposal would corrupt their victory.

"I returned to the council. I said, 'Dharmateja Vidura is not acceptable. My recommendation is to take his offer seriously. His clan's leaders want trade not war. The man has been sent to negotiate peace, and they offer a path to it.'

"The rest of the council did not share Suyodhana's belief in the inevitability of victory. The result was an impasse, and Dhritarashtra wavered between giving in to his son and accepting the advice of the council. Dhritarashtra said, 'Uncle, you have the greatest experience of war and strategy. At the same time, my son has shown his mettle and knowledge of tactics by winning a great victory. What is the right balance between strategy and tactics? What should we do that maintains the greatest freedom of action?'

"Suyodhana groaned. He said, 'Father, you have never taken part in a war. Without any experience of either tactics or strategy in war, you are spouting theory. There is no need to think about strategy. After we win, we will raze Kampilya to the ground and erase all knowledge of Panchala. That is our strategy. As far as tactics are concerned, we do not need this man's help.'

"Dhritarashtra shrank even further into his seat. I felt sorry for him. I said, 'Whatever your strategy might be, you cannot ignore any tactical advantage, however small. I have met the man in private and my opinion has not changed. There is benefit in his proposal. There is risk as well.

"'Kutaja Drona is our arms-master and war strategist. I rate him more valuable than myself. We cannot send him as an emissary. If we cannot agree on any other emissary, we should get whatever advantage we can out of his presence here. But, that is not my recommendation.'

"I continued, 'We must suggest another name.'

"Suyodhana and Karna went into a huddle, ignoring the rest of the council and me. They looked up smiling broadly, and Karna said, 'The King's father has a companion: Sanjaya. He has the ear of the King's father. Who has greater authority to command the King than his father? Not only that, Sanjaya has claimed for many years that he can see activities from a distance. He will be safe from any kind of trap for he will not fall into it.'

"With each reference by Karna to Suyodhana as King, Suyodhana's smile grew wider and wider. Dhritarashtra's face had darkened, and his eyes were downcast. Suyodhana had taken over the role in public, but until this day, Karna and Suyodhana's brothers had maintained the fiction that Dhritarashtra was the King. That bastion had fallen now.

"Sanjaya accompanied Dhritarashtra everywhere and was sitting behind Dhritarashtra at this time. He looked alarmed. Then he said, 'Sir, I do not claim to see at a distance – I am not a god. I have created a *yantra*, a tool that allows me to watch from a distance. If you wish, I can show it to you and explain it as well.'

"On hearing Sanjaya's words, Suyodhana and Karna sniggered and laughed. They were being impolite and insulting to their own proposed envoy, a close friend and companion of Suyodhana's father. Sanjaya had been a member of the Kavi Sangha who had left when he failed to advance. He was not good at memorizing, his diction was poor, and he was a poor wordsmith. He could not, or refused to, create the archival and historical poetry that was the Kavi Sangha's reason for being. The Kavi Sangha does not expel anyone who had been through its school; underachieving students leave of their own accord and that is what Sanjaya had done. He had become friends with Dhritarashtra and had stayed a loyal friend as the King aged and allowed his son to arrogate royal powers to himself. As Dhritarashtra became more and more of a figurehead, his erstwhile friends abandoned him and finally he was left with Sanjaya. Sanjaya had nothing to gain and nothing to lose from the war. He was not a warrior; he was not a trader.

He cared neither for power nor for wealth. He had no family –
ergo, he was expendable. Nobody listened to him.

"It was not a proposal; it was an insult. Despite that, the council
agreed, while Dhritarashtra said not a word. I was directed to
negotiate with the man again. I did as I was directed and took the
proposal back to the man. He rejected it.

"Despite his discouragement, the man was not ready to give up.
He tried once more, asking for Karna. I was in favor as were
Kutaja Drona and Dharmateja Vidura. This time, Suyodhana
rejected it. 'Karna is my right arm,' he said. 'It is a ridiculous idea
that we will send a warrior from the council. Tell him I refuse.
Ask him to choose somebody lower down the hierarchy – even
one of my brothers, perhaps.'

"I stood up. I said, 'I see no path to agreement. I will send him
back.' I turned to leave the room and could hear Suyodhana and
Karna still sniggering. When I was at the entrance, Suyodhana
said, 'Uncle! Listen to me.' I turned to face him – he was smiling,
a crooked slant to his lips and a sparkle in his eyes. He gave Karna
a sidelong glance and said, 'If you think it is such a good
proposition, why don't you go!' Karna laughed at the suggestion
and slapped Suyodhana's back, saying, 'You are indeed a genius.'

"I was disheartened. I carried the refusal back to the man. In his
turn, he was disappointed and depressed. His disappointment
tugged at my heart. I know now why I was so accepting of this
man – he had reminded me of Amba and so I was willing to trust
him. I recalled past occasions when Karna, Suyodhana's closest
friend, had expressed his opinion of me, 'At his age, he will be
useless in battle.' Kutaja Drona would defend me, saying, 'At his
age, he is priceless in war.' The distinction was lost on Suyodhana.
My counsel was not wanted, and I felt that I could be most
effective if I ended this war. At my age, this was the most I could
hope to do. I made my decision.

THE AMBUSH

Devavrata remembered the fateful moment, "I told the man, 'I
can come.' I had credibility with the council, even when they
voted against me. I could converse with all the elders of the

family. My strategic competence was not in question. If I came back with an agreement, it would be one beneficial to Hastinapura, and Suyodhana would not be able to reject it.

"The man considered my proposal. I don't know what I would have done if he had rejected it. The man said, 'Sir, you are certainly the most senior member of the council. However, it is generally known that you and Suyodhana frequently clash in the council. Will an agreement you make be acceptable to Suyodhana and his brothers?'

"Even though the man said he doubted that I could be an effective envoy, his attitude changed. His demeanor had changed from a gloomy slump to an erect stance, almost a bounce. His eyes lit up with hope.

"I said, 'I am the most senior commander of Hastinapura's forces. I have credibility.'

"'Yes, you'll do,' he said, looking at me as though I were a bird brought down by an arrow, ready to be cooked for a meal. 'I'll take you to the meeting place.'

"He then laid down some rules. 'We will go by ourselves. The meeting place is on the right bank, the Hastinapura side of the Ganga. The four senior leaders of the Panchala clans will come there to meet us. It will take a few days to get there.'

"I said, 'I am not young. I cannot walk at a military pace or carry my own supplies. If we are going into the forest for more than one day, we will need a cart or carriers. Unless, you can carry all we need.'

"He frowned at me. He must have expected a much simpler expedition. He did not seem to have considered the logistics of this conclave.

"'It will be about three days. We will be on the King's Path for much of the way and you can rest in one of the many peddlers' huts along that highway.'

"'I set up those huts, but nobody has been maintaining them during the war. They will be rundown, if not destroyed.'

"'Good!' he said. 'We will not encounter anybody in one of them.'

"'Can you carry supplies for three days? We will need to share sentry duty at night, for there are wolves and tigers in the forest.'

"The lines around his mouth deepened. It reminded me of something, but I could not make the connection. Now I know – Amba had the same lines on her face when she disapproved of something.

"'I cannot take a wedding party to the meeting site!'

"'How are your negotiators coming?'

"'All they have to do is cross the river at a point across from the meeting spot. Not more than one ghati to cross and another to return. They will only be exposed to watchers for a short time.'

"That did not tell me anything about the location. Between Hastinapura and Kampilya, there are thousands of river crossings. Only some were ever put to use, mostly for trading, but even that had stopped. These days all the crossings have been abandoned.

"'We'll take a cart, an onager, and two helpers. We will use the peddler's huts – it is even better if they are rundown as nobody else will be using them,' he said. 'On the last night, we will camp half a kros from the meeting point. We will leave our helpers at the campsite and head out by ourselves. We will plan to arrive a little before noon. I expect the ferry will cross at noon exactly. If all goes well, the meeting will only last one or two ghatis. We will then return and spend the night at the same campsite.'

"That is what we did. For three days, we walked in the forest along a path that the man seemed to know. The cart carried their supplies. They walked when they could to conserve the onager's strength. At the end of the third day, the man, who had been tense all along, was relaxed. He had been concerned that we would be late, but seemingly we were not. We were a short distance from the river, and that morning, all of us took the opportunity to bathe in the cool water. Then the guards replenished our water supply and fed and scrubbed the onager. I waited. In the middle of the morning, the man said to me, 'It is time to go by ourselves. We are only a short distance from the meeting place.'

"My guards looked at me for orders. We had prepared for the eventuality that I would be separated from them, so they knew what to do. I said to the men, 'You will wait here. I do not expect to be back until evening. Set up the tents before the evening so that we can spend the night here.'

"The man said, 'There is no need for that. If all goes well, we will be back by early afternoon.'

"I put on my armor and tied a scabbard for my short sword at my right hip. On the left hip, I tied a small quiver with a few arrows. Armor and swords do not make for easy travel through these forests. The man laughed and said, 'There is no reason for these precautions. See, I am unarmed. So will everybody else be.'

"I look back and think that, under normal circumstances, every one of these statements from the man would have aroused my suspicions. The circumstances were not normal, and I continued to be blinded by the unconsciously seen glimpses of Amba in the stranger.

"The guards set to doing what they had been told to do while the man and I left for the meeting. We walked cautiously for about six ghatis. The sun had not yet reached the zenith when the man raised his hand and we stopped. We were at the edge of a clearing. From the absence of tall trees and a uniform growth of small trees, I guessed that it had lain fallow for a year or two at the most. A Naga band must have lived there, for a large thatched hut still stood there. These huts deteriorate slowly, but this one appeared to be in good condition with an intact roof and fresh mud daubed on the walls. The hut must have been maintained even after the band had left. We headed for it.

"The ground was very dry, and twigs cracked underfoot as we walked on a path through the new growth. I felt uneasy. But there was no reason to suspect anything. I took the precaution of loosening my scabbard so that the sword would pull out easily. The man did not notice my action. I thought I heard a twig cracking somewhere a little further away, not under our feet. I had arranged with my guards that one of them would follow us.

They were experienced trackers and would not have made a noise. But the possibility that it was my own guard led me to down-play it. There was no way to unsling my bow from my back without alerting the man, so I relied on my short sword.

"The man, who had been cautious about making noise up to this point, walked as though the need for caution was over. I tried to stay cautious. The man glanced at me and smiled. He said, 'We are at the meeting point. We appear to be early; they will come at noon. You can relax.'

"I said, 'Maybe. Will you be careful and alert, even if you think it is safe?'

"He shrugged and said, 'As you wish.' He was still smiling. We had been together for three days and I had seen his smile before, but not the smile that now appeared on his face.

"He was still smiling as he slowed down, and it was a fortunate thing. Just as we entered the hut, a branch shook slightly to the right of the hut. But when I turned, I saw nothing. The hut was empty, so I turned around and backed into it, watching the clearing.

"As a result, I saw what I would not have seen otherwise. Right in front of me, across the clearing, an armed man moved from behind one tree to the cover of another. To the right and left of the tent I heard something that sounded like an animal moving through the brush. We were early, and Shikhandin had said his negotiators would be here at noon, not for another ghati or more. This was a trap. There were no talks to be held on an impossible future peace.

"I had to deal with the man right away, not when the trap had closed. I turned around to face him, and drew my sword from its scabbard. Shikhandin – I can pronounce his name now – had entered the hut a few steps ahead of me, expecting me to follow behind him. He began to turn to the right to face me when he heard the sword being drawn. He was too slow, and I did not give him any time. I lunged at his back and drove the sword through his chest. It was a fatal blow for it went in the right side of his body and pierced his lung. Fortunately, it did not reach the heart. He would die a slow death. He fell towards me. When I was younger, I would have sidestepped the dying body. But these days, I am not fast enough and I only managed to catch him as he fell.

"I intended to use him as a shield if anybody entered through the door of the hut. He lay gasping in my arms, his one good lung trying to keep him alive. I wanted to know who would be leading the ambush, but a gold chain that I had noticed around his neck was constricting his throat. I loosened the chain and found that it was attached to a pendant. I glanced at the pendant as I pulled the chain free.

"The tent seemed to glow with a bright light. I felt as if I was in a field after the first monsoon rains when the earth sings with joy at the sight of the sun. Amba. Amba? Amba! Amba had chosen to re-enter my life at an inopportune moment.

"'Where did you get this?' I said. Shikhandin answered. He was dying, and there were so many things he could have thought about. But he answered my question.

"'From my mother,' Shikhandin said, sucking air with every breath.

"'Where did she get it?'

"'From my father.'

Impossible! That was impossible. I had to know who his father was.

"'Who is your father? Where is he?'

"The man took another deep breath, but it was not enough. He would be losing consciousness soon. *He had to answer my questions.* I had many unanswered questions. *Was Amba dead? Had she been killed in the forest and her jewelry scattered among thieves? Or was she alive?* There could not be another pendant like it. We had designed it together, the motif of a lotus with two snakes wrapped around its stem. I put one hand over the wound to prevent the air from escaping his shattered lung. It may have helped, for with his next breath he said, 'I don't know.'

"I groaned. What did that mean? That he did not know his father? Not know where he was? What did he mean?

"Then he said, 'Hastinapura.'

"That was when I noticed what I had missed all these days when he had worked to build my trust in him. His eyes, the shape of Amba's eyes; his lips and nose like my father's; his hands, large with shaped nails, also like my father's; his stance with the tilt of the head with which Amba expressed puzzlement. *Was it these familiar features that had made me trust a supposed renegade from Panchala?*

"'Who is your mother?' I asked, though I knew the answer.

Did he say *Amba*, or did I imagine it? If he said *Amma*, wouldn't it sound like *Amba*? That was the last question he answered before he closed his eyes and lost consciousness.

"It is possible that if I had not wasted time with that question and its answer, I would have been prepared for the ambushers. Unfortunately, he had delayed me enough. I had planned to use him as a shield, but I had not moved his body around when I saw movement at the periphery of my vision. There was a sword by my left hand, and I reached for it. I recognized Arjuna, the Pandava, and Krishna, the Yadava, entering the hut. Arjuna's bow was drawn and ready. It seemed to me that time slowed at that moment.

"In my mind, the scene is played out on a stage. I reach out with my left hand for the sword, but even before I can touch it, an arrow, moving, oh, so slowly, has cut through the seam of my front and back armor pads under my left armpit. I pick up the sword but the pain is intense. I gasp. I command my mind to ignore the pain, but there is no strength in my arm as my breath leaves my body. I stand up with the sword dragging in front of me, the first time a sword has felt like a burden. I let it drop. This scene plays itself out repeatedly, in an endless cycle.

"Arjuna and Krishna held their bows ready but kept their distance. Some part of me could not understand. *You can come closer*, I tried to say. Pain radiated from the wound. Breathing intensified the pain. I reached around the front of my body with my right hand and could just barely reach the shaft of the arrow. I wanted to pull it out, but my hold was very weak. Even then, any movement of the arrow worsened the pain. I must have fainted. The next thing I knew, I was tied to the bed here, with my son Shikhandin's body at my side for me to contemplate. My first thought on regaining consciousness was, 'I have found Amba!'"

The Archivist was quiet after that. Devavrata and he contemplated each other. *If I had become a memorizer, I would have been like him,* Devavrata thought.

The Archivist turned his head for he did not want Devavrata to see the tears in his eyes. *A long life with so much power and he pines for a lost love.*

The door flap was pulled aside, and the Vyaasa came in.

"Let us break for the day," he said, taking in at a glance the emotional exhaustion of the two men. "Tomorrow we can get to the next generation."

END OF BOOK 1

APPENDICES

A. ANNALS OF THE KAVI SANGHA

BACKGROUND: THE FLOODS OF HASTINAPURA

Thirty-six years after the Great War was over and all of its primary participants had passed on, the King Parikshit, son of Abhimanyu, grandson of Arjuna, Emperor of Hastinapura, proclaimed the beginning of a new Yuga. This was to be the Fourth Age of humanity on earth. Despite all the predictions that the Fourth Age would be an age of strife marked by war, Parikshit proclaimed that the peace achieved by Hastinapura was eternal and whatever happened in the rest of the world, Jambudvipa and Bhaaratavarsha would be a center of peace. Parikshit's era has come to be called the "Kali Yuga", the era of Kali, and the Kali Yuga has been all it was predicted to be. Throughout this period, the Kavi Sangha has maintained its oral archives. Hastinapura fell and was replaced as the imperial capital by Mathura of the Yadavas. Then Mathura was superseded by Pataliputra of the Rakshasas, who called their land Magadha. Still, the archives remained housed in Hastinapura, maintained by the bards of the Kavi Sangha.

One thousand and two hundred years had passed, and Hastinapura suffered another crisis. A flood destroyed the city, killing most of the kavis, and the oral archives were in danger of being lost. The Vyaasa Vaishampaayana, the head of the Kavi Sangha at that time, initiated a project to write down the oral archives.

In addition to stories with heroes and heroines and gods and goddesses, these archives contain information of interest to historians. The answers to Yudhishthira's questions given in this novel fall in this category. These questions and answers are rarely recited in public, but they are an important piece of the archives.

Below are excerpts from the Annals of the Kavi Sangha that were responses to King Yudhishthira's questions. They were committed to writing after the Great Flood of 1201 Kali Era under the direction of the Vyaasa Vaishampaayana with the help of Bhargava the Kambhoja trader and his son Chandrasekhara.

A.1.   A Trader's Education

A trader is a glorified peddler selling goods to faraway cultures on behalf of manufacturers and merchants. A peddler within a culture travels in a cycle of six to nine months – a trader plans a cycle that might last two or more years. A peddler brings back goods to sell at home – the trader also takes orders from buyers for items and quantities and promise delivery. The trader may be trusted to negotiate exchange offers from foreign sellers. A peddler travels alone and must be constantly on the alert – he listens well, speaks little, remembers everything – well, not as much as bards, but still almost everything. The careful peddler makes friends who travel with him or who host him – that is how a peddler becomes a merchant. He makes friends along his route, who will receive him and help him on the next step. He may marry a local woman and establishes a household that supports him when he visits. A merchant welcome in every destination along a well-worn path becomes the leader of a caravan for a trading family. The families that support him are also trading families. These families build up links with each other and often consider themselves a single family even if they speak a different language, follow different customs, eat different foods, bow to different gods, and perform different rituals.

Some members of a trading family choose to stay and distribute the imports as peddlers in local markets. Some, usually loners, become explorers who travel to strange lands looking for new products. In the course of time, some of the traders become leaders of caravans – their extended families will help them put together syndicates of manufacturers and sellers and buyers at every stop.

Considering all this, the training for a trader, at least in the first year, is not that different from the training for bards. For instance, both traders and bards learn to memorize long lists. A trader trainee or apprentice might be asked to recall a manifest of objects for trade such as a lapis lazuli necklace, a choker of pearls, earrings of copper and tin, gold ornaments for the nose, a pendant for the forehead, a jar of unguent for the lips, a whitening cream for teeth, rings for the fingers and toes. A second list might be the directions for a trip of two months with choices to be made every day and distances to be travelled. A third list would be a list of people's names that is then expanded to include how they relate to each other. The difference is that bards are trained with a much wider variety of memorisation tasks while traders focus on the marketplace. For instance, a good trader will learn many languages and customs, while bards develop their skills in the customs, and language or dialect of one city.

A.2.   THE FOUR AGES OF THE WORLD

Yudhishthira said, "What did people believe about the state of the world, in particular, the belief that we are on the brink of a Fourth Age of extreme evil, that the transition from one age to the next would be calamitous and traumatic, and that all humanity would be destroyed at the end of the Fourth Age. The scholars of Panchnad had created this explanation for the troubles that followed the earthquakes that had destroyed the cities of Panchnad."

Devavrata's answer:

Human history on earth could be divided into three past "Ages" during which Panchnad had progressively deteriorated. This was proposed as a Law of History: The future would be a Fourth Age and, therefore, the Fourth Age would be lesser than the Third Age, just as the Third Age had been lesser than the Second, and the Second in turn had been lesser than a glorious imagined First Age.

The Kavi Sangha records show that the belief in these four Ages of civilization was widespread in Panchnad in its last days. The Third Age was ending and the Fourth Age was beginning; they just did not know exactly when. A thousand years later, we know that the current Age is indeed the Fourth Age, the Kali Yuga. It has been called the Dark Age; the Iron Age, for iron is black; the Age of Strife, for war is its way of life; and, sometimes, the fourth and last Age. At the end of Kali Yuga, the world will be consumed by fire and water, and all human beings shall die, except for the seven immortals whose duty it will be to repopulate the world. The name for the Age comes from the game of dice. In a dice game, a throw of one is called 'kali' for it is always a losing throw, and the Kali Yuga is the era of complete loss.

This story of the Great War is the story of how the Third Age, the Dvapara Yuga, ended. Devavrata lived during that Age. It has been called the Red Age and the Yellow Age, for those are its colors; the Copper Age, for copper is red; the Age of Bronze, the hard yellow metal that emerges from the mixing of soft ores; the Age of Settlement, for the matriarchs ended the wanderings of their clans and put down roots; and, sometimes, the Third Age in the cycle of four ages that make up a kalpa. At the end of the Dvapara Yuga, mountains move, rivers overflow their banks, and people are compelled to abandon their homes and seek new lands to settle in, for human settlement tires the land and drains its soil of life. The land must rest lest it become desert. In a dice game, a throw of two is called 'dvapara' – it loses to all throws except 'kali.' As such, the Dvapara Yuga is the age of little victories and big losses.

This is the common belief, that many scholars see fit to agree with. The Kavi Sangha takes no position on the matter. We use the Kali Yuga calendar that begins in the year of the Yadava civil war that would make Hastinapura the sole center of power in all of Jambudvipa. As to how the belief in the Four Yugas came about, even the archives of the Kavi Sangha have little to say.

A.3. THE RARITY OF WAR IN PANCHNAD

Yudhishthira said, "All my life, the prospect of war has never been far. How did Panchnad settle conflicts without war? All the foreign cultures that I have heard about, from travelers and traders, engage in war. How did Panchnad become a war-free culture?"

Devavrata's answer:

The Panchnad civilization was a trading civilization. Ships sailed from the ports on the Western Sea to Dilmun and other lands inhabited by Mlecchas. Caravans crossed the mountain passes into the lands of the Asuras, the Medes, and the Parsakas. They left the land of peace and entered a world in which war was endemic. There, gangs of thieves might attack an unprotected caravan. The caravan might blunder into the middle of an armed conflict between cities in foreign lands. The caravans and the ships needed to be protected and a guild of warriors existed that raised competent fighters.

These warriors were a cost when trade was slow. During slow times, they were employed as paid guards who protected settlements from foreign gangs. In Panchnad, land and water was plentiful. No settlement aspired to dominate the others. Why did Panchnad need mercenaries at all if there were no causes for conflict?

As Panchnad grew and expanded, conflicts occurred. You could say it is natural to fight over resources, such as land and water, even if there appears to be enough and even if the residents of a settlement were cousins. The conflicts did not lead to the kind of war we have now, the kind of war that is ubiquitous in the rest of the world. Two settlements in conflict would be encouraged by their neighbors to negotiate. Panchnad had been settled by the steady splitting up of bands with a daughter band settling the frontier with help from its new neighbors as well as its parent band. Neighboring settlements were tied to each other by familial as well as economic and cultural bonds. Conflicts affected everybody, and everybody had an interest in resolving them. The result was that negotiations rarely failed.

Negotiations rarely failed, which is to say that sometimes, often enough, negotiations did fail. Then, neighboring cities would try to help resolve conflicts peacefully. Those too could fail. When reasonable means failed, the practice was to try unreasonable means. For instance, the unreconciled parties would be encouraged to decide by a competition. The winner of a race or a competitive game or the winner in a game of dice would get a favorable decision. These unreasonable means sometimes worked when everybody agreed that there was no fair resolution possible.

War was the most unreasonable of means and as such, the last resort. When the opposing parties were adamant in their positions and would not accept the result of random chance that games or a throw of dice represented, the parties would be allowed to go to a managed war.

Nobody wanted war, even a managed war. More than anything else, the matriarchs who governed each band and clan understood that dependence on uncontrolled war to settle conflicts would change the culture by creating the need for an army. On average, a man was stronger than a woman, and a very strong man was stronger than a strong woman. The difference was slight, but it would be enough to create a preference for an army of men, led by men. Such a force soon became an army for men that would treat women as lesser, weaker beings. This would pose a danger to the power of a matriarch. Neighbors collaborated to prevent or eliminate such developments.

A managed war was a war that felt like another game, like a game of dice. The difference was that warriors could still die. That was the price, and settlements embarked on war with that foreknowledge. A few deaths were preferable to uncontrolled war that might kill the entire culture. A managed war was ritualized to heighten the enormity of death. This is how the practice of ritual war came into being.

Fighting a war is a skill, like any other skill. The guild of guards expanded to become a guild of mercenaries who could be used to conduct war games. The guild of mercenaries provided the warriors, the advisors to the opposing settlements, and the arbitrators who decided who lost and who won.

If negotiation failed to settle a conflict between settlements, the settlements would go to war with mercenaries hired from the guild of mercenaries. This was ritual battle. The settlements stated their demands before the battle and the side that won the battle would dictate terms restricted to those demands. Since a wealthier settlement could always hire better and more mercenaries, a poorer settlement would rarely choose this path, preferring to negotiate instead, or to create a coalition that might oppose the wealthier settlement. As a result, even managed war, when it happened, was between approximately equal coalitions of settlements.

The modern reader would not recognize a Panchnad war as war. One side would issue a challenge by announcing a goal of capturing something of value from the other side, for example, its commander-in-chief. The judges would assign a value to this challenge, specify the time within which the task was to be accomplished (ghatis, days, or other time period), and determine if the challenge had been successfully overcome. The defenders would announce their strategy, perhaps an armed formation to protect its commander for the time specified by the judges. If capture was successful, the challenger won and the challenger's client might declare victory. If enough judges did not accept the claim of victory, the challenge would be reversed. (The required number of judges would be agreed on before the war.) The defending side would issue a challenge in its turn. It did not have to do so; possessing the disputed resource and keeping it secure during the original challenge might be enough to claim victory. The judges might uphold such a claim. There was no limit to the number of challenges a losing side could bring. The cost of such challenges could become unsupportable even for the wealthiest city.

The members of the guild of mercenaries, even those on opposing sides of a battle, were often related to each other. They preferred to capture an opposing warrior rather than kill or even maim them. At every engagement, the goal would be to capture, not kill, one or more senior commanders of the other side. The mercenaries did not overtly change their own behavior. Their clients would get nervous by the loss of the trusted commanders. The arbitrators might make a snap judgement if one side lost enough senior commanders (by capture or, occasionally, death). The result of a Panchnad war was peace.

The trading families taught some fighting skills to their members so that they could protect a caravan under attack from bandits. That is not to say that they were trained as warriors. A trader would never become as expert a fighter as the traditional mercenary of Panchnad.

A Panchnad war was also the training ground for the guards of a caravan. When raiders attacked a caravan, its guards would create a defensible encampment and ward off challenges and try to wound the attackers until they left. Only rarely would a Panchnad troop chase and destroy raiders. They preferred to wait out the raiders or negotiate safe passage, paying tax if it seemed feasible.

Between the Panchnad preference for negotiated agreements, aversion to a standing army, and the guild of mercenaries' preference for bloodless battles, war was rare in Panchnad.

A.4.   THE END OF THE THIRD AGE

Yudhishthira said to Devavrata, "I want to know more about Panchnad and the world in the Third Age. Tell me what you know of the Third Age: the world at large and Panchnad in particular."

Devavrata's answer:

This is what the world looked like in the Third Age. At the very center of the world, that unmatched mountain, Meru,[54] rose into the heavens where the gods keep their secrets. That sacred mountain peak is home to Amaravati,[55] the city of the gods. To the extreme north of Meru lies Uttara-Kuru,[56] the original northern home of the legendary Pururavas, ancestor of Puru, who left that home in a time lost to memory. Just south of that is the

---

[54] Mount *Meru* is a legendary mountain believed to exist north of South Asia, approximately in the centre of the Pamirs in Tajikistan.

[55] *Amaravati* was the city of the gods, located at the top of Mt Meru.

[56] *Uttarakuru* is the mythical "Arctic home of the Pauravas" covered by ice all through the year. The Pauravas claimed to have come from a land far to the north of Mt Meru. Some optimists have located this in the North Pole.

frozen northern wasteland where the Danavas,[57] asuras by nature, hide from the wrath of Indra in the summer. Through this ice-bound land flow the unnamed mighty rivers that empty into the northern sea. When the sun goes south, these asuras emerge to freeze the rivers and inflict pain on the unfortunate denizens of that land. Still further south, closer to Mount Meru, we find the homes of the brutal, horsemeat-eating Shakas,[58] who range from the eastern desert to the western lakes, from the foothills of Mount Meru to the northern wasteland. To the east of the great peak lies the plateau of the Bo[59] and the Ronga and then the plains of Su-wa-Xia.[60] Through this plateau flow great rivers: the mighty river Lauhitya,[61] also called the Bo Ganga; the Xia Ganga that flows to the land of the Xia; and other great rivers called the Ganga because they purified whatever they touched. Immediately to the west of the mighty peak lie the lands of the Mlecchas and the Parsakas; further west are the lands of the brown, the red, and lastly the black people of Egypt. The rivers that flow here are deep and fast, hence called Sindhu (swift) – the Arvand,[62] beloved of Indra; the River of Egypt, sometimes called the Krishna[63] for the color it imparts to the land, sacred to the blue-necked Eashwara; and the Supurna[64] that fulfils all desires. Finally, to the south of Mount Meru lies Jambudvipa,[65] the most fortunate of continents,

---

[57] *Danavas*, pronounced Tha(r)-nu(t)-wo(rm)(-s), are demons, children of Danu, one of the wives of the mythical sage Kashyapa who fathered all beings (except the highest gods).

[58] In historic times, the *Shakas* are identified with the tribes that the Greeks called Scythians.

[59] The Tibetan plateau inhabited by the *Botias* and the *Ronga*.

[60] *Xia* refers to the plains of China, through which flow the Yang-tze (Xia Ganga) and the Huang Ho (the Ho Ganga).

[61] *Lauhitya*, meaning the child of Lōhita (iron), is one of the names of the river Brahmaputra; other names include Bo Ganga and Tsang-po.

[62] The *Arvand* is the Tigris (the Swift River, also Sindhu).

[63] The *Krishna* (the Blue/Black River) is the River Nile (also called "the Black River") that flows through lands sacred to Osiris (translates to *Eashwara*, the Lord in Sanskrit). These were the Black Lands, also called the Land of the Temples of Ancestral Spirits. (The Egyptian word translates to *Pitr-vihara-naadu*.)

[64] The *Supurna* ("fulfilling" or "completed well" in Sanskrit) is the Euphrates (meaning "well-fertilised" in Greek).

[65] *Jambudvipa* (The Island of the Jambul) is the ancient name for South Asia (from the Hindukush to Assam and from Ladakh to Kanyakumari).

watered by the rivers Sarasvati, the giver of wisdom, the Sindhu, the swift river, and the Ganga, the purifier of the soul. Many more rivers, of various merits, water this land and empty into the southern ocean, the Brihatsagar,[66] either through the Western or the Eastern Seas.[67] To the east of Jambudvipa beyond the Lauhitya are the rivers Iravathi,[68] mother of the Mahanaga Airavatha, and the Hme-Ganga,[69] the great river that vanishes into the unknown world of the east. To the north, the Himalayas, the snow-covered White Mountains, are an endless source of water and a barrier impassable by enemies.

Panchnad, the center of Jambudvipa in the Third Age, is, settled by the most honest, the most honorable, the most peaceful, and therefore the richest and most prosperous people in the known world. Panchnad can be divided into regions, each settled by an ancestral clan. In ancient times, the Bhaarata-Pauravas resided to the west and north of the juncture where the Drishadvati and the Sutudri joined the Yamuna to form the Sarasvati, a wide, swiftly flowing river of legend that has disappeared. Further south, the Vanara,[70] the Raishyava,[71] and the Mayura[72] clans have settlements along the banks of the numerous lakes that slow down the Sarasvati. Having slowed down, the river widened across the flat plain it flowed through. Finally, the southernmost settlements were those of the Yadavas, all the way to the place where the river enters the sea. Over two thousand such settlements lived in peace. The citizens considered themselves fortunate to have been born to such prosperity.

---

[66] *Brihatsagar* is the Great Ocean surrounding Jambudvipa (referring to the Indian Ocean).

[67] The Western Sea is the Arabian Sea; the Eastern Sea is the Bay of Bengal.

[68] The Irrawady, which originates in the Himalayas and flows through Burma to the Bay of Bengal.

[69] The Mekong, named for the Hme/Hmu/Hmong people, that flows through Thailand, Cambodia, Laos, and Vietnam and empties into the Indonesian sea, a region not known to the people of Panchnad.

[70] *Vanara* means "ape", probably the langur.

[71] *Raishyava* means "unicorn". The myth of the unicorn is believed to have originated from this source.

[72] *Mayura* means "peacock".

Each settlement was independent of others. Each settlement governed itself in the traditional manner, with a matriarch advised by a council of the wisest and most experienced dwellers. The citizens were consulted through assemblies called when requested. The council advised the citizens who were informed and engaged. The seven independent guilds were disciplined, and guild members obeyed the rules and norms established by their guild and the government in performing their tasks. The guild of bards witnessed the acts of the current assembly and reported truthfully on the important events during the time of the last seven matriarchs. Six other guilds – weavers, potters, smiths, builders, farmers, and doctors – reported on their activities, successes and failures, and knowledge of distant events that might affect the settlement. The guild of mercenaries, traditionally not considered a part of any settlement and whose members disavowed allegiance to any settlement, sent observers who would participate if guild-relevant matters were discussed. All the major families participated in trade under the leadership of the founding family. Trade was the usual source of wealth and power and entry into the guild of traders, which controlled by the leading family. The guild of traders did not need a separate representation in the councils of the state.

A settlement might contain more than one family headed by a matriarch. The matriarch of the first family, the family that had established the settlement, considered herself the chief and headed a council of matriarchs. The families were usually related to each other, and conflicts among the families of a settlement were rare.

There was one aspect of settlement life that was not dictated by matriarchs. The eldest son of a matriarch could expect to be the next male head of the family supporting his oldest sister as matriarch. Consequently, the eldest son was trained to be a chief. Sometimes, one of his brothers might also be similarly trained in case the candidate for chief died prematurely. The other sons of the matriarch did not have that opportunity.

It was the duty of the father of a boy to manage his son's education. The simplest way to do this was to enroll the son in the father's guild as an apprentice. Similarly, the younger daughters of a matriarch, the ones not destined to be matriarch, would be guided by an aunt into an appropriate guild. That aunt would often be performing the same guiding role for her own daughters as well. As a result, entrance into a guild was largely passed on from father to son or from mother to daughter.

The survival and well-being of the settlements depended on all these guilds, but prosperity depended on trade. The settlements traded with each other, of course, and with the far-off lands to the west and northwest. They shipped their fine clay pots, rice, wheat, barley, rice wine, pepper, sesame seed oil, and other goods west to Dilmun[73] and sometimes directly north of Dilmun, to Susa,[74] the capital of Elam, and all the way into Ur.[75] The smiths manufactured faience beads, the most colorful in the world, and fashioned jewelry that was greatly in demand in Dilmun. They exported textiles of cotton that were in great demand. In turn, they imported gold from everywhere, for the people were fond of glittering decoration. They imported tin from secret mines in the far north and exported it to the western world through Dilmun, paying a fortune and making a fortune. They imported decorative objects made of alabaster from Egypt, the land of the Black River, and imported dates from Elam and woolen textiles from the cities of Sumer on the Arvand. The land was at peace and had been at peace for many generations. During the Third Age, in a period long before the events leading up to this war, the Sindhu and the Sarasvati held pride of place among the people of Panchnad. The Master trader Ilina wished to expand the trading for which his clan was famous. Ilina was directly descended from the beautiful Pururavas through the prideful Nahusha,[76] the self-indulgent

---

[73] Dilmun was either Bahrain or Oman. The Sumerians considered it an incredibly prosperous trading centre that allowed them to trade with the mythical land of Meluhha to the east. Meluhha could have been a Sumerian pronunciation of "Malaya", i.e., mountain land or plateau, and referred to the region north of modern-day Gwador on the Makran coast (possibly pronounced "Maghan" by the Sumerians). The name "Himalaya" is a conjunction of "Him", snow and "Malaya", i.e., "Snowy Mountains"; the traditional Sanskrit etymology is Him/Snow and Alaya/Home, i.e. Abode of Snow.

[74] Susa still exists as the city Shush in modern Iran.

[75] The first city of ancient Sumer.

[76] *Nahusha* was a legendary ancestor of the Pauravas. Nahusha's pride led to his downfall.

THE END OF THE THIRD AGE | 319

Yayati,[77] and the self-restrained Puru.[78] The land available in Panchnad on the banks of the Sarasvati was limited, hemmed in by other settlements, and not usable as a trading hub. If he left the banks of the Saravati and headed east, he would reach a great river, the Ganga. If he settled there, he would be leaving Panchnad. The Ganga flowed east into uncharted territory and did not connect with any Panchnad settlement at all. Ilina vacillated between staying in Panchnad and increasing trade with the West, or going to the Ganga and developing new markets in the east. Ultimately, Ilina hedged his bets and established Kaalindini,[79] named after his mother, on the upper Sutudri, almost at the foothills of the Himalayas. Kaalindini was close to the other Panchnad settlements. Though the Sutudri was not navigable, the residents of Kaalindini would still share its waters with Panchnad. Kaalindini was closer to the Ganga and within the reach of the forest-dwelling Nagas. It was positioned to monitor and manage any trade with the east. Ilina was certain that such trade would come about, and he wanted his family to be prepared to benefit from it. Kaalindini was not as hospitable as other Panchnad towns, and the decision to stay was a strategic bet on the future of trade. Ilina's ambivalence about this decision could be considered a family trait. Every generation after him considered the question of moving east (and abandoning Kaalindini), or declaring failure and returning to some Panchnad town, or staying put, doing nothing. The residents felt that migrating to the banks of the Ganga would break their links to Panchnad. They also feared that this separation from Panchnad would make it difficult to attract immigrants who would be needed to grow the frontier town.

Ilina's grandson Bharata was successful in trading with the West and ignored Kaalindini. Interest in the east declined and

---

[77] *Yayati* was a legendary ancestor of the Pauravas. At the end of his life of over a thousand years, he is not satisfied and asks his sons to give him their youth in exchange for his age.

[78] *Puru* was Yayati's youngest son. He grants his lustful father's desire for one more youthful year. As a reward, he is designated his father's heir.

[79] *Kaalindini* was probably close to the current town of Ropar, just before the point at which the Sutudri changed direction and flowed west to the Indus. It was positioned to be an important trading centre for Panchnad.

was not revived until Bharata's great-grandson Hastin determined to try his fortunes in the east.

Hastin stayed on the Panchnad side of the watershed at first, intending to reassure the Nagas that the traders did not want to displace the forest-dwellers but wanted to trade with them peacefully. Previous attempts to settle on the Ganga had threatened the Nagas. The Nagas avoided conflict and did not try to evict the settlers, but they had refused to trade or cooperate with them. With the establishment of Kaalindini, the threat seemed diminished and relationships with Naga bands immediately to the east improved. The bulk of the Nagas still lived a long distance (and past dense forests) from Kaalindini, and trade was not as central to the Naga way of life as it was for Panchnad. Despite that, more Naga-produced goods came to market to barter for Panchnad's products. Nagas would bring unusual produce – fruits, vegetables, or animal meats and pelts; and minerals – rock salt or other minerals used by smiths, but occasionally copper and very rarely, small quantities of tin. They wanted tools, ceramics, and utensils of bronze. Bronze was scarce in Panchnad and not easily found in the market, but an exchange for a larger weight of copper could be profitable. By persistence and some sacrifice, the traders of Kaalindini maintained a monopoly on the Naga trade as it became profitable.

The Panchnadis were familiar with monopolies. They approved of monopolies as a valuable strategic tool for a trader dealing with foreign cultures. Any Panchnad trader could ask to share in the monopoly. The Kaalindini monopoly was different. The Naga trade was risky and intermittent, hard to share, and the profits came from importing into Panchnad, not exporting. The Nagas consumed little, and almost the only product they asked for was bronze. They gave too much in exchange for bronze. This roused both jealousy and anger among traders in other Panchnad cities. By comparison, the Yadavas, who settled around the delta of the Sarasvati, established the great port city of Tripura and controlled the trade with destinations reachable by sea, such as Dilmun, Elam, and Egypt. The Yadava monopoly, though vastly more lucrative than the Kaalindini monopoly, was seen as a service benefitting all of Panchnad. Small things can have magnified effect in society. The Kaalindini traders were considered miserly and grasping, while the Yadava traders were considered generous benefactors, even though the two groups behaved identically.

The traders of Kaalindini were concerned that the other cities of Panchnad were jealous of their success. Hastin, a Bhaarata,[80] addressed this by deflecting that resentment away from Kaalindini. He set up a caravanserai on the banks of the Ganga southeast of Kaalindini. Usually, a caravanserai was a place where caravans stopped on the way to a market or city. This caravanserai was a destination in itself, for there were no known markets or cities to be reached from there. The caravanserai was not a settlement but a service center for trade. It provided a marketplace for Nagas to barter with peddlers and traders from Panchnad. Little changed as far as Kaalindini was concerned, for the profits still flowed there. However, the caravanserai provided a service in a potentially hostile environment, and its fees were not resented.

Hastin collaborated with the local Naga clans in establishing the settlement and called it Nagapura in their honor. This further insulated Kaalindini from the disapproval of other Panchnad towns. Nagapura was intended as a trade center that all Panchnad traders could use and nothing else. It was organized like a caravan rather than like a settlement, the leader of the caravan being a male trader who exercised absolute powers. Nagapura did not even try to become self-sufficient as an urban settlement would. Instead, it bartered for food from the surrounding Naga bands. The Nagas became partners in the success of Nagapura, and it succeeded where previous, more conventional, attempts to settle on the Ganga had failed.

A.5. NAGA REACTION: PANCHALA AND NAGAPURA

Yudhishthira said, "You said that the Nagas of Panchala and the other Naga bands as well did not welcome Hastin and his traders. How was Hastin's settlement of Nagapura established,

---

[80] *Bhaarata* means a descendant of the legendary emperor Bharat, who was said to be the first ruler of a unified Jambudvipa–Bhaaratavarsha.

why did it flourish, and why did you make it the center of an empire?"

Devavrata's answer:

The historian will find it curious that an otherwise unremarkable trading post became a city so different from the rest of Panchnad. The changes are extraordinary. It was governed by a Master, not a matriarch. The Kauravas were warriors, not traders. The settlement first collaborated with the Nagas, then became the ruler of some of the Nagas, and, finally became their oppressor, all the while asserting the sincere desire for extensive trade with them. The historian would note that this transition to a militarized state occurred after the Nagas of Panchala tried to destroy Hastinapura.

Hastin, the great-grandson of Bharata, founded the frontier outpost of Nagapura on the west bank of the Ganga. Naga bands were sparse, but the location was near a convenient ford that the Nagas used to cross the river. It was an ideal trading location, and Nagas came to Nagapura often. By the time of our forebear Samvarana, Naga settlements had appeared around Nagapura, for their population had increased. Conflicts were rare as the Panchnadi settlers of Nagapura avoided agriculture and relied on the Nagas for food. The Nagas were used to growing just what they needed and had to be encouraged to grow more so that there would be a surplus to support Nagapura. The exotic cotton textiles, the bright jewelry made from silver, faience beads and lapis lazuli, and the superior metal tools of Panchnad were bartered for food and other products. The Naga population had expanded towards the north on the east bank of the Ganga, despite the thick forest near the river.

Over ten yojanas to the west was the Yamuna, but as it went south, it turned west at the northern ridge of the Aravalli[81] range to join the hundred little streams of the river we call the Sutudri. The unfortunate land to the south and west of Nagapura was protected from rain by the Aravalli range. Deprived of water from

---

[81] The *Aravallis* are a mountain range in Western India stretching from Ahmedabad to Central Delhi.

the rain as well as from the snow melt, the land was bone-dry. This wild and arid land, unsuitable for cultivation in the Naga manner or for Panchnad settlements, we called Khandavaprastha. This cursed desert land stretched south up to the Charmanavati[82] River, which is also monsoon-fed but drains a vast plateau in the Vindhya mountains.

Nagapura was prosperous because of trade and only because of trade. The Bhaarata Hastin had recognized a valuable opportunity in settling it. Occasionally, the Nagas would come into Panchnad with small quantities of almost pure copper and some tin. The Westerners consider tin to be the most precious metal. It was scarce in Panchnad and in the rest of the world. The Panchnadis had discovered a source far to the north past the north-western plateau and across the valley of the Vakshu. It had been a secret, but eventually that secret was revealed and Panchnad lost its monopoly. Hastin thought he might be able to establish a more lucrative trade in tin and other ores. That was how Nagapura succeeded. It became the destination for tin and copper ore brought by the Nagas from the east in small boats. Nagapura prospered with increasing trade.

In the beginning, Nagapura was managed like a caravan, not like a Panchnad settlement. The head trader was a man who managed all aspects of caravan life and negotiated barter deals with his Naga counterpart. Over many generations, the head trader's post became the entitlement in perpetuity of the descendants of Hastin. Nagapura never became a Panchnad-style janapada ruled by a matriarch and her council. The head trader's family wanted to retain control and the position of head trader passed from father to son, a practice imported from the Parsakas across the snow-covered Himalayas west of Panchnad.

The settlement was not completely peaceful. On the east bank of the Ganga was Panchala, a confederation of Naga bands. Panchala had slowly but surely extended its rule over other Naga bands of the east bank. Panchala wanted to rule over the Nagas on the west bank as well. The Ganga was too wide to construct a permanent bridge, so such dominance would not have been easy

---

[82] *Charmanavati* is the river Chambal.

to maintain. When Nagapura emerged, it became practically impossible to dream of unification of all Naga bands. Nagapura's success led to prosperity for the Nagas who allied with the Panchnadis and traded with them. Panchala refused all interaction with Nagapura. The Naga bands on the west bank did not want to join Panchala. Shortly after our ancestor Samvarana, Hastin's great-grandson, became the head trader of Nagapura, he faced an ultimatum from Panchala: You are on Naga land; pay tax on all your deals. When Samvarana laughed off this demand, the Panchalas did the impossible. Their army went north, found a place to cross the Ganga, and invaded Nagapura. They drove a surprised Samvarana and the Pauravas out and took over Nagapura. Samvarana sought refuge in Kaalindini. He did not find support from the other Panchnad cities, for external war was not their forte. Nor did he get support from the guild of mercenaries, for the war to recover Nagapura was unlike anything they had executed in a long time.

The cities of Panchnad dotted the banks of the Sarasvati from its beginnings at the merge of the Sutudri, the Drishadvati, and the Yamuna, all the way south to the western sea. Cities like Moolasthan and Takshashila similarly flourished on the banks of the Sindhu and its tributaries many yojanas to the west. The population was still growing in all these settlements. The great teacher and strategist Vasishtha had established the Kavi Sangha to address the expected problems of growth. Vasishtha believed that expansion to new regions to the south and to the east was essential, but neither he nor the Kavi Sangha managed to persuade anybody.

Samvarana's exile proved to be an opportunity for Vasishtha to establish the credibility of the Kavi Sangha. Vasishtha offered his advice to Samvarana. He and the Kavi Sangha helped Samvarana train an army of warriors, the first such army in Panchnad. It did not consist of mercenaries. Mercenaries fought for an employer. This army was an organization managed, maintained, and pledged to fight for Nagapura and owing allegiance to Samvarana. The Kavi Sangha borrowed one innovation from the other cultures that the Panchnadis knew about: It was an all-male army that did not include any mercenaries or other guild members. This allowed them to build the army without requiring approval from the matriarchs of Panchnad.

In the meantime, the Panchalas had troubles of their own. They did not understand how to run a market or a trade entrepôt. Nagapura's prosperity faded, and the surrounding Naga bands suffered. The takeover of Nagapura was a disaster for Panchala, and as the years passed, they maintained a smaller and smaller force to keep control of Nagapura. When Samvarana returned with his army, he found a disaffected population that welcomed him. The small Panchala force was routed, and Nagapura returned to Samvarana's rule. Vasishtha and the Kavi Sangha gained in stature, and this victory marked the acceptance of the Kavi Sangha as a formidable strategic, political, and intellectual force in Panchnad. Under Vasishtha, the guild of bards merged with the Kavi Sangha. Vyaasa, the title of the head of the guild of bards, became the title of the Panchnad-wide head of the Kavi Sangha as well.

The Panchalas, by evicting Samvarana and then, in turn, being evicted by him, sowed the seed of an empire. Nagapura with its new standing army became the hegemon in its immediate surroundings. Samvarana's army did not consist of mercenaries but of career soldiers who stayed together. The troops remained in the army when the fighting was over and were supported by taxing the surrounding Naga communities in exchange for 'protection' from Panchala.

Samvarana's son Kuru used the army to send expeditions to the east to find the source of the tin and copper. Many yojanas to the east, the Ganga encountered a great plateau to the south and then turned north.[83] A monsoon river, which we call the Hiranyaganga,[84] emerged from the plateau to join the Ganga. At that juncture, Kuru established a small trading post called

---

[83] Modern Varanasi/Kashi is located a little east of this turn to the north. Kaushambi is also close by (about 75 kilometres from Allahabad). After flowing past Varanasi, the Ganga turns east again and joins the Sone at Patna (old Pataliputra, the capital of Magadha).

[84] *Hiranyaganga* means the "Golden Ganga", possibly because gold was brought down this river from the plateau. Later the name would change to "Son-ganga", further shortened to Sone.

Laghu[85] Nagapura. The plateau was peopled by a different forest-dwelling culture. The Nagas called them Defenders, which Kuru's men translated as Rakshasa. The Rakshasas of the plateau followed two different ways of life. Some lived in permanent settlements that depended on the surrounding forest for game and food. Others lived as miners, whose settlements were located next to a lode of ore – copper, silver, gold, and other tradable minerals. They had developed techniques for extracting almost pure copper from the rich lodes they treated as owned by their settlement. The plateau Rakshasas had access to tin, though they would not, or could not, explain where it came from. Laghu Nagapura became the market in which the plateau Rakshasas exchanged almost pure copper and tin ore for products from Panchnad, such as cotton, textiles, bronze tools and utensils, and fine clay pots.

Laghu Nagapura was not considered a suitable site for smelting arsenical bronze. The Rakshasas did not know how the shiny golden metal was made, there were no local sources of arsenic, and Kuru did not want to create an incentive for raiding. Instead, bronze foundries were established around Nagapura, to smelt arsenical bronze and further work it into tools and jewelry. Nagapura produced copper and bronze items such as cooking utensils, carpenter's tools, expensive armor, and hunting weapons. Smiths and artisans from the rest of Panchnad came to Nagapura. Nagapura prospered as a Third Age manufacturing site, and its surroundings were dotted with foundries in the middle of growing swathes of clear-cut forest. Nagapura began to look more urban, like a traditional Panchnad settlement, and less of a nomadic caravan stop. To recognize this evolution, Kuru renamed Nagapura. The new name was Hastinapura in honor of the founder Hastin.

Later, Kuru's son Viduratha and grandson Arugvata, the latter also called Anashwa, found a source of arsenic ore in the plateau of Laghu Nagapura and moved the manufacture of bronze ingots there, while the artisans remained in Hastinapura. Arugvat gave the Rakshasas a stake in the production and protection of the

---

[85] *Laghu* means "Little."

bronze by handing over the furnaces to them. A Rakshasa band that raided the site to steal the stockpiled bronze would only hurt another Rakshasa band and the response would be immediate and devastating.

The Rakshasas responded to the new technology and new production methods by increasing native copper production in order to produce more value-added bronze. They also increased cooperation with the Hastinapuris and exchanged information of mutual interest. Arugvat discovered that the tin came through traders who hiked from the headwaters of the Hiranyaganga to the head of a river the Rakshasas called the Great River, which the Hastinapuris translated as Mahanadi.[86] The Great River flowed east out of the plateau and emptied itself via a delta into the Eastern Sea.[87] The traders were met at the delta by ships that claimed to come from the other side of the Eastern Sea. The ships carried tin ore as well as linen, salt-water fish, unusual fruits, and coconut oil and other palm by-products. They took back copper ore and gems – lapis lazuli, beryl, and shell – as well as animal pelts. Live animals – tamed elephants and domesticated dogs – were favorites.

The demand for arsenical bronze, tin, and tin-based bronzes in Panchnad led to the establishment of a great trading route from the unnamed land[88] across the Eastern Sea to the mouth of the Great River, across the plateau, to Laghu Nagapura, then up the Ganga to Hastinapura and thence to the plains of the Sarasvati and the Sindhu. Hastinapura, as the entrepôt, controlled the trade and prospered – more than prospered, for Kaalindini and Hastinapura came to be respected in the councils of the Panchnad cities.

Kuru's explorations increased Hastinapura power and profile in Panchnad. Hastinapura had been a caravan. It was going to be a city while retaining its unique features. One difference would prove to be important. Hastinapura was not a matriarchy. The

---

[86] *Mahanadi* means "Great River."

[87] The upper reaches of the Mahanadi are a few days' trek from the upper reaches of the Sone.

[88] Probably Malaysia or Siam.

legacy of its long existence as a caravan outpost, headed by a male trader, continued. To conform to Panchnad customs, the chief's sister, or sometimes the chief's wife, was called the Matriarch, but the lineage and power passed through the male chief to his sons and not through the Matriarch to her daughter and son. Kuru, in turn, was recognized as the patriarchal dynast. Hastinapura was no longer the trading outpost of a glorified caravan, but a successful city, controlled entirely by his descendants called Kauravas.

This change in inheritance seemed a minor change. It was expected that when the crisis was past, the traditional Panchnad model would be followed. The Kavi Sangha did not expect the change to last more than a generation or two. However, not only did the new model of patriarchy continue past the next few generations, it has been the standard. Your own claim to the throne rests on your father inheriting from Vichitravirya.

Many Hastinapuris resented the lack of support from the Bhaaratas of Panchnad during Samvarana's exile. Kuru's success in establishing Laghu Nagapura gave him the wherewithal to declare independence from Panchnad and make Hastinapura a state, called Kururashtra. With its standing army of trained warriors, this state could assert its rights in hostile surroundings.

A.6.   AN ARCHIVE SAVED

The Vyaasa explained in the Annals of the Kavi Sangha how the archives contained the story of the war as seen from the Pandava side.

The Kavi Sangha was accused of trying to please both sides in the conflict. That was not true. The Kavi Sangha was centered in Hastinapura and maintained the archives of the city. The Vyaasa Shukla, also the brother of the Queen Mother Satyavati, King Shantanu's second wife and Devavrata's stepmother, had wanted the Pandavas to return to Hastinapura. He thought they would be easier to manage if they stayed close by, in Hastinapura. His attempts at forging a compromise collapsed with Suyodhana's intransigence on the one hand and, on the other hand, the alliance the Pandavas made with Hastinapura's ancient enemy Panchala. Once the war started, it looked like a foregone conclusion that the

Pandavas would lose. When the Pandavas eliminated Devavrata Bhishma, they created a slim possibility that they might win the war, but it was still very unlikely.

The presence of kavis in the Pandava camp was unplanned, if fortunate. (Nobody expected the Pandavas to win.) There were rumblings that the kavis were spies, could not be trusted, and should be expelled, especially as they took directions from Hastinapura.

When the Kavi Sangha, and for all practical purposes that means the Vyaasa, decides to archive history-in-the-making, it appoints an Archivist. The Archivist is expected to interview key persons at the beginning of the major events and debrief them regularly thereafter. The people involved rarely decline the interview request for they know that it is a rare honor for their thoughts to be considered for the archives. In the case of a war with an enemy of Hastinapura, it would have been unusual for the Kavi Sangha to have an Archivist in the enemy camp. An enemy of Hastinapura would not be expected to welcome an Archivist. Even if they did, they would place restrictions on the Archivists to prevent spying.

The Vyaasa Shukla thought that there was no point archiving events on the Pandava side. The Pandavas were on the run, unlikely to win. The rebellion was historic, but the Pandavas were expected to lose, and the events to be documented would happen in the city.

The Vyaasa appointed an Archivist in Hastinapura to memorize and organize the history of the Kuru family. No Archivist was appointed for Indraprastha, nor was one sent to the Pandavas. It was a miracle that they had one in Lomaharshana.

This is how the miracle came about. Many years earlier, when the Pandavas had been allowed to re-establish the settlement of Indraprastha, the Kavi Sangha and its then newly-elected Vyaasa Shukla had offered archival support to the Pandavas. (Hastinapura and Indraprastha were not enemies yet.) When war broke out, the bards and archivists of the Kavi Sangha serving in Indraprastha came under suspicion of spying for Hastinapura and were not allowed to leave Indraprastha if they knew of

Pandava war plans. The Pandavas' advisors, many from Panchala, had recommended imprisoning the kavis. Some proposed killing them; feelings against the Kavi Sangha ran high in Indraprastha. The Kavi Sangha had been Devavrata's ally in developing policies for the empire he was building, which were anti-Naga in effect. The Panchala viewed the Kavi Sangha as the instrument of Panchala's defeat so many generations earlier.

Yudhishthira rejected the advice and allowed members of the Kavi Sangha to leave Indraprastha, if they so wished, or to stay if they were willing to archive the events in the Pandava camp. Two of the senior-most members left, leaving behind only four kavis, headed by the young Lomaharshana. The younger ones, being with the losing side, found it difficult to communicate with their leaders and get approval from the Vyaasa. But they stayed on. They would do their job, with or without the Vyaasa's approval at every step. It was some time before the Vyaasa was able to convey his approval and commendation: "Do your job – memorize. You will never be asked to become spies. If asked, pledge loyalty to the Pandavas." In later years this policy of loyalty to the host of the archivists would become part of the ethos of the Kavi Sangha.

This small team initiated the Pandava archives as an extension of the Hastinapura archives. The expulsion of the Pandavas from Indraprastha was followed by a quiet period during which Hastinapura forces hunted for the Pandavas in the forest. Meanwhile, the Pandavas stitched together their coalition and re-built their army, recruiting unhappy Nagas and older residents who felt displaced by immigrants. During this quiet period, Suyodhana declared that any contact with the Pandavas was treason, and even the Vyaasa Shukla felt constrained not to visit the Pandava camp openly.

Since Shantanu's time, the Kavi Sangha had admitted many Nagas as members. This practice began during Parashara's term as Vyaasa and continued under the next Vyaasa, who recruited Shukla. When Shukla became the Vyaasa, he continued the policy. Shukla recruited Lomaharshana, the Archivist who memorized and organized the Pandavas side of this history. Even though very young, Lomaharshana had already built up a reputation as an Archivist. Suyodhana had demanded that this recruitment of Nagas stop, further alienating the Nagas from his rule. The Kavi Sangha deployed its Naga kavis outside Hastinapura. Lomaharshana had been sent to Indraprastha to be Archivist for the Pandavas. He was more than an expert memorizer. He was a skilled elicitor of facts – of the events, conversations, actions that a person had experienced. He was a poet and a storyteller with a keen sense for what had to be archived.

The unresolved debate question is: Is the story of the Kavi Sangha a part of the story of the War?

The Kavi Sangha maintains its archives separately from the archives of the city; the history of the War will not tell the story of the Kavi Sangha. The Kavi Sangha is invisible. The Kavi Sangha is always present.

A.7.   THE DISASTER

Yudhishthira said, "Gurudeva! The Regent will not speak on this matter and threatens to become silent forever. Tell me what you know of the history of the Disaster and how it led to Devavrata's vow of celibacy."

The Vyaasa Shukla's answer:

The Disaster took place in multiple acts. The first act was the shaking of the earth. Prithvi, the Earth, shook. It was in the time of Pratipa, great-grandson of Arugvat, the grandson of Kuru. Some said that such shaking showed Prithvi's anger with humanity. The truth of this accusation was incontestable, for there was always something that could have angered Prithvi. She is a capricious mother who hugs her children and in the next instant turns against them. That must be what happened here. The earth shook, and it changed the world.

The star-gazers have their own language. The quakes, they said, marked the end of the Age of the Bull and the beginning of the Age of the Ram. They pointed to a starry outline in the sky and said it was a bull. Next to it, they pointed out the outline of a ram. If a wise man is one who can see through obscurity, the star-watchers certainly qualify as wise. I frequently wonder, why these two animals and not any other? Do not all animals have a body with four legs, a head, and a mouth? If you can see one animal in the sky, why would someone else not see a different animal? No matter, it is their mystery. They will tell you that the change of Age denoted by the stars is a subtle observation first made by a Samavedin and verified by other Samavedins. Samavedins are bards who specialize in maintenance of clocks – managers of time, if you will. All bards study the Samavedins' art, but only the most skilled who have the greatest fortitude, patience, and focus go deep into that art. A sad consequence of their training is that many Samavedins go mad as they age. Occupied in incessant measurement, they become even more obsessed. They become counters who see numbers in everything. The Samavedins say, and there is no cause to disbelieve them, that this cosmic observation has taken centuries to make and it could only be made because Samavedins, too, maintain archives of their observations. When asked about the significance of the transit from the Age of the Bull to that of the Ram, they defer to the astrologers who see future history in the stars. The Samavedin measures time, not history. In any case, the heavens moved from one Age to the next and shook the world; the world changed.

It is the case though that neither the priests nor the philosophers, neither the star-gazers nor the star-readers predicted any particulars of the Disaster. The shaking of the earth surprised everybody.

Prithvi shook. The river Yamuna, the great tributary of the Sarasvati withdrew her blessings from the people of Panchnad and turned at the northern ridge of the Aravalli range to flow eastward. The river Sutudri, which had flowed in a hundred streams to join the Sarasvati, now abandoned those channels. It no longer went south after it emerged from the Himalayas. It turned sharply to the west to join one of the tributaries of the Sindhu many yojanas away. Kaalindini, less than a yojana away, lost its water supply and, in time, would be abandoned. The River Drishadvati, rain-fed along the western slopes of the Aravalli range and flowing south of the old Yamuna, continued to flow as it did and arrived at the meeting place with the Sarasvati, only to find itself alone. It could only pour into the Sarasvati a fraction of the water that that great river had once received. Other tributaries flowing down with the monsoon rains that fell in the Aravalli range continued to feed the Sarasvati. But it was not enough. The die had been cast and showed kali, the losing throw.

The consequences in the east were tremendous. That year, the east was flooded. The southwestern corner of Kuru territory, once called Khandavaprastha, which had been arid scrubland in the rain shadow of the Aravalli range, became a wooded swamp. The Yamuna's water flowed along the eastern foothills of the Aravalli range as far as where the Sahyadri range was visible and the land sloped up to the south. The Yamuna then turned to the east (many yojanas south of the Ganga at this point) and entered forested regions populated by new Naga settlers along the banks of previously monsoon-fed rivers now overflowing with the snow-fortified Yamuna. The floodwaters then continued parallel to the Ganga until they reached the Charmanavati River emerging from the Vindhya mountain range. The Yamuna-augmented Charmanavati followed its old bed until it merged with the Ganga at the place we call Prayag. Nowadays this stretch is called the Yamuna. For many years there was no fixed riverbed in the upper reaches of the river; it was a floodplain and the course of the river was very unstable. Over the years, as the river made its way through the Naga-occupied forests, a stable bed was formed. The occasional depression collected water to become a pond. Some of these ponds grew to form lakes. For many generations, though, the Yamuna remained an unstable rogue river.

The Kauravas continued to call the river by its old name, the Yamuna. The first region that was traversed by the new Yamuna had few inhabitants, mostly a small number of Naga bands. The Nagas dealt with the new situation as they had always done when displaced by floods or other natural threats to their settlements – they moved to a new location, burned a new clearing for their plantings, and started afresh. Their biggest problem was that they might not have food stores to carry them through a new crop cycle. In this case, the availability of water in an otherwise arid region would increase arable land, but only after the river settled down. A few years later, dormant seeds sprouted, grass and reeds appeared, followed by tadpoles, insects, small fish, and then, finally large fish. When the fish became plentiful, the river dolphin, a gift of the mother-goddess, would appear and it would be time for the Nagas to return. Many Naga bands on the banks would switch to fishing, like the Meena-Nagas in the northeast of Jambudvipa who lived by rivers.

Downstream from where the Yamuna merged with the Ganga, a few yojanas from our settlement here in Kaushambi, the increased flow almost doubled the width of the Ganga. Much of this widening was towards the flat northern bank as the southern bank sloped up to the Vindhya range. This was the territory bordering Rakshasa country that saw conflict when Naga bands expanded into this area and met Rakshasa bands also seeking to settle there. Both sides traditionally avoided such conflicts by turning away, so a sparsely occupied no-man's land extended from this juncture to Laghu Nagapura where a river emerging from the plateau, called the Hiranyaganga, joined the Ganga. From that point on, Rakshasas were found on both sides of the river, but the increased water flow of the Yamuna split Rakshasa society into two – one on the north side and the other on the south side of the Ganga. The two communities found it harder to get together and interacted much less. The settlement at Laghu Nagapura flooded and was moved to higher land.

Back in the west, the Sarasvati dried up slowly, its waters disappearing into the sand at its southernmost point just before the point at which it used to split to form a delta to the sea. A slight ridge about five yojanas from the sea had created the last of the Sarasvati lakes. The water would flow over the ridge and find multiple paths to the sea. When the water level in the lake fell permanently below the ridge, the saltwater of the sea moved into the delta but was still a long way from the lake. The land in between was dry and salty, and would become a saltwater marsh in the rainy season. The lake itself dried up slowly as the Sarasvati brought in less and less water.

The other lakes that had dotted the river's path to the sea also received less and less water and slowly dried up. The southernmost lakes dried up first and then the other upstream lakes dried up as the stored water evaporated and was fitfully replenished by monsoon water. The southernmost settlements were abandoned first. Some émigrés went north towards other Panchnad towns, where they were initially helped, but as the magnitude of the disaster became clear, they were asked to move on. Some went to the northwest to the towns on the Sindhu, in particular the great city of Moolasthan, but here too they only received temporary help as these north-western towns struggled to cope with their own floods and shifting rivers. Those émigrés kept going northwest through the passes that lead to the Kubha River, where they stayed and settled. Some émigrés went south to Saurashtra and then proceeded down the shores of the Western Sea.

The émigrés who went north past the other Panchnad towns reached the place where the Yamuna and Drishadvati once joined. Now there was only the trickle of the rain-fed Drishadvati. The Sutudri used to flow through innumerable channels. Its swift flow prevented it from depositing silt; it left shallow beds covered with rocks and gravel rather than soil. The Drishadvati, though slower, did not bring down much silt. Agriculture was not feasible in the areas watered by these rivers. The emigres then went east towards Hastinapura, expecting help but worsening the situation in the host communities. Having come that far, they stopped. The prognosis was poor for going further. The land on either side of the Ganga was clayey, difficult to till. Anyone going further would have to become pioneers opening up uninhabited lands, which they considered a lowering of their status. Some of the area was occupied by Nagas, who would object to losing their land. The Panchnad refugees did not want war nor did the Nagas; they were not eager to start a war whose outcome they could not guess.

From Saurashtra, a large faction went north along the eastern side of the Aravalli range. In the beginning, there was a belief – a hope, rather – that the Yamuna would return to its original course and the Sarasvati cities would regain their wealth and power. That hope faded as the years passed. Moolasthan and the cities on the Sindhu were not in a position to help the Sarasvati refugees. The Sutudri's flow into the Sindhu had increased significantly, and all along the Sindhu, embankments had overflowed and the river had moved to a different channel. The disruption was small in comparison to the lot of the Sarasvati settlements, but the Sindhu towns could not be of much help to the refugees.

Notwithstanding all the differences between the older Panchnad towns and Hastinapura (militarized with a standing army, patriarchal, ruled by warriors not traders, and so on), there had always been a substantial faction in Hastinapura that thought of the city as an outpost of Panchnad. Many citizens still considered themselves the children of Bharata or the children of Puru, who settled by the Sarasvati, and not only the children of Kuru who had secured power in Hastinapura on the Ganga. The Kauravas, who ruled Hastinapura, and their leader Pratipa, recognized that the cities of Panchnad were collapsing and were concerned that they would take Hastinapura down with them. At this point, the Kavi Sangha concluded that the changes in the Sarasvati were permanent and the Sarasvati settlements doomed. Hastinapura was already their stellar success; they made a critical decision to abandon Panchnad and move to Hastinapura and begin the process of creating an urban civilization.

First, a key action was considered necessary. Pratipa[89] was persuaded to justify his name and formally declare the independence of Hastinapura from its Kaalindini parent and from the Puru homeland; independence too from the Sarasvati, to be replaced by a permanent commitment to the Ganga. The significance of that declaration was that he was formally reneging on the implicit promise to support the parent settlement in times of need and to follow their ways of conflict resolution. He would be free of commitments to submit to a matriarchy. This made it possible for Hastinapura to treat the refugees differently from its own population and the Nagas. Though supported by the Kavi Sangha, Pratipa's declaration was not welcomed and caused much debate in Hastinapura. Ultimately he compromised by postponing complete emancipation, leaving it to his son to complete the break-up.

Of Pratipa's three sons, the oldest, Bahlika, objected to the Kavi Sangha-inspired decision and decided not to accept the leadership. He led a batch of refugees to the Northwest, crossed the Sindhu and entered Gandhara via the Kuberakuta[90] road.

---

[89] *Pratipa* means "rebel" or "adversary" (among other meanings).

[90] *Kuberakuta*, meaning "Kubera's Fort," is the Khyber Pass.

They intended to return to the old tradition of rule by traders rather than warriors. His group of emigrants crossed the Kubha River into a plateau north of Gandhara. There they discovered that collapse of civilizations was not limited to Panchnad. All over the West, drought and famine had devastated ancient trading networks and wars had become ubiquitous. The people they were expecting to settle with were themselves impoverished by the changing climate and the collapse of trade. Further migration west would have to be postponed by a few generations. They went as far west as they could and named their settlements and themselves Bahlika. They sent back word of this discouraging development. It made Kururashtra look like the only alternative for all of Panchnad.

Pratipa's second son Devapi was declared Yuvaraja, heir apparent.

A.8. THE PANCHNAD MIGRATION

The Annals of the Kavi Sangha describe how the population of Panchnad abandoned the towns on the Sarasvati and migrated to other parts of Jambudvipa.

In less than a century after Samvarana's return to Hastinapura and the creation of Hastinapura's standing army, patriarchal government and patrilineal inheritance of power were entrenched in Hastinapura. Pratipa's declaration of partial emancipation from Panchnad, followed by the use of the army to control the behavior of immigrants, extended Hastinapura's rule. It became universally recognized as the hegemon of the stretch of land from the western bank of the Ganga to the fluctuating eastern bank of the Yamuna and from the northern foothills of the Himalayas to an undefined boundary with Naga allies to the south. This region came to be called Kururashtra. Trade had been disrupted during the early years of the crisis but was expected to rebound when the crisis was over and normalcy was restored with Kururashtra in full control of trade between the east and the west.

The Panchnad towns were emptying, and a million people were migrating in all directions. To the north and west were other cities that shared their culture, but the earthquakes and the great changes in the flow of the Sindhu had hit them hard. The émigrés who went south established themselves in Saurashtra where the rivers Narmada and Tapti made the land productive. Further south, along the coast of the Western Sea, they established ports and cities that could attempt to continue the commerce that had once been the lifeblood of Panchnad communities.

For all its promise, Saurashtra was suffering from many years of drought. The water in the monsoon-fed Narmada River varied greatly, but it had a large watershed and potentially could enrich the land. For the time being, it could not support a large population. Many migrants, led by the Yadavas[91] of Panchnad, went northeast along the eastern slopes of the Aravalli range in the direction of Hastinapura. The land here was hilly and unpromising. Where it was flat, there was not much water. The Yadavas continued north and east between the Aravalli range to the left and the Sahyadri range to the right into the valley of the Charmanavati. They then followed the Charmanavati River into the Gangetic plain to the meet the new River Yamuna. This land, receiving both rainwater and snowmelt, looked like promising territory.

As the Yamuna was unstable, the Yadavas tried to go upstream as well as downstream in search of a place appropriate for settlement. Upstream, the river was still not stable and the situation looked bad. When they tried to go downstream, they met and came into conflict with the Nagas near the river and with Rakshasas in the forest. They compromised as well as they could. They wanted to establish a city, to be called Mathura, the "City of Honey".

The Yadavas made many attempts to establish Mathura. The river's constant shifting was only one problem; the opposition from Nagas and Rakshasas never ended.

The last group to emigrate from Panchnad was from the upstream cities. The most numerous, the most ancient, and the poorest clan called themselves the Pauravas; then there were the powerful Bhaaratas, who ran most city councils; and a small

---

[91] *Yadava* means "a descendant of Yadu."

sprinkling of Kauravas, who were largely up-and-coming traders. These refugees could go north along the old bed of the Yamuna past the point where the river's course had changed and cross it closer to the Himalayan foothills. There was an ancient bridge, but it had been damaged during the earthquake. The local Naga fisher-folk, called Meena (or Meena-Nagas), ferried the refugees over in exchange for textiles, weapons, ornaments, and jewelry. Then, going east, the Panchnad emigrants would first come to the Ganga and continuing southeast along the right bank, they would reach Hastinapura, where they would request refuge for they were family. The familial relationship meant that the request could not be refused. The declaration of emancipation was intended to enable Hastinapura to decline such requests.

A.9. THE REFUGEES IN HASTINAPURA

Yudhishthira said, "Why was it so difficult to manage the refugees who came to Hastinapura seeking help? What did they expect, and what did they get?"

Devavrata's answer:

Hastinapura did not have the resources to support all the refugees, so a bad situation was becoming worse. The Kavi Sangha suggested a tough stance. Pratipa's oldest son Devapi[92] had been crowned King but did not have the stomach to deny shelter to the refugees. Reclusive to begin with, Devapi became more isolated when he rejected Kavi Sangha help. Increasingly, he attempted to solve all problems by himself and failed. The common opinion was that Shani had infected him with depression at an early age. This could have been true for he was often melancholic and pessimistic.

One day, Devapi's clothes were found abandoned by the edge of Khandavaprastha. He was nowhere to be found. A message had been left with an attendant: The King had abdicated. He did not want to do it publicly as he knew the counselors would try to dissuade him. He wished his brother well.

---

[92] *Devapi* means "friend of the gods" or "beloved of the gods"

The third son of Pratipa, Shantanu, became the leader of Hastinapura. Shantanu realized the magnitude of the refugee problem and requested more help from the Kavi Sangha.

The refugees were from an urban society and lacked the skills needed in building new settlements on uninhabited land. The Vyaasa at that time was Bharadvaja, who preceded Shukla, the Vyaasa who recorded these annals. Bharadvaja was a pragmatic realist. He responded to the disinclination of the refugees to settle new land by proposing positive and negative inducements. In the process, Bharadvaja invented new policies, including harsh ones that were disliked.

It is necessary to note that there were many reasons why the refugees did not want to be pioneers. Their view of themselves as a sophisticated and urban people and not forest-dwellers like the Nagas; their unfamiliarity with the land and the limitations on its use; their knowledge and the skills that they would need to start afresh as pioneers.

First, their view of themselves. They did not want to live like the existing population. That existing population, the Nagas, consisted of nomadic, loosely allied bands that did not build permanent settlements and occupied central and eastern Jambudvipa, that is, the plain of the Ganga from the foothills of the Himalayas and points south. There was fear that the Nagas would not allow any settlement on their land.

Second, their familiarity with the land. Even if the Nagas were amenable to sharing their traditional lands, the methods of farming known in Panchnad could not be used in the new land. The land of the Ganga was heavily forested and the Ganga was the year-round source of water, but irrigation systems would have to be constructed to sustain agriculture far from the rivers. In Panchnad, with the many lakes on the Sarasvati, it was easy to irrigate farms.

The third category of reasons for the refugees not wanting to be pioneers was knowledge, especially of appropriate technology. There had been past attempts by individual Panchnad adventurers to settle along the banks of the Ganga. These failed because the work was hard and the returns meagre. Those settlers in the past had to spend years learning the slash-and-burn agriculture practiced by the Nagas. They discovered that slash-and-burn agriculture was not productive enough to support the Panchnad manner of living in solid houses of brick in a permanent settlement. It wasn't just individuals had to change – systems would have to change. The refugees believed that sooner or later they would be able to return to Panchnad and resisted learning what they needed to learn.

A.10. PANCHNAD FAILS TO COME TOGETHER

The crisis caused by the drying up of the Sarasvati and the problems of the refugees broke down the historic unity that the people of Panchnad had been proud of. The settlements became unable to cooperate to address the problems.

Well before Devavrata's renunciation, Panchnad was a troubled land. The saving grace was that despite the troubles, there was no war as peace was a way of life. The Sarasvati had begun drying up in the time of Pratipa, Devavrata's grandfather. Pratipa wanted the Pauravas and Bhaaratas in the oldest parent settlements to work together and restore the Yamuna's flow to the west. He offered all the help that he could – this was limited as the Yamuna's sudden appearance in the east was radically transforming the Gangetic plain as well. Hastinapura itself was not in the path of the flood as it skirted along the boundaries of Kururashtra. Naga (and Rakshasas further downstream) bands had suffered the brunt of the flooding in the beginning, but now they were responding to the opportunities created by the new river. Naga bands in the heartland were moving up the Yamuna with new settlements. Rakshasa bands further to the east were preparing to move into the no-man's land that separated them from the old Naga boundaries to exploit the new source of water. The only opponent Pratipa faced who might choose war were the Panchalas who had not been touched by the change. Pratipa had his hands full keeping Panchala from crossing the Ganga again in a reprise of their ancient confrontation.

The upper and middle classes of Panchnad, the Pauravas and the Bhaaratas, were traders first, and builders second. They could not see the need to undertake, at current cost, a huge project with no immediate return. There was no profit to be made in diverting the course of the Yamuna. It was possible that the monsoons might make up the deficit in water. The river might return to its previous course on its own. The communities dithered, and while the impasse continued, migrants from further south overwhelmed the central Panchnad towns. Faced with a population crisis, the towns of central Panchnad were unable to finance such a project. The Bhaaratas repeated their earlier mistake; they considered action only when the southern and central cities failed to handle the refugees. But it was too late, and the Bhaarata cities succumbed to the exploding population of migrants. Pratipa could see the juggernaut building up and wanted to stop it before it arrived in Kururashtra. But he did not control the Yamuna upstream where the problem might have been resolvable. Pratipa felt helpless and failed to take decisive action. In the first years of Shantanu's reign, more refugees arrived at the Kuru borders seeking help. The people of Panchnad were abandoning their settlements as the drought spread north.

Shantanu sought the counsel of the Kavi Sangha and its Vyaasa (Bharadvaja, before Parashara) on developing a long-run strategy to deal with the refugee situation. Something had to be done immediately that would choke the flow. The refugees imagined an unpopulated land with a bounteous river like the Sarasvati on whose banks settlements could be raised. The reality dismayed them. But by then, they were already in Hastinapura and had nowhere else to go. Hastinapura itself had to become unattractive.

The broad outlines of the strategy Shantanu and the Kavi Sangha developed were thus: Recreate the Sarasvati-centric way of life of Panchnad on the banks of the Ganga and the Yamuna. Change the pattern of use of arable land from slash and burn to permanent settlement, even if it meant that the Nagas would have to change or would have to leave. Encourage the refugees to be the pioneers in settling the new land. Police the roads from the west along which the refugees came and control their entry. Oppose the work breakdown that the guilds enforced in the old Sarasvati settlements. Slow down the growth of the population to match the rate at which new settlements were established.

The democratic organization of the old settlements would have to be abandoned and a unitary state like the empires of the West that traders described (such as Parsaka, Sumer, and the land of the Black River) would have to be established.

To implement this long-term strategy, it was necessary that in the short-term, first, Shantanu maintain and expand the army so that it could deal with the societal unrest that might follow, while watching the Panchalas, and, second, population growth in Hastinapura and in the camps be tightly managed. The first and immediately contentious result of those plans was the 'one child per person' policy. This provoked unrest that had to be put down by the ever-expanding army. The reported suicide by Shantanu's wife magnified the unrest.

A.11. SATYAVATI'S AMBITION

There are no good answers to the questions about Satyavati's ambitions. What did she want, and how did she try to get it? Despite her brother Shukla's rise to the role of Vyaasa, it is generally believed that he was too close to her to be objective.

How are we, looking back at a distant past, to judge the actions of Devavrata and Satyavati. Devavrata's mind must have been in a whirl when his father married the woman he loved. Was avoiding Satyavati's eyes enough? What if they encountered each other on the street? When he visited his father, how could he avoid seeing his stepmother?

Similar questions arise when we think of Satyavati. Shukla reports that she announced to him and their father: *I might as well be dead*. But then she goes ahead with the marriage. How did she find the will to lie with Shantanu? How was it that Shantanu failed to detect her lack of love for him?

Shukla's explanation as recorded in our archives of the time was:

Satyavati was born to be a matriarch, a leader of an independent clan. Matriarchs did not follow the norms of ordinary women in our culture. Men were not the all-powerful beings that we have portrayed, nor were women the fragile weaklings of later stories.

The Vyaasa Vaisampayana's reaction was to avoid looking for explanations. He said, "This was the story that has come down to us. It is history, not melodrama. Even if accidental meetings occurred they were not consequential. Otherwise, the Kavi Sangha would have recorded them as well. So we must accept Shukla's assessment."

Shukla's explanation continued:

Why did Satyavati go ahead with the marriage? She was ambitious, and she thought she was going to be the matriarch in Hastinapura. She knew that Hastinapura society differed from the Nagas in the primacy of men in governance. But she may not have been prepared for the extent of male domination. There were no women in superior roles in the state, something unthinkable in Naga bands. All she could be in her new role was the founder of a dynasty. When Devavrata met her and impressed her, she was just beginning her transition from a young girl and early motherhood to an adult. She may have wanted to die at the prospect of losing Devavrata, but she was a pragmatic woman. She may have realized the silliness of her announcement and did not act on it. Devavrata's impulsive vow was similarly silly. It would have impressed her as extremely foolhardy, if not foolish, and she would have been amazed when nobody attempted to dissuade him and the seriousness with which he followed it. She had compromised and found other reasons to live. He should have found other reasons to back away from his vow. She had not asked for celibacy, she had not asked that he never make love to another woman, just that he not have children who aspired to be Crown Prince. Even then, as Queen, she would have managed the expectations of his children if he had had any.

It is interesting to observe the reactions of the audience when this story is narrated. They do not question Devavrata's impulsive and daunting vow. Nor do they question his father's behavior. Would a father leave on a trading caravan while the son he left behind exhibited dangerous tendencies? But Satyavati is judged.

A.12.   SHANTANU MODIFIES KAVI SANGHA POLICIES

The older Annals of the Kavi Sangha are incomplete when discussing the changes of policy under Shantanu. The Kavi

Sangha went through some difficult leadership transitions and failed to record the archives completely.

This is a summary of what the Annals of that time say:

After Shantanu married Satyavati, the Kavi Sangha retreated on some of its policy directives. Part of this retreat was forced; the one child policy had to be abandoned, and that decision was controversial. Meanwhile, Devavrata saw himself as the only person who could bring balance to the absence of empathy in the Kavi Sangha's approach to managing the crisis.

Parashara's policy of bringing Nagas into the Kavi Sangha was intended to make it more acceptable to the Nagas and not appear as an imperialistic extension of Panchnad. But the process of the Nagas participating in the discussions inevitably led to compromise, sacrificing the immediate reward for a future promise.

For instance, the Kavi Sangha approach to creating new settlements effectively took land away from the Nagas. It is reasonable to wonder why the Nagas in the Kavi Sangha did not object, especially given the high ranks they reached. Shukla was the first Naga to become the Vyaasa, and after him, there would be many.

The Nagas who joined the Kavi Sangha often felt that the policies proposed were in the best long-term interest of the Nagas. Like all such policies, much would depend on honest and sincere implementation, even though we know that the implementers are human, error-prone, and corruptible. The war broke out because the sons of Mahendra Pandu decided that the Nagas had been treated unfairly, extremely unfairly. Meanwhile, their opponents, the sons of Dhritarashtra, refused to see unfairness in practice but theorized about principles. As this benefited them, they objected to any change.

Everything would be sacrificed on the altar of fairness – the selfish who stole from the poor; the refugees, now called immigrants, who wanted to restore their old way of life; and the Nagas who were short-sighted, focused on the present, and refused any compromise. The Pandavas would sacrifice everything on this altar of fairness.

When Shantanu married Satyavati, he abandoned one element of the Kavi Sangha strategy. He backed away from the short-term plan to stop population growth by limiting family size. Such impulsive individual decisions, usually by male decision-makers, have often created problems for the plan.

The alliance that the Pandavas cobbled together to oppose Hastinapura included Panchala, even though there was still enmity between the Naga city and Hastinapura. Panchala had been opposed to Hastinapura from its founding as a trading outpost. The Yadavas were in the alliance too. Their leader Krishna kept his own counsel but wove a path to a Yadava empire that would rival a Kuru empire centered on Hastinapura. In principle, the Kavi Sangha was not opposed to the Yadava plan. The rise of the Yadavas under Krishna had not been anticipated. Though the Yadavas, descendants of Yadu, were cousins to the descendants of Puru, Yadu's brother, their imperial plans would not mesh with Devavrata's goals. Those plans were also inimical to Yudhishthira's goals, but the Yadavas allied with him to oppose Hastinapura and Devavrata. Added to this incongruous mix were the southern Nagas represented by their army chief Virata, who styled himself King of the Matsyas, that is, the Meena-Nagas. The Meenas may be Nagas, but their interests diverged from those of Panchala. They had fared well under Hastinapura's policies, so why did they oppose Hastinapura? All they saw, like many others, was the unfairness of Kavi Sangha policies.

A.13. DEVAVRATA'S SPRING PROJECTS

Some of Devavrata's projects, especially those that failed, were:

One proposal was to build channels that would divert the Yamuna back into its old channel to the west. Then the Sarasvati could become a great river again, instead of the monsoon-fed, drought-prone stream that it had become. These channels were difficult to cut for the mountain-fed rivers never dry completely. During the winter, the cold, white snow freezes in the mountains, creating glacial ice dams at unexpected locations. Melted water from higher grounds accumulates behind these natural dams. When the dam bursts, a torrent of water is released. We cannot predict when such a dam might break upstream. The breakage of a dam deeper in the mountains might release enough water to break the next ice dam downstream, setting off a chain of dam collapses. When that happened, the floods overwhelmed our best efforts. The best times for constructing water-works are late fall, after the first ice dam forms in the mountains and holds back some water, and early spring before the ice-dams break releasing gushers.

Unfortunately, spring was also the best time for the refugees to leave their homes or temporary shelters and migrate. The weather was not too hot or too cold or too wet, though fearsome animals ranged in the forests. A spring migration could end in settling down on fallow land and creating a permanent settlement. A fall migration followed a summer spent accumulating supplies to last through the winter before continuing east. Many of the water projects were right on the migration route to Hastinapura, and Devavrata planned to use the refugees as laborers. But he miscalculated. The urban refugees were in no sense ready to labor on a canal project. A settled urban life changes people; they become unable to perform physical tasks or work with soil. These refugees were repelled by physical labor as a child shrinks from the fire that burnt it once.

A.14. Devavrata's Early Plans for Empire

Yudhishthira said, "Grandsire, you've mentioned plans for creating an empire as early as Chitrangada's reign. What were these plans?"

Devavrata said:

After Chitrangada's death at the hands of the Shaka, I concluded that the only way we would repel future invasions was by presenting the Shakas with a united defensive line across the foothills of the northern mountains. I needed support from the Panchnad republics on the Vipasa and Jahnavi rivers. Even if the far western republics of Moolasthan and Takshashila would not join me – they had their own refugees – I would at least prevent the Shakas from establishing a foothold on the gateway between the west and the east. To create such a defensive line, I needed to have a unified entity, an empire, if you wish. This empire would have to command the loyalty of the Nagas, the original Kuru settlers of Hastinapura, and the new Panchnad refugees.

These days the idea of an Emperor is bandied about easily – Emperor Yudhishthira and Emperor Suyodhana, as they call themselves. In those days, there was no 'Kuru Empire', even in fantasy. The refugees from the west brought along their ideas of running cities by guilds organized around critical functions, but this did not sit well with the Nagas who wanted to live in bands. It was not even acceptable to the immigrants settled in border areas, who could not wait for service from a guild member with the authority and training to perform a specialized task. The Nagas had no concept of empire, though Panchala, the hostile Naga confederation across the river, was developing into a military state with imperial ambitions. To this day, we point to the Shakas and what they did to a peaceful Naga band to define and justify the empire I have created.

The best argument for a Kuru empire came from the work I had done. As I built dams and lakes along the Ganga and tried to control the Yamuna, I realized that the local residents, whether new immigrants or older residents, had to be organized to maintain the waterworks. How were we to convince these local people – urbanites, farmers, Nagas, and even traders – of the value of long-range planning and long-term maintenance? I could see it and acted to foster it through my waterworks projects. These hydraulic systems would survive forever if they were kept in good repair. The taxes collected on the produce of the farmers and the goods shipped by traders would more than pay for the maintenance. The problem, as always, was finding qualified people to do the work.

My focus on the long-term issues created an alliance between Hastinapura and the new immigrant-turned-farmers, who saw their interests tied to the interests of Hastinapura. If they could be trained as fighters, we could rely on them for defense. When defense was not needed they would rely on the empire to support them and their economy as needed.

A.15. CARROTS AND FATHERHOOD

There is an explanation for Satyavati's demands that puzzled Devavrata. The source of this information is not named, but it must have been a bard who knew both agriculture and the medicine used by women.

This is what the older Annals say:

Devavrata had been confused when Satyavati imported carrot plants as medicine for Ambika and Ambalika. The Queens had been secluded and then Satyavati had asked Devavrata to spend time with them so that their sons would inherit Kaurava features.

The carrot, a small purple root that comes from the northern hills, can be used to produce an abortifacient that causes a fetus to be expelled prematurely from the womb.[93]

Satyavati did not want Devavrata or anybody else to suspect that the children were not the sons of Vichitravirya. She used the wild carrot plants to produce a concentrated liquid that was administered to Ambika and Ambalika in the seventh month. Thus the two babies were born prematurely in the seventh month. Satyavati let it be known that the babies were full-term but because they had received some of the poison that killed Vichitravirya, they were weak and needed special care. She prepared the warm room and other facilities knowing that the two boys would need special care. After two months in the warm room under special care, the two sons of Shantanu were ready for a regular diet based on their mothers' milk.

The maid-servant who also had intercourse with Krishna Dvaipaayana bore Dharmateja Vidura as a full-term baby two months later (in the ninth month). Vidura was born healthy. Vidura's mother started producing milk just in time for the premature royal babies to drink.

---

[93] The carrot's cousin called "Queen Anne's lace" can be used to produce an abortifacient which causes a foetus to be expelled prematurely from the womb. The modern carrot has evolved greatly from the original, which was a small purple root that originated in South Asia.

The use of the wild carrot as an abortifacient was not known to Panchnad, but may have been a Naga secret. The beliefs about how the father's characteristics are inherited were common Panchnad knowledge. Heating rooms with hypocausts was ancient knowledge in the Sindhu-Sarasvati culture and the plateau of Gandhara. Unfortunately, Devavrata had no knowledge of what was going on. His goal was to keep the peace. He wanted Vichitravirya's sons to be born so that he would not be forced to reign as King.

B. NOTES

B.1. STANDARDIZATION

A recurring theme in Panchnad culture was *standardization*. This can be seen in the archaeological sites of Mohenjo-Daro, Harappa, Chanhu-Daro, Lothal, and others, where uniformity reigns to a far greater extent than other contemporary urban cultures such as Sumer. Bricks were manufactured in sizes in a standard ratio of 1:2:4. Weights are found in the sequence 1, 2, 4, 8, 10, 16, and 32. (It is surely a coincidence that the #2 weight is within 10 per cent of the British ounce.) Towns are constructed on a precise north-south axis. Every town's architecture is very similar. There are other such standard features.

I have assumed that this approach to standardization applied to other areas of endeavor, such as the calendar, seasons, time, distance, arts, and even the conduct of war.

B.1.1. Annual Calendar of Panchnad and Hastinapura

Melas (fairs) are held on the occasions of the two equinoxes and the two solstices. The winter solstice marks the Sun beginning its journey north, but it also marks the beginning of the winter harvest period (January to March or April, depending on latitude). The spring equinox heralds the arrival of spring and is considered the start of the year. The summer solstice is the beginning of the monsoon planting season. The autumn equinox marks the end of the monsoon harvest and the beginning of the winter planting season, ending with the winter harvest. In the parts of South Asia where three crops are possible, the summer planting and harvest season extends from March to June (spring equinox to summer solstice). Traders leave home after the winter harvest to reach their destination(s) before the monsoons begin (a leading separation motif in Sanskrit love poetry) and start on the return journey after the monsoons end to arrive home in time for the winter harvest.

B.1.2. Seasons of the Year

Sanskrit Season	English Season	Gregorian Months
Vasanta	Spring	Mid-April–Mid-June
Grishma	Summer	Mid-June–Mid-August
Varsha	Monsoon	Mid-August–Mid–October
Sharada	Autumn	Mid-October–Mid-December
Hemanta	Winter	Mid-December–Mid-February
Sishira	Prevernal	Mid-February–Mid-April

B.1.3. Measures of Time: Ghati and Vighati

$G^{h}a\underline{t}i$ and $Vig^{h}a\underline{t}i$, pronounced "Gut-e" and "We-gut-e", and spelled "Ghati" and "Vighati", are the measures of time that have been used in India from ancient times (with regional variations, such as *nāzhi* and *vināzhi* in Tamil). I have appropriated them for this period though we do not know what terms were used then.

The day is defined as the time from sunrise of one day to the sunrise of the next day. A day was defined as approximately 60 ghatis. The measure is approximate because the "day" defined in terms of the sunrise varies during the year. Each *ghati* in turn was divided into 60 *vighatis*. For comparison, one *vighati* is 24 seconds and one *ghati* is 24 minutes.

B.1.4. Measures of Distance: Yojana

The earth rotates once every 3600 vighatis (through 360 degrees, the modern measure of angles of a circle). In one vighati, the earth will have rotated one-tenth of a degree. In that one vighati, a vertical rod that casts a small shadow pointing north at high noon (say local time in New Delhi, India) will cast a slightly bigger shadow angled slightly east by one-tenth degree with respect to north. At the same time, some distance to the west, it will be high noon (local time) and a vertical rod placed there will cast its smallest shadow pointing due north. The distance between these two rods was considered one *Yōjana* (pronounced "Yo(re)-ju(t)-nu(t)" and spelled "Yojana") in Panchnad.

The above definition of yojana as a measure of distance is dependent on latitude. Such a dependent definition, while useful in a culture spreading in an east-west direction (such as Europe, West Asia, the Russian steppes), is not useful for a culture oriented from north to south (such as South Asia or Egypt). A definition based on a north-south orientation would be a constant, but establishing it would depend on the exact determination of longitude (or, the circumference of the earth), which requires the use of synchronized clocking. Such a capability did not exist until late in the history of Panchnad, when the Samavedins perfected their techniques for keeping time.

A standard definition of yojana can then be obtained by selecting a well-known spot, for instance, Takshashila. Takshashila was the famous center of learning and thought in historical ancient India, and in this book is depicted as the Panchnad center of learning, culture, and philosophy, where Kavi Sangha members went for their advanced education. The standard yojana is measured on the ground at that latitude and composed of smaller standardized units, such as the hasta (or cubit). The latitude can be determined easily by measuring the declination of the sun at noon on the spring or autumnal equinoxes, and other spots at the same latitude can be identified if necessary.

If measured at the equator, one-tenth of a degree would be about seven miles (11.13 km). At the latitude of Takshashila, it would be the "standard yojana" of about six miles (9.24 km), or 21,120 hastas or cubits (see below). All of Panchnad used this definition of yojana.

An average "casual" walking pace is about fifty steps per vighati or three thousand steps per ghati. The average stride of the average South Asian is about two feet. So the average walking speed is approximately one mile per ghati. In six ghatis (one-tenth of a day of sixty ghatis), an average person could walk about one yojana.[94]

Allowing for meals and other breaks, and by walking only in the daytime, a traveler could hike between three and four yojanas, i.e., about twenty miles in a day. Walking at that pace, it would take about three months to go from Kamarupa in the east of South Asia (in Bangladesh) to Takshashila in the west of South Asia (in Pakistan), a distance of about sixteen hundred miles.

Another measure integrating time and distance is the cartwheel. A fully loaded cart with large wheels (about four feet in diameter) pulled by a single bullock or onager makes between one to five turns of the wheel every vighati. The smaller wheels of two feet in diameter make about four to eight turns in the same time. A peddler's cart pulled by either animal moves four to eight miles/hour, not an unreasonable speed. But a single bullock will work less than four hours a day at that pace. A caravan of such carts will go slower, perhaps half the speed, at eight to sixteen miles/day. The trader can make the outbound trip starting in early to mid-October (after the monsoons end) and arriving in mid-April (just before the summer heat makes it difficult to travel).

B.1.5. Measures of Distance: Classical Sanskrit

These definitions are from Kauṭilyā's Arṭaśāstra (approximate equivalents in inches are also provided):

1 angula = a finger-width, 3/4 of an inch

4 angula = 1 dhanurgraha [bow grip], 3 inches

8 angula = 1 dhanurmushti [fist with thumb raised], 6 inches

12 angula = 1 vitasta [a handspan], 9 inches

---

[94] Note that this definition of the "standard yojana" is speculative and based on average speed of walking. At the latitude of Takshashila, the sun will "move" in one vighati a distance that a person walking east (or west) can go in six ghatis.

4 vitasta = 1 aratni = 2 hasta [cubit], 18 inches

4 aratni = 1 danda or dhanus [bow], 6 feet

10 danda = 1 raja, 60 feet

2 rajas = 1 paridesha, 120 feet

2000 danda or dhanus = 1 krosa or gorutta = 4000 yards or 2 1/4 miles, nearly 3.66 km

4 krosa = 1 yojana = 9 miles, nearly 15 km

Note that, by the time of Kauṭilyā, believed to be around 300 BCE, a yojana is no longer defined using the motion of the sun but is composed of smaller measures built on human dimensions.

B.1.6. Fine Arts

Centuries later, the *Natyashastra* of Bharata-muni would codify the theatrical arts and techniques, establishing *standardization* in theatre. This began, I assume, in the cultural ideal of standardization inherited from Panchnad before 2000 BCE. The techniques and methods of instruction used by the guild of bards became the pattern of all theatrical instruction. Speech sounds had been classified into *swara* (vowels) and *vyanjana* (consonants) and systematized. This made it possible to teach memorization in a uniform manner. Every bard was capable of reciting an epic poem in exactly the same way, and development of the skill of learning and reciting was attributed to the mode of instruction.

This mode of instruction was applied to all the elements of the theatre. Hand movements were named *mudras* and became the basis for a semi-secret alphabet of signs and signals. Exercise routines that actors practiced were named *adavus* and standardized for formal instruction. Emotional states were named *rasas* and there were eight, arguably nine, of these. The art of expressing the rasas on stage was named *abhinaya*.

B.1.7. *Vyuhadyuta*: War by Mercenaries

A *vyuha* described the deployment of an armed force intending to attack or to defend against an attack. The Panchnad mercenaries' guild had developed a theory and classification of vyuhas that suited their mode of battle in which troops hired by two cities would set up challenges or duels to determine victory as efficiently as possible. Actual battles between armies only occurred if one side developed an overwhelming superiority in numbers or position, but this was rare. Thus, the Sarasvati-Sindhu Culture had standardized war, with the result that full-scale all-out war never happened. Until the Great War.

B.2.   PANCHALA VERSUS PANCHNAD

The names are, unfortunately, very similar.

Panchnad is the land defined by five rivers. These are the Sarasvati, the Sindhu, the Sutudri, the Yamuna, and the Drishadvati. This region extends from approximately today's Ropar (Kaalindini) in the north to the Arabian Sea in the south, the Aravalli range in the east to Multan (Moolasthan) in the west. Note that Panchnad is not the same as "Punjab." That province, divided between India and Pakistan, overlaps with Panchnad. Punjab also means the land of five rivers. But as it turns out, only the Sutudri (today's Sutlej) and the Sindhu (renamed Indus) are common to the two regions. Punjab also extends further northwest into the Himalayan range, but stops well short of the sea in the south, whereas Panchnad goes all the way south to the sea.

Panchala is the name of a confederation of five Naga clans. The clan is a unit much larger than a band or a family. Panchala became the name of the region controlled by these five clans. The region lies on the northern side of the Ganga from Ahichhatra in the north to (possibly) as far as modern-day Kashi to the south.

B.3.   CULTURAL ELEMENTS

B.3.1.   Dress

Both men and women dressed in two primary pieces of cloth, usually made from woven cotton. A longer piece was wrapped around the waist to form a skirt. (It would be called the *panchagacham*.) Another piece of cloth was wrapped about the upper body, which would be called the *angavastram*. The guild of weavers produced these to order and decorated them as required by the wearer.

A bard at a recital of a historic poem would wear a new white (undecorated) panchagacham and angavastram.

Men and women tied the panchagacham and angavastram differently. The male style of panchagacham used a longer cloth whose first section was used to gird the loins, while the woman's style was more like a skirt hanging off a girdle. The men used the angavastram as a kind of shawl, while the women used the central section as a crosspiece to support the breasts.

An angavastram padded with cotton and wrapped securely around the chest and shoulders functioned as rudimentary armor. Cotton armor was the main protection of the "Indian"[95] infantry of the Persian Empire under Cyrus the Great as described by Herodotus. I believe that one of the earliest uses of felted cotton may have been as armor.

B.3.2. Renaming the Characters

The reader familiar with the Mahabharata might be puzzled by some names. I believe that during the composition of a *jaya* (a lay celebrating a victory), the names of the participants were modified to highlight some attribute of or action by the character. In addition, as the jaya is composed by the winners, the names of the warriors of the losing side might be changed to denigrate them. Occasionally, these became the name by which they were later remembered.

For instance, the martial arts teacher *Drona* may have been renamed from Kutaja, meaning "highest mountain peak." An alternative meaning of *kutaja* is "born in a jar." The word *drona* also means "jar". More specifically, the drona was a wooden jar that held soma during a fire sacrifice. As soma was an intoxicating drink, the jar and the people who handled it were supposed to be drunk from its fumes. So "Drona" may have been a mocking

---

[95] The soldiers in this infantry division were from the provinces ("satrapies") of Arachosia and Gandhara, which lie to the west of the river Indus. The men were most likely mercenaries.

name for the teacher of the vanquished Kauravas. Similarly, Duryodhana ("bad warrior") may have been renamed from Suyodhana ("good warrior").

The reason for such transformation by a poet is that a person can be identified by names as well as attributes. Using a descriptive name that tells of some action by the character keeps the audience interested and signals what to expect. It allows the poet to avoid repeating a name multiple times in a single verse. In addition, names can be used to signal to the audience what they should think of a new character that appears on stage.

B.3.3. Naga Culture as Imagined in This Book

The Hastinapuris gave the name "Naga" to the forest-dwelling, matriarchal bands living along the Ganga. These bands occupied the forests along both banks of the Ganga, ranging from south of Hastinapura to a little east of Kashi. They translated the matriarch's title as "Nagini" ("Mother or Female Serpent"), and the title of the male chief, usually the brother of the Nagini, to "Great Serpent", i.e. "Mahanaga". This was the origin of the name "Naga" as applied to the culture. It is likely that the bands had a different name for themselves.

The Nagas practiced slash-and-burn agriculture. Each band would burn a grove in the forest near a source of water for growing food plants and raising chickens and barley. They would settle nearby, usually at the edge of the grove, for a few years, from five to twenty, depending on the fertility of the grove's layer of ash. Then they would move to a new location not adjacent to the exhausted grove. The old grove was left fallow for at least two more cycles, generally over twenty years.

The women made most decisions in the band, which was a haven for the women and the children. The matriarch's brother was the traditional head of the men's fraternity. Except for the matriarch's brother, the rest of the men joined the band on invitation. The popular men often moved from band to band, while the others acted to keep the matriarch and the women satisfied. Boys were expected to leave their bands after puberty and find other bands to join, but matriarchs and other powerful women could keep their sons in a band indefinitely. The men who were not invited by any band were considered "rogue." They lived by their wits without social support and usually died soon after leaving their mother's band. Rogue men who survived for a long time could be dangerous, as they were often anti-social or otherwise had difficulty in social settings. If a group of rogue men formed a gang, they could be a big threat to bands. But most rogues could not cooperate with each other and found it difficult to form a large band of rogues.

There were a number of rituals that the Nagini and the Mahanaga were expected to perform. Four of these had to do with the equinoxes and the rest divided the quarters evenly. At the spring equinox, the Nagini and the Mahanaga emerged from a sacred fire and led a bacchanalian nine days. Most children were born about nine months later (around the winter solstice), and the number of children born was an indicator of the matriarch's inner strength.

B.3.4. Redistributive Festivals Among the Nagas

Naga bands often celebrated parties with other Naga bands, both close and far. A group of nearby bands (typically five) would get together once a month. A larger group of twenty-five bands might meet twice a year. Festivals involving even larger groups might be held every few years. These events were organized by the men of the hosting band, sometimes in collaboration with the men of other bands. It provided an opportunity for the men to display their ability to organize, collaborate, make friends across bands, and create alliances that crossed family boundaries.

The word "potlatch" is derived from a redistributive feast held by the Trobriand Islanders of New Guinea. Similar festivals occur in other cultures as well, usually as part of a transition to settled agriculture. In the beginning, all the clans or bands would bring food and gifts for exchange. Later, a clan might host the entire event by itself, and the attending clans would acknowledge the host's "big man" superiority. A feature of the Trobriand Island culture was that the men of one tribe led by a "big man" would challenge other tribes through potlatch events. Occasionally, conflicts broke out, and even though their conflicts rarely led to actual battles, the more successful "big men" or those with bigger teams would usually win by intimidation. "Big Men" whose teams won often grew in prestige and with time became "Big Chiefs", leaders of larger groups of men. From time to time, a prototypical "Big Chief" would host a potlatch to show off his superior organizational capabilities as well as breadth of popularity. Over time, Big Chiefs became kings and did not have to sacrifice themselves to host a potlatch; taxes would pay for redistributive feasts.

The confederation of Panchala came into existence by a military merger of five Naga clans. The men of these five clans got together to handle the menace of "rogue males," who had been organized into a gang by a charismatic leader. Such cooperation between bands is an example of how the ritual of potlatch maintained a critical skill and makes possible coordinated responses to unusual events.

B.3.5. Language Questions

We do not know what language was spoken in 2000 BCE or, for that matter, in 850 BCE. We know that after 850 BCE, many texts were written, though few samples from that early era exist. Those we know of are in Sanskrit, and after 300 BCE, in Pail. I have used Gondi in a few places for personal and intimate forms of address (such as "Avva" for mother, and "Bābō" for father) used by Shantanu's children. Satyavati's brother, a Meena-Naga, uses the Dramila (or Tamil, as Tamil speakers are called in many ancient texts) word "akka" for his sister. For the more formal words (e.g. ghati, yojanas) spoken by the upper classes in 850 BCE, I have used terms from Sanskrit, translated when it seemed necessary. I've used "Namaskar" and "Guru" as well as "-deva" and "-ji" as honorifics. This too may be an anachronism. In addition, Sanskrit does not use "-ji", so it assumes a vernacular language that was not Sanskrit. Keep in mind that over four thousand years, a language will drift along with its speakers. Some of the changes are well known. For instance, 'k' drifts to "w". There are many such changes possible, and not all that is possible happens.

On the whole, I don't believe that this experiment in trying to convey an imagined language has been wholly successful. Whatever language is used in this book as the base, including

English, some results struck me as ill-fitted. So I only use a non-English word when a candidate word or concept is first used, and a footnote provides the meaning. Subsequently, I use the English form.

B.4. MYTHS AND HISTORY OF THE KAURAVAS

B.4.1. Myth: Pururavas the Handsome

Pururavas loved Urvashi, the semi-divine *apsara*, who agreed to live with him on the condition that he would never show himself to her naked. Indra, the king of the gods, was unhappy that Urvashi no longer graced his assemblies but lived with a human. He used his *Vajra* (the thunderbolt) one night when Pururavas and Urvashi were lying together, and she saw Pururavas naked and immediately left him.

B.4.2. Myth: Nahusha the Proud

Indra, the King of the gods, had committed the sin of killing a brahmin when he killed Tvastr and Vritra. As a result, he could no longer appear in the courts of heaven and hid himself in shame. After many years, the gods chose Nahusha as their King. Initially a good king, he became proud and lusted after Indra's wife Sachi. Sachi prayed to the great god Shiva and was told to ask Nahusha to come to her on a palanquin hoisted by the seven Sages. The Sages were old and slow, and Nahusha was in a hurry. He kicked the shortest one, Agastya, and shouted *"Sarpa! Sarpa"!* meaning "Faster! Faster"! Agastya lost his patience and cursed Nahusha to become a *sarpa* (another meaning: 'snake'). Immediately, Nahusha fell to earth as a giant python.

Later, Agastya modified his curse and allowed Nahusha to be freed by his descendant Yudhishthira, who would then counsel him about life and death. Centuries later, the python Nahusha attacked Bhima and they fought. When Yudhishthira appeared and tried to save Bhima, Nahusha was freed of the curse. This is clearly a myth as the young Yudhishthira then counsels the aged Nahusha and helps him attain liberation.

B.4.3. Myth: Yayati, the Needy

Yayati figures in two myths, the first being about his marriage to Devayani, the daughter of Shukra, the preceptor of the demons, and the second about cheating on his wife by making love to Sarmishta, the daughter of the king of the demons, punished to be Devayani's maidservant. Yayati had two sons with Devayani (Yadu and Turvasu) and three sons with Sarmishta (Druhyu, Anu, and Puru).

The second myth is the founding myth of the people of South Asia and the rest of the world. It begins when Yayati was granted a thousand years of youth by the gods. When he reached the end of that period and began to suffer from the debilities of old age, he found that he was still unsatisfied. He wanted a few more years of youth to satisfy his desires. He had an additional gift from the gods, he could extend his youth if he could find somebody to exchange their youth for his old age. Yayati asked, but nobody would give up their youth. Finally, he asked his own sons. Yadu, Druhyu, Turvasu, and Anu refused, with particularly harsh words from Anu.

Puru freely gave up his youth. After a few more years of extended youth, Yayati felt sorry for the son whom he had deprived of youth in this manner and gave Puru back his gift. He then made Puru his heir and sent Puru's brothers to other parts of the world. The oldest, Yadu, remained behind to go to the south of Jambudvipa and became the ancestor of the Yadavas. Druhyu's descendants are the *Bhojas*, the clan that Kunti comes from (though the Bhojas also claimed descent from Yadu, and were one of the Yadava clans forced to migrate from the banks of the Sarasvati).The other brothers gave rise to other people, generally classified as Mlecchas, Yavanas, and so on.

B.4.4. Myth: Puru the Obedient

Puru gave up his youth to his father, Yayati, and in exchange became the dynast. His descendants, the Pauravas, settled on the banks of the Sarasvati and established the first cities of Panchnad.

B.4.5. Pauravas: From Puru to Bharata

This book reimagines the history of the Pauravas from Ilina, a descendant of Puru to Bharata. They developed the trade routes from Panchnad in all directions and made Panchnad a well-known trading culture.

Puru's descendant Ilina founded the city of Kaalindini (named after his mother Kaalindi, the matriarch) among the foothills of the Himalayas on the banks of the Sutudri (Sutlej). Kaalindini was on the trade route to the north into Kashyapura and points further north. Ilina developed long-distance trade to the north and to the south across the Western sea. Ilina's grandson, Bharata, began the first tentative moves towards the east, but he encountered dense forest populated by Nagas not used to long-distance trade. He pulled back and continued Ilina's work of creating a single integrated trade route from northern Gandhara and northern Vakshu (the land around the river Oxus) to the port of Tripura in the south and across to Dilmun. Tin, lapis lazuli, and cotton textiles became staple exports from the Sarasvati-Sindhu culture to the western world.

B.4.6. Bhaaratas: From Bharata to Kuru

This book reimagines the history of the efforts by Panchnad to trade with the Nagas to their east in the Gangetic plains.

Bharata and his descendants continued their attempts to trade with the Nagas. It was not until Hastin's reign that a trading center was established on the banks of the Ganga at a point where the river expanded and slowed down. They sold cotton textiles and felted cotton pieces in exchange for exotic animals and fruits. Occasionally, almost pure copper ore would turn up, and there was great excitement once when a small sample of almost twenty-five per cent pure tin ore was brought in. There was little explanation of how or where this was obtained nor of how much was available.

This trading center, managed by a head trader, was called Nagapura. It would grow to become the capital of a great empire, but it began as the outpost of a trading caravan.

The Naga polity had been changing during these years. "Rogue males" had always existed among the Nagas, but their inability to cooperate with each other meant that they lived lonely lives and died young. However, many generations before Hastin, a band of rogue males led by Takshaka had begun to threaten normal Naga life. To counteract Takshaka's band, a confederacy of the Nagas called Panchala had been formed. After much difficulty, Takshaka was defeated, his band dispersed, and he was killed. In the process, a settlement called Kampilya was established on the northern bank of the Ganga about 150 miles[96] south of Hastinapura. Kampilya functioned as a cantonment for a permanent standing army. Like the other Naga bands, Kampilya was ruled by a matriarchy, but it had a special status among the Nagas and continued as a training center for a permanent army. The confederacy also grew by absorbing more and more Naga bands within its protective umbrella.

Trade expanded slowly, and Nagapura grew in prosperity. By the time of Hastin's descendant, Samvarana, it had become the single biggest settlement on the Ganga. The Nagas around Nagapura had refused to join the confederacy. That made Panchala feel threatened. Panchala attacked Nagapura, and Samvarana was driven out. Samvarana did not retire to a Panchnad city. Instead, he started working on regaining control of Nagapura.

Meanwhile in Panchnad, a teacher named Vasishtha had been developing new ideas of governance. This was in response to the observation that the world outside Panchnad was different. Traders returned with stories of great wars, of fortified cities

---

[96] One hundred and fifty miles is a critical span for many Bronze Age empires. A messenger walking twenty-five to thirty miles a day would take about a week to go from one end to the other of such an empire. (A riverboat could cut that time by two or three times at most when rowing with the current and a favorable wind.) This creates a two-week round-trip time for administrative actions in response to events, probably a limiting factor in managing such empires. Only after the arrival of the horse did larger empires become feasible, Mesopotamia being a good example.

For what it is worth, the distance from Kaalindini to Hastinapura was approximately 150 miles and so are the distances from Hastinapura to Kampilya, Hastinapura to Agra, Agra to Kanpur or Jhansi, Kanpur to Allahabad, and so on, all of these being ancient sites of settlement after the disappearance of the Sarasvati.

under siege, of drought and famine and mass migrations. It was all a bit too much for the ordinary Panchnadis to believe.

Samvarana proved to be an excellent pupil. Having suffered a loss to war, he could believe in Vasishtha. An army was organized with the help of Vasishtha's Kavi Sangha, with the help of the ex-mercenary Vishvamitra. The soldiers were all men, trained to fight and committed to the aims of the Kavi Sangha and to recovering Nagapura. After ten years in exile, Samvarana returned and found a demoralized Naga force defending Nagapura. Trade had dropped to nothing, the settlement was decrepit, and the surrounding Nagas no longer looked to Nagapura for luxuries obtained through trade. The Panchala army melted away, and Samvarana was back in power. The Kavi Sangha's and Vasishtha's reputation for wisdom soared.

After Samvarana returned to power, a steady, if small, stream of ores, mostly copper, but occasionally tin, would come by boat from the east. Tin, in particular, was extremely valuable, but there seemed to be no way to increase its supply. Samvarana's son Kuru took up the challenge to extend Nagapura's trading network to the east. Far to the east, he discovered a plateau south of the Ganga from which the river Hiranyaganga flowed. The ores came from the plateau. A small settlement called Laghu Nagapura was established. Laghu Nagapura was positioned to satisfy an increased demand for ores.

The Panchnadis encountered a new forest-dwelling culture of hunter-gatherers – the Rakshasas – whom they had only heard about until then. The Rakshasas were hostile to trade, and this hostility took many years, almost two generations, to overcome. In the meantime, Laghu Nagapura could only be used for shipping the ores out to Nagapura for smelting into bronze.

Kuru renamed Nagapura as Hastinapura after his ancestor who founded the settlement.

B.4.7. Kauravas: From Kuru to Pratipa

This book is the reimagined history of the Hastinapura trading settlement as it gained power over the local Naga inhabitants and the city's role changed from being only a trading center to being a hegemon.

The first few generations after Kuru were peaceful ones. Hastinapura grew in prosperity, but maintained its army because Panchala continued to be a threat. The presence of a standing army made Hastinapura the most powerful proto-state entity in its neighborhood, the effective hegemon over the surrounding Naga bands. The surrounding Nagas had also become integrated into the trading network. The biggest problem in moving away from the slash-and-burn agricultural way of life was the difficulty of agriculture on the heavy clayey soil of the Gangetic plain.

Many local Nagas found it simpler to switch to fishing as a source of livelihood, becoming Meena-Nagas. There were many differences as well as similarities to the old way of life. Settlements tended to be permanent. Building on stilts was expensive, and so old settlements were not abandoned. In addition, the river's ability to provide fish did not degrade as fishing continued, so frequent moving was not necessary. It was harder to spin off a new band. A new site had to be found, and it had to be located along the riverbank. There were fewer places available for sites.

The new way of life was a riskier way of life. It would be put to the test by the crisis.

B.4.8. Kauravas: From Pratipa to the War

This is the period of the crisis caused by the tectonic events and the resulting changes in the flow of major rivers.

The crisis broke out very early in Pratipa's time. His son Shantanu took the lead in trying to solve the problem. However, personal issues and weaknesses dominated the family. Shantanu's first wife died, leaving a son Devavrata. The story of Devavrata from an early age is the subject of Book 1 of this series.

Spoiler Alert: What follows is a summary of this book and a commentary on some aspects related to the crisis.

Wishing to marry again, Shantanu disinherited Devavrata to fulfil a promise to his second wife Satyavati. Shantanu had two sons with Satyavati. While Shantanu abandoned his duties in the pursuit of pleasure, Devavrata administered the state in consultation with the Kavi Sangha. Steps were taken to help the thousands of migrants, but the crisis grew in magnitude every year. Waterworks were constructed along the Ganga to provide water for agriculture. Land was set aside for new settlements. Disputes with the Nagas over land rights increased, and the Hastinapura military had to be deployed. The Nagas were not a combative culture. If two Naga bands came into conflict over land, it was usually easier for one or both to move. Therefore, the Nagas moved, and moved again. Lands they would have left fallow did not remain fallow but were occupied by migrants. Though Devavrata tried to be even-handed between Panchnad immigrants and Naga inhabitants, the Nagas were slowly pushed away by a growing circle of immigrant settlements centered on Hastinapura.

When Shantanu died, his son Chitrangada was crowned king but died childless. Chitrangada's brother Vichitravirya also died, leaving two sons, Dhritarashtra and Mahendra. The older son, Dhritarashtra, being blind, could not be crowned, so Mahendra became King. Mahendra was nicknamed *Pandu* (meaning "the Pale") and this name stuck. Dhritarashtra had many ("a hundred") sons. They were called the Kauravas to distinguish them from the sons of Mahendra Pandu, the five Pandavas. Suyodhana was the oldest Kaurava, and Yudhishthira was the oldest Pandava. Yudhishthira should have been crowned King, but in a compromise, the Pandavas left Hastinapura to rule half the kingdom from Indraprastha, a settlement originally founded by Mahendra Pandu. Suyodhana, the oldest Kaurava, was declared heir to his father Dhritarashtra, but he could not be crowned while his father lived. Nevertheless, he titled himself King while Devavrata continued as Regent.

In summary, after Shantanu's death, Devavrata was Regent for about four years. After Chitrangada's death, Devavrata was Regent for about six years. After Vichitravirya's death, Devavrata was Regent for sixteen years, the regency ending when Mahendra Pandu was crowned. After Mahendra Pandu went into exile, Devavrata acted in his stead, acting as Regent for over fifteen, possibly as long as twenty, years. This regency should have ended when the Pandavas returned and Yudhishthira crowned. The compromise that sent the Pandavas to Indraprastha averted conflict but did not resolve the succession dilemma. It allowed

Devavrata to continue as Regent de facto until the end of the Great War.

B.4.9. The Great War: Pandavas and Kauravas

This story is dealt with in this series of Books.

B.4.10. Pandavas: From Arjuna to Janamejaya

This is also dealt with in this series of Books.

B.4.11. The Family Tree

The Kuru family tree is shown in the end of the book. It shows the chain of ancestors from the mythical era – Pururavas to Puru. Some of Puru's descendants, the Pauravas, are identified in the yellow box. The list only identifies the rulers whose actions are mentioned in this book and skips over many intervening rulers.

To the left is the "Vyaasa Chain" that names the sequence of Vyaasas, the head of the Kavi Sangha. The extent of a Vyaasa's role is approximately parallel to the Hastinapura ruler they were associated with. Vasishtha, for instance, is associated with Samvarana. Samvarana's ancestor Hastin founded the town of Nagapura, and Samvarana's son Kuru renames the town Hastinapura.

Kuru, a Paurava, i.e., a descendant of Puru, is considered the dynast for the Kauravas, his descendants. The label "Kaurava" denotes all the descendants of Kuru, referring to the sons of Mahendra Pandu as well as the sons of Dhritarashtra. However, in the most common usage, "Kaurava" denotes only the hundred sons of Dhritarashtra and "Pandava" denotes the five sons of Mahendra Pandu.

The crisis described in this book began towards the end of Arugvat's reign – a trickle of Panchnad refugees that slowly grew into a population problem in Shantanu's time. Shantanu's two wives (Ganga and Satyavati) are shown along with their children, including Satyavati's child with Parashara (who also appears in the Vyaasa list).

Kunti, the Bhoja Matriarch, who comes to live in Mahendra's settlement of Indraprastha, is shown with a dotted line back to her ancestor Druhyu, skipping many generations. Kunti does not have daughters. Her three sons grow up in Indraprastha with the twin sons of Madri. These five are, of course, the Pandavas, named after Pandu, the male head of the settlement.

Colored boxes surround the warring cousins, the Pandavas and the Kauravas. The five Pandavas are joint husbands of the Panchala Matriarch Krishnaa Agnijyotsna. She and her children are not shown. Arjuna is also husband to Subhadra, the daughter of Devaki, the Matriarch of the Vrishni clan, by Vasudeva, army chief for the Bhojas and brother of Kunti. That is, Arjuna and Subhadra were first cousins. Subhadra's ancestry from Yadu is also indicated by dotted lines.

Arjuna's son by Subhadra is Abhimanyu. He died young during the war. His son Parikshit is the only descendant of the Pandavas who survives the Great War. Following the patrilineal model of Hastinapura, Parikshit becomes the ruler of Hastinapura.

B.5. A BRIEF HISTORY OF THE KAVI SANGHA

The Kavi Sangha is a completely invented organization. The names of its leaders (the Vyaasas) have been chosen to correspond with sages in Hindu mythology, but everything else is invented.

B.5.1. Vasishtha

The first Vyaasa was Vasishtha. Vasishtha was a bard. Bards had always been a key part of Panchnad society for they provided the memorization and archiving service that was used to manage the marketplace in the oral culture of those days. The demand for bards was growing and the guild of bards was not able to expand fast enough. Vasishtha established a school to teach these skills to any student, and the best graduates of the school were organized into the Kavi Sangha. When Panchala drove Samvarana out of Nagapura, he came to Panchnad looking for help. Vasishtha took him under his wing and trained him to be a warrior. He then helped the newly minted general to put together an army of men prepared to fight a real war, unlike the mercenaries of Panchnad. The martial arts teacher Vishvamitra was an ex-mercenary, but one with experience in the Western world, and knew about fighting such wars. Vishvamitra's unusual intellect had got the attention of Vasishtha, who made him a protégé.

The Kavi Sangha's role in restoring Samvarana to Nagapura greatly enhanced its prestige and Vasishtha's reputation for wisdom. After the restoration, the Kavi Sangha and its members, especially the Vyaasa, became much sought after and every Panchnad town invited them to participate in civic affairs at the highest level. Vasishtha was the head of both the guild of bards and the school, which he managed as a single operation. He received support to train more bards and in response, he increased the range and extent of the archives maintained by the guild, now merged into the Kavi Sangha.

Many Kavi Sangha members aspired to succeed Vasishtha in the role of Vyaasa. As Vasishtha grew older, the virus of patriarchy had begun to infect him and he wanted to make his son Shakti the next Vyaasa. Shakti had been born very late in Vasishtha's life and was still a child when his father died, and another Vyaasa, Vishvamitra, was selected.

B.5.2. Vishvamitra

Vishvamitra was the obvious next candidate, but many bards objected to him as he was not a bard but had been a mercenary. Vishvamitra had to prove his qualifications many times, but finally succeeded in obtaining universal approval. After Vishvamitra, Bhrigu became the Vyaasa.

B.5.3. Bhrigu

Bhrigu was a systemic institution builder. He established practices and precedents that made the Kavi Sangha a permanent institution in the life of Panchnad and Hastinapura. During this period, Hastinapura grew in power and established itself as a major trading center. After his death, Bharadvaja became the Vyaasa.

B.5.4. Bharadvaja

Bharadvaja was the Vyaasa when Pratipa was King and the crisis of refugees began.

The Yamuna and the Sutudri changed their course, the Yamuna going east and the Sutudri further west, and both were lost to the Sarasvati. A worldwide drought that lasted almost four hundred years coincided with the riverine changes. As a result, the Sarasvati also lost the other source of water and started drying up. Refugees streamed into Hastinapura. Hastinapura was overwhelmed, and Pratipa asked the Vyaasa Bharadvaja for help.

Bharadvaja was a pragmatist and realist who looked for rational solutions to all problems. The flood of refugees had caused hardship. There was not enough food to go around, and the Naga mode of production precluded ramping up food production rapidly. The Nagas could not be displaced easily, but their practice of leaving groves fallow for two generations made it possible to house the refugees there, even if the land was not productive. However, that was not enough, and the population had to be controlled. Already, babies were dying of starvation. Bharadvaja suggested the "one child per person" policy, that child preferably a son. A girl would contribute much more to population growth a generation hence than a boy could.

This law would apply to refugees in Hastinapura, creating a disincentive to settle in the city. Bharadvaja wanted to encourage the Panchnad refugees to go as far east as possible, well beyond Laghu Nagapura into Rakshasa land or beyond, or to go as far west as possible, to Bahlika or even Parsaka and lands beyond. He floated a proposal to work on diverting the Yamuna back into its old channel. This would be backbreaking and dangerous work, but it would restore the Sarasvati and allow the refugees to return to Panchnad. In order to encourage the refugees to participate in the diversion project, workers on this project would be exempted from the one-child-per-person policy. This concession aroused anger in the older residents of Hastinapura as it was seen to favor the immigrants.

The diversion project was given up and the one-child-per-person policy applied without exemption. Thus began the policy disputes that led to the Great War. Shantanu applied the policy to the whole population of Hastinapura in the spirit of equity, but the policy was only enforceable because Hastinapura had become a permanently militarized state.

Bharadvaja began to use the army to construct waterworks in areas deemed fit for settlement by immigrants. Conflicts with local Nagas were addressed quickly. As the land being expropriated was lying fallow, the Nagas frequently let the land go without a fight. Among Nagas, conflicts only occurred when two groups wanted to move to the same place at the same time. Such a coincidence was rare, and most often, the conflict was settled by one Naga band going somewhere else. The Nagas took the same approach towards Hastinapura. But the Hastinapura-supported settlements were permanent, and the Nagas were being slowly pushed out of the region. When conflict did become worse, the army dealt with the uncooperative Nagas harshly.

Bharadvaja died a few years after Shantanu's wife Ganga died. He was succeeded by Parashara.

B.5.5. Parashara

The Vyaasa title returned to Vasishtha's family when Parashara, son of Vasishtha's son Shakti, became the Vyaasa. Parashara was known as the "walking Vyaasa" for he walked everywhere. He had been asked by Bharadvaja to assess if the Nagas would tolerate being thrown off their land to make room for the immigrants. Parashara concluded that the Nagas would not tolerate it. In the course of his travels, he also encouraged many Nagas to join the Kavi Sangha, with the long-term goal of extending the Kavi Sangha to the Nagas. Parashara had hidden his involvement with Satyavati from the senior members of the Kavi Sangha. The affair was not a problem, but hiding it was, and he was sentenced to a vow of silence for a few years, even though he was the Vyaasa. During this period, Satyavati married Shantanu through Shukla's machinations.

Parashara died before the term of his punishment ended. He was followed by Jaimini.

B.5.6. Jaimini

Jaimini became Vyaasa a year or so before Chitrangada was born. He was the opposite of Bharadvaja. Where Bharadvaja had been practical and hard-nosed, Jaimini was compassionate and flexible. In particular, Jaimini objected to the use of the army to build the waterworks that helped settle immigrants and dispossess Nagas. But there seemed to be no alternative. An army was needed to keep Panchala at bay. The army had to be fed. The only way to feed it was to use it to increase food production or enforce laws that controlled the population. Some years after the death of Shantanu's first wife, the one-child-per-person policy was annulled. That left the army only one choice, increase food production by replacing Nagas with settlers.

Jaimini continued the recruitment of Nagas into the Kavi Sangha. As Devavrata expected, this made the process of settling immigrants a little harder, as Naga concerns were taken into account in each project. However, addressing these concerns reduced the conflict in the colonization of Naga lands.

Jaimini died a few years after Vichitravirya's death.

B.5.7. Shukla

Jaimini's successor was Shukla, the brother of Satyavati, and the first Naga to be named Vyaasa. He was the Vyaasa through the period of this novel (*The Last Kaurava* and *The Making of Bhishma*). When he died, his nephew Krishna Dvaipaayana, son of Parashara by Satyavati, became the Vyaasa.

B.5.8. Krishna Dvaipaayana Paaraasharya

Krishna Dvaipaayana as Vyaasa worked with the Archivist Lomaharshana to create order out of the archives of the war years. He composed the *Jaya*, a poem about the war, and performed it at a Spring Festival at King Janamejaya's request.

The Archivist Lomaharshana (introduced in this book) followed Krishna Dvaipaayana as Vyaasa.

B.5.9. Lomaharshana

Lomaharshana made it his mission to spread the story of the Great War. He made its recital an annual event coinciding with the Spring Festival.

B.6. NEOLOGISMS

Terminology invented by the author.

B.6.1. Nishkamkarnarpana

The Kavi Sangha's bards and memorizers learned early in their education to enter a trance state in which they would listen without judgement and without attachment to what was being said. With practice and experience, the memorizer would learn to dispense with the trance state when listening, but the skill was available for use under unusual conditions. I have named this skill *niṣkāmkarṇārpaṇa* (pronounced "nish-calm-cur-narp-un-u(h)", and spelled "nishkamkarnarpana"). The word means "paying attention without attachment."

B.6.2. Nishkamsmaranadharanam

The Kavi Sangha's bards and memorizers practiced a collection of mental exercises and practices to erase unneeded memories while retaining the important ones. These exercises and the skills developed were called *niṣkāmsmaraṇadhāraṇam*, pronounced Nish-calm-smu(t)-runner-th(e)-ah-run-um,   and   spelled nishkamsmaranadharanam, "holding on to memory without attachment."

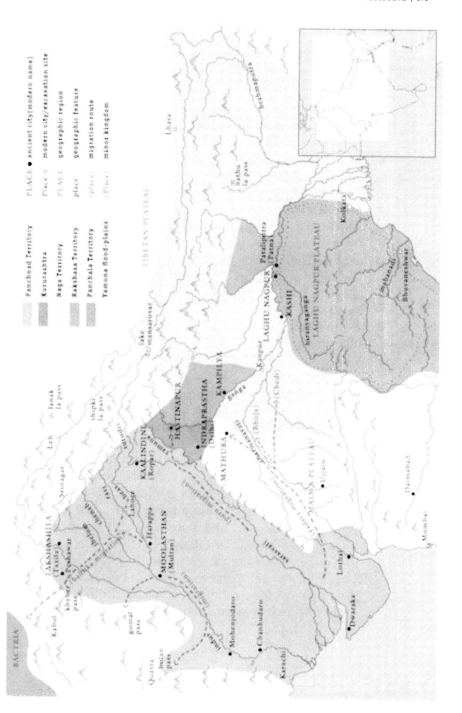

Panchnad Territory

Kurukshetra

Naga Territory

Rakshasa Territory

Panchala Territory

Yamuna flood-plains

PLACE ● ancient city/modern name)

Place ○ modern city/excavation site

PLACE geographic region

place geographic feature

place migration route

(Place) minor kingdom

B.7. GEOGRAPHY, POLITICS, AND HISTORY

A map of Panchnad and Northern South Asia is shown in the front of this book. It shows the geopolitical situation in 2000 BCE (the time of the events in this book). The following conventions have been followed:

- Regions occupied by different groups and/or cultures are shown as shaded areas.
- The Laghu Nagapura and Malwa plateaus are demarcated using a dotted line.
- Cities and regions mentioned in this book are labelled in uppercase.
- Some modern cities are marked to help readers orient themselves. These names are in lowercase with initial capital. The label is placed within parentheses if an ancient town, village, or city was close by.
- Rivers' names are in all lowercase and are placed alongside the river.
- A number of cities outside South Asia are also indicated.
- Some of the major passes (Khyber, Gomal, and Bolan passes in the west, the Lanak-La and the Shipki-La passes in the north, and the Nathu-La in the northeast) are shown. They were major routes into South Asia for both trade and human migration.
- Lake Mansarovar in Tibet is shown. It is generally held to be the source of the four great rivers of North India (the Sindhu (Indus), the Ganga, the Yamuna, and the Brahmaputra) and is a place of pilgrimage for both Hindus and Buddhists. A number of other great rivers of China, Myanmar, and Indochina also have their watersheds within a short distance of this lake.
- At bottom left, Mumbai and Daimabad are shown. Daimabad's claim to fame is that it is the southern-most point of the sub-continent where "Bronze Age" Sarasvati Sindhu Culture artefacts have been found.

B.7.1. Nagas and Rakshasas

The map shows a light brown region to the north and east, extending from Lake Mansarovar in the west to the eastern end of the Brahmaputra (Tsang-po) river and incorporating the delta of the Ganga and Brahmaputra. This area was heavily forested and sparsely populated by the Nagas who were slash-and-burn agriculturalists. They had migrated here from the north (Tibet) and east (China and Indochina through Myanmar) many thousands of years earlier and spread over the Gangetic plain.

The region colored reddish-brown contains the Laghu Nagapura (now called Chota Nagpur) plateau and extends south into the South Asian peninsula. This region, too, was heavily forested and sparsely populated by the hunter-gathering culture Rakshasas (the name the Nagas used for them). The Rakshasas were descended from the earliest human migrants out of Africa (~60,000 BCE) who had left bands in settlements along the shores of the Deccan peninsula (probably 40,000 BCE to 20,000 BCE. These bands had slowly expanded into the plateau and up north into Laghu Nagapura where they may have first encountered the Nagas. The Nagas initially responded by retreating. They avoided conflict, and the land seemed unlimited. As a result, the Rakshasas had come down from the Laghu Nagapura plateau, crossed the Ganga, and occupied land all the way to the Himalayas. Meanwhile the Nagas, who had discovered that land was not limitless, began to resist, leading to the situation shown in the map.

The Rakshasas in Laghu Nagapura had developed significant mining and copper smelting skills.

B.7.2. Panchnad

Panchnad is the brown region to the west on the map, extending from the Sarasvati in the east to the Western Himalayan foothills in the west and from the northern Himalayan foothills to the Western Sea (now called the Arabian Sea) to the south.

The city of Kaalindini (near the modern town of Ropar or Rupnagar) in northwest Panchnad is located on the banks of the Sutudri ("Hundred rivulets") as it leaves the Himalayas. Before the crisis brought on by the earthquake, the Sutudri drained to the south. The land being a very flat alluvial plain, the Sutudri split into a multitude of streams (hence the name). The crisis changed the Sutudri into the modern Sutlej, which turns west at Kaalindini/Ropar (and is not shown in this map). The map shows the approximate ancient course of the Sutudri as it heads south.

Before the crisis, the Sutudri merged with the Yamuna to form the Sarasvati. Tectonic events, i.e. earthquakes, changed the course of the Yamuna as described. It turned east at the northern ridge of the Aravalli range. As a result, the Sarasvati lost its two primary sources of water from the Himalayas. It did not dry up immediately as a third monsoon-fed river, the Drishadvati (not shown here), came from the Aravalli range to join the Sarasvati.

B.7.3. Kururashtra

The Yamuna (in its old course) formed the northeast boundary of Panchnad. The river Ganga flows parallel to the Yamuna. The town of Hastinapura (begun as the trading center Nagapura) was founded on the western bank of the Ganga. Hastinapura controlled the land between the Yamuna and the Ganga all the way to the northern foothills. To the south, Hastinapura's control extended just past the Aravalli ridge into a scrub forest that was called Khandavaprastha. The Hastinapura-controlled area called Kururashtra is shown in pink.

B.7.4. Panchala

The eastern bank of the Ganga was under the control of Panchala, a confederation of five Naga clans that considered Hastinapura a dangerous foreign interloper. Panchala, shown in purple, was managed from the military cantonment of Kampilya. It extended along the northern foothills of the Himalayas past Hastinapura to the point where the Ganga emerged from the mountains.

B.7.5. Migrations out of Panchnad

The map shows the routes that the refugees leaving Panchnad followed. To the northwest, they went through the major passes towards the Afghanistan plateau. From the northern settlements on the Sarasvati, the refugees went towards Hastinapura. From the southern end of the Sarasvati, the refugees, who called themselves Yadavas, went east past the southern end of the Aravalli range and into the Malwa plateau (shown in white). From the Malwa plateau, the Yadavas split into four branches: The Andhakas stayed in Malwa. The Chedis went east towards Kashi. The Bhojas went along the Charmanavati River gorge and tried to settle the region between the rivers Charmanavati and the Betwah. The Vrishnis headed north and tried to create settlements on the banks of the re-directed Yamuna.

The Chedis and Bhojas came into conflict with the Nagas on their territory. The Chedis responded by allying with Rakshasas. The Bhojas retreated to Malwa after many failed attempts to establish settlements. The Vrishnis were lucky. The instability of the Yamuna meant that neither they nor the local Nagas had much to fight over right away. But that same instability frustrated the Vrishnis' wish to create their urban center Mathura.

The Vrishnis followed a different model for settlement. Led by their army chief Gopala Krishna (son of the matriarch Devaki by her husband the Bhoja army chief Vasudeva), they tried to create alliances with all the local powers – Hastinapura in the north, Panchala on the other side of the Ganga, and the Meena-Nagas who had migrated up the Yamuna streams. But that caused rifts with their cousins the Bhojas and Chedis.

B.7.6. Prehistory

This map does not show the other ancient migrations that led to the tripartite division of South Asia between the urban civilization of Panchnad, the hunter-gatherer Rakshasas, and the slash-and-burn Nagas. This division had come into being well before the time of the Sarasvati disaster.

B.8. JAMBUDVIPA

The traditional name for all of South Asia is *Jambudvipa*, the Island of the Jambul. Unfortunately, South Asia is not an island, and there is some debate over the identity of the Jambul fruit.

B.8.1.   The Jambul

Wikipedia describes two different "Jambul" fruits. One is a purple berry, tart and sweet (*Syzygium cumini*[97]), that grows at higher elevations all over India. The other is a pear-shaped but smaller fruit (*Syzygium samarangense*[98]) with a melon-y pulp ranging in color from white to red that grows all over South Asia and South East Asia. The Wikipedia reference calls both of them "Jambul", but it also calls the latter the "rose apple". It seems that the rose apple may be called "Jambul" in some parts of South East Asia as well. However, Indians asked to describe the "jambul", will describe the berry. To add to the confusion, the jambul berry is called "naga pazhum" in Tamil, i.e., "snake fruit", or "fruit of the Nagas".

So, is "Jambudvipa" the "Island of the Rose-Apple" or is it the "Island of the Purple Berry" or "Island of the Snake Fruit"? It is unclear to me why most Western authorities in Indian mythology prefer one meaning ("rose-apple") over the other. The Tamil name conjures the possibility that the name Jambudvipa connotes the original possession of the land by Nagas.

B.8.2.   The Island

A Kashmiri legend says that in the center of Kashmir was a great lake with an island paradise in the middle. When the Earth was kidnapped by the demon Hiranyaksha and hidden in the depths of the Sea of Milk, Vishnu, incarnated as a boar, killed Hiranyaksha and retrieved the earth from the milky depths by carrying it on the tip of his tusk. The tip of the tusk punctured the edge of the great Kashmiri lake at a place called Varahamoola, which drained the lake and created the land of Kashmir. Varahamoola is now identified as Baramulla.

I have "extended" the Kashmir myth to cover all of South Asia: A hypothetical Panchnad myth identifies South Asia as that central island and the draining of the lake with the emergence of

---

97 See http://en.wikipedia.org/wiki/Syzygium_cumini
98 See http://en.wikipedia.org/wiki/Syzygium_samarangense

the subcontinent of South Asia (then called Jambudvipa) from the drained lake.

There are problems with this unification as a solution to the myth as with others. Jambudvipa is clearly not an island, so some people believe that it refers to all of Asia or Eurasia. Others believe it refers to Asia, Europe, and Africa as a single landmass. And then (a deep breath is called for here) there are people who believe that this name is a residual race memory of ancient Gondwanaland, from a time when India, Africa, Antarctica, and Australia formed one island, a mere one hundred and eighty million years ago. This is, of course, conclusively proved by its name, which translates as *Land of the Forest-Garden of the Gonds*.

B.9. GEOGRAPHY OF THE WESTERN WORLD

B.9.1. Egypt

B.9.1.1. Names

From the Wikipedia entry for "Egypt"

The English name *Egypt* is derived from the ancient Greek *Aígyptos* (Αἴγυπτος), via Middle French *Egypte* and Latin *Aegyptus*. It is reflected in early Greek Linear B tablets as *a-ku-pi-ti-yo*. The Greek forms were borrowed from Late Egyptian (Amarna) *"Hikuptah* of Memphis", a corruption of the earlier Egyptian name *Hwt-ka-Ptah*, meaning "home of the KA (soul) of Ptah", the name of a temple to the god Ptah at Memphis.

The god Ptah was considered an ancestor of all Egyptians. One variation of the name of Ptah's temple was "Home of the Temple of the Ancestor." In Sanskrit, this would be *Pitr-vihara* ("temple of the ancestors"). Adding *"naadu"* ("land" from vernacular languages) as a suffix to make *Pitr-vihara-naadu* might be a culturally appropriate way to refer to Egypt.

Other names of Egypt include "The Black Land," "The Red Land," and "The Land of the Black River." The word "black" or "red" refers to the color of the silt that the Nile carries and deposits on the land after floods. This soil is responsible for the extraordinary fertility of the land bordering the Nile, converting a desert into one of the most productive agricultural lands in the world. The ancient Egyptians also referred to themselves as the "black" or "red" people.

The "Black River" is the Nile and it would be translated to "Krishna" in Sanskrit.

B.9.1.2.   Egypt: Places, Gods, and People

Osiris (the Greek pronunciation of "Au-ser") is the great god of the ancient Egyptian religion. Indian interpreters of Egyptian religion have made much of the similarity between "Au-ser" and "Eashwar" (as the great god Shiva is known in Hinduism). There are many similarities. Au-sera could mean "the great prince or lord" and Eashwar means "lord". Au-ser could mean "the receiver of ritual offerings," while "-eashwar" as a suffix could mean the one who has the right to a sacrifice (or ritual offerings). There is no known link between the two names, but they are ancient names in two civilizations that traded with each other.

Egyptian history mentions a people called "Punit" or "Punt" from before 1500 BCE who traded with Egypt, but came from an unknown homeland to the "east". Around 1500 BCE, the Queen-Pharaoh Hatsepshut sent an expedition to Punt with a guide. They came back with stories that could have been from eastern Somalia, but could also describe the land around Kerala in India. Later Egyptian chronicles mention the attack of the "Sea People," who are said to be related to the people of Punt. The Sea People, also called Panit by the Egyptians, came to dominate trade on the Mediterranean Sea and were called Phoenicians by the Greeks. I've called them the "Western Panias", the "Pani-s" or "Bani-s" being the traders of ancient India, forerunners of the Banias in later times.

B.9.1.3.   Egypt: From Matriarchy to Patriarchy

Egypt's transition from matriarchy to patriarchy took place in many ways. One example of a transitional structure is the inheritance model of the Pharaohs of Egypt, which was followed for almost four thousand years. The successor to a Pharaoh would be his son who was a *stepson* of the Great Queen (the senior-most wife of the Pharaoh). The son had to marry the Great Queen's *daughter* (not stepdaughter) to establish his legitimacy, and she would become the next Great Queen. (This is the source of the claim that Pharaohs of Egypt married their own sisters; they married a stepsister to establish their right to the throne. In practice, the system was frequently abused as some Pharaohs, once established in power, would marry other women, declare one of them the Great Queen, and usurp the stepsister's title.

One collateral effect of this mode of inheriting power was that any other sisters of a Great Queen would be barred from marrying *anybody*. In the few cases they were married, it was to men incapable of being a Pharaoh. In many cases, these sisters died of unknown causes, possibly murdered by their brother to forestall a husband from challenging the Pharaoh's fitness to rule (as *any* daughter of a Great Queen could lay claim to be her successor as the Great Queen).

B.9.2. Rivers

The land of the Shakas (said to be descendants of Druhyu, a son of Yayati) was called Scythia by the Greeks. North of Scythia, the Danavas (the children of Danu, one of the wives of the Sage Kashyapa) were said to occupy Siberia and Eastern Europe, through which some of the greatest rivers of the world flow, though they are frozen for several months of the year. Many of these rivers were not known in India, though by coincidence a number of great rivers have names beginning with "D-n". Some river names from Iran to Mesopotamia are easily translated into the Sanskrit names used in this book. The Euphrates ("Well fertilized" in Greek) becomes the Su-purna ("Fulfilling well" or "Completing well"); the Tigris ("Swift" in Greek) becomes the Sindhu-of-the-west.

All the rivers to the east of India that came out of Tibet are given names that are a variant of "Ganga." The Bo Ganga is Tsang-po or Brahmaputra or Lauhitya (Lohita's child). The Shia (Xia) Ganga is the Yang-tze. The Ho Ganga is the Huang-Ho. The Hme Ganga is the Mekong. The Naga Ganga is the Irrawady (also mother of the Great Naga Airavatha). The rivers that flow west are fast rivers and are called Sindhu. The rivers to the northwest were known but do not appear in this book. The Syr Darya was called *Yaksh-arta*, which means the *Pure Pearl* in Persian, which is close to *Laksha-Rta* in Sanskrit, the Greek name being *Jaxartes*. The Amu Darya, was *Vakshu*, possibly meaning "good or beneficent river", the Greek name being Oxus.

B.9.3. Names of Countries

Afghanistan is part of the South Asian cultural landscape, but is difficult to reach, so its cultural connections with mainland India were intermittent and driven by trade. Gandhara (Kandahar in modern Afghanistan) had the closest relationships. Further north, Shantanu's brother Bahlika is said to have settled in Bactria (the Greek form of Bahlika). The similarity of the names "Bahlika" and "Baluchistan" could be mere coincidence, but note that Brahui, spoken only in Baluchistan, is one of the oldest Dravidian languages known. Bactria forms part of the Vakshu (Sanskrit name for the Oxus) civilization, also called the Bactrian-Margiana Archaeological Complex (BMAC). BMAC was an extended civilization of fortified towns contemporary to Harappa and Mohenjodaro. The design of the settlements of BMAC could arguably be a response to the hostile conditions under which Bahlika left Panchnad.

B.9.4. The Khyber Pass

The name Khyber is supposed to be derived from the Semitic/Hebrew word for "fort". There is no other name used by the West. Unfortunately, I have not been able to find a Sanskrit word for the pass. A plausible derivation is that the word "Khyber" is a translation of the name used by the residents. This would be "kuta" meaning fort (among other meanings). Kubera is the god of wealth in the Hindu pantheon. The Khyber was a pathway to wealth for traders going west and for raiders coming south. Hence the name "Kuberakuta", i.e., Kubera's Fort. The translation in a Semitic language to "Kubera's Khyber" is a bit strange because it sounds like "Fort's Fort", and it was simplified to "Fort", i.e. Khyber, by the Westerners.

B.10. FATHERHOOD

The reader of this book may consider incredible my assertion that the ancient culture of South Asia did not understand the connection between sexual intercourse and fatherhood and did not understand how the baby developed, how it inherited the characteristics of the father, and so on.

This claim is not limited to South Asia, but is generally true for many, if not all, Bronze-Age cultures. The evidence for my claim can be found in various stories and rules found in religious myths, scriptural documents, and other ancient writings. An example of such a story is Jacob tricking his father-in-law in the Torah. An example of such a rule is Manu's rule, "Any child born in the 'field' owned by a man is his."

When I discuss this, I have found many listeners unwilling to listen carefully and jumping to conclusions about what I am saying or not saying. Their view is that we know the following:

1. A single act of intercourse, about nine months earlier, makes the woman pregnant
2. That a child has exactly one father and cannot have zero or multiple fathers
3. One and only one of the sole father's sperm cells fertilized a single egg/ovum of the mother
4. That the child inherits characteristics from the mother through the egg
5. The child inherits characteristics of the sole father from the single sperm cell.

Multiple births are a bit more complex and raise other possibilities than single births – we still do not know all the different possibilities that can occur. So the following observation is limited to single births.

To many people it is incomprehensible that three propositions listed above is not known to humans "naturally", i.e., without any kind of experimental or other verification. People want to believe, apparently, that we are all born with this knowledge and that fathers know who their children are by some non-conscious and non-deliberate chemical or alchemical process.

There is no question about motherhood as the mother's role in creating the child is very obvious.

My claim is that observation #1 above is not innate to humans but had to be discovered by some empirical observations. The observations became possible when humans domesticated animals, specifically the dog, which has a short gestation period. This still does not establish the knowledge of #2, #3, #4, and #5. If the mother had sexual relations with more than one man in the critical period (just before the first missed menstrual period) then maybe the child has multiple fathers. The seminal fluid is the visible product of the man that enters the woman and is the "obvious" source of the foetus. The knowledge of spermatozoa requires the invention of microscopes. It is "obvious" that the mother's characteristics are inherited because the foetus grows in the woman's womb. This leaves us with the conundrum of #5 – how does the baby inherit the characteristics of the father? It has to be more than just the seminal fluid because then a woman who had multiple sexual relationships would give birth to children with the characteristics of many fathers – not a usual occurrence. The environment is an "obvious" choice, as exemplified by the story of Jacob in the Torah. In that case, the father can also influence the child by being part of the environment.

One feature of #1 – it is based on empirical data collected by women! The knowledge that a period has been missed following a sexual act would not automatically be conveyed to a male observer. I propose that this requires a settled or partially settled community, not a frequently moving nomadic band. In such a band a minimum number of men are needed for hunting and for protection from other predators. An excess of men creates instability and cannot be tolerated as they are expensive to maintain.

C. GLOSSARY

Name of Person or Place/Pronunciation Guide	Definition of Word and Description of Person or Place
Amba / (H)um-ba(h)	Member of Naga band; goes to Hastinapura; escapes
Angavastram/(H)ung-gov-us-trum(p)	Upper cloth or covering; covers the torso and shoulders
Arjuna/Urge-june-u(h)	Son of Kunti and Mahendra Pandu; third Pandava
Bahlika/Bah-lick-u(h)	Shantanu's brother who abdicates and migrates to Bactria or Baluchistan
Bakakula/Buck-ark-cool-u(h)	Name ("Family of Baka") of Shantanu's driver
Bharadvaja/Burr-oth(er)-va(st)-ju(st)	One of the Vyaasas
Bharata/Burr-rut-u(p)	Ancestor of Samvarana; in legend the first king to unify all of Bhaaratavarsha (eponymous "land of Bharata)
Bhima/Beam-u(p)	Son of Kunti; the second Pandava
Bhishma/Bee-schmu(ck)	"The Terrible," a title attached to Devavrata's name
Charmanavati /Chur(l)-mon(day)-(c)arver-thi(ef)	River; now called the Chambal

Name of Person or Place/Pronunciation Guide	Definition of Word and Description of Person or Place
Chitrangada/Chit-ra-(su)ng-othe(r)	Son of Satyavati and Shantanu; rumored to have been killed in a battle with a Gandharva
Devapi/They've-up-pea	Shantanu's brother who walks off into the forest
Devavrata/They've-of-(b)rothe(r)	Son of Ganga and Shantanu; earns the name "The Terrible" (Bhishma)
Dhritarashtra/Thee-ri-the-ra-sh(h)-tru(ck)	Son of Ambika and Vichitravirya; blind at birth; father of Suyodhana and his brothers, the Kauravas
Drona/Thee-row-nu(t)	Possibly pejorative name for Kutaja, the martial arts instructor of the Kaurava and Pandava cousins and others
Duryodhana/Thee-ri-yo-the-nu(t)	Bad Warrior; pejorative name of Suyodhana
Dvaipaayana/Thee-why-pa-yen-nu(t)	"Born on an island," Krishna Dvaipaayana is the son of Satyavati and Parashara
Dvapara Yuga/Thee-va(st)-purr-u(h) You-gu(t)	The third of the four Ages of mankind
Gana/Gun-nu(t)	The masses; the people at the bottom of the social hierarchy
Ganapathi/Gun-nup(tial)-per-thie(f)	Lord of the Gana(s); also a god in later times; patron god of Hastinapura, who removes obstacles to trade and business
Ganesha/Gun-hey-shhh	Another name for Ganapathi; meaning "Lord or God of the masses"
Ganga/Gun-ga(h)	Devavrata's mother; also, the river called the "Ganges" by the ancient Greeks and modern Englishmen
Hastinapura/Hus(h)-tea-na(h)-poo(h)-ru(m)	A trading post established just beyond the frontiers of Panchnad on the banks of the Ganga, in Naga territory; also called Nagapura as it was built with Naga help
Himavat/Him-marve(l)-th(ief)	"White Mountain Range," the Himalayas
Hiranyaganga/Here-un(do)-near-gun-gu(t)	A tributary of the Ganga coming from Chota Nagpur; now called the Sone
Indraprastha/In-the-ra-pr(op)-us-thu(d)	Settlement founded by Mahendra Pandu; capital of the Pandava kingdom before the war

Name of Person or Place/Pronunciation Guide	Definition of Word and Description of Person or Place
Jambudvipa/Jum(p)-boo-the-vee-pu(n)	The Island of the Jambul Tree
Jaya/Ju(mp)-yea(rn)	"Victory;" also a victory lay; when capitalized, as in "Jaya", it is a lay of the Great War that is the central story of this novel
Kaalindini/Kaa-lindy-nee	Panchnad settlement in the Himalayan foothills closest to the point where the Sutudri emerged from the mountains; possibly, the town of Ropar/Rupnagar (though "kalindi"'s meaning "from the Yamuna" makes this dubious)
Kali Yuga/Cull-ea(se) You-gu(t)	Fourth age of humanity, supposed to be in the future for Panchnad
Kampilya / Come-pill-yea(rn)	The capital of Panchala
Karna / Cur-nu(h)	Friend, supporter, and provocateur to Suyodhana
Kaunteya / Coun(t)-The(odore)-yeah	Descendant of Kunti, generally used for Yudhishthira, Bhima, and Arjuna, the three oldest Pandavas
Kaurava / Cow-ru(n)-ver(se)	Descendent of Kuru
Kaushambi / Cow-sharm[ǀ ǀcalm]-bee	Site occupied by the citizens of Hastinapura escaping the floods of 850 BCE
Kavi Sangha/Cu(r)-vee Sung-gu(t)	Means "Society of Poets"; established by Vasishtha to fulfil his plan to prevent Panchnad from possible stagnation
Khandavaprastha/Khan-dove-up-russ-thu(d)	Land to the southwest of Hastinapura, suddenly inundated with the waters of the Yamuna when it changes course; over a century, Khandavaprastha changes from scrubland to green and fertile forest, setting the stage for conflict
Krishna Dvaipaayana/Cree-shhh-nu(t) Thee-why-pa-yen-nu(t)	Krishna Dvaipaayana is the son of Satyavati and Parashara, Krishna means "black"
Krishna Vaasudeva/Cree-shhh-nu(t) Vas(t)-sue-they've-u(p)	Leader of Yadavas who supports the Pandavas' claim to half of Hastinapura's land

Name of Person or Place/Pronunciation Guide	Definition of Word and Description of Person or Place
Kuru/Coo-roo	Dynast of the family ruling Hastinapura; changes name of Nagapura to Hastinapura; establishes Laghu Nagapura; establishes riverine trade between Laghu Nagapura and Hastinapura
Kutaja/Coo-touch-u(p)	"Mountain peak" or "jar"; may have been original name for the martial arts teacher of the cousins
Lomaharshana/Low-mu(ss)-her-shun-nu(t)	Storyteller who makes hair bristle or stand on end; Kavi Sangha Archivist in the Pandava camp
Mahanadi/Mu(ss)-ha-knee-thee	"Great River;" so named by the Rakshasas; goes east from Chota Nagpur plateau to the Bay of Bengal
Matsya/Mu(tt)-th(ud)-sir-yeah	Panchnad name for Meena Naga clan
Mayura/Mu(tt)-you-ru(t)	Peacock; totem of Yadava clan
Meena/Me-nu(t)	Naga clan
Meru/May-roo	Mythical mountain; the home of the gods; often located in the Pamirs of Tajikistan
Moolasthan/Moo-lus(trate)-sthan	Panchnad–Gandhara settlement near Bolan pass and Gomal pass that enter modern-day Afghanistan; one of the oldest urban settlements known in the Sarasvati Sindhu Culture.
Naga/Na(h)-gu(t)	Forest-dwellers occupying most of the Gangetic plain except towards the east, where Rakshasas lived; organized as matriarchal bands with a male war-chief; slash-and-burn agriculturalists
Nagapura/Na(h)-gu(t)-poo(h)-ru(t)	"The City of the Naga"; later renamed Hastinapura by Kuru after his father
Nagaraja/Na(h)-gu(t)-ra-ju(t)	Chief or ruler of a Naga clan
Nishkamkarnarpana/Niche-calm-cur-nerve-pun-nu(t)	"Focused listening" practices taught by the Kavi Sangha
Nishkamsmaranadharanam/Niche-calm-smur(f)-run-u(h)-thar-run-(dr)um	"Memory management" practices taught by the Kavi Sangha
Panchagacham/Punch-ugh-(m)uch-(dr)um	Lower cloth or covering; covers the body below the waist; predecessor of today's "dhoti" or "veshthi"

Name of Person or Place/Pronunciation Guide	Definition of Word and Description of Person or Place
Panchala/Punch-ah-lu(ck)	Naga confederation of five clans controlling the land north of the Ganga up to the foothills of the Himalayas
Panchali/Punch-ah-lea(d)	Title of Matriarch of Panchala; the Matriarch Agnijyotsna whose consorts are the five Pandavas
Panchnad/Punch-na(h)-d	Land between Sindhu and Sarasvati rivers; center of modern-day Pakistan; home to more than two thousand settlements from the Bronze Age (3000 BCE to 1500 BCE)
Pandava/Pa-(u)nder-vu(h)	Descended from Pandu
Pandu/Pa-(u)ndo	Named Mahendra at birth but called Pandu because he was very pale (albino); considered the father *de jure* of the five Pandavas
Parashara/Per-harsher-u(h)	One of the Vyaasas; father of Krishna Dvaipaayana
Paurava/Pow-ru(t)-vu(h)	Descendant of Puru; describes people of Northern Panchnad and settlers of Hastinapura
Pitr-vihara-naadu/Pit-r-we-har(sh)-un-na(h)-du()	Land of the Temple of Ancestors; Egypt
Pratipa/Pru(ssian)-tea-pa(h)	Father of Shantanu; the name means Rebel or adversary;
Puru/Poo-roo	Ancestor of Kuru; Yayati's youngest son; gives up one year of his youth to his father Yayati; becomes the heir
Raishyava/Wry-she-eve(r)	Unicorn; one of the iconic totems of the Sarasvati-Sindhu Culture, portrayed on many seals
Rakshasa/Ruck-sus(tain)-si(r)	Hunter gatherers; "Defender" in the Naga language; name given by the Nagas to the hunter-gathering tribes who dwelt in the forest to the east of modern-day Patna
Samavedin/Sa(ga)-mu(d)-way-din	A Kavi Sangha bard specially trained to keep time; the "chronometers" of Panchnad
Samvarana/Some-vu(h)-runner	Driven out of Hastinapura by Panchala; returns under Vasishtha's guidance ; establishes a standing army

Name of Person or Place/Pronunciation Guide	Definition of Word and Description of Person or Place
Sanjaya / Sun-ju(t)-yu(m)	Guru and advisor to Dhritarashtra
Sarasvati/Sir-russ-vu(h)-tea	Hidden river of Hindu mythology; river bordering Panchnad on the east; dried up when it lost the snow-melt from the Yamuna (before the events in this book)
Sashidhara / Su(m)-she-the-ru(n)	Name of Shantanu's Chief Minister or Advisor
Satyavati/Su(m)-tea-yeah-vu(h)-tea	Naga wife of Shantanu; has two sons Chitrangada and Vichitravirya; co-Regent with Devavrata; politically ambitious and capable
Shani / Shun-ea(se)	The god of destiny; traditionally associated with the planet Saturn in Indian astrology
Shaka / Shucke(r)	Scythian
Shantanu / Sha(rp)-(hu)nter-noo(se)	King of Hastinapura; husband of Ganga; father of Devavrata, Chitrangada and Vichitravirya
Shikhandin / Chic-und(id)-in	Pandava spy who leads Devavrata into an ambush; killed by Devavrata
Shukla / Shook-lu(g)	Brother of Satyavati; the Vyaasa at the time of the Great War
Sindhu / Sin-do	Ancient local name for the river Indus (which is the name given by the Greeks)
Sutudri / So(me)-(s)tood-ree(l)	Ancient name of the River Sutlej; Himalayan river that used to flow south to the Sarasvati; changed direction near the town of Kaalindini (Ropar) to flow west and is a tributary of the Sindhu (Indus)
Suyodhana / Sue-yo-the-nu(t)	Also called Duryodhana; mortal enemy of Pandavas; son of Dhritarashtra; leader of the Kauravas
Takshashila / Thuck-shush-ill-a(hh)	One of the oldest settlements in the world; center of learning established by Vasishtha
Vaishampaayana / Why-shum-pa-yen-u(h)	Vyaasa in 850 BCE; charged with writing the archives of Hastinapura

Name of Person or Place/Pronunciation Guide	Definition of Word and Description of Person or Place
Varahamoola / whirr-aha-moo-lu(st)	From Vishnu's incarnation as a Boar, this refers to the tip of the Boar's tusk that held the Earth at this point ; ancient name of the modern town of Baramulla in Kashmir
Varanavata / Whirr-runner-vu(h)-tu(b)	A town west of Hastinapura on the northern bank of the Yamuna river; founded by Devavrata
Vasishtha / (L/W)ush-ish-ta(h)	The first Vyaasa and head of the Kavi Sangha, created by merging the guilds of bards, poets, and archivists
Vichitravirya / We-chit-ru(n)-vee-riya	Son of Shantanu by Satyavati; marries Ambika and Ambalika; uninterested King; dies young
Vidura / We-do-ru(t)	"The Wise;" half-brother of Mahendra Pandu and Dhritarashtra; born of a maidservant, therefore not a citizen but a commoner; named "Dharmateja" at birth; considered both learned and street-smart
Vyaasa / We-yeah-sir(ilst)	Title of the Head of the Kavi Sangha; also arranger, organizer, or editor, capturing the many roles of the Head of the Kavi Sangha
Vyuhadyuta / Viewer-d'you-ta(h)	A duel between two armies that consists of setting up opposing battle formations but not actually fighting
Yadava /Yeah-the-vu(h)	Descendant of Yadu
Yamuna / Yum-moo-nu(h)	A river; changed direction and created a crisis of flooding in Khandavaprastha and of drought in Panchnad
Yayati / Yea(rn)-yeah-tea	Ancestor of Kuru; enjoyed a thousand years of youth but wanted more
Yudhishthira / You-dish-tea-ru(t)	The oldest Pandava; the King of Hastinapura after the Great War

ABOUT THE AUTHOR

Kamesh Ramakrishna grew up in Bombay (now Mumbai) and completed his undergraduate studies at IIT-Kanpur. He went on to obtain a Ph.D. in computer science from Carnegie-Mellon University in Pittsburgh, specializing in Artificial Intelligence. He worked as a professor and a software engineer; received some patents; was software architect for some foundational products; was CTO for a startup; and in recent years, has been a consulting software architect.

For over twenty years, Kamesh has been an avid student of history, archaeology, science, and philosophy, and the interconnections between these disciplines. This interest has had tremendous influence on this book. The core ideas underlying this novel have been published in two peer-reviewed journals – *The Trumpeter* (Canada) and *The Indian Journal of Eco-criticism.*

Kamesh lives with his family in Massachusetts.

The Kuru Family Tree

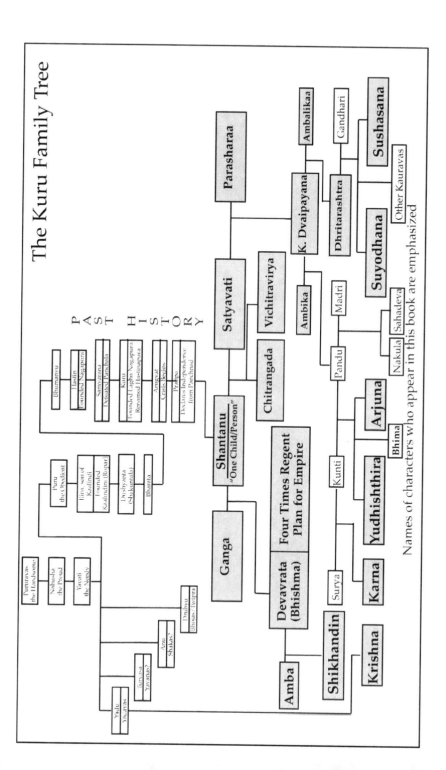

Names of characters who appear in this book are emphasized